WILD LIKE US

BOOK 8 IN THE LIKE US SERIES

KRISTA & BECCA
RITCHIE

First Edition - Print

Cover Image ©Shutterstock
Cover Design by Twin Cove Designs

ISBN: 978-1-950165-28-5

CHARACTER LIST

Not all characters in this list will make an appearance in the book, but most will be mentioned. Ages represent the age of the character at the beginning of the book. Some characters will be older when they're introduced, depending on their birthday.

The Security Team

These are the bodyguards that protect the Hales, Cobalts, and Meadows.

KITSUWON SECURITIES INC.

SECURITY FORCE OMEGA

Akara Kitsuwon (boss) – 27

Thatcher Moretti (lead) – 29

Banks Moretti – 29

Farrow Keene – 29

Quinn Oliveira – 22

Oscar Oliveira – 32

Paul Donnelly – 28

PRICE KEPLER'S TRIPLE SHIELD SERVICES

SECURITY FORCE EPSILON

Jon Sinclair (lead) – 40s

Greer Bell – 30s

…and more

SECURITY FORCE ALPHA

Price Kepler (lead) – 40s

Tony Ramella – 29

…and more

The Meadows

Ryke Meadows & Daisy Calloway

Sullivan – 21

Winona – 15

The Cobalts

Richard Connor Cobalt & Rose Calloway

Jane – 24

Charlie – 21

Beckett – 21

Eliot – 20

Tom – 19

Ben – 17

Audrey – 14

The Hales

Loren Hale & Lily Calloway

Maximoff – 24

Luna – 19

Xander – 16

Kinney – 14

The Abbeys

Garrison Abbey & Willow Hale

Vada – 15

A NOTE FROM THE AUTHORS

The Italian used in this book is an Italian-American language developed by Italian immigrants. It is an incomplete language and uses Italian, English, or both. Different Italians speak different dialects in certain areas, and what is used in the Like Us series is prominent on the East Coast. Words may vary in pronunciation and spelling in different communities. A glossary with pronunciations for Wild Like Us is included at the end of the book.

Wild Like Us is the eighth book in the Like Us Series. Even though the series changes POVs throughout, to understand events that took place in the previous novels, the series should be read in its order of publication.

Wild Like Us should be read after *Charming Like Us.*

LIKE US SERIES READING ORDER

1. Damaged Like Us
2. Lovers Like Us
3. Alphas Like Us
4. Tangled Like Us
5. Sinful Like Us
6. Headstrong Like Us
7. Charming Like Us
8. Wild Like Us
9. Fearless Like Us
10. Infamous Like Us
11. Misfits Like Us
12. Unlucky Like Us

Sullivan Meadows

THE BEST WAY TO DESCRIBE this situation is *fucking comical.*

I have to pee.

Like I might piss my pants if I don't find a toilet kind of pee, and I'm nowhere near a toilet. I'm in the middle of a *field* that's landscaped with flashing lights, a giant Ferris wheel, thrill rides, cotton-candy stands, and too many beady-eyes that follow me as they wonder what the fuck I'm up to.

Where are you running off to so quickly, Sullivan Minnie Meadows? Why are you not with your little sister or your parents at the Carnival Fundraiser? Why'd you leave them at the Tilt-A-Whirl?

Because I downed five bottles of orange cream soda. For a good cause: a belching contest with my fifteen-year-old sister. Which turned into a "first to not puke on the Tilt-A-Whirl" contest. The squirt and I were both victorious, as life should be. Our mom would say, *sisters at war is the saddest adventure of all.*

Thankfully I've never been on that gloomy voyage. Winona is all the tendons that hold my heart together. A life without her would break me.

The carnival is packed tonight, and I go from a clench-the-thighs trot to a full power-walk, quickly bypassing a corn dog stand. The reality of my situation would disappoint many gossip blogs.

You mean to say the oldest daughter of thrill-seeking Daisy and Ryke Meadows isn't *leaving for a rendezvous with a secret boyfriend?*

Nope.

You mean to say that she's never *had a boyfriend before?*

That was true until last year. First boyfriend at twenty. First kiss at twenty. First break-up at twenty-one.

I could've waited longer for those good firsts if the right guy didn't come around. Not that Will Rochester was Mr. Forever. He was Mr. Back Then. Mr. Good for Now.

Growing up, I always sidelined the idea of romance in favor of my first love.

Swimming.

Boys were big fucking distractions, not that many tried to distract me, but I refused to cheat on my first love, my drive to win. Myself. But once I retired from swimming, my focus expanded beyond reaching Olympic gold. *No time for romance* became *all the time in the world to fall in love.*

I honestly don't have much faith in myself in the romance department. It's not like I have a lot of fucking experience there, and you can't really train for the dating game.

At least not when the pool of people I trust is *small.* Like Fisher-Price plastic fishing toy-set small.

But the secret boyfriend is long-gone now. Will Rochester is in the past, and our relationship wasn't totally secret to everyone. Just the public. Thank fucking God. I couldn't have imagined dealing with the scrutiny of a million eyes while dating for the first time.

Water guns squirt clown targets at a nearby game booth, and all I hear is the forceful splash of water. My need to pee intensifies. "Oh fuck that last sip of soda." I pick up speed into a slight-jog, and I'm going to outpace the two men in front of me if they don't haul ass.

I place my hands on their backs, and at the exact same time, they glance over their shoulders. They look downward to meet my eyes, and I'm really fucking tall—especially in my worn-leather boots, I crest over 6-foot—but they're taller.

"Go, fucking *go,*" I say strongly, pushing them towards the bathrooms.

They easily lengthen their stride, but they're on the cusp of full-bellied laughter.

Akara's brown eyes twinkle, his lips lifting as he looks to Banks, his six-foot-seven Italian-American friend. "You hear that running water?"

Banks cracks a smile at me. "You mean the waterfall between her legs?"

I'd probably laugh if I weren't so afraid of wetting myself. "Hardy-har-har." I twist my long brown hair into a messy bun to distract my bladder. Putting my hands on their lower backs again, I shove them forward as they skillfully weave between carnival attendees.

Akara teases, "Hey, Sulli, I hear that waterfall right now." He glances back at me. "You hear it? Goes something like *woooosh*."

I almost tinkle. Fucking God. "You're going to regret that when I piss myself and jump on you."

Banks is laughing his ass off.

I playfully slug his side. "Why are you laughing? I'd jump on you first."

Akara bursts into laughter now.

Banks bites down on a toothpick, mouth curved up. "You wanna jump on me, just don't miss. It's a long way from my body to the ground, and I wouldn't want you to break your ass."

I laugh hard at that, and we're all smiling on the trek and the urge to piss actually recedes for a second.

And then we pass a long, winding line for funnel cake. Teenagers—boys and girls around my sister's age—eye me, and their heads shift in eerie unison. Like something bizarre from *Black Mirror*.

I wince at the thought. Only because that's Beckett's favorite TV show.

We'd binge-watch all the episodes together between his ballet schedule. Since we're not really talking that much right now, I try to push my best friend (ex-best-friend?) out of my head.

"Is that Sullivan Meadows?" a girl yells loudly from the pack of teenagers.

I do the dumb fucking thing and look. As I make *slight* eye-contact, they all start shouting my name.

"SULLIVAN!"

I can't stop and chat.

"SULLIVAN!"

"CAN WE GET A SELFIE?"

I really will piss myself in that photo.

And I'm not Jane or Moffy—my older cousins are so willing to sacrifice their time and heart and energy to fans. To strangers. Who I know could turn on me in a second if I do anything they deem "unacceptable"—I've seen them turn on my mom and dad as easy as the flip of a pancake. And I'm not good at small talk with people I can't trust. I'm constantly in my head wondering if I said the right or wrong thing. One wrong move, one slip of the tongue, and they could blast private info to the world.

And of course I want to do the right thing. I want to be as fucking *good* as Moffy.

But my dad is good and so selfless, and the media still calls him "inappropriate" and a "disgrace" because he dated my mom when she was only eighteen.

Because some people still believe he had an affair with my Aunt Lily, and they believe that Moffy is actually his son.

It's not true. He'd sooner die than cheat on my mom.

So I *don't care* to try to prove anything to anyone but myself. Tabloids can call me standoffish and disrespectful when I decline photos and autographs. I just march on.

"SULLIVAN!" another teen screams, and they begin to detach from the funnel cake stand and follow my tracks.

Akara slips Banks a silent look, and then Banks falls back behind me.

I joke, "Boobs and ass coverage."

Banks lets out a laugh. "Looks like you're covering Akara's ass, mermaid."

Mermaid.

My lips rise, but from behind, he can't see my smile. As Akara walks ahead of me, my eyes fall to his ass.

He has a nice ass. Round. Perky.

He has a nice *a lot* of things. A sharp, heart-shaped jawline, thick black hair that's grown longer in the summer, an athletic build highlighting long hours spent at Studio 9, the MMA gym he owns, and also kissable lips (that I've obviously never kissed).

With my *limited* experience in kissing, I just think his lips look like they'd do the job fucking well. The same way that Banks' long tongue looks good for eating girls out.

Some lusty observations aside, I focus on Akara. "Kits," I call out to him. "You should turn around and cover Banks' ass. Spread the love."

Akara smiles back at me. "Your boobs are more important, Sul."

"Amen," Banks chimes in.

I laugh, but the sound slowly fades. A part of me wishes they were actually flirting and not just cracking crude jokes with me.

They quiet down as the teens gain speed. Banks edges closer, his chest almost brushes up against my back. He maintains a sliver of space and seems aware not to touch me.

I can't help but focus on him. On the closeness. On the not-yet-there touch. His body heat prickles my skin, and my pulse thumps.

Hot guys can become ugly the second they open their mouths and heinous shit comes out. So I don't put a lot of stock in good looks, but Banks Moretti is a beefcake at first sight.

Scruffy jaw and a strong pairing of muscles with an imposing height.

After getting to know him, he's a sweeter, beefier beefcake. He can make me double-over laughing, and he's only ever been considerate and nice to me.

Banks' and Akara's vigilant eyes rest on the teenagers, then up ahead to our destination: a row of porta potties near a kiddy train-car ride. Akara speaks softly in his mic, and Banks adjusts his earpiece.

With our easy banter, I forget that they're not just two buddies. Two of my friends.

They're my bodyguards.

Akara Kitsuwon is the one who acts like *Sullivan Meadows on the verge of pissing herself* is the funniest crap since last week where I ate asphalt doing a shitty trick on a skateboard. What's funny is that Akara looks more like a twenty-seven-year-old pro-skateboarder. He's even wearing a pair of scuffed Vans and a black tank that shows his lean-cut muscles. But he's worse than even me at attempting an ollie.

His skills are in Muay Thai, snowboarding, rapid-fire texting, and being a badass boss.

To think *he's* the leader of an entire team of men would shock a lot of people. Not just because he looks ready to hit a skate ramp. But because he's younger than five of the six men he leads.

As far as how he fits in my life…I can barely remember a time where he wasn't there. He's been my permanent bodyguard since my ripe teenage years of *sixteen.* Where I was determined to win gold.

Banks Moretti, on the other hand, I've gotten to know more personally in my ripe adulthood of twenty. Where I've free-spirited my way into new experiences: my first international trip without my mom or dad, my first kiss, my first failed romance.

He's the floater on Omega who always seems to float towards my detail, and he's really good friends with Akara.

They've never said it explicitly to me, but I can tell in so many different ways.

Like how they speak through single glances. How they feed off each other's jokes. How they know exactly what'll push the other one's buttons—and they seem to not only appreciate the raw honesty, but they rely on it.

Making friendships outside of my family are often anxiety-ridden and fucking hard. Seeing theirs in action sometimes causes real envy. Internally, I feel like I turn into a six-foot green goblin, but they help smother those feelings because they pull me in like I'm part of their clique.

Buddies.

Pals.

Friends.

It's what I've always wanted. True and real, long-lasting friendships, but I think I've literally friend-zoned myself with two of the hottest guys on the planet.

I'm a fucking moron.

Be kind to yourself, I hear my mom's sweet words in my head. She's said them a lot to me, and I think the first time might've been when I was leaving for first grade.

"Do I have to go?" I pouted. "Can't I stay with you?" Colorful finger-paints streaked our faces from a messy arts-and-crafts morning.

She wiped some paint off my cheek with a damp washcloth. "It'll be fun, Sulli. Think of first grade as an *awfully* big adventure." Her smile was radiant, like I was about to embark on life's greatest journey.

It sounded like a fucking hell-scape. "But I suck at school."

My mom squeezed my hand. "My peanut butter cupcake, you *don't* suck. You're brave, amazing, smart, beautiful, and capable of *anything*. You're just a beginner. We all start somewhere." She pressed a kiss to my forehead. "Remember—be kind to yourself."

I always try to remember.

When we finally roll up to a long row of blue porta potties, my bursting bladder catapults me into this rancid sucker.

I shut the blue door without glancing back at Akara or Banks.

Oh…*fuck*. Someone pissed all over the black toilet seat, and moths fly aimlessly above my head, trapped inside this literal shithole with me.

I plug my nose with two fingers and use my other hand to unzip my pants. A girl's gotta go when she's gotta go, but porta potties are an invention made from Hades' ass-crack. I'd rather pop a squat in the woods than be in this hot, stinky, cramped contraption. At least in the woods, you're not five centimeters from some stranger's excrements.

Don't think about it.

I squat and pee.

And I stare at the locked porta potty door and picture Akara and Banks right outside, guarding the facility I'm using.

There is nothing about this situation that screams, *romance me.*

My thighs burn as I hold a squat position, but I don't dare touch the seat. After what feels like an eternity, I finally empty my bladder, wipe with a tiny piece of toilet paper, pull up my panties and jeans, and I kick the door open while I zip up.

I'm outside.

I could pump my fist to the sky like the end of *The Breakfast Club.* Fucking hurray.

The brisk night air cools off the bathroom stench, and I realize fast that Akara is MIA. Only Banks is waiting near the porta potties for me.

"How was it?" Banks asks as I roll up to his side.

"Utter fucking relief and totally disgusting." I dig a travel-sized hand sanitizer out of my back pocket and squirt some on my palm.

One side of his mouth curves up. His smiles aren't like Akara's, which almost always sparkle his eyes. Banks' smiles are darker, almost half-hidden and fleeting.

His observant gaze skates across the bustling carnival, but he cocks his head to me. "You hate porta-shitters?"

I smile at his name for the boxed shithole. "Yeah, I'd rather go behind a bush or dig a fucking hole than pee on someone else's crap."

Banks laughs. "I was planning on defending them, but you've got a point." His South Philly accent comes out more than his twin brother's.

"You really like porta potties?" I eye his height.

He hoists a shoulder in a slight shrug. "After two deployments, porta-shitters are like churches. The only place to have one moment of silence." He plucks the toothpick from his lips. "You dig a hole and some knucklefuck is gonna come annoy you for ten minutes about a rumor they heard from another platoon." His eyes settle on mine for a softer beat, and I almost forget about the flash photography.

Kids are snapping photos of me while they wait in line for face-painting.

Banks asks, "Did I sway you to my side and beauty of porta-shitters?"

How do you flirt well?

I wish I knew at times, but I don't want to be someone I'm not just to get his attention.

So I sink into the casualness of our conversation. "I'm still team shithole." *Fuck, Sulli.* That wasn't cute at all—the thought is abruptly cut off by his laughter.

"Yeah?" he says between laughs. "My metaphor or analogy or whatever literary thing didn't do it for you?"

I smile and elbow his side. "What? That a toilet is like a church?"

"It's godly enough to be called a fucking throne."

"The hole is my throne," I say with an outstretched arm, knowing full well this is a sexual innuendo.

Banks bounces his head, his laugh deeper in his chest. He surveys the kiddy train-car ride and the families helping their children in the caboose. "Even if some knucklefucks come walk up and shoot the shit with you while you're shitting?"

"Yeah, why not? I fucking hate being alone most of the time anyway."

His brown hair is long enough to brush the back of his neck. He curls a strand behind his ear. "Isn't swimming more solitary?"

"I had Moffy growing up. We went to swim meets together—he's the closest thing I have to an older brother. I could've done any sport without him, but it wouldn't have been the same. I think..." I scuff my boot on the dirt and stare out at the bright Thrill Drop, an adrenaline tower, in the distance. "I think that I would've been lonely. With how many cousins I have, I'm just used to being around people, even if I'm not that good with people."

Everyone knows that I'm not that great with words like Jane. She's a witty princess. I feel like the foul-mouthed voyager sailing the ocean blue, who'd reroute back home too quickly. I'd miss everyone too much, too fucking badly.

"You're telling me," he says huskily, "I'm twenty-nine, and I've never really been alone. Never lived alone. Never spent more than a day truly *alone*." He catches my gaze and lifts another shoulder. "Maybe people like you and me are just meant to be in the company of a buncha knucklefucks—or we are the knucklefucks."

I slug his arm. "Probably the latter."

We share a smile, and our attention finds the same spot. The same person. Akara is pacing slowly near the miniature train caboose, a phone to his ear.

Business calls.

I've been slowly growing used to Akara's abrupt, unexpected departure from my detail. Ever since he created his own security firm, he's been too busy to protect me 24/7. I'm proud of him for building something big, and I don't want to be the reason he fails.

"He looks really stressed," I say to Banks as we watch Akara.

"Yeah," he nods. "He's grown an extra wrinkle overnight. Right above the third and fourth one."

I laugh into a snort.

His lip lifts too, but our humor weakens as concern mounts.

Banks is here to protect me for these moments, when Akara has to step out, and he cares just as much about his friend.

A second passes when I realize that I'm just waiting around the fucking porta potties. *For what?*

Not, *for what?*

For whom?

My eyes flicker to Banks. "You're not going to mention that I don't need to wait around for my bodyguard since I have you?"

He shakes his head once. "I know what he means to you." His gaze sweeps the area. "But you don't have to wait around for Akara if you don't want to."

My stomach tightens. *He's my bodyguard.* Wherever I go, Akara will eventually catch back up to me. But I feel like we've been hanging out at the carnival as friends, and even if he just briefly left, I'd want to spend the next few minutes with him.

So I wait.

Banks doesn't even bat an eye at my choice.

And not long after, Akara pockets his cell and jogs back over. "Sorry, Sul. Had to take the super, important phone call about *taxes.*" He sighs. "It was riveting." His sarcasm is all over his face.

"Oh hey, at least you're important enough to take important calls." I smack his well-defined abs.

He steals my hair tie out of my bun. Fuck! My long hair falls, and he flings a strand at my face and walks backwards, just as I try to steal the hair tie back.

He raises it above his head. "At least I'm important enough to protect a very important person."

I try to grab the hair tie again, but Akara hides it behind his back. I tell him, "Banks must be more important since he's clocked in more hours protecting me."

Banks laughs, and Akara snaps the hair tie at his friend's face.

We're all laughing again, and Banks returns the hair tie to me. "Thanks," I say as I fix the strands up in another messy bun, and I spot bright bulbs that spell out *American Circus Funhouse.*

"Want to check it out?" I ask them.

They're already leading the way.

I follow them up creaky metal stairs and into a tight hallway. It's actually weirdly *quiet.* The outside sounds of laughter and the music from amusement rides are more muffled here.

Banks messes with his earpiece. "Comms are jammed?"

"No service," Akara tells him. "It's fine. Thatcher is keeping tabs on everyone." *Thatcher Moretti.* He's the SFO lead. Banks' identical twin brother is actually higher than Banks on the security hierarchy.

Metal disks line the hallway, and they spin Akara 360-degrees when he steps foot on one. He keeps complete and total balance.

Like a badass.

Banks trips. "Jesus, *Mary*—"

Akara catches Banks' wrist and pulls him onto the second spinning disk. They're hugging to stay on the same metal plate.

I grip the side railings and use my upper-body strength to avoid touching the disks. Leaping my way through.

Akara cups his hand over his mouth. "Cheating!"

"Hey, I'm being fucking resourceful. Why else put railings here?"

"For people like Banks," Akara quips, stepping easily on the next disk.

Banks follows and laughs. "She's allergic to land, so she'd know how to avoid it. I'm a fucking tree. I actually like *standing.*"

"She's not a mermaid," Akara says as we pass the rest of the spinning disks.

Banks looks a little ticked. He even shoots Akara an annoyed glance.

Akara frowns back like, *What?*

I look Banks over, my pulse quickening, and I bite my lip, feeling a smile. He came to my defense. Feels like some type of romance—or I could be really fucking playing myself. How far-fetched is it that Banks could see me as more than a friend?

He's never even made a move.

I get that there are bodyguard rules. Close but not *too* fucking close, but some of my cousins have *decimated* those rules.

Maximoff.

Jane.

They deserve a round of applause for doing the fucking impossible and making it all work.

We enter a much larger blue room. Polka-dot-painted boxing bags hang like a maze. And I tell Banks, "Don't mind Kits. He doesn't believe in mermaids."

Banks cocks his head at Akara. "You don't believe in beautiful women who swim in the sea?"

"With a tail?" he asks incredulously. "No, man. That shit is for *Disney* movies. Anyway, Sulli is more like a…" He eyes me. "String bean."

My mouth falls, and I'd slug his arm if he were closer.

He smiles teasingly. "No muscle. Can't lift a five-pound weight. Way too tall. Definitely a string bean."

I push a boxing bag aside, trying not to zero in on the "too tall" part. I am taller than the average woman, but the rest of his words were bullshit. I have a lot of muscle and a fucking *six*-pack that I worked hard for.

Plus, I can lift over a hundred-fifty pounds.

I mean, fuck, I can lift *him.* "Let me carry you out of here and we'll see how much of a string bean I am."

Akara just laughs.

Banks grips the top of a boxing bag, and when my eyes meet his, it feels like he can see right through me. Heat blazes my neck because I'm not totally fucking sure what he's thinking. But I just know I wish I could hear it.

We loiter around for a second. Standing among the colorful boxing bags. And I look between them while they joke about redecorating the Studio 9 gym with polka-dots and stripes.

Would I like Banks or even Akara to pull me closer? *Yeah.* But not just in playful jest. Not just to protect me. In actual, real *want.* Desire. Fucking *passion.*

Things I've only ever seen as a bystander and on TV shows like *Roswell* (thanks to Luna's obsession). I don't want to make out with an alien though.

I want to be devoured by a hot fucking *man.* Who I trust, who makes me feel so completely comfortable and confident even in my inexperience.

I'm picky about guys. I won't physically let just anyone *in.* I crave those comfortable, trusting pieces while being mixed with the *I wanna bang you* attraction.

But it's right here. They're beyond bangable.

And I trust Banks.

I trust Akara.

They'd never take advantage of me. Never hurt me. I know they'd take care of me before, during, and afterward. They're completely different guys, and I should be lucky that I've made two friends out of them, out of bodyguards.

Two friends who I'm attracted to.

"What's that look?" Akara asks me with playfulness.

I won't lie. "You're both fucking hot."

Banks smiles, one of those shadows of a smile.

Akara laughs brightly.

They know they're hot.

I wrap an arm around a boxing bag. "I feel comfortable and safe around you two, and I figure if I never have another boyfriend in my life, I could totally see myself losing my virginity to either of you."

Akara's face drops.

Like plummets.

Like I took a needle and popped a fucking balloon.

Oh my *fucking* God.

Banks scratches the back of his head. His eyes are on Akara.

We joke all the time! This isn't that different, right? Boobs, tits, ass, penis, cock—what's so different about me mentioning my virginity? It's not a joke to me, but they should at least respond like we're friends, right? I said everything really casually, right??

RIGHT?!

I stammer, "I mean…I…um, it'd be like doing me a favor—I mean, not like that. *Not* a favor." My face burns. "I'd hope you'd want it too. Don't just sleep with me out of obligation. *Fuck*, what am I saying?" I'm boiling up. "It's just…I want it to be good, and I think you'd both be really good—you're experienced, and yeah…" I want to disappear. "It's something…something to consider. Losing my virginity to one of you…?"

I can't even look at them.

Silence.

All there is is utter fucking silence.

2

Sullivan Meadows

I'M SUFFOCATING BENEATH their lack of *fucking* words. It might only last a second, but my embarrassment clocks this moment at *fucking* eternity.

I realize now that I didn't friend-zone them.

They've friend-zoned *me.*

I'm the un-bangable one.

And even then, maybe we're not as friendly as I thought. Friends should be able to respond to me!

"I, um…" I can't recover.

Abruptly, I bolt to the right.

I run through the heavy bags. They smack my cheek as I push through.

"Sulli!" Akara shouts.

"Wait!" Banks calls. "Wait!"

I can feel them behind me, but I'm faster.

I'm always faster.

Shoving a few more, I come clear to a door marked *3.* There are three fucking doors. Of course there are. I choose the one in front of me, and I dart inside…

"No," I mutter.

Mirrors.

Dozens upon dozens of *mirrors.*

I'm surrounded by my horror-stricken, wide-eyed face. Everywhere, my reflection stares back at me, some misshapen and distorted by the curved and bent glass. My breathing is rapid, but not from exhaustion.

I sprint to the left, meet a wall, then to the right. Meet another dead-end.

Let me fucking out of here!

I rest my hands on my forehead.

Concentrate, Sulli.

I touch my lips. Thinking.

"Sulli!"

I hear them call my name, but they sound distant. They must've chosen a different door. After I collect my shit, I see a sign that says, *no running.*

Hilarious.

And then I spot another door, hidden behind a mirror that warps my face, so my panicked eyes look humongous.

Racing out of the door, I crawl through a yellow rotating barrel, then thrust open an *exit* door to the outside. Inhaling a lungful of crisp night air, I move forward. The carnival is still in full swing like I never left. I skip down metal stairs without slowing.

"Sulli!" Jane calls.

I turn my head and see Jane waving her hands. Without thinking, I sprint towards her. She's like my big sister, so instinct says, *go to Jane.*

But she's not alone.

Outside the funhouse, a larger group of mostly bodyguards surround her and Charlie on a patch of grass.

Keep running.

Keep going.

I grab onto Jane's arm, not wanting to stop, and I say quickly under my breath, "Let's fucking get out of here. Right fucking now." My eyes dart to camera phones.

So many fucking camera phones. Carnival attendees are recording us, but our families have always been the spectacle. Bodyguards are barring the audience from physically reaching us. So I can focus on Jane as her eyes pop out.

"Why?" She speaks hushed.

I'm burning, and it pours out fast, "I opened my big fucking mouth. That's why. I told Kits and Banks they're really fucking hot and they make me feel safe and comfortable, and that if I never have another boyfriend in my entire life, then it'd be cool to lose my virginity to one of them." I nod forcefully. "Yep, and I thought they'd take it like pals, you know like buddies. But they were fucking silent!" I wave a hand. "So I ran, but then I ended up in the mirrors and I got lost and they were looking for me…and oh my fuck." *The funhouse.*

Akara and Banks are jogging out of the funhouse.

I'm not ready to meet their condolences. Their, *it's okay, Sulli. We just don't like you* that *way.*

"We're going," Jane tells me. "Right now. Let's go. Charlie?"

Oh fuck, what's wrong with Charlie? Thatcher is keeping him upright. Charlie seems to be favoring his leg, the one he hurt in the car crash a while back.

"I'll leave with Jack and Oscar," Charlie says. "You go ahead."

"Are you positive?"

"Yes." He stands on his own.

Jane hugs her brother. "We'll meet you at the hospital."

The hospital?

My attention is pulled in seven-hundred different fucking ways. To Charlie and Jane. To Akara and Banks. To Jack and Oscar. The carnival attendees. The phones. The blinking lights.

Screams off of thrill rides.

Pinging of games.

Laughter that feels too close. Like I'm the butt of a joke.

I'm the joke.

My chest rises and falls heavily.

Run.

Run.

"Right in front of you, honey," Thatcher says to Jane as he starts leading us to the parking lot. Everything is a fucking blur.

I end up at Jane's baby blue Land Rover. I can't speak. Seeing Jane with Thatcher—her bodyguard-turned-boyfriend who she's now engaged to—is like another pie in my face.

Romance with a bodyguard—*not for me.*

Friendship with a bodyguard—*did I just fuck that up?*

Did I just ruin it all?

I made things weird.

Fuck.

Fuck.

And I run.

I hear my name from more than one person, but I don't stop. Legs pumping beneath me, my feet and strength carry me through the graveled parking lot. Knots in my chest try to loosen. I pick up speed.

Bolting past the *$5 for Parking* sign, beyond the carnival entrance, I sprint onto a dark empty road out in Pennsylvania. My hair spills out of its bun. Flying messily, wildly around me as I push and push to go faster.

Farther.

Muscles searing.

Angry, frustrated tears slip out of my eyes and catch the wind. Angry with myself. Frustrated with myself.

And then, footsteps pound the concrete.

Someone is running towards me.

I don't look back because they're fast. Easily, they reach my side. I can feel them keeping exact pace, exact step in line with me.

And I turn my head to see my dad.

My dad is running beside me.

He never tells me to slow down. He never tells me to stop. He sprints on the deserted Pennsylvania road in the middle of the night. No words, no fucking questions asked.

We run together.

We push harder.

Air fills my lungs. With all my training, with every morning run with my dad, I don't *think* about inhaling and exhaling. I just *do.*

I feel like I'm flying.

One hundred and fifty miles per hour.

The knots unwind. Bursting. Whatever rattled inside me is being set free. For a moment, anyway.

And when I finally skid to a slow jog, then to a walk, breath comes easy and my muscles ache from not stretching. I glance painfully at my dad.

His darkened, concerned expression says, *are you fucking okay?* He's already bringing me into a hug. I hug tighter.

"I'm a fucking idiot," I mutter.

"Hey," he snaps, pulling me back to meet my eyes. "Don't fucking talk about yourself like that. Your mom would say—"

"Be kind to yourself," I nod. "I know. I fucking know." I exhale, and I notice the bright beam of headlights. A car crawls towards us but maintains distance.

Bodyguards.

Maybe it's just my dad's bodyguard, but with how tonight is going, it's probably Akara *and* Banks.

I focus back on my dad. "I made things so weird."

His face hardens. "How?"

"I'm bad at friendships, Dad." I outstretch my arms, then set my hands on my head. "I don't know how to even maintain one with a *bodyguard* without screwing it up. And that's like a built-in friend. I didn't even really need to *try.*"

He gives me a hardass look. "You're not giving yourself enough fucking credit, Sulli." He messes my already messy hair.

It makes me smile.

"You ready to go back?"

I sigh. "Can't I run forever?"

"Your feet will bleed."

"I'll bandage my toes."

"You'll fucking cramp."

"I'll limp."

"You'll be alone."

My face sobers. "Won't you be there?"

He shakes his head. "My knee is bad, Sulli. I can't keep up with you forever."

Then Moffy will, I want to say.

Moffy will be with me forever. I wipe my nose that drips snot, but my eyes are dry now. Growing up is fucking hard. Even if there were no cameras, no spotlight, no fame—I think I'd still struggle.

I'd still want to run forever.

When I change directions, we walk towards the bright headlights.

My dad tells me, "You're going to have fights with your friends. It fucking happens. You know how many times me and your Uncle Connor wanted to rip each other's fucking head off?"

But I doubt my dad asked Uncle Connor to take his virginity. The thought makes me snort, and my dad smiles like he made me feel better.

He did, just not exactly how he thinks.

Turns out, the car isn't a security vehicle after all. The three SUVs behind it are, though.

We approach the green Subaru from the passenger side, and the window rolls down. Revealing my mom, a blonde bombshell. Her smile pulls a long, old scar that weaves across her cheek. "All aboard," she calls and unlocks the car.

"Hey, sweetheart." My dad kisses my mom through the window.

I climb into the backseat. A young Golden Retriever lets out a happy whine from the trunk. My mom's service dog for PTSD goes almost everywhere she goes, and I give Goldilocks a scratch behind her ears.

Winona spins around from behind the wheel to get a good look at me. With flyaway dirty-blonde hair, friendship bracelets, and a utility vest and cargo shorts, my fifteen-year-old sister looks like an ad for Patagonia or Wolf Scouts. She's the whole outdoor package. "What'd Akara do this time?" Her eyes flame.

I can count the number of fights Akara and I have had on one hand. Not fucking many, but they've all been recent enough that Winona has grown more protective.

I should be the protective one. I'm older by six years, but she's so much cooler. Even driving on a learner's permit, she somehow seems like she can do anything. Scale any mountain, swim any ocean.

I *can* do those things, but I don't exude the same effortless *coolness.*

"He was quiet," I say in a wince.

"What?"

"It was dumb." I can't even rehash the event without feeling secondhand embarrassment from my own embarrassment.

Her eyes soften.

My dad has swapped seats with my mom. She scoots in beside me, and when I lean into her, she lovingly cups the side of my head.

"It'll be okay," she whispers.

I breathe in.

Yeah.

It'll be totally okay.

How am I going to face them tomorrow? They're my bodyguards. Inescapable.

As though reading my anguished face, my mom asks, "You want us to drop you off at the penthouse or would you rather stay with us?"

"Spend the night with us," Winona says fast. "I *whale-y* miss you, sis."

I sit up more. "I *whale-y* miss you too, Nona." And I'll gladly take a night with my family. Avoidance can't be that fucking bad for the soul. Not when I'm with my sister and my mom and my dad. "Let's go home."

"Groovy," Winona smiles, stepping on the gas.

Windows down, wind whips through the car, and I wonder if it's strange that I call my childhood house *home.* I haven't lived there for a couple years, and still, it feels like home.

Where I'm safest. But if I want to experience more out of life, how much higher do I really need to fly from the nest?

Pulling out my phone, I type out a text.

I'm spending the night at the cottage with my fam

I add a thumbs-up emoji and send it to Akara.

My phone buzzes in a second flat.

K. Call me if you need anything or if you leave. – Kits

It's so formal.

No emojis. No gifs.

I can't tell what's happening to my friendships, except that they're changing. I wanted them to in a way, but not like this. And I don't have many left to destroy, but they're all imploding around me.

3

Sullivan Meadows

10 DAYS LATER

I WAKE UP BEFORE THE crack of fucking dawn.

Sleep and I are mortal enemies. If I'm being particularly honest here, *Sleep* can go fuck itself. There's so much I can do in those hours of slumber. So much I can accomplish. But my time is thieved away, and I hate that sleep is a requirement to function at full capacity.

It's what I think every time I wake up in the early morning. Today—it's 3 a.m. My retro alarm clock glows a pale blue light as I roll out of bed.

A small smile inches up my lips.

Sometimes it feels like I'm giving *Sleep* the middle finger every time I wake before sunrise. *Fuck Sleep. Fuck it good in the ass.* I let out a soft, quiet laugh.

In middle school, I was sent to the principal's office more than once for my crude humor and…flowery language. Most of the time the other kids ratted me out. "Sullivan just called the class fish pussy lips!" was probably the loudest and most blatant act of throwing me under the bus. I still have those tire marks on my back.

In my fucking defense, that goldfish totally had big ole pussy lips and if the teacher had a funny bone attached to her body, she would've let out a fraction of a giggle.

My mom at least laughed when she picked me up from the office.

I guess I was just raised to not give a shit. To say fuck it all. Cursing. Crass humor. All the profane things were never profane to me. They still really aren't.

My feet fall to the ground, careful not to make too much noise. Habit, really. From the time that I roomed with Luna in the small townhouse.

Now in a monster-sized Philly penthouse with a monster-sized bedroom all to myself, I have less reason to be quiet. But I still tiptoe to my dresser and wrestle through the neatly folded shorts and tops.

Normally, I'd wake Akara up at 3 a.m. He's used to my odd-hour wakeup calls to go for a run. But I have major news to unleash, and I'd rather deliver it at an appropriate hour.

4 a.m. seems more doable.

I try not to think about the other reason I'm biding time to interact with my bodyguard.

The funhouse.

My stomach twists. I haven't spoken to Akara *or* Banks about that night. Really, we haven't had any serious conversations since the Carnival Fundraiser.

They've just done their bodyguard thing, and I've been happy to pretend that night never existed.

Fuck, that's a lie.

Did I mention I'm a shit liar? Can't even formulate one in my own head.

To be fucking crystal clear, I totally, sincerely wish that I could just look them both square in the face and ask, "Are you fucking attracted to me?" Sometimes…most of the time…it feels like no one ever is.

I'm every guy's friend.

Best buddy.

The girl pal.

Someone to shoot the shit with but not someone to bang. It didn't ever used to bother me this much. Because I'm raised by a mom that taught me not to put my worth in the hands of what men think about me. But it's hard to be the daughter of a former high fashion model, the daughter of a *sex* symbol, and not feel like maybe I didn't inherit one tiny piece of her beauty. Her charm.

I'm charmless.

I'm just crude.

I blow hot breath out of my nose.

Too bad I'm also stubborn as hell, and like fuck will I be less crude for anyone. I take another check of the clock. With an hour to kill, I quickly change into a sports bra, gray muscle shirt and some turquoise nylon shorts. A weight bench is pushed up against the far side of my room, and I start slipping on the plates to each end.

I can get a solid workout in before I confront Akara.

Confront.

Wrong choice of word. I sit on the bench.

Talk.

Better.

I grab the bar over my head, and as soon as my fingers curl over the metal, I let all the thoughts drift out of my head. After years of training for the Olympics, I've learned how to focus. To empty the invasive thoughts to make way for the here and now.

I count in my head with each rep.

The ache in my muscles goads me to keep going and sweat builds up along my skin. Halfway through, my breathing heavies and it takes more energy to do the same movements.

When my arms start quaking like jelly, I set the bar back in its rack. I may love pushing my limits, but I don't have a spotter. And an injury is a worse outcome.

I wipe the sweat off my forehead with my arm, and my eyes flit to the clock.

3:45 a.m.

Close enough. The longer I prolong talking to Akara—the more I'm going to be chicken-shit scared and back out. I can't back out.

I made up my mind last night. And that's that.

Grabbing my water bottle from the nightstand, I make a quick exit from my room. I wind through the hallway and leave through the front door, entering a foyer with an elevator.

Akara lives three floors below the penthouse in a two-bedroom apartment with some of the other Security Force Omega bodyguards.

His roommates: Banks Moretti, Paul Donnelly, and Quinn Oliveira.

As the elevator drops me off, and I walk down the hallway of the 30th floor, I type out a quick text to Akara. At your door. Can we talk?

I don't overthink it before I hit send, and then I slide my cell into my shorts pocket.

Waiting for a reply, I pop the lid to my water bottle. At this early hour, it's no surprise that the hallway is empty and dead quiet. Water rushes down the back of my throat.

The door suddenly opens—

A very shirtless Banks Moretti exits the apartment.

I inhale quickly and *choke* in surprise.

"You alright?" Banks whispers in concern and softly shuts the apartment door behind him. *That's strange.* But it's hard to focus on his actions when I'm coughing into my elbow.

I nod vigorously. "It just"—I motion to my throat—"went down the wrong way." *Because I was expecting someone else. Not you.*

And not a half-naked *you.*

Gray drawstring pants hang low like he threw them on quickly to meet me in the hall. Dog tags lie against his unshaven chest. More hair leads down his sculpted body, a trail right to his package.

Oh, fuck, I'm looking at his crotch.

I raise my gaze and catch his shadowy smile. He leans against the wall next to the shut door, muscular arms threading loosely. "You used to swallowing water?"

Pool water, yeah. My natural makeup is probably half-chlorine by now. But that response flits away as I take a sip from my water bottle, then I reply, "Probably not as much as you're used to making girls choke." I let out a weak laugh because I can't tell if we're buddy-buddy still. Maybe we never really were…

I'm so fucking confused.

Banks shuts one eye. "You'd be surprised." His other eye tightens like fluorescents suddenly beam at him. But the hallway lighting is dim at best.

I'd be surprised? "It was a blow job joke," I say, thinking he didn't get it.

"I know." He rubs his temple. "Don't love blow jobs as much as other things." His nose flares while he takes a long blink.

"Hey, are you alright?" I step forward.

"Yeah." He expels a heavy breath. "No…actually I've gotta grab something." He stands off the wall, but hesitates to go back inside the apartment.

And that's when I realize, "Akara sent you?"

Banks bounces his head. "He just needs five minutes, then he can talk."

Five minutes?

Doing what?

"Is he taking a shit or something?" I ask.

Banks almost laughs. The sound catches in his chest. "Or something." He shuts another eye again. Is he in pain?

I frown, my concern building like a snow-packed avalanche. "Don't let me hold you up. Go do your thing."

Banks glances down either side of the hall. *I'm famous.* It's easy to forget when it's almost 4 a.m. and I'm standing in a ghost town of a hallway.

Totally safe.

But I can understand how he'd feel responsible if someone snuck up on me while he's gone.

"Come with me?" Banks asks. "I don't wanna leave you out here alone."

I nod. "Scared a big bad wolf will devour me?"

He turns the doorknob and shakes his head. "You were raised by wolves. If anything, you're going to devour some poor bastard one day."

I can't take my eyes off him. What I'd give to know how Banks actually sees me. The saddest thought: I'll probably *never* fucking find out.

Opening the door, he tells me, "I just know you hate being alone. I don't like the idea of you standing out here waiting for him by yourself."

That literally causes words to evaporate in my head. Leaving pure emotion. Something swells inside my throat, my chest, and I walk dazedly behind Banks while my heartbeat sputters.

Thanks for not leaving me alone, I want to say.

Words are trapped, and instead, I focus on where he's going. I follow his footsteps into the darkly lit living room (brown leather furniture galore), then over to the nearby tiny kitchen.

The microwave and oven light cast a soft glow over the counters. Banks opens several drawers. Quietly shutting them.

"What are you looking for?" I try to whisper.

"This." He snatches a bottle of Tylenol, then tries to twist the child-proof cap. "It's just a small headache."

Doesn't seem that fucking small. His jaw muscle tics like he's gritting his teeth. He grunts out a frustrated breath, struggling to open the bottle. His headache must be like a rock concert in his temple.

I come closer and take the Tylenol from his hand. He lets me, and I easily unscrew the cap. "How many?"

"Three."

I dole three pills into his palm.

He tosses them back, and I hand him my water bottle.

Banks takes a swig with a short nod and thanks, then washes down the pain meds. He wipes his mouth with the back of his hand. "You want something to eat?" He rests against the counter. "I was making rigott' and toast earlier—before Akara asked me to get the door."

I notice the bread bag near the toaster. "Rigott'?" I ask, picking up the canister of what looks like sour cream.

"*Ricotta*," he enunciates.

"You're eating ricotta cheese on toast?"

He tries his hardest to look at me, but his headache lowers his tightened gaze. "My brother is the good cook. This is the best I got."

"Seems like a weird combo for breakfast."

"Says the girl who eats jellybeans on waffles."

"I've only done that twice." I untwist the bread bag. "Jellybeans are better with chocolate syrup on a spoon."

"Anyone ever tell you that's fucking disgusting?" He tucks his hair beneath his left ear, then right.

I take out two slices. "All the fucking time. Don't knock it till you try it."

"Same here," he nods to the ricotta. "My grandma eats rigott' and toast every morning." He plucks the bread from my hands and pops the slices in the toaster.

"I can finish breakfast for you since you're not feeling that great."

"It's just a headache, not a coma." He rubs his eyes though, and the smile he tries to give me is brief and weak.

Still, I grab a knife for the ricotta. "I've never seen you complain when Thatcher does stuff for you."

"He's my twin. He's duty-bound from birth to do shit for me." He watches me pop the ricotta lid. "Look, I'm not that much of a gobbadost'—I just don't want you to think I'm dying here."

He's said that Italian-American word before. *Gobbadost'*. For the life of me, I can't remember what it means. So I guess, "You're not that much of an idiot?"

Banks almost laughs. "Hardhead."

"Fuck, I was not close." The toast ejects. "And I don't think you're dying, so can I?" I reach for the warm bread.

He nods and lets me spread ricotta on the toast. "You gonna try it?"

"Just a bite." I cringe as I keep spreading. "It looks gross, like cottage cheese." *Which has the consistency of curdled sour cream.*

"Food doesn't need to look pretty to be good."

I drop the knife in the sink. "In my case, food that looks like a unicorn farted all over it is the best food." I just stare at the bland finished product on the paper plate. Like maybe in a couple fucking seconds it'll look more appetizing.

Banks picks up the toast. "Close your eyes."

I zero in on his closeness. My breath shallows because his eyes flit around my features in a way that I almost believe he thinks I'm pretty to look at. While he towers above me, a feat in itself, I gently close my eyes. For a moment, I pretend he's about to kiss me.

Not a gentle peck either. Like a grab your face, push you against the counter, leave you utterly fucking breathless *kiss.*

"Take a bite."

Definitely not about to kiss. But I smile as the toast nudges against my shut lips. I take a tiny bite. Tasting mostly *plainness.* So I take a bigger one, and the ricotta is just…

My eyes open, face contorting. I chew slowly. *Ugh.*

Banks laughs, then uses his foot to pry open a sliding drawer to a trash bin. I spit out the half-mashed bite of toast.

"You sure that's not in the cottage cheese family?" I sip from my water bottle.

"It's…" He trails off as we hear footsteps towards the bedrooms.

The noise stops.

My eyes skim the width of their apartment. I'm not here a lot, if ever. Usually they'll just come hang out at the penthouse. It's clean for four guys crashing here, but this is about how clean security's townhouse was too. No crushed, empty beers cans, no panties or bras lying around. It looks more like a professional sleep-space.

So maybe Akara is just taking a 4 a.m. business call?

A door creaks open. Just as I take a swig of water, a shirtless Akara Kitsuwon saunters towards the kitchen.

I *choke* again.

"You okay, Sul?" Akara asks with furrowed brows. He comes up to the bar counter that separates me and Banks from him.

His shoulder. His chest.

Wide-eyed, I wipe dribble off my lips and zero in on the fresh *tattoo.* Colorful ink covers his shoulder, upper bicep, and part of his upper-chest like a plate of armor. The design is mesmerizing: a snake winding around budding red roses and some type of yellow flower. Scales a rich green.

Beyond the new tattoo, sweat casts a glossy sheen over his bare chest and abs. His black hair—grown out enough to curl behind his ears—is a little damp.

My face begins to slowly fall.

It's not wet like he took a shower. It's damp from *sweat.*

Oh fuck me…

Five minutes.

Though, I ask hopefully, "Were you just getting tattooed?"

"What?" he frowns and glances at his fresh ink. "No, I got it a few days ago." He'd been talking about getting a tattoo, so I shouldn't be *that* fucking shocked. But I guess I always thought I'd be there. That he'd *want* me there. Before I ask if it's Donnelly's work, he explains, "I was around Old City and passed a tattoo shop. It was a spur of the moment thing."

I just nod, not sure what to say.

Banks bites into the toast I nibbled.

"What's up?" Akara asks me.

I texted him to talk. But I can't shake how tense he looks.

He checks over his shoulder. "Can we go in the hall to chat?"

Someone's in his room. He's not sweating from weightlifting like I'd been doing.

Sex.

He was 100% having sex. The fact settles heavy in my stomach for some strange reason. Am I seeing mid-fuck Akara right now? Or is this his post-nut high?

My thoughts aren't making this any better. A knot twists inside me.

"Um…" I stumble for a second before settling on a decision. "You know what, it can wait. You go back to Bone Town. Finish strong."

I've actually said these words to him before—but today, *after* the funhouse, it feels a little different. I go fast for the door.

Nearly there, Akara reaches out and grabs my wrist. "Wait—" he starts.

"Akara?" a woman calls out.

Akara and I spring apart like an electric shock.

A blue-eyed, auburn-haired beauty has strolled out of his bedroom. She looks older than me. Probably closer to his age. Late-twenties. Freckles splatter her flushed cheeks, and a sheet is wrapped around her curvy, naked frame. Like she could be modeling for a half-nude oil portrait.

Suddenly, I'm highly attuned to my sweat-stained gray shirt, messy ponytail, and frumpy running shorts. My lack of shower this morning shouldn't be *that* regretful, but the dark hair on my legs is longer than the usual prickly layer.

My leg-hair is obvious in a way that sends alarm signals in my brain.

Sulli the Sasquatch.

Insecurities fucking suck ass.

So I think, *W.W.F.M.J.*

Luna and I coined the acronym last year. *Wise Words from Maximoff & Jane.* I go to them for advice all the time, and right now, Jane would tell me to try not to compare myself to anyone. *I'm myself.* She's *herself.* And we both can be fucking awesome…in our own ways.

I'm just the hairy one.

Fuck. I want to bathe in a vat of confidence. I know it's there. It's within me. It's just washed off for a second.

Akara lets go of my wrist, his eyes on her. "Give me a second, Jenny."

Jenny.

Slowly, I back up towards the kitchen.

Is Jenny short for Jennifer?

Is he already on a nickname basis with this girl? If she's more than a casual hookup, why don't I know anything about her? He'd tell me if he was dating someone. Right? We're supposed to be friends.

Jenny plants her eyes on me. Luckily, she's not cutting me with a death-glare for interrupting what I'd bet is an epic night of sex. Not that I know what getting fucked feels like. But I'm sure from Akara it'd be rated 5-stars. No deductions.

Bitterness rises to my mouth. Discomfort roasts me all over. So I open the freezer. Cool air blasting my hot skin, I grab a bag of frozen broccoli as something to do.

Jenny smiles a friendly smile. "You must be Sullivan. I've heard so much about you."

What? I frown deeply at Akara.

He's shaking his head. "Not from me, Sul."

Jenny laughs softly. "Right, definitely not. He told me there's a bodyguard-client confidentiality thing. I totally get it. But I know a lot from online. My little sis just started competitive swimming, so she looks up to you a lot."

"Oh, fucking rad," I say into a single nod. Jenny seems…nice. Like really nice. I don't know why that aggravates me even more. It really shouldn't especially since she has a little sister just like I do.

Weight sinks further in my gut.

Jenny returns her attention to Akara. "I'll be waiting, Kits." She winks flirtatiously before slinking back into his bedroom.

My stomach has tossed five times.

Kits?

Kits!

She called him KITS!

What. The. *Fuck!*

I've never heard a single person call him that but me. My mouth dries, and I feel a hand on my shoulder. "Breathe, mermaid," Banks whispers beside my ear. He pries the frozen broccoli out of my iron-grip. My hand is pink and numb.

Akara runs his fingers through his black hair a thousand times before rooting his palm on his stiff shoulder. Like his muscles are too tight. His gaze is on me, at least. He's not avoiding me. But then he drops his hand to say, "What do you need, Sul?"

Oh no.

"Oh no," I actually say. "We're not going to talk about her?" I realize how loud I'm speaking. "Sorry," I whisper. My eyes ping down the hallway to the other bedrooms. "I didn't mean to shout." Disturbing a sleeping Donnelly and Quinn wasn't on the agenda when I decided to come here at 4 a.m.

It wasn't a well thought-out plan.

Fucking obviously.

Akara comes closer. "She's a friend of a friend. It's just casual."

"But she called you *Kits*?" I frown deeply.

Banks places the frozen broccoli on a shelf behind me.

Akara cringes. "It happens. Some people have seen *We Are Calloway*—and there are times that you've used the nickname on air."

Honestly, I haven't really watched a lot of the aired segments since I joined the docuseries. Watching myself on TV is fucking weird.

I swallow a lump in my throat. "That makes sense." But I'm burning alive, a heartbeat from stepping into the freezer and shutting the door.

Because the more territorial I seem over Akara, the worse I feel. He's not mine.

We're not dating. We're barely even *friends* at this point. Whatever we were is dangling on a cliff by a cheap friendship-bracelet string. The kind that frays after one hot summer.

I tuck my water bottle under my arm. Step away from the freezer. And try to salvage what's left here. So I nudge his arm. "I hope you gave her an orgasm. Rocked her world. Stroked her clit. All that good stuff."

Banks hangs his head, eyes on the ground with a soft smile.

Akara is trying to read my features. Maybe to see if I'm sincere. His eyes are asking, *you're okay? We're better?*

Banks lifts his head. "Yeah, Akara." Humor laces his voice. "You stroke that clit?"

Akara smiles, flips off Banks, then turns to me. He opens his mouth. Closes it. Rethinking. Before he says, "If you really want to know, I made her come four times. So you can stop worrying about that."

I'm really not worried about it.

Just trying to re-knot the friendship bracelet of our friendship.

It feels like a little too late.

"Yeah, I won't worry anymore," I tell him.

He frowns. "We're okay?"

"I don't know," I say honestly. "You tell me, Kits."

He rakes a hand through his hair. "What can I do?"

"Nothing. You've done nothing wrong. You're allowed to have a girlfriend—"

"She's not my girlfriend—"

"Friendly casual date, whatever."

Akara sighs, hating this place we're at, but of the few times we've fought or entered awkward territory, he's always tried his hardest to repair the damage. It means a lot to me. Because at the very least, I know he doesn't want to lose me completely.

Maybe that's why his silence after the funhouse felt so fucking different. I'm usually the one who avoids and he's the one who insists on working through the mess.

"Can we just start over?" I ask him.

He massages his hands, but his eyes never leave me. "How far back? Do I need to reintroduce myself to you?" An attractive smile inches up his face. "Hi, I'm Akara." He extends his hand. "Born and bred in Northwest Philly, fourth-generation Thai, son of a broker and of a former-pro Muay Thai fighter. I hate people who walk too slowly on sidewalks, and I've had the honor of protecting a competitive string bean."

It makes me smile.

And I shake his hand with a firm grip. "Sulli."

"Just Sulli?"

"You can look me up on the internet."

"Ouch." He touches his heart.

I pat his sweaty shoulder. "I do have to tell you something that can't be found online." I look around for Banks. He's tossing his paper plate in the trash, about to leave. "Wait, Banks," I say fast. "You should probably hear this too."

He leans a hip on the stove.

Akara grows more serious. "This is why you texted me?"

"Yeah," I nod. "I want to leave for the mountains today. The earlier, the better. And you can't tell my parents."

It's going to be a covert road trip out west. With Akara.

And most likely Banks.

There's no running away from this one.

4

Sullivan Meadows

MY DAD HAS BEEN ON the cover of *National Geographic* more times than I can count. He'll be the first to say it's a stupid fucking accomplishment—that the personal goals are the ones to strive for.

Personally, I thought he wouldn't have taken it so hard when I told him my new goal. That I wanted to free-solo climb his old routes.

He taught me how to climb before I even learned how to read. Plastic anchors and footholds spindled up my childhood bedroom wall like I lived and breathed inside a jungle gym. I loved the difficulty, the challenge, and the euphoric feeling when I reached the top.

My dad would swoop me up in his arms, and we'd cheer together.

As soon as I was old enough, I gripped real rock and ascended. While I trained for swimming in my teens, I climbed as a way to condition on dry land.

Rock climbing has always, *always* been a part of my fucking life. Swimming is my first love, but climbing is something else. If families gather around the TV every night to watch *Survivor* or *The Amazing Race*, my family gathered around cliff faces. It brought us closer. Bound us together.

For me and Winona, climbing became a part of our DNA.

Our dad taught us how to sport climb, using preplaced bolts.

He taught us how to trad climb, placing our own safety gear as we ascended.

He taught us how to free-solo when we craved to learn. No rope, no harness. No safety equipment. Just your body, the rock, and a sack of chalk.

My dad—Ryke Meadows—is considered the greatest free-solo climber in the world. He'll be the first to say, *it's not true.* That others are better out there. He's just the most recognizable. The one who's shown his face to the media.

But at the thought of his daughters learning to free-solo from someone else, he caved under our wishes and longing. He taught us the *safest* way. To never put ourselves in a situation where we couldn't accomplish the task.

Because if you fail at free-soloing, you're either gravely injured… or you're dead.

Due to the high-risks, I've only attempted to free-solo smaller faces. Mostly, I've spent a good portion of the past few months speed-climbing. Breaking new personal records. Clocking in faster and faster times. Until the allure slowly fizzled out, the challenge completed, and I needed to set another goal.

So a couple days after the carnival—on my dad's fiftieth birthday—I told him, "I want to free-solo climb all of your old routes."

After the words left my mouth, he just stared at me for a long moment and then said, "Fuck no."

Despite my dad's public reputation as a foul-mouthed, aggressive dude, he's actually a soft teddy bear at heart. I can count on my hand the number of times he's actually told me *no.*

My throat closed that day. "You can't be serious."

"I'm dead fucking serious. You're not climbing *all* my routes."

"I'll put in the time and work up to the more advanced ones—"

"Sulli, it's not fucking happening." He shot up from the couch, brown eyes blazed with heat.

"Dad—"

"Do you even realize who you're named after?" His voice rose and he paused quickly to breathe through his nose.

In his silence, my veins iced. "Adam Sully." I said *his* name.

My namesake.

I watched my dad's eyes glass. He took a full minute to formulate words. "I'm not losing you to the mountain, too."

I touched my chapped lips. "I'm not going to fall. I'm smart. I'm calculated. You know this about me. I'd *never* take a risk that I couldn't complete." Injuries were death knells for me growing up. Being careful is something that Meadows aren't known for, but I broke that mold a long time ago.

"You wouldn't do the ultra-marathon without Moffy, but you want to go do this?"

I wanted to complete the ultra-marathon because my dad had accomplished the same run. The Atacama Crossing in Chile. Maybe I have something to prove to myself. That I'm as strong as he was at my age. Maybe I'm sentimental and just driven by a connection to my dad and these moments in life that are so beyond reason.

The spiritual feeling of accomplishing something that takes every ounce of heart, grit, and mental fortitude, I want that with each goal. And to know that I understand *that feeling*—that I share this with *him*—it drives me to go after the things he once did.

With his bad knee, he couldn't run the ultra-marathon with me. I felt like it'd be too dangerous for me to run alone. No bodyguard would be able to keep up.

Only Moffy could.

"Free-soloing is different than the ultra," I told him. "Bodyguards can be at a cliff site if something happens—but *it won't.* I'm going to climb the route with gear first. Over and over." I'd never free-solo without practicing with safety equipment.

He kept shaking his head. "No. You're not doing it. End of the fucking story."

"You can't force me not to," I said stubbornly. "I'm twenty-fucking-one."

He went pale. "You're still my *kid.*"

"And you know me better than anyone," I said. "You know that when someone says, *you can't.* I'm going to prove them wrong."

He ran a hand through his hair and then dropped it to his side. "You step foot in Nevada, California, Montana"—he listed the states off his fingers—"Wyoming, Colorado, Utah, Arizona…I'm coming to collect your ass."

That left the smaller rock faces. Easier climbs. Less preparation and training. Ones I could do in a few hours.

I frowned deeper. "You've always believed in me. I don't fucking understand."

His face shattered for a second. "I still believe in you. But Sulli… you drive his fucking *Jeep*." He pointed at the door. "You have his fucking name."

I waited for him to add another fact that we both knew. The one that would send a blade through my heart. *My birth almost killed my mom.* And even before that, *my conception was harder than hell.* It took a lot for me to make it into the world, so I don't hold my life in my hands with carelessness. I understand the toll it took to bring me here. And my mom's fertility struggles meant she couldn't even get pregnant again after me. Winona is biologically my mom and dad's daughter, but she was carried to term by our Aunt Rose.

I waited for those words from my dad. *Sulli, your birth almost killed your mom.*

But they never came. A silence hung in the air, and I realized that no matter how angry my dad was, he'd never hurt me that bad.

I breathed in harshly. "So if I were Winona, you'd be okay with this?"

He didn't say anything.

It was a resounding *yes.*

If my name weren't Sullivan.

If he didn't give me Adam Sully's Jeep.

If I hadn't been so wrapped inside his best friend's death, then maybe my dad would've given me his blessing.

Instead, it's seven in the morning and I'm currently riding in that old green Jeep, the one I treat like my baby.

And I'm on the way to Montana. To Yellowstone Country.

My dad and my mom have no clue.

It's fucking killing me.

I don't think I've ever lied to them. Growing up, they've been my best friends and being "rebellious" feels like a suffocatingly tight swimsuit. It crushes my ribcage. Cuts off my circulation.

To circumvent the guilt that gnaws, I've been busying myself with rechecking supplies and mapping out the first few climbs. With winter approaching, I need to knockout several major climbs in Yellowstone before bad weather hinders what I can do.

Tablet on my lap, I scroll through some of the popular climbing forums and focus on various areas around the Yellowstone region, including south Montana (aka Yellowstone Country), Wyoming, possibly Grand Teton.

If I filled my dad in on this trip, I think he'd be at least glad I'm not hitting the most difficult climb first. California—Yosemite National Park—that pit stop is dead-last. Possibly even *off* my radar. The Yosemite Triple Crown, three cliff faces, were the hardest climbs my dad ever free-soloed, and I can't imagine climbing those behemoths without safety gear.

I know what I'm capable of with the time I'm given to practice. Yosemite—I'd need *years* to master those rock walls. Research is a big part of climbs, and I'm not going into this blindfolded.

I'm also not going to Montana alone.

Banks mans the wheel and chews on a toothpick, while Akara messes with the air vents in the passenger seat. They're broken…again. The Jeep is old, and normally, I'd just roll down the windows, but paparazzi are still trailing us.

I'm used to the muggy, too-warm feeling from winters at indoor heated pools, but Banks and Akara are noticeably sweating.

"Hey, Kits," I call up to him. "I swear if you rub the dashboard and whisper to the vent, *you're not a piece of crap*, three times, cool air will come out."

Akara glances back. "You're fucking with me?"

Banks nearly smiles. "Sounds legit to me."

"It's worked *almost* every time," I assure.

"I've been with you almost *every time* and I've never seen you do that," Akara refutes.

"It was in private," I say. "She's shy."

"What'd you name her?" Banks asks me. It's not the first time we've all ridden in the Jeep together, but lately, she hasn't had as much attention as family gossip.

"Wait for it," Akara tells Banks with a wiseass smile. Kits was there when my sister and I coined the nickname. Plus, he's heard me use it.

"I named her *Booger*—said in love," I add quickly while they both break into laughter at my green Booger Baby.

I find the nearest thing to throw, a pair of old dirty hiking socks and I chuck one at Banks and one at Akara.

They laugh more.

"She's going to break down if you keep making fun of her," I point out.

Banks strokes the wheel. "I'll fix her real good." He's touching Booger more than he's ever touched me. The thought sinks my stomach.

Fuck that—my car is *not* more attractive than me. But Booger is hot old metal.

Akara scoots closer to the vent. "You're not a piece of crap." He rubs the dashboard, trying to cage laughter. "You're not a piece of crap. You're not a piece of crap."

We wait in silence.

And then cold air blows out.

I smile. "Told you. She just needs some reassuring." I'm about to return to my climbing research, but Akara looks disturbed.

"How did that happen?" he asks Banks, probably since Banks is a skilled mechanic and understands cars.

Banks lifts a shoulder. "Maybe somethin' to do with you putting pressure on the dash." He makes a face at himself though like that's bullshit. "Or God."

Akara leans back. "I don't like fucking with the dead."

Because the Jeep belonged to someone who passed away.

"Amen," Banks says.

I edge toward the middle console. "You're both overreacting. The spirit of Adam Sully doesn't live within this car. He's in the fucking sky and in peace, so you both can stop freaking out."

I'm actually pretty superstitious, so their uneasiness is making *me* uneasy. And I love this green Booger too much. If anything, the spirit of my dad's best friend would only want to protect me.

Banks is driving casually. "I'm not freaking out."

Akara nods, but he's busy texting.

What if he's texting Jenny? I could just ask...as a friend to a friend. Staying close to the middle console between their seats, I say, "So how'd you leave things with Jenny?"

Akara rotates slightly, his deep brown eyes locking onto mine. "Why do you want to know?"

I accidentally glance at the phone.

He already puts two and two together. "I'm not texting Jenny."

"I just wanted to know if I should expect to see her around. I mean, it's okay if I do—"

"You won't," he says quickly. "She's not a girlfriend."

My stomach flip-flops. Not sure exactly what I feel, I just say the truth, "I'm glad that you're finding time for yourself, Kits." I lean more towards Banks and tap the back of his headrest. "Banks, I hope you're finding time to get laid too."

That seemed casual, right?

The car sobers though. No laughter, no grinning. A strange tension winds through the Jeep. Should I call this part of my life: The Death of All Friendships?

I draw further back.

Banks moves his toothpick with his teeth. "I'm doin' alright." He glances in the rearview at me. "Out of the three of us, you're the one we should probably be concerned about."

I pull my knee up to my chest. "Because I'm a virgin?"

"Because of what you told me and Akara. That you'd want to lose your virginity to one of us."

My chest collapses in shock, and my smile flickers in and out because I'm thinking, *fuck yes! We're finally talking about the funhouse!* And then *oh my fucking God, we're about to talk about the funhouse.*

But Akara suddenly slides Banks a harsh look. I've found the tight-lipped one of the two.

Banks goes quiet. He uses one casual hand to turn down a road. Booger bumps over a pothole. And the silence is tearing up my nerves.

I feel like I'm on a swim platform and constantly taking false starts. I just want to rewind.

Go back.

Back.

Please.

"I'm withdrawing my virginity offer," I say suddenly. "Neither of you need to be concerned about my V-card. If I don't have a boyfriend again, I can just die with my virginity intact."

Banks now shoots Akara a glare.

Akara turns to me. "Why do you think you won't have another boyfriend?"

"I don't trust people that easily," I say, resting my chin on my knee. But really, I'm thinking, *maybe because the guys I like are the ones who don't even want me.*

"You'll trust someone enough again," Akara encourages, but his Adam's apple bobs, and I wonder if he's hoping I won't. I always had the feeling that he didn't love Will Rochester when I started dating him, but he never told me to break up with him either.

My insides twist. "I'd rather just be friends with you two than ruin that with some virginity thing."

Akara nods tensely.

Banks barely reacts.

I just take both responses as the damage is done. We've crossed the Rubicon, and there's no turning back. Not even Akara's "shake the hand, reintroduction trick" could really change that.

Fan-fucking-tastic.

I'm headed to Montana, and this endless car ride is going to be four-fifths full of *awkward* tension that I can't erase.

Akara eyes the road as a paparazzi vehicle hugs too close to us.

I buckle my seatbelt and pick up my tablet again.

"Take the next right and circle around," Akara tells Banks. "We'll lose the last one and then you can jump onto the freeway."

"Right on." Banks swerves to catch the next turn.

I tune out their security talk.

"Shit, it's blowing heat again," Akara says after a minute or two, but he doesn't fiddle with the vents. We're all just sitting in an uncomfortable swelter, which is not all my Booger Baby's fault.

I break the quiet. "We're still headed to REI?"

"Yep," Banks says.

"Alright, good." I try to focus on the checklist, but I can feel their eyes ping to me every so often. My neck is burning. My face is burning.

My whole fucking body is burning.

Concentrate, Sulli.

Right, we have to pick up more supplies before hitting the official road to Montana. I have most of the climbing gear—stuff I picked up from my parents' house last week—but I didn't want to grab the camping equipment. My mom would ask questions, and I'd spill every last detail. Hell, I *still* want to spill even without her asking.

"Fuck this heat," Akara complains as he pushes his hair back with two hands and then reaches for the vents again. I think he's being kind by not saying *Fuck this Jeep.*

I barely glance up. "I can take her into a shop once we're in Montana."

"I'll just take a look at her," Banks says to me, and he catches my eyes in the rearview. "My ma's a mechanic. Spent my teens working in the shop with her."

I knew he had the skills, but didn't know how he got them.

"That's cool that you did that with your mom."

The corner of his mouth lifts. "Yeah, I didn't see it like that until I got older. Back then, I didn't have a choice, really. Needed the money, and I didn't want to work as a busboy like my brother."

His brother is going to marry my cousin.

The fact rolls up to me now and again. Sometimes I wonder if it'd complicate anything between me and Banks. So far it hasn't, but I guess we're not much of anything anyway.

"Weren't you a lifeguard?" Banks asks me.

"When I was fourteen," I say. "It was at a local community pool, but kids kept fake-drowning so I'd save them."

"Can't blame them," Banks says.

"Why? You'd want to be saved by the famous Sullivan Minnie Meadows too?"

"Not 'cause you're famous, mermaid."

Is he…is he flirting? My pulse skips. *No way.* My brows pinch, and Akara shifts uncomfortably in his seat. He switches a knob on the air conditioning.

No luck.

Akara glances back. "Maybe those kids were trying to see if you'd grow fins and a tail." He tosses the dirty sock that I threw at him right back at me.

"Jokes on them because I quit after a week." I chuck it back again. "And I thought you didn't believe in mermaids."

"I don't." He has trouble facing forward, away from me.

I'm about to speak when a text pings my phone.

> Morning, my peanut butter cupcake. Hope you have a wonderful day! Guess what? That new donut shop you'd been talking about is opening up down the street from Superheroes & Scones tomorrow. We should go next time you're free. Love you to the moon and back xoxo – Mom

My stomach sinks into the fucking Earth.

"Sul?" Akara's concern leaks from his voice.

"It's just my mom."

"Everything alright?" Banks asks.

I swallow hard and toss my cell between my hands. "Yeah, it's all normal. Which, I guess is the problem. I just..." I exhale into a deeper frown. "I don't like keeping this from my parents. It feels wrong." I hug my legs to my chest.

Banks wipes sweat off his brow. "If it's eating at you, just call them."

"Exactly," Akara chimes in, wafting his shirt which looks damp.

"What if my dad shows up and demands you return me?"

Banks nearly smiles.

Akara shakes his head. "We didn't kidnap you, Sulli. We're not going to listen to him."

My brows raise. "You wouldn't listen to Ryke Meadows?"

Akara rotates more fully to face me. Confidence eking from every small movement. His eyes lock onto mine. "I won't listen to Ryke Meadows."

More heat bathes me. As does skepticism. "You remember Red Rocks when I wanted to go off on the long trail by myself. Without you, even. And my dad said, not that day because I'd already done a hard morning swim. You agreed with him."

He barely blinks. "You were seventeen."

"So?"

"You're twenty-one now." He tilts his head, hair falling over his forehead. "An adult."

I've always wanted to hear him say those words.

You're an adult now.

My parents had an epic, soul-mate kind of love that started out as a beautiful friendship, and my mom met my dad when she was fifteen. He was twenty-one. And he never even let himself love her in that way until months after her eighteenth birthday.

When I was sixteen, I dreamt of Akara saying those words to me once I was older. *You're an adult now.*

When I was seventeen, I kept that dream.

When I turned eighteen, I threw that dream in the fucking garbage.

He never fell on his knees and proclaimed his love for me. Never made the grand gesture and chose me over being my bodyguard. Never told me we could be together because I was older and *an adult.* Hell, he never even checks me out or makes an indication that he thinks I'm attractive. I've heard him call women *babes.*

She's a total babe.

What a babe.

But never to me. Never about me.

In his eyes, I'm probably as sexy as a hairy little caterpillar.

Since then, I thought I've accepted what we are. He's just Kits to me. But recently, lately, I guess I wanted to test the waters. I'm not sixteen-years-old holding onto a fantasy, but I did have some hope that two friends could find a morsel of romance.

Even if it was just for a single night.

Akara must read my silence as indecision because he adds, "Your dad can't force you back home, Sul. He knows that. He's just scared."

My dad's not scared of anything, I almost say. I stop myself because I know if anything *could* freak him out, it'd be losing me or Winona or Mom.

I open up my contacts on my phone. Am I still flying too close to the nest? Should I *really* call my parents just to snitch on my own whereabouts? But I can't stomach lying about this. Not for a thousand more miles, not even for *ten* more.

I dial my dad's number.

I'd rather confront his anger than carry the weight of this lie.

5

Banks Moretti

GETTING LAID IS EASY for me. I'm six-seven, built like a god, and my deep voice could melt the fuckin' sun. But easy is boring. I've had more fun trying to explore the ways to make a woman come than by having a pair of lips around my dick. The longer the roadmap to her orgasm, the better. But I can count the number of times I've truly been challenged in bed.

Zero.

Big ball of nothing.

And I'm not so arrogant to think that maybe the problem doesn't lie with me. If sex bores me, then that's got to at least be a fifty percent *me* problem. I'd blame my issues on not having enough time to cultivate real relationships beyond the first lay, but Akara has the same time-sucking job. And he does just fine going out on dates. I'm the one that shuts anything down after one night.

But I'm not that shocked Akara called it quits with Jenny. He's the kind of guy that hates to end things the morning after, but *Sulli* saw Jenny.

And Akara Kitsuwon is in love with Sullivan Meadows. He just hasn't fully accepted what's right in front of his face yet.

The past few months, I've thought to myself: *Banks Roscoe Moretti, you old fool, why don't you play cupid and put these two dummies together?* I've played Mother Goose to my first-ever client, young Xander Hale—my little chickadee.

Playing cupid can't be that hard.

Except Akara hasn't just dug in his heels. He's cemented his ankles in the fucking core of the Earth. The more I try to chisel him out, the more I look over at this strong-willed goddess of a woman. In leagues with Athena and Aphrodite. Joyful, funny, tough-as-nails Sullivan Meadows. And I wonder what the hell I'm doing.

No one ever warned cupid of accidentally shooting himself with an arrow. Never been good with a bow, anyway. Should've seen this clusterfuck coming.

Because I love Akara.

I love him too much to ever fuck him over.

And Sulli—she deserves to be swept off her feet. Probably by Akara. He's driven like her. He has money. A business.

He can offer her more than I can.

All I have is love to give, and seeing as how Akara *can* give that if he gets his head out of his ass, I'm going to come up short in the horse race.

I know that.

I know that.

Taking a deeper breath, I try to be okay with the state of things. *Semper Gumby.* Always flexible. I go where the wind blows me. Where I'm needed most.

Today it's in an REI.

Akara and I stand at the end of a shopping aisle. Both our eyes are planted on Sulli as she searches through a bin of plastic camping plates. Out of earshot of our client, Akara whispers to me, "Why were you flirting with her in the Jeep?" If we weren't friends, he'd have skewered me by now. And I'm not all innocent. I do enjoy busting Akara's balls now and again.

"Better question is why *you* were flirting with her in the Jeep."

He adjusts his earpiece. "I wasn't."

"That's horseshit," I whisper back, our eyes never leaving Sulli. "You threw a dirty sock at her."

"You insinuated she was hot enough to fake-drown for."

"She *is*," I say. "Tell me fourteen-year-old Akara wouldn't fake-flail in the deep-end hoping she'd dive down and rescue your ass?"

"I wouldn't. Because when I was fourteen, she was *eight*."

I grimace. "Alright, alright, that's *not* where I was going, man. She's *twenty-one* now."

He whisper-hisses, "And I've known her since she was *sixteen*, Banks. She's like a sister. I've told you that. It's different for you—it'll always be different."

Yeah, I haven't been her bodyguard for years. I'm not the one she really wants. I joined security right after the Marine Corps and became a bodyguard to Xander Hale. I've *seen* Sulli since I was twenty-two, but I didn't know her. Didn't spend time with her. Not like Akara.

I scratch the back of my head, frustrated, and I lean an arm against a shelf of tin can pots. "Maybe you should go find a mirror and reflect."

His eyes flit to me. "Maybe you should go find some cotton swabs and clean your ears out so I don't have to repeat the same shit a billion times."

I nod. "Who wants to tell her we're making a detour to Bed, Bath, and Beyond after this?"

Akara smiles.

I smile back before our gazes return to Sulli.

"She's Oscar Mike," I say, telling him she's *on the move* in military lingo. She can't hear us, but she's tossing some plastic camping plates into a shopping cart and heading to the next aisle.

As we walk, a soft thump bangs against my temple. God, I could use a cigarette right now. A few minutes pass, and I've gone quiet next to a rack of sleeping bags.

"What are you doing?" Akara asks, more at my silence.

"The usual." I put a toothpick between my teeth and bite down. "Waiting for my best friend to admit to his feelings."

"Hey, while you're waiting, you should go grab a canteen, some water, meal kits for a few dozen years—because it's going to be a long fucking time."

I lift my shoulder in a stiff shrug. "I have forever."

He laughs into another smile. "Funny, so do I."

My mouth curves up. "You're almost as stubborn as my brother."

"That's not possible."

Thatcher at least acknowledged his attraction to Jane. Akara won't even admit to himself that Sulli is beautiful. No bodyguard-client boundary forbids him from making a move. He's the fucking boss, and she won't fire him.

Denial—he's so far in fucking *denial* that I'm starting to think this is all a lost cause.

Maybe Akara does just see her like a sister, and my dumbass is putting too much energy in the wrong direction.

A buzz vibrates my pocket. I pull out my phone. "Speaking of that handsome devil." Checking the text, my jaw tightens.

> Uncle Joe wants me to invite Tony to the bachelor party. Put him on the list. – Cinderella

Yeah, I have Thatcher in my phone as *Cinderella* ever since Donnelly tattooed it on his ass. Barely makes me laugh after reading *that* text.

"Fuck," I mutter and show Akara the message. It's bad enough Tony Ramella is invited to my brother's wedding, and now the prick is going to the *party*.

Akara looks irritated too. "He'll probably decline the invite. Right?"

"He won't for the same reason Thatcher has to invite him. It's a family obligation. Uncle Joe is trying to glue-stick everyone back together so there's not a Capulet and Montague situation."

The Ramellas are married into the Morettis and Piscitellis. Tony is family.

I hate that he's family as much as Thatcher. Because I'd do anything for family, but Tony…after my brother saved his ass in a fire…he's still a raging prick.

He couldn't give a fuck about my brother or me.

But I'm not gonna be the one to create a war among my family. My mom is married to Nicola Ramella, and rifts with the Ramellas will directly affect her. She's had enough hardship in her life. I'm not giving her more.

I type out a text. Rah.

That's it.

Rah.

Short for *oorah*.

My brother can definitely feel my irritation in those three letters.

I shove my phone in my pocket. "As if planning this party wasn't hard enough."

Akara glances at me. "You know I can help—"

"No," I cut him off. "You have enough on your plate, *boss*." Akara needs me. It's why I'm here in the first place, watching over his client.

"Not enough that I can't make time for you," Akara says. "The offer isn't evaporating."

"Roger copy." *I'm not taking it.* For his sake.

Truth: I never thought throwing Thatcher's bachelor party would be hard. I figured it'd be a cake walk. And yeah, I always knew I'd be my brother's best man one day.

He's my twin—he's been a part of my life before I knew what *life* was. What he means to me is greater than air, than water. Almost losing him in that fire this year...that was the worst pain I've ever felt.

I'd rather be burned alive.

Being a best man, *easy*.

Organizing a bachelor party, *easy*. Buy some booze. Some wings and pizza. Probably go to Uncle Joe's row house, the biggest place among our family that'd cost us nothing.

Do it cheap.

Not that I wouldn't want to spend a lot of money on Thatcher. It's just not fucking sensible. It's a party. We grew up saving cash for practical shit. Clothes, toothpaste, the bad-luck day where you get in a wreck or the water heater breaks.

But Thatcher isn't marrying some good ole Italian-American girl our grandma introduced him to. Come November 1st—less than two months from now—he'll be married to a Cobalt.

American fucking royalty, and now I need to throw a bachelor party that includes *Cobalt brothers* on the guest list.

Thatcher has told me, "Let's not do it at Uncle Joe's row house."

Fuck me.

Anything for my brother. But opulence isn't something I understand. Like a gold brick fucking another gold brick, it makes no damn sense to me. Somehow, I gotta pull a rabbit out of a hat so this party looks made-for-royalty.

Akara and I fixate on Sulli as her phone rings.

She does a quick 360, making sure no one is in eyesight or earshot. Her eyes sweep me, then Akara for a brief second before answering her cell.

Squatting, Sulli hides behind a display of mountain bikes, phone to her ear.

She does that in public sometimes.

The squat and talk.

It's hotter than she knows because she squats with her legs spread open. It takes all my unholy energy not to stare at her so that I can focus on her AO. And her *area of operations* right now is as riveting as water dripping from a spigot.

The store is practically empty.

Too easy.

No targets, no shitheads, no threats.

Akara's eyes are rooted on Sulli. I can't tell if he's staring at her pussy, and I'm not about to triple-fucking check like a tennis match to figure it out.

She talks quietly enough that we can't hear her call. And the tension from the car ride to REI swarms me like a bad memory. The suffocating heat, her *revoking* the offer to take her virginity after we were little church mice, silent as can be.

I tuck hair behind my ear, and I slip Akara a glare.

"What?" he asks calmly and quietly under his breath.

"You know you're an asshole." My voice is deep and hushed.

He picks a bright neon-yellow bike helmet off a shelf in reach, and then reaches up to put it on my head. "In what way?" He smiles a little, even as he eyes his four o'clock, scanning the aisle.

The straps dangle by my chin. "You literally ordered me not to answer her declaration or question—whatever it was in the funhouse. And you're ignoring her too. Now she's retracting her offer—and she's allowed to change her mind," I add fast, "but how much of that is because we've made her uncomfortable by staying silent?"

Her statement was a moment of sincere vulnerability.

She said she was comfortable with us.

Trusted us.

And we've nuked it.

A groan dies inside his throat, and he places a closed fist on the shelf next to him. Eyes still on Sulli. "There's no good way to answer it without ruining...what we have."

I smack his chest. "Which is?"

"We're friends." He licks his lips, pushing back his black hair. "But it's not like *you* and *me.* The two of us are closer in age. We're both men. I've been friends with you longer. She's older now...but it's..." He sighs, confused, then shakes his head. "Her statement was hypothetical anyway. She's going to have a boyfriend who'll take her virginity. Let's just thank whoever it's not the fucking Rooster."

Yeah. Her ex-boyfriend, Will Rochester, is a cock.

I almost smile, remembering our exchange with Sulli when she found out her boyfriend's code name on comms.

"He's not a cock!" She slugged Akara's shoulder.

I laughed, then she slugged mine.

"His cock is probably ten times bigger than both of yours," she said in defiance.

"No way in hell," I told her.

She stared at our crotches. Unabashed, brazen as fuck.

This was almost a year ago. Akara reassured her she wasn't the butt of a joke, but I get the feeling she's thinking she's one now. Left out.

And we can't help that sometimes. Akara and I are older, like he said. We have a friendship that's different than when she joins us.

Not better or worse, just *different.*

In REI, Akara tells me quietly, "She doesn't need me or you to do it." *To take her virginity.*

"Then tell her that," I say. "Tell her something."

He shakes his head. "She wants me to say yes."

"Then say *yes.*"

He goes quiet.

"Mary Mother of God," I groan. "Then I'll say yes."

He shoots me a look like *no you will not.* And we've returned to square one.

Back in the funhouse, I was so close to replying to Sulli, *if that's what you want, I'd be of service.* But against better judgment, I turned to Akara. He gave me one of his classic *shut the fuck up, Banks* looks. So I shut down.

It wasn't until Sulli ran out of the funhouse that Akara told me hand-to-heart not to reply to her. Ever. To let her statement languish until it doesn't exist.

I'm not a coward. Neither is he.

But this is fucking cowardly. He's just so afraid of changing his dynamic with Sulli. He's gripping onto the past and trying to piece back the remnants, but it's already gone.

Probably for the better. She's not the teenager he used to protect anymore.

Sulli stands up and pockets her cell.

We grow quiet as she approaches.

"My parents called," she explains. "They'll be here in ten minutes." She nods a lot to herself, maybe nervously.

We're not scared of her parents. Akara and I were bodyguards to minors before, so we've had to deal with their parents throughout the years. He just has more experience with the Meadows than me.

Sulli pulls her cart closer. "We should finish shopping." She glances at my helmet, her lips inching in a smile. "I don't think that one's your color."

I snap the buckles, then eye Akara. "She's insulting your shopping skills."

"Hers aren't any better." He places a bright pink helmet on Sulli's head. "Gotta protect this one." He knocks the helmet with a light fist.

"Careful," I tell Akara, as we walk to the center of the store. "You break it, you bought it."

Sulli pushes the cart, staying quiet. She even removes the pink helmet and places it on a rack of lanterns. Red patches roast her cheeks.

My pulse nosedives. I should've just flirted back with her instead of making a joke to Akara. *God fucking dammit.* She looks more aware like it's the two of us versus her, and not just the three of us joking around.

Her neck is flushed, and she actually tries to outpace us. The wheels screech on the cart, and we let her go ahead.

"Shit," Akara mutters and fits a baseball hat on backwards.

We roll to a stop.

Sulli has halted in front of a display of tents. Two fingers rest to her lips in her iconic *concentration face.* An expression that has graced sports magazine covers.

Brown hair falling over her shoulder, she turns to Akara and me. "How fucking big should the tent be? Do I need two—?"

"Protocol is one," Akara reminds her. "But if you'd be more comfortable with—"

"One is fine," she cuts him off, her voice tight. "Just fucking fine." She tries to whisper but she's terrible at it.

I hang my head, smiling.

Akara meets my gaze, smiling too. Even in her frustration, she's really cute.

"Hey, string bean," Akara calls to Sulli. "Maybe up it to a four-person tent for this one." He squeezes my shoulder.

I smile again, biting on the toothpick.

She sizes me up, starting from my feet. No, really—she *lingers* on my feet, on my hands, then my dick. "Yeah, Jane said your brother has a big shoe size." It tenses the air. "I mean, I'm just guessing your size is the fucking same."

"Shoe size, yeah, but we're not the same."

"Oh hey, I know."

I nod more. *Christ*, I feel like a jackass for assuming she might see me like a carbon copy of Thatcher. I hate being treated like we're the same person.

We're two separate human beings with individual thoughts and desires, and I forget we even look alike half the time.

I motion to a teal four-person tent. "That one looks good."

"This one?" she points and looks for confirmation.

I nod.

She reads the tag for details.

Comms crackle in my earpiece, and I hear the Alpha lead. "Price to Akara and Banks, we're heading inside the store."

Akara clicks his mic. "See you."

My focused gaze diverts to the entrance. Two bodyguards are escorting a scruffy-jawed fifty-year-old Ryke Meadows and his forty-three-year-old bubbly wife. She's not bouncing on her toes like usual. Daisy Calloway searches left and right for her daughter. Concern etched in her eyes.

"Ca-caw!" Daisy calls out.

Sulli cups her hands over her mouth. "Ca-caw!"

Daisy spins around in the wrong direction.

Being six-seven, I'm the only one who can see over the shelves. I wave a hand until Sulli's mom spots me. Her face lights up, she speaks to Ryke, and they both sprint over to the tents.

When I was Xander's bodyguard, I dealt with Ryke's half-brother: Loren Hale. Xander is a particular client, and mostly Lo was grateful for me and Thatcher.

Ryke is different. He's told me, *"Don't get too fucking close"* when I was already standing four hockey sticks away from Sulli.

He has more guards up around me than around Akara.

Because A.) two bodyguards have *fucked* clients. One of them is my brother. And B.) Ryke hasn't known me like he knows Akara.

So again, I'm coming in at a disadvantage.

I'm coming up short.

Usually, I wouldn't be that aggravated. I'm useful to security, to the team, to people—to Sulli. *They need me.* But I'm starting to feel more second-rate than ever before.

RYKE ASKS TO SPEAK ALONE WITH ME AND AKARA.

His daughter was about to take a secret trip out west and rock climb without a fucking harness. Most parents would want to pack their kids up and ship their ass back home.

I get his fear.

But I've been on Sulli's detail while she's climbed, and she's careful. Is out west different? I don't know. Taller cliffs, a greater ascent, a worse fall—but danger isn't something anyone should look to me for an opinion.

I served in the Marine Corps. I've been in firefights and screamed in frustrated rage when my NVGs busted and thought I'd lose a buddy more than one night. Danger was a constant, living thing, and the only way to mitigate it was to come home.

While Ryke, Akara, and I leave for the bathroom, Sulli stays back at the tents with her mom and Alpha bodyguards.

Swiftly, Akara and I check the toilet stalls—all clear—and then we face Sulli's intimidating dad. No other way to describe him than *intense.*

His stare is hardened with history and grief. He reminds me a little of my twin brother. Stoic, stone-faced, an expert on hell but a lover of heaven.

Ryke adjusts a Patagonia backpack across his shoulder. "I'm going to make this as short and fucking sweet as I can because I don't know how else to do it." His nose flares for a second and he grinds on his jaw. "I have to let her go."

He looks physically pained by those words.

I imagine my own dad saying them. *I have to let you go.*

But there's no pain. No heartbreak. My dad walked away when I was twelve and never cared enough to create a bridge back.

Ryke is a good father, someone I respect.

Someone Akara respects. Hell, someone every man in security *respects.*

He takes a breath. "I made a fucking promise to myself…" He pauses, the words stuck in his throat like normally he wouldn't say them out loud, not to us, but he's forcing himself to speak. "I promised that I'd give my daughters what Daisy's mom never gave her. That I'd never fucking control them." He smears a hand over his mouth. "Sully—*Adam* Sully would've hated if…" He shakes his head at himself. "*Fuck,* he would've *hated* if I quit climbing after his death and he would've *hated* if I kept my daughters from climbing because of him." He wipes angrily at his eyes. "We live for the ascent, and if Sulli needs this, she has my blessing." His eyes darken on me more than on Akara. "But I have to make this painfully fucking clear—I was on that mountain when my best friend died. It wasn't a free-solo. We were roped in. *Tied together.*" His voice tightens in pain. "I held him in my arms as he was dying. So understand that she can be the best climber in the fucking world, but when it's time for her to go, she's going to go. Just like him. Just like me."

He takes an agonizing breath.

My chest hurts. Burns. Most people I love keep dying or sitting on the brink of death, so his declaration is like seven-tons of lead in my body.

Just don't fall in love with her.

Maybe then she won't die.

What a dumbass thought.

I keep picturing Thatcher. He's gone through something like what Ryke described. My twin brother held the dead body of our oldest brother. Life isn't everlasting. I've felt that since I was a kid and asked God why He had to take Skylar.

I wasn't there.

I wasn't there when he died.

A part of me hates that Thatcher has to carry those memories alone. We're twins. I'm supposed to carry half the weight. Half the burden. But he's shouldering it all.

Akara steps forward. "Ryke, we won't let anything happen to her."

"She's going to be up on that fucking mountain, Akara. You can't promise me her safety. So this is where I'm at." He swings his head from me to my best friend. "If I lose her while you're with her, every time I look at you two, you'll remind me of the daughter I fucking lost—so I want *nothing* to do with you two after that. I don't want to ever see your faces again. You'll be dead to me."

Dead to Ryke Meadows.

None of that will really matter—because if Sulli died on our watch… it'd kill me in the end. My duty is to protect her, and I wouldn't…I'd never go back to security.

I couldn't.

I'd be done.

A withdrawn fucking hermit fixing beat-up Hondas for a living.

Akara can barely keep his head upright; his eyes are bloodshot. Chest collapses, but he fixes his gaze on her dad.

Ryke looks to Akara. "I love you like a son, but I love her more." He pauses. "So now's your chance. You can give her another two bodyguards for this trip."

The risk has always been clear to me.

To Akara too. Strongly, he says, "I'm not giving this to someone else, Ryke."

Her dad turns to me.

"Respectfully, sir, I'd rather be there for Sulli."

We're all living on the edge of death. And Ryke nods in acceptance of the road we're driving down with his daughter.

If only he knew about the funhouse. My brain is trying to crack a joke, and it lands flatter than a fucking pancake.

6

Akara Kitsuwon

I LOVE YOU LIKE A SON, *but I love her more.*

Ryke's words stay with me as we exit one state and enter another. Miles and miles away from the REI, from Philly, they still sit inside my head. Even as we stop at a gas station in the Ohio, Midwest countryside.

Fathers.

I used to have one. He was the kind of father that would watch morning cartoons with me. That would pick out all the oat pieces in the Lucky Charms, leaving me with a bowl of colorful marshmallows. I'd see him in the early mornings before school and then in the late evenings after long hours at his office.

He was the kind of father that demanded *he'd* be the one to teach me how to drive, even though he barely had the time. So I learned in the dead of night, and he was right by my side. I rammed the Mercedes straight into a trashcan on my first try. He laughed.

After his death, relatives would come up to me and tell me that I was lucky. He passed away when I was seventeen. I made memories with him that I'll remember *forever.* But it was a load of shit. In those memories he's faded. Like a blurred image that I can't quite make out.

What good is remembering, if I can't even have the full picture?

I'm twenty-seven now.

No one can replace my dad.

But I can't deny how much Ryke's words have crashed into me. I've been on Sulli's detail since I was twenty-two. I've traveled the world with the Meadows family. They don't have legions of children like the Cobalts. They're not rooted to Philly like the Hales. I was the youngest bodyguard to be on a Meadows detail.

Ever.

In a way, I always *felt* like a part of the family. Ryke would tell me over and over *and over* how he sees me as Sulli's big brother. How I'm that protector in her life.

But I've never actually heard him say those words until today. *I love you like a son.*

My phone rings in my back pocket just as I remove the gas cap to Sulli's Jeep.

Sulli jumps out of the backseat, saying, "We're going to have to put a *No Fucking Phones* policy on this trip."

Hey, I'll take any jab at my phone and workaholic nature, especially since half the car ride has been spent in excruciatingly hot silence. Awkward shit that I could hardly bear. Her virginity statement was the first time where I sincerely didn't know how to answer. So the silence is my fault.

The other half of the journey here was spent in something more familiar. Easy, friendly banter, but it kept dying on impact with each hour. Like it had a constant expiration date.

I prefer teasing her because it feels like Sulli and I are on a path towards rebuilding *something*. But it might be too much to ask for it to travel back to how it used to be. Before the funhouse.

I'm good at juggling *everything*. At managing time. Split between being a leader and a friend and someone's short-term date, the almost-boyfriend, but I can barely pinpoint *when* it all changed between me and Sulli.

I've been rapidly trying to bandage something between us since before last week. Shit, even before Scotland when she had a boyfriend. Maybe it was sometime around Greece.

When she was questioning what we are to each other, and my emphasis and reassurance of our friendship never felt like enough.

Near me, Banks shuts the driver-side door. Stretching his arms above his head, he tells Sulli, "Take the new policy up with the boss."

Sulli is tying her Timberland boot. While I put the nozzle in the tank, her green eyes rise to mine. She says, "You work too fucking much."

I work more now than I used to, and Sulli was the first one to notice the difference. But I'm building something beyond myself, and it takes time. Energy.

I begin to smile. "You curse too much."

She stands up and nods her chin at me. "You lick your lips too much." *Did not know that.*

"You worry too much," I counter.

Banks smiles softly at that one, then pulls out a pack of cigarettes from his jeans.

I'm quick to steal the carton. "*You* smoke too much." I chuck it into the garbage beside the gas pumps.

He rests a tensed hand on the Jeep. "We all have vices; you don't see me throwing yours in the trash." His gaze pins on my ringing cellphone.

"Mine isn't killing me," I say in a friendly tone.

Sulli grabs her wallet. "That we know of." Her voice sounds icier with me, and I deserve the arctic storm. Part of me *likes* when she's all frost because it's better than nothing.

I want her anger over apathy.

Is that bad?

Yeah. Because I shouldn't want to enrage Sulli.

Shit, I am an asshole. *Banks is right.*

"It's *not* killing me," I say again. "I can easily go without answering it."

Banks and Sulli watch as I let the call ring out in the next three seconds.

"See?" Though, on instinct, I pull out the phone to see which call I missed.

Fuck.

I need to call them back. Like *now.* When I look up, they both can read my expression too well.

Banks is near laughter.

"You were saying?" Sulli jokes, her smile peeking.

I smile, then glance at Banks and laugh. I shove his arm. He tries to capture my phone and toss it in the trash. We side-arm wrestle, shoving more, grunting, and then with one hand to his chest, I hold the cell behind my back.

"I love you, Banks, but you trash this, you die."

He laughs lightly at my glare. I can skewer men with *one* look, but Banks—Banks never takes them to heart. It should piss me off, but I usually end up smiling. He has a way of making the absolute worst days somehow full of life, and I love him for that.

"Screw you," I say at his laugh.

"Hey, hey, hey, *you're* the one who threw my cigarettes out. I should file a workplace complaint." He's full of shit.

I push my hair out of my eyes. "Take it up with HR."

"Who is?"

"Your brother."

He rolls his eyes in a groan because if anyone would've trashed his cigarettes besides me, it'd be Thatcher.

I look for Sulli.

She's watching us, and her smile…it's completely vanished. Like we left her out of our exchange. Forgot her. *Not possible.* "Hey, string bean—"

"I'm going to get some snacks," she cuts me off and jabs a thumb to the gas station. Turning on her heels, she walks away from us.

I shoot Banks a look like *guard her.* He doesn't need the instruction—he's already following her footsteps—but I always feel better giving it.

As he passes, Banks nods to me, then catches up to Sulli. He opens the door for our client. Leading her into the store. I needed a second bodyguard on this trip for times like this, and I could have picked anyone. Even a temp. Shit, it might have even made more sense to choose Farrow since he has a medical background. But the idea of spending hours upon hours in a car with Farrow sounded less than appealing. I enjoy Banks' company the most, and I trust him to protect her.

It was an easy decision. Probably easier than the phone call I'm about to return.

More tensed, I walk to the edge of the poorly paved road. Cool wind blows long grass stalks, and I unclench my fist where my phone lies. The missed call stares back at me.

Michael Moretti.

Fathers.

This one is Banks'.

He's supposed to be flying into Philly tomorrow, and with his unexpected call, I'm afraid he's bailing on me. I'm the one who offered Michael a position in Kitsuwon Securities. When he finally took me up on it, I was *relieved.*

Michael left training Navy SEAL recruits in Coronado to help *me* train temp guards for my start-up security firm. Banks thought his dad would never leave his cushy military job for private security.

I feel indebted already.

Even if I do know the main reason Michael Moretti took the job offer was for the pay. I doubled what he made in Coronado, and the raise motivated him enough to make the jump.

What if he is quitting before he's even started? Banks kept telling me his dad has more bad blood over here than the west coast. He burned every bridge with his family, and it'd take "*an unholy fleet of effort*" to permanently pull him back here. Those were Banks' words, at least.

If Michael does actually fly to Philly tomorrow and join my company, it's going to be a double-edged sword. Positive: I now have the best guy around to train temps. No more taking my full-time guys off their clients to put in those hours.

Negative: I will have proven Banks wrong.

That his dad did come back for more than just Jane & Thatcher's engagement party. He'd be in Philly permanently. Because I asked. Because I paid him a shit ton of money. And I know it's going to wound my friend. I don't like choosing my company over my friendships, especially the ones I have with Thatcher and Banks. But this is different.

Since the moment I created Kitsuwon Securities, I've been pushed into a corner, and I need to stop feeling like I'm five-steps behind Price Kepler's Triple Shield. I need to start feeling like I have a chance and I'm not some underdog coming into a fight with a broken leg and a hand tied behind my back.

I redial Michael's number, and he picks up on the second ring. "Kitsuwon, I've got some crummy news," he says in a matter-of-fact voice.

My fingers clench tighter around the cell. "You can't make it."

"Not on tomorrow's plane. Something came up. But I'll be out there this weekend. You can count on it."

Not good. Not horrible.

"Alright, thanks for the update, Michael."

He laughs dryly. "Gonna have to get used to that."

"Used to what?"

"Being called *Michael.* Everyone out here calls me Moretti."

I can't call him that. "I'm sure you'll get used to it," I say. "Send me your flight information when you've got it. I'll send someone out there to pick you up from the airport." *Probably Thatcher.*

He harbors less resentment towards his dad.

Michael says a quick thanks and we end the call.

I circle back to the Jeep, and my gaze cuts to the gas station. Through the glass windows, I see a plastic bag around Banks' arm like they've checked out. But they loiter inside while Sulli stacks gummy worms on a donut.

They talk but I can't hear what they say—she laughs more than once. I watch as Sulli lifts the gummy worm donut up to his lips. He bends his head a little. I think...she's telling him to shut his eyes.

He closes them.

Sulli feeds him the donut—*why are you watching this, Nine?*

My chest falls.

I turn my head away, but I look back. I'm a glutton for punishment. For pain, because I'm standing alone beside a Jeep, the gas done pumping, and I'm watching my two friends *flirt.*

It's okay.

It's okay.

I try to remind myself that my life has changed. It changed the moment I signed the papers to create my own security firm. I've had lawyers all tell me the same thing: *you should quit being a full-time bodyguard.* Even Connor Cobalt, my mentor, told me that I was going to overwork myself if I'm not careful.

That conversation was a hard one.

Connor has given me business advice since I joined his detail.

I was nineteen. Ambitious. He was my first client in security—at a time when I was a full-time bodyguard and struggling to keep my new gym afloat. I put my dad's life insurance money into the gym, and if it failed, it felt like I was failing him.

I needed everything to work out. And I would've taken any advice, from anywhere, but it just so happened that I had access to the CEO of a Fortune 500 Company, who's graced *Forbes* more than once in his lifetime.

Sometimes I joke that I graduated from the University of Connor Cobalt with a Master's in Business. He taught me how to rely on people that I trust, that I need. That *the best* hire the best, and *the best* lead the best, and I can't do everything myself.

After two years protecting Connor, I was transferred to his oldest son's detail. The fact that I couldn't cut it protecting Charlie—it bruised my ego. Because I thought I'd proven myself.

So I fought harder to be better.

For an entire year and a half, I was the bodyguard to Tom Cobalt, and then I was transferred to *the* position—the one that told the rest of security, *I'm good enough to be here.*

For the security team, that's always a Meadows detail.

For me, that was always going to be Sulli's. The girl that was bound for the Olympics. The one with enough drive and passion to light the world on fire.

She's what I wanted.

She's what I got.

But I've known that I can't have her forever, it's just that I didn't think my time would be cut short this soon. Connor told me, "As long as your gym and your security firm keep growing, you're going to have to make a decision one day. And that day is coming soon, Akara. Be a full-time bodyguard or be a businessman. There's a great chance you won't be able to do both."

I've always wanted to be in business.

To build my empire with what my dad left me when he died. The more my companies grow, the more I'm honoring him.

But some part of me is resisting the giant leap towards *business.* When the opportunity came knocking to franchise my gym, I rejected it. Too much work. Too big of a project away from security.

I didn't want to leave Sulli then.

And now—it's not any easier. I've loved *every* moment being her bodyguard, and a gnawing, bittersweet feeling overcomes me when I consider walking away from her. It's the end of a huge chapter of my life.

It's the end of a fucking era with her, and how am I supposed to say goodbye?

So I thought having Banks gradually fill in for me would ease the transition, but it's not easing a damn thing. It still feels like pouring salt on an open wound.

Back at the Jeep, I tear off the gas receipt. And instinctively, I look back at the store for Sulli. She's laughing while he motions her forward. And then she stuffs the rest of the donut in Banks' mouth, smiling. He's near-laughter and trying not to choke.

Banks likes her.

It's not the first time I've *seen* it. Not the first time I've thought about it. Shit, I've thought *a lot* about the idea of Banks & Sulli together.

Romantically.

My jaw tenses at that word. But at least my glare isn't drilling fifty holes in the cement parking lot. *Fuck.* If Banks were *any* other guy—if I didn't know him so well—I'd be running into the gas station and twirling her towards me. To protect her from the bastards of the world.

She's like a sister. I rest against Booger. Yeah, she's like *a sister.*

But Banks is the kind of guy I'd pair with my sister in a heartbeat. He's considerate, honorable, selfless—he treats women like they're gods among mortal men. He'd worship her.

I'd run to the ends of the earth for her.

I shake the thought away. Why the hell does that matter? Banks isn't Will Rochester. He's not a shitstain or a prick like her ex-boyfriend. If she likes him, she *should* be with him.

But even trying to picture their first date deadbolts my brain. I go blank and self-eject.

I'm not jealous.

My chest sinks. I can't be jealous…

More likely, I've never been a real third wheel with Sulli. Even with Will, she chose to hang around me over him. She'd constantly turn to me.

Talk to me.

Play with me—teasingly, *friendly*.

Being a third wheel—this is just new to me. Something I'm not used to. It's making me feel weird shit. That has to be it.

Banks leads Sulli out of the store, a plastic bag in his hand and in hers. I nod to Sul, "What's the damage?"

She bypasses me with a short, fleeting look. "Donuts, Ho Hos, and gummy worms." And then she climbs into the backseat.

Banks makes a face at me while he swigs a Ziff sports drink. Washing down the donut Sulli crammed in his mouth.

Am I bitter?

Something rises to the back of my throat.

While I screw on the gas cap, Banks hands me another Ziff out of his bag. "Unless you want to spend another hundred miles with Sulli the Iceberg, you're gonna want to go unfuck that."

"I'm already there." I down a strong gulp of Ziff, heading to the window of the backseat. Every time Thatcher and Banks say *unfuck*, I picture a dick exiting a pussy.

So that's what I'm picturing.

My dick. Exiting *her* pussy.

I blink and blink to get that shit out of my head. Strolling up to the window, I rap my fist on the glass.

Sulli rolls it down, and I rest my arm on the sill, eyeing the bag of snacks she just bought. All sweets. Her dietary habits lie solely at the top of the food pyramid. With her hand halfway in the gummy bag, she says, "Hey."

"Hey," I smile, trying to ease back in her good graces.

She bites a gummy. "What do you want, Kits?"

"Just to talk, say *hey*."

I can't help but see a faint look of disappointment cross her face. Like I'm not giving her enough, but I can't be...we can't be...

A breath catches in my lungs, and I exhale and nod to the gummy worm she's eating. "What flavor is that?"

"Cherry."

I picture her on a bed. For a split-second. I picture Sulli on a fucking *bed*. Legs spread. *Her cherry*—it's just my brain. Means nothing.

"Taste good?" I wonder.

She shrugs. "The green ones are better." She tears one with her teeth. Sulli is tender-hearted, but with a single, serrated slice, she will cut out anyone from her life that hurts her. She cut out her ex-boyfriend without second thought.

She cut out Beckett, her best friend.

But she hasn't cut me yet.

"Green ones taste like lime?" I wonder.

"Yep."

I lean more into the window. Teasingly, I smile, "Where's my gummy worm?"

She rips off another piece with her teeth. "Between your legs."

Banks laughs hard, climbing in the driver's seat.

I shoot him a middle finger.

Sulli twirls the gummy. "Only totally hot *babes* know what that worm tastes like."

"Where's the lie?" I tease, then I slyly and quickly reach for the gummy worms through the window, stealing the bag.

Sulli smiles, "Kits!" She tears the bag out of my grip. Gummy worms go flying, but I grab a few out of the air.

"Thanks for these." I slide into the passenger's seat.

"Asshole!" she shouts, kicking the back of my seat.

I turn around, staring at her while I eat a green gummy worm. "Mmmhh."

She tries hard not to smile. "Fuck you."

I mime grabbing the *fuck you* out of the air and swallowing it.

Her humor fades pretty fast. Too fast, and I watch as she concentrates on the scenery out the window over our interaction.

Well, that lasted point-five seconds.

Great.

I face forward while Banks pulls out of the gas station. "I'll drive next stop," I tell him.

He nods. "Who called earlier?"

I lean back, more tensed.

Being the boss, I don't share everything with everyone in security. I could easily shut out Donnelly, Oscar, and Farrow (the Yale boys) and say, *it's nothing you should worry about.* They'd understand. But the Moretti brothers are different. I've always confided in them.

And I've known Banks since I was twenty.

He was twenty-two, fresh out of the military, brand new to security, and I just clicked with Banks and Thatcher. At the time, not many guys were around our age on the team. We hung out off-duty. Relied on each other.

Thatcher Moretti became my best friend. We were both eventually leads. Our problems were the same, and we understood each other. Banks...Banks was the friend who added *needed* levity to the shit that Thatcher and I faced.

Most days would've been total hell without him.

So I won't lie to Banks. We're on the same side. Always.

"Your dad called," I tell him.

Banks grips the steering wheel tighter with one hand.

Sulli stiffens in the backseat.

And just like that, I've siphoned off all the remnants of a good mood. I'm used to that. I pull switches often. One minute we're all fun and games. The next, it's serious.

"Yeah?" Banks frowns. "He bail on you already?"

"No. He's just coming in a few days late."

Banks blinks hard a few times, gaze hot on the road. "Don't set your hopes and dreams on that, Akara. All that man is good for is disappointment." His eyes flit to me, softening.

He's worried for me, I realize. He's worried his dad will be a no-show and fuck me over in the process.

I'm worried for him.

That his dad will show up and prove something worse to his son. Money drove him here. Not love for his family, his sons.

Sulli scoots up between our seats. "Is your dad really that bad?" She drops a bag of powered donuts in the drink console for us.

I open it.

"Yeah." Banks glances at her, then the road. "The last thing he ever said to me before he left was, *You're the dispensable one.*" He shrugs like it's nothing but I know it's everything. "I'm the second-born twin. The dispensable one." He grits down on his teeth. "He can go fuck himself."

7

Akara Kitsuwon

SULLI YAWNS INTO HER bicep as she reverses out of the third campsite we've marked on the map. We called ahead to two, and they were full by the time we showed up. First come, first serve is not on our side tonight.

"I fucking hate when you have to have *reservations* to campsites," Sulli grumbles. "Camping is half-spontaneity, and there's nothing wild and free about a fucking reservation." She flips off the *At Capacity* sign on the bulletin board before peeling the Jeep away.

"Jesus, *Mary*," Banks startles awake with the sharp turn. He was lying down in the backseat, my baseball hat over his eyes, and he grabs hold of my headrest, pulling himself up. "What the fuck was that?"

"Not Jesus or Mary," I say with a smile.

"Thank God." He sits up more, rubbing his tired eyes. "I don't expect to see them until I'm six-feet under." He glances out the back windshield. Where our tires kick up dirt against the bulletin board. "Campsite all full again?"

"Yep," Sulli yawns.

"Pull over," I tell her from the passenger seat. "I'll drive."

"You just drove, Kits. It's my turn." She readjusts her grip on the wheel. While Banks has been sleeping, we've talked…not a lot.

It's been just great.

Really, *really* great.

Outside of mentioning campsites, the last we spoke was through the McDonalds drive-thru, and I told her Oreo McFlurries tasted like concrete paste.

She said nothing until she dropped the McFlurry on her lap. And then she muttered, "Cumbuckets," and gave me a look, "Can concrete paste, do that?" Her whole lap was wet with ice cream. Teal running shorts drenched. I handed her a roll of paper towels and helped wipe up the stream of ice cream that trickled down her leg.

She tensed.

I pulled back a little bit, wadding up the paper towel.

She used to always let me help her, but now—now it's weird. Is it because she's older? Because she's dating—or she's willing to date? I wish I knew. Things are stranger than I can even comprehend. Heat smothered me, and I just nodded to her.

Sulli mumbled a *thanks* and scrubbed the rest of the ice cream off with harsher, frustrated force.

"I can drive," Banks offers.

"No," Sulli and I say in unison, but I add, "You've clocked in the most hours behind the wheel."

"I'm better at staying awake longer," Banks reminds me.

He's not wrong. Sulli and I have chaotic sleep schedules. She rises at odd hours. We always nap a shit ton, but I've caught Banks popping Tylenol like they're Skittles today. When I asked him about it, he said, "Just a headache. It's nothing."

He *needs* rest too. Beyond being my friend, he's one of my men. I'm not driving his health into the ground by leeching his sleep.

"Sul, take the next exit," I say, like an order.

She switches lanes. "Do you see another campsite?"

"I saw a sign for a motel." And it might be the last one for a while. "We're getting some sleep. *All of us.*"

"And that's an order," Banks jokes light-heartedly.

I smile, but my face slowly morphs in a grimace when we arrive at the motel in nowhere Wisconsin.

"What a shithole," Sulli mutters, parking beside a beat-up truck.

The neon *vacancy* sign is half-busted. Only the *V* and *C's* are glowing. The single-level motel looks grimy and rundown: paint chipped, overflowing trash bins, and a few broken windows on rooms 3 and 5. Safety hazards, definitely, but with me and Banks on her detail, she'll be protected all ways around. No matter where we crash for the night.

"As long as it has running water, should be fine with me," Banks says as we all unmount from the Jeep.

I pop the trunk. "You need some help raising your standards, Banks."

"At least my standards are higher than Donnelly's." He pulls his rucksack out of the back. "I wouldn't have slept in the Lost & Found room."

"The what?" Sulli asks, slipping her Patagonia backpack on her shoulders. The one her dad gave her before we left the REI.

"The Lost & Found room," Banks says. "It used to be a guest bedroom in security's Hell's Kitchen apartment. Stunk like stale beer and piss."

I explain, "Bodyguards would crash there when they were in New York for the night."

Sulli looks surprised. "And Donnelly wanted to sleep there?"

"I heard he was willing to," Banks says. "I would've just crashed with my family before sleeping there." He goes quiet, his gaze dropped.

I understand the somber shift. So does Sulli.

Donnelly doesn't have a home to run to. Not like the Moretti brothers, who have an army of uncles in South Philly at their disposal. These days, I don't have a home anymore either.

It's gone.

It's not gone, Nine.

With my mom living back in New York, sometimes it feels that way. Shoving those thoughts aside, I grab my red duffel.

Sulli fits on her Philly baseball cap, even in the dead night. "I know my sister couldn't come because high school started back up, but you think I should've invited my cousins to Montana? Like Moffy or Jane or Luna?"

I'm about to answer, but when I turn, I realize she's asking Banks.

My stomach sinks.

He lifts a shoulder. "You want them here?"

She stares off at the flickering vacancy sign. "The FanCon tour was one of the coolest adventures I've ever fucking had—when we were all together. But Beckett was there too and Charlie..." Her frown deepens. "I guess I just miss how close we all got. Anyway, if I asked them, I think they'd just say *sorry, we can't.*"

I chime in, "I doubt that, Sul."

Sulli rests her hands on her head. "You would say that, Kits, but nothing stays the same with friendships. Everyone is growing up and growing apart." Her words sound pained. "No one has time to travel to Yellowstone to watch their cousin free-solo some cliffs." Wind picks up the dirt on top of the graveled parking lot. "And I get it. I get that everyone has their own thing going on. Luna is taking more online college courses. Moffy has a fucking *baby.* And Jane is getting married. *Married.*" She laughs like it seems unreal. "To your brother." She points at Banks. "And it feels like just yesterday we were all kids, piling into a canoe at the lake house. Trying not to tip it over." Sulli exhales strongly, then stares at the ground, adjusting her backpack strap. "Maybe it's good they're not here. Flying higher from the nest, right? I need to do this on my own—with you two, obviously."

Banks and I nod, trying more or less to be impartial. But with her cousins come their bodyguards. Omega. My men. Of course we'd like them here, but Sullivan is right.

It's better it's just the three of us.

I don't need SFO to rib me about my relationship with Sulli right now. Not when it's being electrocuted every ten minutes.

"So what now?" Sulli asks me and Banks.

Hey, she included me. Love those good signs.

I pass them. "I'm going to check to see if they have a room available." I walk backwards and say, "Grab what you need. Cover her ass, Banks."

"On it," he says.

As I walk away, I hear Sulli ask him, "Who's going to be in charge of your ass tonight…?" Her voice tapers off as my shoes crunch gravel.

I walk faster.

And faster.

Not wanting to hear Banks' reply for some reason.

I blink back invasive thoughts.

Cherries.

A bed.

Her body.

I blink.

Sulli.

Thighs spread.

Virginity.

I blink and blink. Gusts of wind whip my black hair.

Sheets.

Her long brunette hair.

Greenest green eyes.

Legs that never end.

I blink.

Her arched back.

Shallow breath.

Shit.

Shit.

Shit.

My stomach tosses in guilt. I shouldn't see her that way. Not even if she *asked* me to take her virginity. Not even if the world was burning down.

She's like my little sister. Ryke said it himself!

He told me *that.* He has constantly said:

"That's your fucking sister, you know? Protect her."

"You're a big brother to her."

"Thanks for being her big brother."

For *years* that's what I heard from her dad.

It'd be so screwed up if we did something…

I run a hand through my hair, kick away those thoughts, and survey the area. For a random motel stop, a surprising number of cars are parked here.

I just hope the *vacancy* sign isn't wrong.

When I enter the office services, I'm hit with an overpowering smell of lavender. Like someone lit the flower on fire and perfume-bombed the room. The scent burns my eyes as I approach the empty desk.

I tap a bell, and while I wait, my phone buzzes. Pulling out my cell, I check the text.

> Let me know dates & times when she starts climbing. I'll pack my equipment & bring Jesse out with me. –Jack

Sulli's cousins might not be here, but Jack Highland-Oliveira is scheduled to arrive at some point—looks like his teenage brother Jesse Highland will be joining.

Jack—I didn't really trust at first. He's just *too likable.* And he has so many secrets about the families that he could spill. It always put me on edge. Being cautious is a bodyguard's job.

But somehow, some way, we became friends. Shit, we've even gone on double-dates with girls he's introduced me to. He has an endless supply of acquaintances, contacts, whoever that always show up when we're out together, even if it's to grab coffee on a quick pass to say *hello.*

I'm not even the one who invited Jack here. Sulli agreed for her free-solo climbs to be filmed for *We Are Calloway*, and he's in charge of her segments for the docuseries.

A camera is going to be on Sulli while she free-solos. All I can think is that her death might be filmed for the whole world to see.

She's won't die.

I believed that.

When she announced her free-solo plan on her dad's birthday, the reaction was heavily mixed. For the parents, she might as well have announced she was pregnant with the devil's spawn.

They were horrified.

But I was in the "let her do it" camp. I'm still there. I *have* to be. Sulli is too determined to drag her to a halt, and I've always known her as the girl who goes for gold.

I send a quick text back: For sure, I'll keep you in the loop. We're on our way to Yellowstone Country. You won't need to come out for a few days at least. She still has to practice the climbs with a harness & rope before free-soloing.

As soon as I look up, an older white man shuffles out from the back of the office. Wrinkles sagging his neck, he adjusts a pair of reading glasses on his slender nose. "You need a room?" he croaks.

"Two. Adjoining if you have them."

"Only have the one," he says. "Would you like by the night or by the hour?"

By the hour...

That reminds me of Banks.

He told me in high school, he'd fuck in motels if he had the cash to "go all-out" for his date. Pay by the hour, buy her flowers, light some Dollar Store candles.

I never had an issue finding places to have sex.

Perks of growing up wealthy, thanks to my dad's lucrative job. I was an only child in a humongous mansion-sized home with a nice pool house. Perfect for those nights alone with my high school girlfriend.

Banks slept on a pullout couch most of his childhood. I realize we're different in a lot of ways, but similar in ones that are needed to protect Sulli.

To the old man, I say, "For the night, not by the hour."

"Forty. Cash only."

I slide a few bills out of my wallet and pass them over. Before I can ask how many beds there are, he's handing me a key. Guess it doesn't matter anyway. It's the only room.

But shit, what if there's only *one* bed?

That scenario plays on loop with every footfall back to the Jeep. Banks and Sulli are out of view behind Booger, but the closer I approach, the more I hear.

"I bet you I can do twenty," Sulli says competitively.

"You know what I weigh, mermaid? If I sit on you while you do push-ups, I'd break your back before you hit *five.* And then Akara will shred me to pieces."

"He's not here, Banks."

I'm right here.

Really, I'm actually still thirty-some feet away. Sulli is just loud. It doesn't take a lot of strain to overhear her.

With a kicked-up pulse, I vacillate between walking faster. To interrupt them. And slowing down…just to see what happens.

"Tell you what, get on my back," Banks replies to Sulli. "If I can't do forty push-ups with you on me, then I'll do whatever you want."

"Deal."

I move faster.

Reaching the Jeep, I round the bumper and see Sulli straddling Banks' back, his palms digging into gravel as he does perfect military push-ups.

Noticing me, they freeze for a second.

"Hey," I cut in, trying to sound casual. "We have a room." I dangle the key.

Banks goes to stand, and in a seamless maneuver, he clasps the backs of Sulli's thighs and hoists her up higher on his back as he rises to his feet.

Her lips part with heady breath. Her arm instinctively curves around his collar. Legs tightening around his muscular waist.

Banks has Sulli secure in a piggyback.

And my heart has stopped pumping blood. Because I can't *get over* how she's looking at him. Her eyes roam over Banks like he just *made love* to her in a motel parking lot.

A knot lodges in my throat.

Banks doesn't have view of her face. He can't even see her expression. Or the way she drinks in his hands that grip the bare flesh of her legs. He's just hawkeyed on me, and slowly, he sets her feet on the ground.

For my sake.

Why does Banks have to be such a good dude? I wish he were a complete *bastard* so I'd have reason to separate them. To protect her.

I'm just the asshole keeping them apart.

"There's only one key?" Banks asks.

"Just one," I nod. Coming up to Sulli, I steal the Philly baseball cap off her head and try to fit in on mine, but it's tight.

She smiles a little, and I tell her, "Banks and I will take the floor."

Sulli passes me and Banks, then grabs a couple sleeping bags from the trunk. "If the bed is big enough, we can all just camp out on the mattress in sleeping bags."

Banks' hot gaze is on me. Waiting for me to make a decision. I am the leader, and I don't want to make a big deal out of this right now.

She pauses in my silence. "If that's...fucking cool with you?"

I wipe all thoughts about popping cherries and *Sulli* clean.

"Yeah, it's cool with me." I take the sleeping bags from her. "We'd need these anyway. Who knows what's living in the sheets?"

She grimaces. "This is why camping is fucking superior."

"Not a fan of motels?" Banks asks her and tosses me my backpack.

I sling it on.

"Tents are better," she replies.

"Five-star resort hotels are *even* better," I pipe in.

Banks cocks his head. "You are the bougiest of the three of us."

"Can't disagree," I say easily, wanting to smile. But I keep replaying the way Sulli looked at Banks.

It stays with me as we all gather the rest of our overnight things. I lock up Booger, and we make the short trek to room 4.

When I open the door, the verdict is in.

One bed.

A full.

Not even a fucking queen mattress could come out and save this situation.

Banks and I sweep the room quickly for recording devices in the lamps and drawers, while Sulli drops her Patagonia backpack on the ground.

Coming out of the bathroom, I see her tear down the blankets and inspect the state of the sheets and mattress. "Um…fuck, what is that?" She inspects a stain with a cringe, then catches my gaze. "Hey, if you don't mind, Kits, I think I'll take the floor."

"That bad?" I ask.

"It's beyond fucking gross." She assesses the room. "There's enough space for all of us to crash on the ground, I think. I can grab the sleeping pads from the Jeep."

"I'll do it," Banks says. "You said you wanted to shower."

She must have told him that when I was grabbing the key.

She smiles, her cheeks and neck reddening. Absentmindedly, she runs her fingers through her hair but tugs on a tangle. "Yeah, thanks…I need to shampoo this mess."

"Looks pretty to me."

"Pretty dirty."

"Nothing wrong with that, mermaid," Banks says before he leaves.

She stares faraway at the closed motel door, at his shadow. And as soon as she turns to me, her smile falters. "What…?"

What expression am I even making? Horror? Concern? Jealousy? Some unknown emotion that keeps ravaging my insides? My stomach has coiled into a tight fist.

All I can say is, "You like him."

It slams into me now more than ever before.

She really likes Banks Moretti. My friend.

That's a good thing, Nine.

Sulli bends down to her duffel, resting near a dusty nightstand with a broken digital clock. "Yeah, I thought that was fucking clear when I told him it'd be cool if he took my virginity."

What is air?

I'm barely breathing.

But I walk closer to Sulli. "I meant that you like him as more than just a friend."

Her brows pinch, staring at the discolored carpet. Then she takes out a toiletry bag. Standing up, she faces me and steals her hat back, taking it off my head. "So what if I do?" She fits on the baseball cap. "It's not like he likes *me* as more than a friend."

I frown.

She doesn't think Banks likes her?

Really?

I shift my weight. Sulli hasn't realized he's *blatantly* flirting with her. How? How is that fucking possible? It's so obvious, it smacks me in the face on a daily basis.

She tries to read my screwed-up expression. "What?"

I should tell her the truth.

Tell her Banks finds her hot, attractive, the sun that sets the earth on fire. But I can't make my lips form those words.

I just slowly *nod.*

She nods a few times back, her head hanging. "I'm gonna go…" She jabs a thumb to the bathroom, then treks there without another word.

Fuck.

Immediately, I feel like shit for letting her believe something that I know to be categorically untrue.

I'm worse than an asshole right now. It's tearing me apart.

And I can't unwind time.

When Banks returns to the motel with an armful of sleeping mats, our eyes collide together, and *guilt* is written all over me. No way can I scrub this away.

Tensely, I sit down on the edge of the stained mattress.

Banks slowly lowers the sleeping mats on the floor like they're tiny bombs. He glances to the cracked bathroom door where the shower turns on. Water pouring.

And then he focuses on me. "You and Sulli had a fight?"

I shake my head, massaging my hands. Running my thumb over the calluses on my palm. My mom has the same habit of kneading her hands. I thought we shared the trait because we shared Muay Thai. Her pro-fighting days left her hands tender and aching. But I never went pro like her, and when we both slowed down competing, *me* as a teenager, *her* after I turned ten—we both kept the quirk.

Banks rests a hip on the wall, arms crossed. With the gun holstered on his waistband, a toothpick between his lips, all he'd need is the hat to be the *cowboy*. What he once joked he was among me and Thatcher.

He surveys me. "You look like someone told you you're not allowed to talk to her for the next twenty-four hours."

I lick my dried lips, eyes descending to the sleeping mats. "I'll help you unfurl those."

Rising from the mattress, I get one step ahead before Banks intercedes and plants a hand on my chest. "First, tell me what's going on." Concern sinks into his brown eyes.

Making me feel like a sewer. Not just a tiny paper bag full of shit. A whole fucking shit-system beneath a city.

I spit out, "She doesn't know you've been flirting with her." It's not what I need to say, but it's a start.

The splash of water from the shower cuts through the brief silence.

Banks' forehead is wrinkling in confusion. "You think this is some revelation, Akara?"

Now I'm frowning. "Wait." I hold up a hand, my voice lowering. "You *knew* she doesn't think you're flirting?"

"Akara, how many fuckin' times do I have to go over this?" He plants his hands on my shoulders. He's five-inches taller, but somehow we feel the same height. His eyes connecting to mine. "*You* flirt with her. *You've* been flirting with her for years, and you keep telling her you're *just friends*. So when some guy like me comes around and *actually* flirts with her—what the hell did you think she's gonna think?"

I push his hands off my shoulders. *I don't know what I thought.* All I know is this... "I haven't been flirting with her."

Banks steeples his fingers to his lips, but his eyes sink deeper into me. It feels almost penetrating. Excavating. I'm vulnerable under his gaze, and I realize it's because he's slowly coming to his own understanding. "Akara," he whispers.

"She's like my little sister," I say quickly, though this time it sounds like I'm trying to convince myself. How much did her dad infiltrate my head? Was it full-on *Inception*? For how many years? *She's like your little sister, Akara. Protect her.*

Shit.

Banks shakes his head repeatedly, almost angrily.

I feel that anger inside me. At myself. I'm so pissed at myself for making this unnecessarily complicated. I end up snapping, "What?"

"What?" He points at the ground and growls, "You *love* her."

"As a friend," I combat.

"A friend?" His voice is hushed but hot with pent-up annoyance like mine. "I've never had friends who are girls and *teased* them like you tease her—"

"Guys can have platonic friends who are girls, Banks. It fucking *exists.*" I spread my arms.

He crosses his. "Sorry, I'm just a little fucking lost here. First she's your sister. Now she's your friend. Is she going to be your cousin tomorrow? Should I start pulling out the cousin-kisser jokes—"

"Fuck you," I say plainly.

"No, fuck you," he whispers hotly close to my face. "I want to fucking *shake you*, Akara. Just accept the simple truth. It's not gonna kill you if you do."

It won't kill me if I do.

His words somehow punch me backwards.

I sink onto the mattress and put my head in my hands. *I've been flirting with Sulli?* I think about how I stole her baseball cap, right after she clearly had a moment with Banks in the parking lot.

Shit.

Shit.

I've been flirting with Sulli. Every time she's been interested in another guy, I've cut in…and teased her, messed with her hair and shoved her playfully.

I've flirted with her.

Will Rochester, her ex-boyfriend, told me to stop *flirting*, and I did back off my interactions with her because I didn't want to ruin her first relationship. I couldn't tell her why I was being standoffish, and when she found out, that almost cost my friendship with Sulli.

She broke up with him instead.

"Shit," I mutter out loud.

Why has this taken so long for me to recognize? My brain...I've just shut off the possibility that I *could* be flirting. Maybe because I didn't want to stop, and now it feels like I have to.

SFO has told me I've been in denial, and it's taken Banks yelling at me to finally see that I have been.

Banks sinks down on the mattress beside me.

I look over with reddened eyes. "This is all my fault. She should know what an advance looks like from a guy. I've screwed with that—with her."

He squeezes my shoulder in comfort. "You're not some Wicked Witch, Akara. It wasn't out of cruelty."

"Is jealousy any better?" I ask him.

Banks shrugs. "She'd understand."

"Maybe she shouldn't," I mutter. "She deserves a better friend, better bodyguard—"

Banks shoves me. He literally shoves me off the fucking bed. My ass hits the floor and I look up at him like he's nuts.

He's smiling this stupid crooked smile.

And I start laughing. "Fuck you again."

"Fuck you thrice." He bites down on the toothpick. "If you try to beat yourself up again, I'll just shove you harder."

I stay on the floor, resting my forearms on my knees. "What would I do without you, man?"

"You wouldn't be on the ground, for one."

I let out another laugh. And I exhale, massaging my knuckles. *What are you going to do, Nine?* I'm a leader, and I have *zero* answers on where I need to go. Or what I even feel...

It's all confusion.

Quietly, I say, "So she doesn't recognize come-ons."

"At least she's not that naïve," Banks says. Motioning to my chest, he adds, "She'd bite a dick off if the wrong guy whipped it out." His smile rises at that image he constructed. Reminding me that he likes everything about her.

Yeah. I nod tensely. "You're the right guy, Banks." My muscles feel taut. "She likes you—she told me."

He doesn't seem that surprised. Just concerned. *For me.*

"And what'd you say?" he wonders.

Here it goes.

Me on the floor, him on the bed, I meet his gaze head-on. "I didn't say anything really. Not even after she told me she thinks you don't like her as more than a friend."

Banks stares at me, expressionless.

So I add, "I let her believe you don't like her."

He blinks. "And why do you think that is, Akara?" I hear the tension in his voice.

"Because I'm an asshole."

Banks rakes a hand irritably through his hair. "Because you love her too."

My brows jump. "Too? You love Sul—?"

"*Like*," he corrects fast, his eyes dragging across the carpet. "I just like her. You know that." He looks back up at me.

"Yeah," I say casually.

"I like her," Banks says, "and you love her."

I shake my head without thinking. "It's not romantic love…" *It hasn't been.* I've been her bodyguard since she was sixteen.

I love Sulli—I will always love Sullivan Meadows—but I've never crossed *that* line. I would never. Could never. Maybe now, it could be different…

Could it?

I glance over at the bathroom door. Steam billows out of the crack. She's older.

A lot older.

If I start really seeing her like the woman she is, then maybe…

"Alright." Banks rises off the mattress. "I don't want to push you one way or the other. From here on out, I'm shutting up about it."

I let out a short laugh. "Really?" My smile dies. I've tried to get Banks to shut up about it for so long. My stomach cramps suddenly, not liking this road.

"Really," he says seriously. "You figure it out."

I push my hair back, but strands fall forward over my forehead. *But I need your help.* I struggle with those words. All this time, I just thought Banks was annoying me on purpose about my relationship with Sulli. Being a pest like the rest of SFO. It's the one sore spot they know they can touch with a wisecrack and a laugh.

Now I think he's been helping me. Because he knows me too well, and I can't sort through my friendship with Sulli without him.

I nod to my friend, thankful for him, for how much he's already done for me.

Banks reaches a hand out.

I grab hold, standing up, and our eyes just impulsively go to the bathroom. Shadows play through the ajar door, and I can almost see the outline of her body against the shower curtain. A glimpse, then gone.

My heart rate goes haywire.

"I'm going to shut the door for her," I tell him.

He nods, unfurling the sleeping mats.

And I head to the bathroom. Every footstep is a pound in my pulse.

Sullivan Meadows

"HEY, SULLI," AKARA calls from outside the motel bathroom. His footsteps stop near the door.

My joints stiffen, a disposable razor frozen in my hand. The grimy shower curtain conceals me from him. Steam cocooning me, I've been avoiding the sheets of scalding water that pound the tub at my feet. For five minutes, I tried adjusting the temperature with no success.

It's still boil-my-fucking-skin-off *hot.*

Now everything suddenly feels catastrophically hotter. "Yeah?" I call back.

"I'm just closing this door."

My stomach tanks.

What were you expecting, Sullivan?

Something *hotter*, fucking clearly.

"K," I say, and I peek my head out of the shower curtain. But I'm too late to catch his expression. He shuts the door. Enclosing me in privacy that I'm surprised to be bummed about.

I like my privacy.

But lately, it's been kind of lonely.

I shake the thoughts away.

Back to shaving. I forgot to pack a new razor, and the one I left in my toiletry kit is dull and sucks. My body hair grows back daily, especially on my legs and armpits, but sometimes I say, *fuck this* and don't shave every single day.

I haven't always taken the carefree route.

But I guess as I grow older, I just care less what people think of me. Sometimes I wish I could transport back to seventh grade and tell myself, "Don't be sad if you're teased for having hairy arms. It's just hair, and kids are fucking cruel."

With a swipe of the razor down my calf, I run my palm over my skin. Ugh, my legs still feel prickly.

"Fuck this," I mutter and ditch the razor. About the same time I throw it beside my body wash, I notice a bug crawling on the tiles near my shoulder.

Fuck.

Fuck.

"Fuck," I gasp and jerk into the scalding water. "Cum—*fuck*." I wince at the stinging heat and edge backwards, but my wide eyes are on the black curled tail of a *scorpion.*

I hate scorpions.

My little sister, however, loves them. Winona adores *every* living, breathing creature—especially the amphibians. Tadpoles are her jam. Even though this is not a frog, my sisterly love surpasses my instincts. So I don't wash a scorpion down the tub drain.

You're an Olympian, Sullivan.

You can save a little ugly scorpion.

My hair wet on my collarbones, I whip open the shower curtain. Assessing. Okay, so a skinny window is slightly ajar above the sink. Big enough for the scorpion to meet freedom and nature. I can usher it there with…the shampoo bottle!

Grabbing my shampoo, I stand on the edge of the tub and create good bodily distance from this tiny, poisonous *beast.* It better not prefer the wonderful amenities of a motel bathroom. Complete with yellow-stained tiles and some type of mold growing out of the air vents.

I try to traffic control the scorpion, nudging him ever so slightly along the tile wall. "Come on, little guy. This way."

He jumps!

What the *fuck*—I jerk back and grab hold of the shower curtain rod for balance.

The metal rod breaks off with barely any force.

I let go fast, catching my balance in a stance, but the rod and curtain tumble to the fucking floor with the loudest, most volatile crash.

"Sulli?!" Akara's panicked shout sends shockwaves down my body—my really, *really* naked body. Footsteps sound just as quickly, and the bathroom door thrashes open.

I solidify. Standing tall and still naked on the edge of the tub.

Akara skids to a halt, eyes on…my eyes, then the window.

Banks slides into the bathroom behind him, realizes I'm in my birthday suit with a short glimpse, and then also eyes the window. "You alright?" he asks me, but I can't read either of them beyond their concern.

Bodyguards.

They're my fucking bodyguards, and of course they were worried about the window. They're being professional—I shouldn't be *this* disappointed, but *fuck*, they didn't even inhale like *wow, that's a babe right there.*

I'm starting to feel like the ugly little beast in their eyes.

"Yeah, I'm fine." Without stepping off the tub, I snatch my towel off the shut toilet lid and hold it up to my chest. "It's secure. No one was trying to kidnap me."

Banks picks up the rod and curtain, setting both in the corner. Akara rechecks the window.

"I was just dealing with an arachnid intruder. A scorpion is in here somewhere." I step down—*fuckfuckfuck*, my foot slips on the slick tile.

With the shower still on, mist wets the floor without a curtain to block the spray, and I go down.

"*Sulli.*" Akara reaches out and pulls me further from the tub. So my head won't meet the edge.

But his feet slide out from under him too.

Now we both go down. My ass hits the ground hard. Butt bone on fire, and the pain is dulled by two realizations.

I dropped my towel.

And Akara falls on top of me.

His hands lie flat on either side of my arms. His biceps flexed, tattoo peeking from his black tank—really though, he's never been *this* close to my bare body. My boobs. My legs are practically spread around him. Open for him.

Oh…

Fuck.

My cheeks roast, but not from embarrassment. His body is hard muscle, and the weight of him on me is dizzying. My pulse drops between my legs.

His eyes search mine. "Are you hurt?" He's more worried than aroused. Hell, *all* worried. *No* arousal.

We're just friends.

It's painfully clear that I'm as attractive to him as the scorpion on the ground, or tile—or wherever the fuck he catapulted to.

"I'm fine," I say again. "Just a bruised butt." *And ego.*

Mention of my ass doesn't change his expression. He's not even looking at my lips. I've glanced at his kissable lips at least three fucking times now.

Suddenly, a sharp pain pinches my foot. "*Ow*, fuck," I wince between my teeth and jerk. "The scorpion." That little asshole is still running around here.

Akara stands up quickly, avoiding looking at me the entire time. He makes a concerted effort to stare at the wall.

I'm *so* over it.

Fuck the towel. I leave it behind as I rise to my feet. One of which throbs from the sting.

Banks' boot lands hard on the tile, his back turned to me. "Got 'em."

"Was trying to avoid that," I say with a shrug. "My little sister says it's cruel to kill things that are weaker than you."

"She'd hate me then," Banks says, then glances at me. "Fuck—" He turns around quickly. "You're—"

"Naked." I rest my hands on my hips, done running away, and I swear, right before Banks drops his head, I catch sight of his rising smile.

Akara is doing an A+ job of avoiding. "You need a new towel, Sul?"

"No." I shrug. "We're pals, right? Friendly friends. I'm sure you two have seen each other's cocks at some point."

They share a look.

"We have," Akara answers first.

"So what does it even matter if I'm naked around you guys?" I wouldn't strip naked in front of just anyone. Even though they're not attracted to me, I'll always trust them, and I'm done feeling like the little girl on the outskirts.

I can play with the older guys.

I'm twenty-fucking-*one.*

With another short, silent exchange through their eyes, they rotate fully to face me. Akara's gaze drips down my body, but I can't read his expression at all.

"Just friends, right, string bean?" Akara asks, his chest rising and falling more frequently.

"Right."

Shower water still splashes at me, but I feel hot from the inside-out.

I look to Banks.

He has his knuckles to his lips. *Is he smiling?* "Where'd it sting you?"

"My foot—"

Akara's cellphone cuts me off. It rings from the bedroom. "I have to take that. Banks, text Farrow about the scorpion sting." He rushes out like a lifeline called and shuts the door behind him.

His quickness shouldn't hurt so badly, but I end up walking backwards in a daze until my ass hits the sink.

Banks stays a few feet away, pulling his phone from his jean's pocket.

When our eyes meet, I ask seriously, "Does my nakedness bother you?"

"No." His mouth curves up, a shadow of a smile returning. "I'm not exactly a Virgin Mary—"

"Virgin jokes," I let out a weak laugh.

"Didn't mean it like that," Banks says softly. "For what it's worth, I'm not uncomfortable by much. I could strip and stand here buck-ass naked without batting an eye."

I skim his six-seven build. "Then why don't you?" I say like a challenge. "We're just a bunch of animals in the wilderness. Clothes aren't necessary to our fucking survival right now, so why even wear them? Right?"

He cocks his head, his smile more and more attractive. It's soft, almost…provocative. "You sure, mermaid?"

Steam billows between us, my breath staggered in real want, and I nod, "I'm sure—but, fuck, only if *you* really want to. I don't want to pressure you or…"

He's already gripping the back of his shirt. He pulls the white tee over his head. Dog tags lie flat against his firm chest. And his fingers unbutton his jeans. Easily dropping them, his navy boxer-briefs mold his package, and he rolls the elastic down. Freeing his length.

As he steps out of his boxer-briefs, I try to be casual about his naked form.

Like he's been about mine.

And I zone in on a tattoo I've never seen before. Across his upper-thigh, the ink looks like bleeding marker, so blown-out I barely recognize the shape of Roman numerals.

My eyes skate across his skin. Tiny scars mar his waist, his legs, and chest. Like the small ones I've seen on his hands before. All look different from the shapes and sizes, probably from different places and times in his life.

I feel his casual gaze on me.

And I'm not nervous or shy or even fucking timid. If bodies are maps to our hearts…to our souls, I've been waiting for someone to travel towards mine.

But fuck, I could have it all wrong, I guess.

I'm not a student of philosophy like Moffy or brilliant like Jane. Bodies could just be vessels to our memories. Not maps.

What then?

I'd still want him to explore me.

I inhale.

His chest rises. Breathing each other in from a distance, my skin feels hot. He's a man my body responds to—like pheromones are circling pungently around us with the steam.

I throb, clenching inside for something I've never had. *Hardness.* Filling me. *Okay, slow down, Sullivan.* And then I take a really good look at his cock, and my lips part in a heady breath.

He's aroused.

I've never seen an erection up-close and personal, but I've watched my fair share of porn. His shaft stands at hard attention, and he's long, *big. Bigger* than my mind even constructed.

Realizing I'm *staring*, I snap my eyes up to his.

He's unbothered, like he said he'd be. Still, I can't stop glancing from his erection to his eyes. And his hardness grows right before me. His face practically says, *yeah, I'm into you.*

"Nice dick," I breathe.

He steps closer. "Nice tits." His gaze slow-burns itself down my boobs, nipples perked. Eyes back on each other, we share a smile among something invigorating.

I feel high.

It's not the steam.

It's not even really being naked.

It's him.

How he's making me feel in this moment. Banks stares at me like I'm a woman. A muscular, strong, powerful, and sexy *woman.*

Still up against the sink, I watch him unfurl his fist. *His phone.* He's been clutching his phone. "I'm gonna text Farrow. How bad does it hurt?"

The sting.

I forgot about it. "Not that bad."

For a second, I think he's about to leave to text Farrow. *Please don't leave me.*

My heart skips.

9

Banks Moretti

SULLI LOOKS PANICKED. Like I'm about to abandon her at a vulnerable time. Akara has had to bail on her more than once since he created his own security firm, but he's never really abandoned her.

Must just be a fear of hers. Hand-in-hand with being alone.

But I'd never leave her right now. We're both naked in a motel bathroom. Not to shower. Not to fuck. It's the strangest, most alluring moment I've ever had with a woman.

"I'm not going anywhere," I tell her softly.

She nods, easing.

I text Farrow: How do I treat a scorpion sting? Along with the text, I snap a pic of the squished motherfucker.

Sulli grips the edge of the sink counter with one hand, her eyes still on my hard cock.

My muscles flex in response. More blood pooling south. *Christ*, I want to paint a portrait of Sulli with my gaze, but I should focus on her wound first.

I'm about a meter away from her and a line I shouldn't be crossing. For Akara's sake. Though—what the fuck am I stalling for? There's a good chance he's never going to see Sulli the way I see her.

Edging closer, I toss Sulli a towel. "Just so I can concentrate on first-aid."

Her lips rise while she wraps the towel around her body. Holding the two ends together at her breasts.

An inch away, I tower above Sulli.

She drinks me in, and I slowly lower to one knee, then the other. "Can I see your foot?"

"Huh?" Her breath is shallow.

"Your foot, mermaid," I say into a soft smile. "You got stung by that pointy shitbag."

She smiles. "Shitbag"—she lifts her foot for me—"that's a good one."

I take her sole in my hand.

She doesn't try to flatten her towel. The fabric spreads open more and more. By the way she's soaking in our positions, she knows I'm at a perfect height to push aside her towel and kiss between her legs.

What lies beneath that towel is my undoing.

Don't I know it.

Legs for days, leading to her unshaven pussy, all brawn in her limbs—in her slender hips that travel up to small boobs and broad shoulders...I can't even blink back the image. Every inch of her is driving me crazy.

My muscles burn, and I focus on the mark on her foot. The skin is a bit swollen around the sting.

"It really doesn't hurt?" I ask.

"Not right now." Her raspy response pumps more yearning in me. Not even just to kiss her. Life's momentary pleasures, I know them well. I'm not looking for just a moment—and for once in my life, can't I have more?

Good grief, I'm *yearning* for something other than a cigarette these days—that alone is a damn miracle.

I gently set her foot down. Steam whirling between us, I'm on my knees in front of Sullivan Meadows.

She's still staring at my length.

It takes everything in me to concentrate on her foot.

My phone pings.

Treat the swelling with ice or a cold washcloth. If any other symptoms come up, take her to the hospital. – Farrow

Any other symptoms. Hopefully it wasn't a venomous shitbag.

"What's the verdict?" Sulli wonders.

"Your foot has to fucking go." I stand up. "Good thing you can grow a mermaid tail or else I'm sure you'd miss your toes."

Sulli stays completely still, our eyes diving into each other while I reach for the washcloth beside her hand.

She takes a short breath. "Akara always says he doesn't believe in mermaids, but one time he told me that if they *did* exist, they'd be those ugly creatures in the sea that eat people."

Akara fuckin' Kitsuwon.

He's unconsciously cock-blocking me. He's been doing it to men interested in Sulli for all her adult-life.

I let out a half-hearted laugh that verges on an agonized groan. "He would say that." Turning on the faucet behind her, I let cold water run over the washcloth. "But just so we're clear, Sulli, in my world, mermaids are gorgeous, out-of-this-world *stunners.*"

She inhales sharply, then shakes her head once like she almost can't believe it.

I leave the washcloth in the sink and grip the porcelain on either side of her athletic frame. "I think you're gorgeous, Sulli." I want to clutch her face. To breathe these words between her lips like eternal air. "A beauty. A smokeshow. The hottest thing from here to the rising sun."

"I'm gorgeous," she says, "but not hot enough to fuck. Right?"

Only a sliver of space separates my body from hers. Vapor swirls around us, the shower still running, tiles warm and wet beneath my bare feet. I stare down at her. "You're hot enough to make love to."

Her green, green eyes.

They fall to my erection that's pointed at her waist in desire. I'm hard for her. Not for the fucking shower curtain.

Her eyes draw into me. "Prove it."

I cut the short distance like a hot bullet. Clutching her cheek in one strong hand, I slide my other palm underneath her towel to grip her bare ass.

An aching sound catches in her throat. She collides against my mouth the same time I lean down. The force of our kiss crashes against my soul. I beckon forward, and her eagerness is as surprising as the way she melts into me like softened clay.

Our tongues explore, the sensation a long, enticing stroke. My fingers knead against the flesh of her ass. I don't even know if she's had a man's fingers inside her. It's tempting to be the first. Lord knows I want to fill her completely. To drive into her and hear the noises she makes.

Her hands feel overwhelmed, zigzagging across my chest. Overcome with a sudden burst of arousal that floods her…and me. Her palms are coarse rather than soft—probably from years in a pool and lifting weights—and something about that just draws a smile.

God, she's a fucking beauty.

Her palms run down my abs, fly up, then to the side, then settle on my ass for a beat. The touch electrifies my senses.

Though I'm remembering, *she's inexperienced.* How many times did she even kiss her ex-boyfriend? Pushing her too far too fast is a fear that almost crashes me to a halt.

But even as I slow our kisses, her arms curve around my waist like, *please don't fucking stop yet, Banks.* I do the next best thing, and mid-kiss, I reach down to the floor. Quickly grabbing my boxer-briefs, I hold the fabric to my cock.

Covering myself so I don't poke the fuck out of her or slide against her pussy.

She notices, but I reignite the moment and clasp her squared jaw. Lips meeting hers, I push her a step back, spin her in a new direction. Like we're kissing and dancing in the small bathroom.

Until I finally just shove her against the wall. An aroused breath leaves her reddened lips.

"You enjoy that?" I ask.

She nods strongly, her green eyes eating me alive. I kiss her again. Roughly. Deeply. Like I could pull the air from her lungs. She reciprocates in kind like she's been yearning for this embrace too.

My hand tangles in her wet hair. I suck on the bottom of her lip. Heat brewing between us, I keep Sulli pinned to the wall. And then I take her ass in my free hand. Still careful to keep my cock covered with fabric. Even more careful to keep space between our waists. Like I'm back in dress-code-wearing Catholic high school, dancing an arm's length away at homecoming.

I'm not making love to her in a motel.

Her first time should be better than mine.

Sulli stares at my eyes and nothing else. Even as I hold her cheek, as I plant hot kisses along the nape of her neck, her collar, back up to her lips—she never stops looking at me like I'm worth more than the Mona Lisa.

I've never felt this rich.

10

Sullivan Meadows

I'M ON FUCKING FIRE.

Lit up from the inside-out.

Banks is kissing me. He's *making out* with me. And his body is so close. *So fucking close.* I'm so tempted to just shift the towel so I can feel his skin against my skin. But I drown into the moment—of how strong he cups my face. How rough he kisses me. I watch him and feel his hunger for me as he pushes forward. An involuntary noise suddenly flies from my lips.

Oh my fucking God.

I almost whimper.

I've never been this aroused.

Never.

Not even touching myself. I'm soaked, and everything about this moment is inducing a mind-rush of endorphins. His kisses are unlike any I've *ever* had. Though, I guess I haven't had a fucking ton to compare it to—but it's so much…more.

More dizzying.

More heart-racing.

I'm overcome with each passing second his lips touch mine. My hands crave to touch Banks *everywhere.* To go on a great voyage across his sculpted body, and they feverishly roam, almost too fast, too excitedly.

I want to savor every bit, but I'm scared this is all I'll ever get.

His large hand is on my ass beneath the towel, clasping my bare flesh, but his fingers have curled closer and closer to my pussy. I wonder if he can feel how wet I am and the warmth I expel.

Above all, I never want to leave his eyes. The way Banks is looking at me—like I'm the only thing that's causing him to lose control—is so intoxicating. It's power I didn't think I possessed. I want him to ravage me. To tear off my towel. To sink his teeth into my skin.

Banks sucks on the nape of my neck. Still pinning me, my breath is lost in each dizzying second.

Keeping going.

Don't stop.

I'm in a dream.

No I'm not. My eyes are still on Banks, and I hate that I'm disbelieving of my reality because all I want is to take fucking hold and never let go.

As his lips draw back up to mine, he stops. He goes really still. Only his chest moves with his breath. And he whispers against my mouth, "Not here."

"What?" I pant.

His hand—his hand carefully, slowly falls off my ass. Even at six feet, I have to look up to meet his eyes. Such a weird thing that I rarely need to do. And I might be more upset by Banks slamming on the brakes if it weren't for his expression.

He looks pent-up and torn-up. Like ending it here is the right thing, but not necessarily what his body wants. Still holding his boxer-briefs against his package, he explains, "I'm not taking your virginity in a motel bathroom. From someone who lost his *in one*, let's just say it's not worthy of praise."

I get stuck on the two new facts.

Banks lost his virginity in a motel.

It sucked, apparently.

"Your first time wasn't that good?" I ask outright, retightening the towel around my chest.

"None of my firsts were. Crossed off a lot of boxes too early, and lookin' back, I wish I would've waited for the person who made me feel…" He lifts a shoulder. "*More.*" He slowly tucks my hair behind each ear. The right. Then the left. Like I've seen him do to himself all the time. "You have a lot of grit, Sullivan Minnie Meadows, to wait until you know you're ready. And I like you a hell of a lot. You don't have to wait for me if you don't want to, but I'm hoping you can."

To wait for a better moment?

A more romantic place?

For him?

He likes me a hell of a lot.

"I can," I nod repeatedly, my lungs inflating with more emotion than I can add up. "I definitely can." I glance down at his sculpted, *naked* frame. Wow…he's still hard. "Uh, so do you need to come still? You can use my towel if you don't want the fucking mess." I'm about to offer the towel on my body, but he touches my hand to stop me.

His lip draws in those almost-smiles as he sweeps my frame head-to-toe. His gaze is fingertips running down my bare flesh. My lips part, a shiver slipping through me. Tingling me.

Fuck, *I* still need to come. My body is begging for relief that I've given to myself plenty before.

He must register the want in my eyes. "Take the shower, mermaid. I'll be out here on land." He already grabs the broken rod and fallen shower curtain.

"The water is super hot," I tell him. "I couldn't adjust it."

Banks easily fixes the shower rod, then skims his fingers through the water. "It's colder now. Been on for a while."

I'm unable to suppress a rising smile. Remembering the last few minutes where we let the hot water run cold. *He pinned me to the wall. He cupped my bare ass. He kissed me.* I can still feel his strong, affectionate hands and lips on me. I'm filing it all in under: Pump My Fist in the Air, a Sullivan Victory. "You take the cold shower," I tell him. "I'll be out here."

"You sure?"

"Yeah. Land isn't that bad."

He nods. Our eyes stay latched for a sensual beat before he steps into the tub. Dropping his boxer-briefs on the tiles before he shuts the curtain, giving us both privacy.

My smile hurts my fucking face. Banks really does want my first time to be more starry-eyed and romantic. But I begin to frown remembering that his firsts weren't what he hoped.

Leaning back against the wall, I shut out those thoughts and slip my hand beneath the towel and between my thighs. More swollen and wet than I even thought. Skidding my finger over the tender, bundle of nerves, my whole body convulses—I shudder.

Fuck.

I close my eyes and picture Banks next to me. Behind the shower curtain, he's stroking himself. Maybe even imagining *me.*

His arousal towards me is like a liquid drug seeping through my blood stream. I'm higher than the fucking clouds.

My back arches, my hips wanting his hands. Imagining is enough to quake my limbs, and I ripple into an orgasm. Noise catches in my throat.

His grunt is also smothered. Maybe by the knowledge of me here.

When I come down, I wash my hands and throw on my clothes: clean underwear, turquoise boxer PJ bottoms, and a long-sleeve yellow top. Banks steps out, shutting off the shower. After he dries off with a towel, he gets dressed too. Jeans and his white tee.

The air is comfortable.

I squeeze out my wet hair. We slip each other smiles, and then the reality of where we are—a motel-stop, on the way to Yellowstone territory so I can free-solo—comes whirling back as we hear the squeak of a door opening.

The motel door.

The front door.

"Akara is back?" I ask Banks.

"Must be," Banks says, slipping his phone in his pocket. SFO has mentioned that comms lose range at a certain distance, and since I'm the only one in Wisconsin, he's not wearing a radio. He'd only have Akara to talk to on comms, and they haven't been apart that much.

Banks is staring at the shut bathroom door like he can see his friend on the other side.

I just kissed Akara's friend. *My bodyguard's fucking friend.*

And Banks just kissed his friend's client. Oh and I'm eight years younger than Banks, which I'm not sure how Kits will take. Considering he didn't love that Will Rochester was *older.* And he wasn't even that fucking old!

"Cumbuckets," I say in a daze.

"What?" Banks looks me over.

"Kits is going to care that we kissed," I realize. "You're different—you're his *friend.* He's going to be so pissed…or worse, *disappointed…* like I did something wrong—"

"We didn't do anything wrong," Banks tells me.

"Yeah," I nod, believing this too. "It's not like I'm married to Akara."

Banks looks suddenly distraught.

"We're not married," I defend. "If we were, then he's already cheated on me a thousand times—"

"Not a thousand," Banks sticks up for Akara. And maybe it should hurt me that he does, but the fact that he values Kits like I do—it stings my eyes. Swells my heart and lungs. Makes me like Banks even more.

"A handful of times," I correct softly, "which doesn't make it any better. Cheating is cheating, and we were never married to begin with. I can kiss anyone, as much as he can be with Jenny or Jessica or fucking beautiful Patricia."

Banks cracks a smile. "Never saw beautiful Patricia. What'd she look like?"

"Imaginary, I guess." I add, "I made her up."

He nods. "I got that."

I want to smile, but it loses strength fast. "Fuck, what are we going to do? I don't want to hurt him. It hurts me thinking about it."

"We're on the same front-line with that one." He scratches the back of his neck. "But we have a whole road trip together. I'm not loving the idea of hiding this from him."

I touch my lips in thought. "Yeah, it'd be better if we tell him right away." How fucking *awkward* is the rest of the trip going to be? Being a third wheel blows. I'm in that seat when Akara and Banks do the whole "we're best friends and guys and you just wouldn't get it" routine.

I wouldn't want Akara to be put in that position.

"Want me to handle it?" Banks asks.

"We should do it together, I think."

He nods. "Alright. Let's do it now. Better than sitting in hell." He slips past me, turns the knob, and he steps *one* foot into the room and dead-stops.

I come up beside him.

Fuck me.

It's not Akara.

11

Sullivan Meadows

GATHERED AT THE MOTEL'S bedroom window, three familiar faces turn around at the exact same time. Like they rehearsed this epic entrance for a *We Are Calloway* promo.

Maximoff Hale.

Jane Cobalt.

Charlie Cobalt.

My three older cousins. The closest thing I have to older brothers and an older sister.

Surprise doesn't even cut what I'm feeling. Fans revere Maximoff, Jane, and Charlie, and I've always held such admiration for them that I've joked with Luna how I'm partly their fan. The other part—I'm just lucky that they're mine. My friends.

My family.

So seeing them in Wisconsin first brings a wave of joy. They traveled miles and miles. For me?

And then I *really* look at them.

They're all zeroing in on my wet hair. Banks' wet hair. And the bathroom we just evacuated *together.*

Moffy wears hard confusion. Luna says her older brother is a quintessential Captain America—a do-gooder soldier and team leader—but in my life, he's the only person able to run next to me and never slow down. To me, he's like his husband's nickname for him. *Wolf Scout.* My mom created the Wolf Scouts, a wilderness & scouting organization. Moffy and I were even in the same troop, until he grew older.

As they always do.

I do too.

Though, in their presence, I feel young again.

"Hey, Sul," Moffy says first, his green eyes pinging between me and Banks.

"Hey, everyone." I nod probably way too fucking much. *Cumfuck, I'm a shit liar.*

Charlie slouches his weight on one leg. His head tilted and eyes roaming like he's Inspector Gadget inspecting all of...*this.*

Jane—lovely, beautiful fucking Jane who always has the best words in the right ways, *please help me.* I widen my eyes at her. She wears the brightest pink lipstick, zebra sweater, and green tutu like the Princess of a Fairy Kingdom that I'm sure is fucking great—but I need her to save me in Wisconsin.

She gives me a furtive nod like, *don't worry.* Her focus routes to Banks. "Thatcher's outside with the others."

The others?

But I see her tactic. Tension will definitely alleviate if he leaves Moffy and Charlie's intrusive gaze. Which is good. I try to exhale.

"Thanks, Janie," Banks leaves in a hurry.

Janie?

I frown. And once the motel door shuts behind Banks, I ask her, "He calls you Janie?"

"Oui. For a while now." Setting her pumpkin-sequined purse on the dusty dresser, she notices my lingering confusion. "I go eat Sunday dinners now and then with Banks and the rest of his family. He's about to be my brother-in-law."

"Yeah, I know." *I just haven't heard him call you a nickname.* Or maybe I have and it hasn't really *registered* how close Jane is with her future brother-in-law. Will she be freaked out that I kissed him?

I'm burning up.

But I pivot and ask, "Who else is here?"

"Akara is outside, and now Farrow and Thatcher are with him." Jane names Moffy's husband and her soon-to-be husband, both also their personal bodyguards. "As well as Ripley."

Ripley is Moffy's eight-month-old son.

"And Oscar." *The tactical badass bodyguard to Charlie.* She nods to punctuate the end.

But Charlie adds, "And the drooling canine. My pants were *wet* for three-fourths of the ride here because of Arkham."

My brows jump. Less on the fact that Moffy and Farrow brought their puppy along. "You rode with their dog?" I ask Charlie.

"Regrettably," he says.

Moffy gives him a look. "You chose to ride with us."

"You did?" My jaw falls. I knew Moffy and Charlie had patched up their fucking horrible feud, but Charlie actively choosing Moffy's car for a road trip is like bridging two sides of the Grand Canyon.

Then again, Charlie did recently oust the CEO of H.M.C. Philanthropies, giving Moffy a chance to be head of the company again. But as far as I know, Moffy is still deciding whether to give up teaching swim classes for the stress of being CEO.

Charlie sighs. "Because I knew my sister would spend every hour discussing wedding details in the other car, and no offense"—he speaks to Jane—"I couldn't withstand that."

"None taken, little brother." She smiles brightly, genuinely, and looks between her brother and Moffy, who's her best friend. Glad that there is less friction between them.

I am too.

But with all three of them merrily together like they were in high school, it makes me feel more on the outs. I'm now the only one with a busted-up friendship. *Beckett.*

He's not here.

Obviously. And I don't even know why Maximoff, Jane, and Charlie have showed up yet.

But I point out, "Couldn't you have just rented your own car?"

"Yeah?" Moffy says to Charlie with a rising smile. "I could've sworn that was an option, wasn't it?"

Charlie clearly *chose* Moffy rather than going off on his own. Instead of acknowledging this, Charlie zeroes in on my face like a target. "Enough about me. Aren't we here for *you*, Sulli?"

"That's fucking news to me." I smile though because I guessed right, and fuck it feels good to know that they're here for me.

Maximoff crosses his arms over his firm chest, confusion knotting his brows. "You and Banks were in the bathroom together?"

My smile vanishes. Cheeks heating. "Because of the scorpion—he was helping me catch it," I say quickly. "It was in the bathroom." I jab a thumb to the bathroom behind me. "I mean, *kind of* catch it. He fucking killed it. But…yeah."

They can't tell that I just had the most epic kiss of my life, right? My lips aren't red or anything. My hair isn't messy. Strands are just damp, air-drying. And I'm in PJs. Nothing out of the ordinary.

It's late.

And it's not like I want to hide kissing Banks. But Akara should know first. Out of respect for him. *As my bodyguard.*

As my *friend.* If we're even still that to each other.

I just don't want to lose Akara.

Charlie plops down on the bed like it's not stained or infested with bed bugs. Do I understand Charlie Cobalt?

Not always, not really.

Some fans think we're friends by my association to Beckett, his twin brother. Paparazzi ask me a lot about Charlie: what he's like; what he's doing. But truth is, being Beckett's best friend growing up didn't provide a gateway into Charlie's mind. We used to hang out, sure, but most of the time I feel like Charlie tolerated me like he would a little sister or a source of happiness to his closest brother.

I love him because of Beckett, who always sees the heart in Charlie.

"That must be why your foot is swollen," Charlie says.

My foot…I totally forgot about the sting. I have a fucking alibi!

Shit, I have *evidence.*

"Yeah..." I trail off, looking down. Wow, the ball of my left foot has *really* swelled up. Tonight's events must've dulled the pain. I wince a little as I put more pressure on it.

Jane drags a wooden chair over from the rickety desk. "You should sit down."

Moffy treks to the bathroom, probably to get a cold washcloth. The one that Banks forgot about.

We both forgot.

I lower onto the creaky chair.

"Your shirt is on backwards," Charlie says from the bed.

"That's unhelpful commentary, Charlie," Jane says to her brother, but her blue eyes flash to me with curiosity and *questions.*

Does she believe Banks and I had sex? She has major reason to think so now than ever before. They all know that I told Banks and Akara it'd be cool if they took my virginity.

Lifting my feet to the chair, I hug my legs to my chest. "Just so we're fucking crystal," I announce, "my virginity is still intact."

Maximoff reenters the bedroom with a washcloth just as I finish that bit. His eyes bug wide. "Were we questioning that it wasn't?" His head swings to Jane for clarification.

Jane perches her hands on her hips. "Charlie was insinuating—"

Charlie cuts in with a laugh. "How was I *insinuating* anything by bringing up her backwards shirt?"

Jane arches a brow. "You can't play dumb with me."

His lip curves upward, then motions to my shirt. "Sulli must have a *reasonable* explanation."

I shrug, my pulse speeding as the three of them stare me down from different ends of the room. "I took a shower. Put on my shirt backwards. Can we just *move on* from the whole Banks thing because it'd be really fucking awesome to know why you're all here? How'd you even know where to find us?"

"Your Jeep has a tracker on it," Maximoff reminds me as he places the washcloth on my swollen ankle.

I stare off at the carpet. "I always forget about that," I mutter. My mom and dad put a high-tech GPS tracker in Booger a while ago. The Jeep is so old they worried it'd go bust on me, and I'd be stuck somewhere without cell service.

"And your free-soloing colossal faces," Maximoff says, adjusting the cloth before rising. He sets a brotherly hand on my head. "You think I'd want to stay home and miss that?"

I smile up at him, my eyes burning with emotion. Years of Moffy joining me on adventures rush back. Snowboarding, hiking, camping, canoeing, white-water rafting, *climbing*. I thought he'd leave me in the dust of time. Because he's married now. And he has a *son*.

I rest my chin on my knee. "So my parents didn't send you here to convince me to come home?"

"No," Maximoff shakes his head, "but after I told your dad that Jane and I were going to surprise you out here, he said he was about to ask me to go meet-up with you." He cracks his knuckles. "He's just worried about you climbing, and he wants us around."

I can see my dad hoping Moffy would be here in his place. My parents also probably think I'll be extra careful with more eyes watching.

Jane nudges my elbow. "Your mom is very excited for you. She handed us a care package to give you for your *grand* adventure."

I smile, remembering how my mom squeezed me in a tight hug at REI. She said she wished she'd made a big box of goodies for me, but she didn't have time then. I already know she must've thrown dozens of chocolate bars in the package.

Thanks, Mom.

Jane shares my smile. "You've done so much for us these past years, Sulli. The FanCon tour."

"The auction," Moffy says.

"Scotland," Charlie adds.

Jane grins more. "It's time we're here for you. We brought enough luggage to last us through most of October."

That hits me like another tidal wave. Jane's bachelorette party is less than a month away. Her wedding is around the corner on November

1st, and she's not batting an eye about being away from Philly for so long.

They're really here for me. Dropping everything to watch me climb.

My smile is uncontrollable, unable to shrink in size. "I'm really glad you're all here. It means a fucking ton to me." I nod a bunch. "Thank you."

Jane gives me a side hug. "Anything for you."

When we part, I watch Maximoff head to my Patagonia backpack near the nightstand. "Your dad gave you this, right?"

"Yeah." While he unzips the bag, I shift the washcloth on my throbbing ankle and ask, "Where's Luna?" I sound bummed, and I already feel *greedy* having three cousins here to surprise me.

Some people would hate this kind of surprise arrival, but they knew I'd love it. I *love* the company of familiar, trusting faces.

I love the company of family. The company of my cousins—they're like other birds in a nest. And maybe I haven't flown too high from mine, but what if we're all just flying together somewhere else? To another nest?

Can that be enough?

Or do I really, *really* need to chart a course away from everyone?

My frown deepens.

"My sister's still in Philly," Moffy tells me, searching through the backpack. *What's he looking for?*

Charlie chimes in, "My brothers requested her appearance at their upcoming shows."

Eliot and Tom. One is a theatre actor, the other a singer in an emo-punk band. The three of them have been best friends since diaper-era, and in the past couple years, I've only recently gotten super fucking close to Luna. We were roommates in the Philly townhouse, but I try to remember she's two years younger.

I'm closer in age to Charlie and Beckett.

Still, I can't help but feel a pang of hurt that I wish would go the fuck away. I'm not in competition with Tom and Eliot for Luna's time and attention. But I guess, now that I don't have Beckett—I just thought I had Luna.

Taking my mind off friendships, I ask Moffy, "What are you looking for?"

He zips the backpack up, empty-handed. "Your dad forgot to mention he packed a gun for you. He wanted me to make sure you stored it right—"

"Akara already did," I interject. "We saw the gun in the backpack." I motion to the nightstand.

Moffy opens the drawer, sees the encased gun, then closes it.

My head whirls, running through all their words. And my gaze beelines back to Charlie, realizing Moffy and Jane excluded him from their big proclamation. "So you're not here to watch me climb, then?"

"Correct," Charlie says. "I'd actually rather be anywhere than watch you fall off a mountain."

"*Charlie*," Jane snaps. "She's not falling off a mountain."

Maximoff rubs the bridge of his nose. "Can we just ban those four words from this point forward?"

Charlie shrugs. "Fine." The fact that Charlie chose not to take the low hanging fruit and rile Moffy is another reminder that their friendship has been solidly repaired.

I look between Jane, Maximoff, and Charlie. They have history together that I don't share with them. High school stories.

Beckett and I—we were the ones that had each other's backs growing up. It was us against the world. We chose to be homeschooled around the same time. Sacrificed family and friendships and everything in between to pursue a dream. Mine was swimming. His was ballet. He's the *one* singular person in my entire life who understands exactly what kind of toll that took.

He was right next to me.

We were together through it all.

But best friends aren't supposed to lie to each other. They're not supposed to keep secrets from the person that matters most to them. It was soul-crushing—*devastating*—to learn about Beckett's cocaine problem from Charlie. And it's not like Charlie intended to tell me, he just blurted it out. How could I be so fucking clueless? I wish I'd known. Maybe I could've talked to Beckett. Been there for him. Done *something* more than *nothing* to help him. And when I did finally find out, Beckett lashed out at me. Said some cruel things that can't be taken back.

The silver lining is that Charlie says Beckett hasn't touched cocaine since Scotland.

I hang onto that.

Maximoff comes closer, eyeing my ankle. "How does it feel?"

"It barely hurts," I tell him.

"That's good," Moffy nods. "Farrow should still look at it though."

I nod, then glance at Charlie. "You still haven't told me why you're here."

"My brother couldn't come because of his ballet schedule," he says. "So I'm here as his proxy."

That's hard to believe. "He sent you?"

Charlie cracks his neck. "In a sense."

"That'd be a no," I state.

"He's miserable without you, and I can't take it anymore. You need to talk to him."

I let out a long breath. Beckett and I have shared the same air since the fallout, but we haven't *cleared* the air. "So that's why you're here? To convince me to talk to Beckett?"

"Basically."

The fact that Charlie had a small influence in getting Oscar & Jack together has *seriously* gone to his head.

"It's not fucking happening," I say.

Charlie shrugs, but he doesn't push the topic. Maybe knowing that it's a lost cause tonight.

Arkham barks from outside the motel room, and for some reason it promotes a yawn from me. Fuck, I forgot how tired I am.

Maximoff watches me, "We're staying in a hotel in the next city over. I can drive your Jeep, if you, Akara, and Banks want to head that way with us."

I glance at the sleeping mats on the floor. Even though this was a gross pit stop, I'd be bummed leaving it behind.

Skipping a step in the journey sounds like taking an easy out to the hard trek I committed to. I can hear my mom encouraging me to stay. *You can meet-up with them soon. Don't fast-track anything.*

"That's okay," I say. "I think we'll probably just crash here. The fucking adventure, you know."

He smiles. "Yeah, I know."

I smile back more. "We'll catch up with you tomorrow though?"

Jane says, "Most surely."

Charlie climbs off the bed and makes his way to the door with Maximoff.

"How'd you all get here so fast anyway?" I wonder.

"Private plane," Charlie says.

My brows rise at Moffy. He hates splurging on that luxury for a random trip. "I lost a coin toss with Charlie," Maximoff admits.

Charlie smiles. "And we arrived on time. So we all win."

I mention, "Winona and Ben would say the Earth lost."

Moffy nods strongly.

Charlie just stares at me, "Then you should take pleasure in the fact that we care more about you than the Earth."

I snort, "Way to spin it."

"Toujours," he replies in French as he leaves the motel.

"See you tomorrow, Sul," Moffy nods and leaves.

Jane remains. Slinging her purse on the crook of her elbow, she twirls to me in her usual breezy way. "So I take it Akara and Banks still haven't given you an answer on the virginity-taking front?"

I think about Banks' lips on mine, and my face heats.

"I revoked the offer," I end up saying.

She squints. "Is that…a good thing? Are we happy about that?"

I shrug slowly. "I…I don't know." Now after kissing Banks, everything is more complicated.

She plants a sisterly gaze onto me. Consoling. Comforting. "Doubt only lasts so long. You'll have a better sense of things in time. I'm sure of it."

I smile. "Thanks, Jane."

We hug again, and when she leaves, the motel room is eerily quiet. I hope I didn't make a fucking mistake telling them to go on without me.

My phone pings.

Heads up, Minnie. The rest of the A-Squad are on their way to you! Sorry I couldn't make it. Tom is freaking about his next show. He had a fight with the replacement drummer
– Queen of Thebula

Luna.

The A-Squad is mostly an inside joke between us. She dubbed the five oldest of the families that nickname, which include Jane, Maximoff, Charlie, Beckett, and me. But with Jane, Moffy, and Charlie as a clique right now, I'm feeling more like a member of the B-Team. Which doesn't even really exist.

I text back: Thanks for the heads up! Just saw them. All accounted for minus Beckett. Tell Tom I wish him good luck xoxo

Huh. Bad intel then. Sorry!!! Thought Beckett was going too.
– Queen of Thebula

How she even gets *any* information is beyond me. I don't have many lines into the family network, and the ones that I do have…I know I'm not the first or second call. Maybe not even the fifth. I'm on the bottom of so many of the family friendship groups.

It didn't used to bother me so much until I lost Beckett. Maybe Charlie is right—I should just talk to him. But the thought of hearing his voice, it brings a sharp pain to my chest.

I don't know how to confront that pain head-on without causing more turmoil.

Akara.

I close my eyes and drop the washcloth off my foot.

How am I going to tell him about my kiss with Banks? It's going to change everything.

12

Banks Moretti

"I KISSED HER."

This confession should probably be made to a priest or a higher being, but right now my brother is the most holy thing I've got in a five-hundred-meter vicinity. In short: I'm fucked.

Thatcher grabs my forearm and pulls me further into the shadows. Away from the motel's flickering *vacancy* sign that's changed to *no vacancy*. Even further away from the motel's parking lot where the rest of SFO linger beside two rental cars.

At the corner of the motel, it's just me and my brother. Half-hidden by an overflowing dumpster and the darkness. In earshot of nobody.

Even among busted streetlights, I can still see Thatcher's expression clear as day. Maybe because I've seen that intense look before.

"Say again," Thatcher whispers, his voice deep and low.

"I kissed her," I reply in the same tone. "You know mouth-to-mouth—"

"I know what kissing is," Thatcher snaps. "I'm just processing the fact that you actually went through with it."

My brother knows I've been into Sulli since I've started spending more time with her, but like me, he's also known that Akara Kitsuwon is in love with her. Unlike me, he's not questioning the true depth of our friend's denial.

The *Do Not Enter* sign in the direction of Sullivan Meadows was torn down tonight. I ripped through it. For better or worse, I'm here.

Just as I open my mouth, my phone buzzes. I check the message.

You're still waiting to tell Akara right? Bc I still want to do it with you – Mermaid

I text back quickly: Haven't told him. I promise I won't without you

Thanks :) – Mermaid

She adds a high-five emoji. My lip almost curves up. When I pocket my phone, my brother gives me a harder look. Like he knows who that was.

"I really like her, Thatcher," I say in an urgent whisper. "It wasn't some impulsive thing." My heart pounds harder, *harder*. "I've thought about it. I waited. *I waited*." I tilt my head back, then forward, then thread my arms over my tight chest, agonized over something. "Akara might be my best friend, but I know I'm not his *best* friend. You're it—"

"You always say that," Thatcher interjects grumpily.

"Cause it's the fuckin' truth." I raise my tensed shoulders. "You and him share responsibilities that I'll never have. You're his go-to. His—"

"Ride-or-die," Thatcher finishes. "What are you getting at, Banks?"

"If you were the one to kiss Sulli, he'd keep talking to you. He'd shove past it. Me?" I shake my head firmly. Seeing Thatcher at the motel just reminds me that Akara is closer to him.

Thatcher doesn't blink. His stern eyes speak words that are hidden somewhere in my mind. "You think Akara makes *more* exceptions for me than he does for you? He'll let you off the hook a thousand times in any ass-backwards, shit-fucked direction."

I'm about to shake my head.

"Banks, he's *seen* you flirt with her and what's he done about it?"

Alright, my brother has a point.

But I drag my gaze towards the rotting trash in the dumpster, then to the motel room where Charlie, Jane, and Maximoff have left. They're talking and walking to their parked rental cars.

We watch them intently. Really, my brother is watching Jane. But he doesn't move a muscle because Farrow, Oscar, and Akara are in range to protect her. Still, we go quiet. Hawk-eyeing their surroundings from afar, our vigilant gazes sweep the outside of the motel.

No threats that I can see or hear.

Sulli didn't leave with her cousins.

She must still be in the room, and I watch as Maximoff gestures Farrow over.

Careful with a sleeping baby in his arms, Farrow slings a trauma bag over his shoulder, then heads to the motel.

I stare at the door. Worried about her foot, the scorpion sting. Fuck, I forgot the washcloth in the *fucking* sink. I didn't even do what Farrow recommended to help decrease the swelling.

I would've remembered. If her cousins hadn't arrived, I would've remembered.

And the longer I stare at the closed door, the more I remember my kiss with Sulli.

How it started with her challenge to *prove it*, and I wouldn't trade anything…except maybe the location. For *her* sake.

"God, I feel like a real jackass kissing her in a motel," I mutter out loud. It's not the same feeling I had when I kissed other girls in a motel. They deserved more too, but I was a broke-as-hell teenager back then. A motel room was the *tippy-top* of what I could actually give, and so it felt like everything.

Looking back to Thatcher, I go rigid.

His face is contorting in a series of emotions—and finally I see that he lands on utter, suffocating *concern*. For me.

Tendons pull taut in my body. Pain bears on my chest.

"You really like her," Thatcher repeats what I said earlier, but with more awareness of the true depth of my affection for Sulli. His concern keeps amassing. "Banks—"

"I know." I'm unblinking now, drilling my gaze into him. *Please don't say it.*

"She's going to choose him."

"I know," I whisper back, eyes burning. Throat swelling. "Once Akara comes around, it's game over for me. But right now, who knows what's going on in his head?" I lift my shoulders again. "Come what fucking may."

"*Come what fucking may*," Thatcher repeats into a shake of his head. "Your fucking motto works on days you're shifted between three clients without so much as a *thank you* or a five-minute warning. Come what fucking may isn't what you'll be saying when you're watching her with Akara and having to stand off to the side."

"It'll be fine."

"It's not going to be fine," Thatcher whisper-growls now. "You're setting yourself up for a damn suicide mission. And I'm going to have to pick up the pieces."

"Then I'll ask someone else to do that." I smack the back of my hand against his chest. "Take it off your hands." I cock my head with a fleeting smile. Trying to add some levity to the quicksand my brother believes I'm stepping in.

I love living life on my toes. So quicksand of any type is a fucking fear—being pulled so deep under that I can't crawl out and move.

Thatcher has trouble smiling on a normal occasion, so drawing one from him now is next to impossible. He's keyed to a *Protect Banks* function.

He lets out an angered breath. "Just reconsider where you're going. It's not too late to change course. You only kissed once. The deeper you get, the worse it'll be coming back up for air. I promise you that." His gaze subtly shifts to Jane.

He's thinking about her.

But there wasn't another man waiting in the wings for Jane. His biggest competition was *himself*. Thatcher Alessio Moretti vs. His Duty.

I'm in a different gladiator match. Unsurprisingly. Thatcher and I take shots at life from different angles, different distances and speeds. Our battles were never gonna be the same.

It's not too late to change course.

I bob my head a few times. His eyes on my eyes as I tell him, "I'm not going backwards."

His pained glare hits the night sky.

I'm setting myself up for misery. "I'll take whatever time I have with her," I tell him. "Whether it's a week, two weeks—hell, it could be a year or three. Maybe it'll be the best three years of my life."

All I know is that I'd rather crawl hands-and-knees towards a future where Sulli exists than hit *reverse* and never know what it's like to be with her.

Either I'm masochistic or an even bigger dumbass, but I'm willing to be both.

"Can you think *longer* about this?" Thatcher pleads. "Take a day or two."

He leads with his brain.

I lead with my heart.

After a breath, I nod stiffly, but thing is, I already made my choice. "Got it."

Thatcher lets out a long sigh, knowing I'm taking his advice and tossing it into the dumpster beside us. Our attention veers over to the sound of crunching gravel. Jane has left SFO behind with the parked rental cars and strolls over to us.

"Don't tell her—don't tell anyone," I whisper quickly to Thatcher.

He brushes a tensed hand over his mouth. His gaze on his fiancée.

"*Thatcher.*"

"Okay." He pinches the bridge of his nose, drops his hand. "Okay." He nods more than once.

"Thank you." The words barely get out before Jane reaches us.

"Well, you two don't look suspicious at all," Jane notes, digging through her pumpkin-shaped purse that hangs on the crook of her elbow. "Just two men lurking in the shadows of a one-star motel."

I weave my arms. "Practicing for Halloween early. Figured we could be ghosts."

Her brow rises. Christ, Jane has a way of staring *through* you. Like my intentions are tattooed from my forehead to my ass-cheeks. "Can you take care of this for me?" She suddenly turns and asks Thatcher, passing him a slip of paper from her purse. The digression almost puts me in a cold sweat.

Thatcher eyes the paper.

"What is it?" I ask.

Jane speaks fast. "The car service that your family is *adamant* I use for the wedding. I want to hire drivers to pick up guests from Philly to the venue in Newtown Square."

The castle-like venue is a stone-built, historic mansion only a half-hour from Philly. When I first saw pictures, I told Thatcher, "It's perfect, Cinderella."

He shoved my arm but actually smiled.

But I haven't heard about the car service drama yet. "It's Uncle Dino's business," I say to Jane. "He's family, so they want you to hire family."

"But he won't answer the phone," Jane says strongly. "It's driving me mad." She looks more stressed than usual.

Dealing with our family can have that effect. Love 'em, but all together, we're like a stampede of stallions. Rambunctious, too chaotic and too stubborn.

Thatcher notices her tension. "I have this, honey. Anything related to my family, let me handle."

She sighs. "I was hoping to stay more in contact with wedding details so they felt like I was including them. Especially after how upset your grandparents are with me."

"Us," he corrects.

Jane nods. "Us."

The last big family meltdown happened when our grandparents on our dad's side heard Thatcher and Jane aren't marrying in a Catholic church.

I'm partly grateful I'm not heading for matrimony like Thatcher. I already have *literal* migraines every other fucking day. I'd rather not add in a figurative one.

"You're already doing enough," Thatcher assures her. He comes up behind her and wraps an arm around her collar, then places a kiss on her temple.

Her freckled cheeks pull in a smile, then she leans against his chest and holds onto his forearm at her breastbone.

It makes me smile because I've wanted *someone* for my brother. Someone he loves more than me. So maybe if I die first, it won't hurt him so badly.

Thatcher stares harder in my eyes, and I know he'd want the same for me. But I also know he'd call me a *stunad* for thinking our bond could be contested. What we share is just different.

It always will be.

"I didn't forget, you realize," Jane says to me.

"Forget what?" I ask, trying not to break into another cold sweat.

"You and Sullivan, *my cousin*," Jane emphasizes, letting go of Thatcher's arm. She tears from his embrace just to step closer to me. "I think she quite likes you."

I eye Jane like she's eyeing me. *Cobalts*. They all must be descendants of Sherlock fucking Holmes. "Well, I *quite* like her."

Jane instantly smiles. "Then do something about it."

Thatcher exhales a heavy breath. "Akara loves her, Jane."

Her eyes grow. "Since when?"

"It's unspoken," I mutter, running a hand through my hair. "This isn't leaving the three of us."

"Oui," Jane nods. "Can I help in any way?"

A phone pings. Thatcher digs his cell out.

I shake my head to Jane. There's nothing she can do. Sulli and I just need to confess to Akara that we kissed and then go from there.

Thatcher texts someone. He must feel me and Jane staring because he says, "It's Donnelly."

I shift my weight. "Is Xander alright?" Xander has had Donnelly as a bodyguard for almost a whole year. Not a week goes by where I'm not thinking about that kid.

"Yeah, he went to Wawa tonight."

I start to smile. That must be the tenth time he's gone to Wawa this month. Donnelly is good for the kid, and I could be a resentful asshat about it. Thinking that maybe I wasn't doing enough for Xander when I was on his detail.

But Thatcher and I protected him during a time in his life where he lacked confidence, sought shelter indoors, and feared most people. A time where he was losing his brother to college. He needed us to be big brothers. Not cool friends.

Thatcher continues, "Donnelly is letting me know he's going off-duty." He hoists his phone, reminding me he's out of comms-range with the two Omega bodyguards back in Philly: Paul Donnelly and Quinn Oliveira. As the lead, my brother has to know our whereabouts and wrangle all our asses.

I crack a smile. "My twin brother, from Cinderella to *Adventures in Babysitting.*"

Thatcher glares more at his phone. "And Quinn is the long-lost child I can't fucking *find.*" He shoves his cell in his pocket. "It's too much to ask for him to send me a text letting me know where he's fucking off to. I have *no* idea where he's been today. Luna could be in a fucking ditch."

Now *he's* stressed out.

Jane whips out her phone. "I'll text her and see what she's up to."

They're a good team.

It's my last thought before I spot Farrow and Maximoff exiting the motel room. *Is Sulli okay?* The single question pushes me off in their direction.

Nodding to my brother in a quick *see ya*, I sprint over to Farrow while he's mid-conversation. Straining my ears, I pick up some on my way.

"You have the keys?" Maximoff asks his husband. "I'm driving next."

"You sure about that?" Farrow smiles, shifting the strap of his trauma bag.

"Let me think." Maximoff barely pauses (the Hale sarcasm, I know well). "Yep. I'm over-my-dead-body *positive.* We agreed to switch off."

"Okay, but I only drove for two hours. I'll swap later, and you have something in your hair, wolf scout."

Maximoff lets out a laugh, like he foiled Farrow's master distraction plan. "No I don't."

Farrow runs his tongue over his bottom lip, grinning. "I'm not fucking with you. You have something in your hair."

"My *bionic* superpower is all-seeing, and I *see* that there's a bucket load of nothing there."

Farrow smiles more. "Just when I forgot how big of a dork you really a—"

"You check out Sulli's foot?" I interrupt the very second I roll up in front of them. Causing them to stop abruptly in place.

Farrow eyes me with raised brows, like I'm a bat flapping hysterically out of hell. "Yeah, her foot is fine. She'll live."

Maximoff slips me a tougher look. The *don't hurt my cousin* warning is something I've seen him shoot more at my brother. I just now realize he's holding his son.

Ripley isn't sleeping anymore. The baby rubs his tired, blue eyes, his cheek on Maximoff's chest.

I nod, "Thanks."

Farrow frowns. "Why are you acting like you stung her, Moretti?"

Maximoff tenses. "Did you do something—?"

"No," I cut in sharply. "I didn't exactly do a knockout job helping her with the swelling. I just wanted to make sure she's okay."

Her cousin eases a bit. "She's alright. Sulli is tough."

I nod, "Yeah, she is."

I kissed her.

I kissed her.

We fucking kissed. I bite down on my molars, hoping the truth isn't raging through my eyes like it's raging through my head.

I can handle this.

Hell, I've *got* this. Yeah, it's fresh on the brain—it literally *just* happened and I've already spilled to Thatcher—but this news can't be that hard to shelter. I've done a twin-switch before and pretended to be *my brother* for weeks on end. Now *that* was fucked up and impossible.

"You took a shower with her?" Maximoff asks suddenly.

"No," I say. "I took one after her." At least I'm not lying. He might only be twenty-four, but this third-degree feels like he's her fifty-year-old father grilling my ass.

So I step out of their faces, and we all head for the same place. The rental cars where Oscar, Charlie, and Akara still talk.

On our trek, Farrow plucks a leaf out of Maximoff's hair. He shows his husband. "You were saying?"

"I saw that," Maximoff replies, trying to suppress a smile.

Farrow keeps smiling until Maximoff breaks his composure. Keeping pace, Farrow cups the back of Maximoff's head, bringing him closer as they walk. Slipping each other affectionate smiles.

They have that storybook love.

What I used to call sentimental, sappy romance when I was a kid.

Attainable for only few. Like my Cinderella brother.

Maybe I thought of *love* as a storybook because it seemed unreal. Something I never had. Something I couldn't grasp because I'd trip before reaching the door.

And the *love* I saw as a child was destroyed by a toxic divorce. One that ripped through my family like shrapnel. Sometimes I still feel the ache inside me, metal lodged underneath my skin.

Storybook love.

Now that I'm older, I know it's just another word for *soul mate.* What the lucky few will find in their lifetime.

At least my brother found his.

I look up at the star-blanketed sky. Wondering if I should ask a higher being or my other brother if I'm meant for more.

My other brother.

I almost roll my eyes at myself. Love and hate tumbles through me in a nauseous mixture. Skylar is a sore subject, even in my fucking head.

"You okay, Banks?" Akara asks as we come up.

I must look how I feel. Christ, his concern puts a pit in my gut. For more than one reason. If I even mentioned the name *Skylar*, Akara wouldn't know who the hell I'm talking about.

No one except *Jane* would.

The death of my older brother is long-forgotten. So buried that it never even leaked online when Thatcher got more famous.

Memories might fade, but *his* memory is still there. Wreaking havoc on me.

I love that Jane knows about him because I never had to vocalize the story. Never had to drudge up the history. Thatcher did all the work, and I reaped all the benefits.

Having someone else know is a weight off my chest. Some days it's even a comfort.

Right now—staring at Akara—the second pit in my stomach is heavier.

I kissed Sulli.

"Yeah, I'm alright." I cross my arms, scanning the parking lot.

I kissed Sulli. Fuck, I want to tell him.

Meeting this impact now and not later sounds way fucking better.

I kissed Sulli.

I uncross my arms. "You about ready?" I motion with my head to the motel room.

Akara nods, clasps Oscar's hand in a goodbye.

"Wait, before you go," Maximoff says to us. "We have a ton of extra food you should take for the car ride. We overbought."

"Moffy overbought," Jane corrects, approaching with Thatcher by her side.

"Overprepared," Farrow chimes in, then explains to Akara. "We have about two hundred cups of applesauce. Ripley won't finish all of it, and we need to make room."

"We'll take it," Akara says. "Saves us from stopping constantly. We'll make better time on the road."

In the next few minutes, they wrap up to leave. Maximoff hands me a heavy grocery bag of applesauce cups and snack-sized packs of Teddy Grahams.

I hug my twin brother. "See you on the other side."

Thatcher hugs tighter. "Stay on comms."

"Is that my brother speaking or my lead?"

"Both."

"Right on, right on," I smile. *It's okay, Thatcher.* I speak the words through my gaze. He'll understand. He always does.

Thatcher nods stiffly.

I'll be okay.

I have to believe I'm headed towards something good and beautiful. I'm headed towards her, aren't I?

Soon, their cars are kicking up dirt and gravel. Leaving me alone with Akara. It'd be easier to tell him about the kiss right now. Not have a second where I'm keeping anything from him. But I understand why Sulli needs to do it, too. It's the same reason I have to. We care too much about Akara. Simple as that.

We're headed back to her now. So the truth will be out there sooner rather than later.

Trekking through the parking lot, I ask Akara, "How'd Jane, Maximoff, and Charlie come into the motel room earlier? They didn't have a key."

His mind seems to be somewhere else. And for the umpteenth fucking time, I wish I were in Akara Kitsuwon's head.

13

Akara Kitsuwon

"I GAVE THEM MY KEY," I answer Banks, a little distantly. "They wanted to surprise Sulli."

He shifts the grocery bag of Ripley's extra applesauce and Teddy Grahams to his other hand. "They surprised *me*," Banks says. "I nearly shit myself." His tone is light-hearted.

I want to smile, but as we walk back to our motel room, I can't stop picturing *Sulli*.

Naked Sulli.

I tilt my head, eyes drifting. Spacing out. Bodyguard 101—do *not* drift. I've ripped into my men for doing what I'm doing. That glazed "where'd you go" feeling is all so…unfamiliar.

But so is seeing Sulli without *panties*. Or a bra.

I thought I'd want to toss clothes at her. Tell her to *cover up* like I'm some prude. Like I'm her *brother*. But I'm not.

I'm not her brother.

The fact has never been more firmly set in my brain. Like concrete, it solidified tonight.

Flinging clothes at Sulli didn't even register. Maybe I was in shock. *Yeah*. I was definitely slack-jawed, stumbled-back *shocked* that she'd drop her towel in front of us. But I kept my composure. Inwardly, I felt more like a Looney Tunes character—where my heart ejected from my body, pumped five-times bigger, then went back inside.

While we walk to the motel, I'm still dazed. "How is she?" I ask Banks, then quickly remember the scorpion, how I left Sulli too quickly. "Shit, I hate that I had to run out on her like that." I wipe a hand down my face. "It was *right* after I saw her naked too. She probably thinks I find her grotesque." I groan and expel a cringing, nauseous breath.

And I'm expecting Banks to ask, *You like what you saw?* But he's pretty quiet. I wouldn't categorize him as a chatterbox, but whenever I bring up Sulli, he's never silent.

Maybe what he said in the motel room is coming to fruition. He's trying not to sway my feelings for Sulli one way or the other. But Banks yelling at me earlier has already chiseled me open. It'd be nice to have his advice, but he's not my moral conscience.

He's just my friend.

"You okay?" I ask him, making sure I'm not assuming too much. He had this same odd look when we were around the other guys and Jane.

Banks nods. "Sulli is alright too. Farrow checked her out."

"I saw." We stop on the stoop to the motel room. Bugs chirp in the night. I dig in my pocket for the key. He's not avoiding my eyes. So there's that. "How are we not talking about this?" I ask, dropping my voice. "When she was with the Rooster, we never hesitated to talk shit about him or discuss Sulli—and now she got naked in front of us and we're acting like it's nothing?"

He scans behind us. "You didn't want to talk about the funhouse."

"Just with her," I retort in a cringe. "Which was stupid. I was scared." *Scared of change.* But I'm more scared of losing her because…

Because you like her, Nine.

My chest knots, the key cold in my hand. I miss Banks flinging the topic of *Sulli* in my face, even if I end up telling him to shut the fuck up. *I can't lose Banks.* I'm afraid of losing him too. "What was your first thought?" I ask him. "When you saw her naked?"

He wears a crooked smile. "Hell have mercy on my soul."

My lips rise, then falter. *He likes Sulli too.* Maybe *that's* why he's being more guarded. I brush a hand through my hair and fit the key into the lock.

"What was your first thought?" Banks finally asks.

I go still. Remembering a very naked Sulli, her nipples perked—and I wanted to throw her on the bed. Tie her up. Kiss her places she's never been kissed, until she's writhing for more. Those weren't my first thoughts though.

It was simpler.

And before I open the door, I say, "She's a babe."

Banks doesn't pat my shoulder. Doesn't look as happy as I thought he'd be for me. Here I am, breaking down walls he's spent weeks forcing me to stare at.

He just nods.

I nod back, sensing his hurt. *How much does he really like her?* But I hesitate to even touch the subject. Because it'll be a reason for me to slam on the brakes towards Sulli, and I'm just now hitting the gas harder.

I don't want to stop.

He switches subjects. "Who called you? When you ran out of the bathroom," he clarifies.

"Price." I crack the door, seeing Sulli lying on a sleeping mat, then close it so we can talk outside a minute longer. "Apparently one of our temp guards tried to call Connor Cobalt for a corporate job recommendation. Which led to Price trying to wring my ballsac." I seethe just recalling the Alpha leads' patronizing voice. I tell Banks, "I don't know how the temp got Connor's number, but it made Kitsuwon Securities look like the Walmart version of Price's firm, which he already thinks is Versace." I exhale. "Hopefully your dad will be able to weed out the bad temps."

Michael Moretti can't come soon enough.

Banks whispers, "Is he still flying in?" I think he's still expecting his dad to let me down.

"Yeah. I'm having a car service come pick him up since Thatcher isn't in Philly anymore."

I asked Thatcher about his Uncle Dino's car service, a mom-and-pop company, but he told me flat-out, *"Uncle Dino hates him. He hasn't talked to my dad since the divorce."*

Hiring Michael is beginning to feel like doing business with the devil.

Before we go inside, I just give Banks a run-down on the plan. How we're linking back up with Thatcher, Oscar, and Farrow in Montana.

"The good thing is they lost paparazzi outside of Ohio, so we should be media-free for a while," I add. "And hey, people may not even recognize any of us out here. It could be the easiest time in security we've ever had." Still, an uneasiness hangs in the air.

I rap my fist to the wooden door frame, feeling like I just *jinxed* myself.

Banks laughs. But he's staring at the door frame like he *needs* to touch knuckle-to-wood too. "Fuck it." He knocks the wood.

And then we enter our motel room. Foam mats are already splayed on the ground, near the foot of the bed.

Banks inhales sharply, then seems to exhale roughly. His shoulders drop. Not sure why.

Gently shutting the door behind me, I slide the deadbolt. Sulli is fast asleep and curled up, she didn't even grab a sleeping bag. They lie in a heap by the window.

I grab one and unzip it like a blanket. Nearing her quietly, I crouch down and lift the green sleeping bag up to her shoulders.

She stirs a little, nestling into the warmth, but she doesn't wake.

Taking care of Sulli and being with Sulli is so natural to me. It's not a routine, I realize. It's a *necessity* in my life, and maybe that's why I've butted in every time someone has tried to fill it.

Banks and I get ready for bed: brush our teeth, change into drawstring pants, then I cut the lights. "You want me by the door?" Banks asks.

I'm the boss. I call the shots.

Including where I want a bodyguard to sleep, and I could be a complete dick and banish him to the door. Far, *far* away from Sulli because my Spidey-sense—what Banks calls a "fuckbag detector"—is tingling. Though, maybe it's broken. Maybe it's off.

Because Banks isn't a fuckbag.

I mean, I was wrong about Jack Highland-Oliveira. He's genuinely *that* nice.

I snap a finger to my palm. *Don't be a dick.*

Don't be a dick.

"You want the door?" I ask.

"It doesn't matter." He makes a concentrated effort not to look at Sulli.

I lick my lips. "Okay, you take closest to the window. I'll take her other side." Basically, we're on either side of Sulli.

Banks nods, not questioning my decision. "Night." He smacks a hand to my arm.

I nod to him. "Night."

A minute later, we're lying down on our backs, covered with our own sleeping bags. Sulli is turned towards me. Resting my hands under my head, I stare at a stain on the ceiling.

Trying not to stare at her. But my eyes flit to her lips, soft breath expelling between them, then I look back up. Every part of today rushes into me. Between what I feel for Sulli and my friendship with Banks, my brain is a rotating planet of thoughts and varying emotions.

I can't even shut my eyes.

So I turn my head and see Banks on the other side of Sulli.

He's awake.

Staring at the ceiling.

Fuck.

It's going to be a long, sleepless night. For both of us.

14

Akara Kitsuwon

MY DREAMS HAVE BEEN unusually vivid these past few years. They're hard to shake out of, and the biggest indicator I'm still dreaming is always the snow.

No matter where I am.

It starts snowing.

Even tonight, Sulli pounds at a steel door. Latched shut. Trapped in a tiny, cramped metal room together, heavy flurries fall from the ceiling. Snowing in an enclosed room.

Dreaming.

I have to be dreaming, but I don't wake up. I'm stuck inside my head. Snow drifts into her long, chocolate-brown hair, and as I try to wrench the latch open, my fingers bleed.

She bangs her fists. "HELP!" Her shrill scream punctures something in me. Swiftly, I draw Sulli back against my chest, wrapping my arms tightly around her waist. Lips to her ear, I whisper, "Hey, it's okay."

She grips onto me.

She heaves for air.

Oxygen depletes from the room.

I struggle to inhale, but I use every strained breath to whisper, "It's okay, Sul."

Still in my hold, she reaches back and cups my neck, squeezing as though to say, *don't leave.* Our eyes rest on that steel door.

Snow packs higher around our bodies.

I barely feel the cold.

"We're going to die here," she chokes. *Has to be a dream.* Sulli wouldn't give up this fast.

"We're not." I don't understand my certainty until I hear two *pops* from the other side of the steel door.

It swings open, and Banks stands there. On a mound of snow. Chest rising and falling heavily as he sucks on the brittle air. His gun looks comfortable in his grip, but he drops it anyway.

He rushes to us, falling to his knees. One hand on Sulli's head, the other on mine.

I breathe in a lungful of air.

I wake up.

Sweat coats me, and I shoot up, gasping for oxygen. I blink and blink, resting my forearms on my bent knees, disoriented after being in such a vivid dream.

I hate and love the snow.

It was snowing the day my father died.

It was snowing the day my mother moved back to New York.

Nearly every shitty day in my life, it's been snowing. Even in my hellish dreams, it snows. But some of the greatest memories I have of my family were on the snowy ski slopes. We were a happy, *close* family. Mother and Father teaching their baby son how to snowboard. Until I became older and I could race them both on black diamonds with ease.

Like Sulli, I grew up with thrill-seeking parents. My dad worked a desk job so he could play harder. He ran marathons. He was healthy. So his heart attack was a surprise to everyone. Especially me.

I sense the rising tide of grief. Flooding me.

Memories are like a mystery bag of emotions. Reach in and you can pull out the bad ones. The sad ones.

Even if you're only reaching for the happy past.

Guess I got the sad past.

"Kits?" Sulli whispers in the motel room, concern all over her voice. *She's awake.* Actually looks like she's been awake for a while. I'm not that shocked. Still on her side, she's propped up on an elbow. A phone glows in her hand, illuminating her face.

"I'm okay." I lick my dried lips and pat her thigh—*that wasn't her thigh.* I just patted her ass.

Sulli goes still. Her reaction is hard to decipher in the dark.

I tense. "Sorry, Sul—I was aiming for your leg."

"Oh hey, I didn't think you were trying to cop a feel or anything," she says easily. "It's alright."

Usually that'd comfort me. Now, the friend-zone is stifling. Like I'm still being packed in an avalanche of snow. I swallow hard, and I wonder if this is what she's been feeling.

I haven't been fair to her.

Sulli sits up. She's more content than in my dream. Her morning hair is messy around her wide, squared jaw.

Quietly, I tell her, "It was a dream."

"Yeah?" She studies my face. "How was the fucking snow this time?"

I exhale a breath. "Heavy."

I've told Sulli about the snow, my dreams—she even knows about the steel room. Only last time I dreamt that one, I wasn't trapped with Sulli. I was trapped with *Banks.* And she was the one to unlock the door.

Before I psychoanalyze myself, I check my phone. Texts are already sky-high. Mostly business-related. I'll answer them later. It's still dark outside. Almost sunrise.

Banks is sound asleep beside Sulli, and I'm glad he's getting rest. Honestly, I hope his dreams aren't as mind-fucked as mine.

Sulli watches as I rise to my feet.

I jab my thumb to the door, and she nods into a smile. No words needed. Just like that, she knows.

Soundlessly, we throw on clothes. I peek over at her while she shimmies running shorts up her toned hips. She's watching me as I pull a tee over my head.

She's twenty-one.

All grown up.

I've never slept with a friend. Never slept with a client, that's for damn sure.

Messy. So messy—but I'm tired of taking wrong turns when it feels like the right one is right in front of me.

I can't lose her.

Can't imagine life without her.

I wonder what it's like to touch her, to kiss her.

The things I want, I go for. And now that I'm wondering about it, I want it.

Sulli digs around in her backpack, and I go to mine. Unzipping the side, I grab a small notepad and pen from the bottom. Scribbling a quick note.

Sulli abandons her backpack. Sidling next to me, she cranes her neck over my shoulder and reads the note.

I wrote: Morning run with Sulli. Be back soon. -9

She motions for me to hand her the pen, and I give it to her. Below my words she draws three little waves.

With a smile, I whisper, "Who said this was a group note?"

"Hardy-har-har." She leans down for another doodle.

I steal my pen back.

She pushes me lightly in the arm, smiling. Her smile expands my lungs. Lifts my chest. Makes me feel really good. I love when I'm in her good graces. Love when our playful dynamic is back in action. Hate when it's all burned to shit in the land of awkward friendship.

Then don't be friends, Nine.

The thought nearly steals my breath. I keep moving. Tip-toeing to the sleeping mats, I leave the note near Banks. Close to his hand.

He'll notice it.

More silently, Sulli and I make our way outside. To the dewy, dark morning. We go behind the motel and into the wooded thicket. I see what she removed from her backpack. She tips a small travel-sized bottle of mouthwash to her lips and then swishes. It's casual, but *fuck* it's sexy.

I've seen her do that a thousand times before.

And each time rushes back to me in a heat wave.

Sulli hands me the bottle, and I take a swig. I watch as she spits on the ground. *Would she spit out my cum or swallow it?*

I think she'd try both.

Cold wind barely pricks my skin. I try to regain some focus by handing her the empty bottle back. I spit the mouthwash in the grass.

She free-throws the bottle into a dumpster we left back at the motel. A basketball court away, and the mini-bottle still lands perfectly in the trash.

I shake my head. "Foul ball."

"Total swish." She walks backwards into the woods, a playful smile on her lips. "Race you?"

"Only if you pretend to tie me," I tell her seriously. "We're shit-knows where. I can't lose you out here."

"Deal." She holds out her hand for a handshake, but I know better.

I go for it, and before she can clasp her fingers with mine, I drop my hand and run past her.

"Cheater!" she calls out with a grin.

"I didn't say I play fair!" I yell back.

Darkness is just receding. Light barely rising from the horizon. This has always been my favorite time to run with her. Early mornings with Sullivan Meadows—they're a strong heartbeat to my life.

Can't live without them.

Can't live without her.

She takes what I said to heart and keeps my pace, which definitely isn't the one she normally sets. She'd be at least a mile ahead of me by now.

We venture further into the woods, on a path that I scoped out last night during my call with Price. Just in case she'd want to do a morning workout.

When Sulli runs, she looks free. Like she's letting go of every stressor. Every worry. She doesn't clock her run times as often as her swims. Though, she's made for the water. That's undeniable. No asshole can say otherwise.

Not even me.

My soles pound the dirt much heavier than hers. She takes measured, controlled breaths, and each foot down is a stronger, lighter foot forward. She's physically stronger than any woman I know. And while we run, I can't stop looking at her.

I skim her up and down. Hot blood courses through my veins. My eyes land on her ass, her legs that flex, her green eyes that give me a *you-keeping-up-Kits?* competitive smirk.

No I haven't kept up, Sulli.

I've fallen really far behind. It hurts to think that it's taken me this long to see *her*. To really see her.

But I know it's good I didn't before.

It couldn't be too early.

I just hope I'm not too late.

Reaching a cluster of trees with moss-covered bark, we both slow to a stop. Fog rolls in, morning light bathing us.

Her ponytail is loose. And she's barely broken a sweat while my chest rises and falls trying to catch breath. But I can't blame that completely on the run.

"Not too slow, Kits. You might be able to outpace me next time." She slugs my arm.

I drink in her strong features.

Her breath hitches.

Inhaling, I say, "I'd only stand a chance if I tie your ankles together." Brushing a hand through my thick, black hair, the strands just fall back into my eyes. My pulse thumps harder.

She touches her lips. "What's that look?" She shakes her head, drops her fingers. "I've never seen you look at me like *that*."

I take a step forward. "Frankly, I should warn you—I'm not a good guy, Sulli."

She frowns. "In what fucking way?"

I let out a short, brittle laugh. "Oh let me count the ways, string bean."

"Is one the nickname you've recently given me?" She crosses her arms. "Because it fucking sucks and only an asshole would call me a lanky vegetable. One thing I'm not and one thing I hate."

I smile. "We can add that to the list."

"How long is the list?"

"Well, I'd probably be getting a lump of coal from *Santa* if I believed in the big guy."

"Kits," she says impatiently.

Stop flirting, Nine.

Okay.

"Seriously," I continue, "I'm not good. I hate when you brush me off, but I brushed you off for a while because your *ex* told me to stop flirting with you—remember that?"

"How could I not," she mumbles hotly.

I nod. "I'm a hypocrite, an asshole, a dick—I'm the bad guy. I don't deserve your attention, but I'm going to fight for it. You need to know that now, okay?"

"Why does it matter now?" Sulli breathes harder, stepping nearer until we're an inch apart. I stare down at her, only a couple inches taller. "It's not like I'm getting with the bad boy. The bad boy doesn't like the hairy Sasquatch—"

I clasp her waist with two hands and walk her backwards. The abruptness steals her words. Our eyes are locked in thirst and history, years we've spent together—the sweetness that she knows from me. What I've known from her.

The heat is on the other side.

When her back hits the tree trunk, my fingers slide up her strong jaw. I lean in, and she eases back, wide-eyed in surprise.

I stay still. Assessing her headspace. My pulse races. I still hold her cheek, and our breath sounds like heavy panting in the woods.

She eyes my lips.

I eye hers.

And then Sulli leans in.

I draw forward in a flash, bringing her mouth to mine. I kiss Sullivan. I kiss her like she's rainwater and I'm savoring every drop in the desert. Achingly slow.

Our bodies shift closer. The crunch of leaves beneath our soles is a faraway noise in my head. Each passing second with my mouth against hers lights up my core. Tasting every breath, my tongue parts her lips, and her hips bow into me.

One beat later, her hand dives to my crotch. Sulli squeezes my throbbing cock. Not to get me off.

Feels more like she's testing how hard I am.

My erection is painful beneath my shorts. *Fuck*, my body thrums to push into her. To have her pressed even harder against this damn tree. With one hand, I clasp both her wrists and pull her arms high above her head. Pinning them while we kiss.

An aroused noise leaves her lips and enters mine.

Suddenly, she jerks away.

I let go.

Her hands fall.

My pulse flat lines at the sheer dread in her face.

"No, no, no, no." Her hands are on her thighs, bent over. She's looking back at the motel.

"Hey, talk to me, Sul." I can't fucking breathe. "Was it me pinning your arms above your head? I won't do that—"

"I liked that—I really, *really* liked that."

I run my fingers through my hair. "I should've asked to kiss you."

"I should've said *hold on* or…something. *Fuck*." Sulli buries her face in her hands. "I knew you were going to kiss me. I wanted you to kiss me. This is all fucked up."

"What's fucked up about it?" My face twists. "Sulli?"

She has a haunted look.

"Sulli?!" I'm freaking out. That I did something wrong. That someone hurt her in the past. *Did her ex abuse her?* Is she okay?

My mind is racing in a thousand panicked directions.

"I can explain." She holds out a hand. "But I can't explain without Banks."

"What?" My face screws up more.

"We need to go to Banks. *Right now.*"

I don't get it. I don't need to get it. I just want answers.

So I listen to Sulli, and we don't walk back to the motel.

We run like we're playing The Floor is Lava. Our feet are on fire. So is my head, my heart, my body—I'm burning alive.

15

Sullivan Meadows

WHAT IN THE FUCK?

How did I go from having *zero* bodyguards—pals, buddies, whatever-the-fuck—who like me to suddenly two who *kissed* me? My mind can't wrap around the fact that not too long ago, I firmly believed Banks *and* Akara would rather kiss an anteater than kiss me.

My experience with guys, dating, kissing—the works—is microscopic. I have one ex to compare all guys to. I'm not sure I'm equipped to handle kissing *two* men in less than 24-hours. Guilt pried my lips off Akara pretty fast. Was I cheating on Banks?

It's not like we solidified anything.

But it felt shitty.

Really shitty.

Because I still really, really, *really* fucking like Banks, and I don't want to hurt him. I don't want to hurt Akara.

What the hell is even happening?

Two guys.

Two kisses.

I am *not* Elena Gilbert. I'm not emotionally prepared for a love triangle. And oh fuck, I can't believe I'm thinking about *The Vampire Diaries* right now.

I totally blame this on my mom and Aunt Willow. One rainy summer at the lake house, they sat my sister, some cousins, and me in front of the TV and *demanded* we binge-watch all seven seasons.

Was I invested in Elena's complicated love triangle with Stefan and Damon? Yeah. We *all* were. There were teams and sides, and the lake house was split for weeks. All I could think is that it'd fucking suck balls to be in love with two people and have to choose one.

Good news is that I'm not in love with Akara *or* Banks.

I just really like them. And it was just a kiss.

From both of them.

My feet pump harder, Akara not too far behind me as I sprint back to the motel with all my might and drive. Leaves and branches whip at my face until my shoes hit pavement of the parking lot.

Already outside, Banks is tossing sleeping bags into the back of Booger. When he turns around and sees me, he reaches down for the radio clipped to his pants. But the cord is wrapped around the battery pack. As he unwinds it swiftly, urgently, his eyes ping to me in concern.

I stop to a breathless halt in front of him. Hands on my knees, I heave for air. I've never been this out-of-breath from a morning run.

Banks steps in front of me protectively and shields my whole body in a snap-second. "What's wrong?" He's in full bodyguard stance. Stoic, alert, and this is so far from a security problem.

It's just a me problem.

A love life problem.

A *friendship* problem.

I try to form words but I just breathe heavier, not able to catch air into my lungs.

He fits his earpiece into his ear and bends down to me. "Sulli?"

"I…" I trail off as Kits comes into view.

Skidding to a stop beside us, Akara has the same hands-on-knees posture. Hair hangs in his eyes in a casual, cool way like he's pretending to expel air for a 90s-style, skateboard photoshoot. He really has no fucking right to look that sexy being so out of breath.

Banks glances between us with mounting worry. He packs on the I'm-going-to-take-care-of-you attitude that draws me in. He really has no fucking right to look that sexy being concerned.

I like them both.

This wouldn't even be such a bad problem to have if I were someone like Jane. She'd multitask like a boss bitch, all in pastels and sequined heels while being surrounded by a hundred fucking cats.

Banks zeroes in on Akara. "Please tell me you two knucklefucks just made a stupid bet and raced over here." His vigilant, unblinking gaze sweeps the woods past our shoulders. He must think we're running *from* someone.

Dead-fucking-honest, we were just running *to* him.

Akara straightens up in a bigger breath. "Sul." His voice is pleading for answers.

I rise more too, a hand on my cramping hip. "We should all clear the air." My lungs feel tight. "Um, starting with…" I motion to Banks, then back to myself. Signaling *us.*

Is there even an *us?*

Is it too presumptuous to say it?

Maybe, because I can't spit out the words.

Banks nods slowly in realization. More clear understanding. *Our kiss.* We meant to tell Akara last night, and Banks is probably connecting those dots.

Not that he can connect the dot that reads: *Akara & Sulli just kissed in the woods!*

Yeah, that fucking dot is off the page. No line can possibly be drawn to it.

"You want to tell him first?" Banks asks me.

"Tell me what?" Akara snaps at *Banks.*

Fuck, this is bad. Hand outstretched to Akara, I cut in fast, "Last night, Banks and I kissed." I look to Banks. "And this morning, while we were out for a run—"

"I kissed her," Akara tells Banks, his voice as taut as a stretched resistance band.

Banks goes rigid.

Akara's muscles are already flexed.

Both guys—both *friends*—are just looking at each other. I can't tell if they're staring each other down, if their shock is riding the edge of a *fuck you* glare.

The tension is so thick, it'd be easier to breathe underwater.

And then there's the silence.

Pure utter fucking silence.

Flashbacks of the funhouse suddenly bombard me, and I really didn't think anything could be more devastatingly awkward than that.

"Say something," I insist, almost panicked. "One of you. *Please.*"

Akara flinches and makes a move to the green Jeep. "We should get on the road. We have a long ride left to Montana."

My stomach nosedives. This can't be the Funhouse 2.0 where we just bury everything underground for ten days before we even speak about it.

"Kits—" I start to *demand* a conversation.

His eyes find mine quickly. "We can talk on the way." He must see my fear because he adds strongly, "I promise we will."

Banks shuts the trunk. "Fine by me." His voice is stilted and strained. "Everything's already loaded up and squared away. We're good to go." With two long strides, he's already in the driver's seat.

Akara barely blinks as he opens the passenger-side door.

They're sitting next to each other.

I don't know what to make of that. I don't know what to make of anything. Part of me would love to just call my mom. Ask her for a pep-talk and maybe how to handle this strange situation. But I can't exactly confess that I kissed my bodyguards without figuring out what this is.

It could just end right here.

At this motel.

They could walk away and realize their friendship is worth more than a future with me. Which—I wouldn't even blame them for. Solid friendships are hard to come by, so they should probably hold each other tight.

Who's going to hold me?

But I don't want to be the reason Akara and Banks fight.

Still, I picture my future where I'm back to the beginning again. No more kisses or make-out sessions or *anything* else.

The thought sinks my spirits.

With one big breath, I open the door and climb into the backseat.

16

Akara Kitsuwon

THE JEEP RUMBLES TO life as Banks starts the ignition, and my head is split open with the realization that Banks and Sulli kissed—and I should've known.

It was right *there.*

Right damn-fucking there!

I knew something was up with Banks last night. I should've pressed him harder and earlier, but screw it—I'm *happy* I didn't. Because who knows if I would've kissed Sulli this morning if I knew about them, and I'm glad I was blissfully unaware so I had the chance.

I adjust the seat straighter. The Jeep is hot, even though it's a relatively chilly morning. Silence is cooking the three of us, and I know I have to break it first.

"So you two are together?" I ask, then turn slightly to lock eyes with Sulli in the backseat. She's snapping her buckle and lifting her legs to her chest. I ask her, "That's why you pulled away from me?"

Banks glances fast at the rearview mirror. "You pulled away from him?" he asks Sulli.

"Yeah, I did," she admits, a hand to her temple like she's witnessing a slow-moving car crash. And to me, she says, "It didn't feel right to keep kissing after I'd kissed Banks."

Conflicting emotions crawl all over me.

It feels like hundreds of ants scurrying across my skin. Sulli is a good person. With the knowledge she had, I'm glad she shortened our kiss. Because I wouldn't want to hurt Banks either.

The actual kiss they shared…I swallow a rock. Shit, I hate that they kissed. Jealousy piles high, bitterness slipping in the back of my throat.

I only have myself to blame.

If I wasn't in such denial about my feelings, I could've had all last year with Sulli.

I run a hand through my hair and mess with the broken air vents in agitation. "When did you two kiss?" *Last night.* Sulli already said last night. But I guess I just want extra confirmation.

"Last night," Banks says, driving out of the parking lot. "When you were on the phone." The Jeep rocks as we roll onto pavement.

Confirmed: this was recent.

Recent enough that they haven't been secretly dating.

Sulli grips her knees. "We meant to tell you right after. But everyone showed up, then I fell asleep. It turned into a big mess, and I'm really sorry, Kits."

I wince with the shake of my head. "You have nothing to be sorry about, Sul."

"Friends don't keep friends in the dark," Sulli proclaims. "We kept you in the fucking dark."

For less than 24-hours.

Real pricks would let this shit fester into something irreparable, but they came clean faster than most would or could. These two are too good to me. Better than I am to them at times, and I'm starting to rethink whether I even deserve their wholesome friendship.

I really am a dick because I want it anyway. And I'd *end* anyone who crosses them.

They're *my* wholesome, good-hearted friends who curse like sailors.

I'll always protect her and him.

Him.

Where is his head at? Because this isn't anything we've been through. Not apart and definitely not together.

"Akara?" Sulli says, and I realize I haven't responded to her statement.

I turn back to her. "I've kept you in the dark for way longer when your ex told me to stop flirting with you. So how about we just call each other even?"

She tries to smile, but some type of sadness washes over her face, downturns her lips and lowers her gaze.

I want to crawl back there and just hug Sulli. Kiss her again. But I glance at Banks. He's eyeing me in his peripheral.

Lovely.

Just lovely.

I can't help but glare. Frustrated at this love-triangle situation. Couldn't I be here with *anyone* but Banks? I'd have no problem slashing through them to get to her.

Which probably says more about me, I know. I can be cutthroat.

Banks catches my hot gaze. "I am sorry, too, Akara."

I clench my jaw, turning my glare to the road. "For which part?"

He laughs lowly. "I'm sorry I didn't tell you sooner. But I'm not sorry that I kissed her."

"Well, I'm not sorry I kissed her," I snap back.

We side-eye each other for an entire minute.

Sulli scoots up to the edge of the seat. Closer to the middle console and us. Our eyes dart down to her, and the air tenses and heats all over again.

Fuck.

I turn A/C knobs.

She leans forward, even closer between our seats. "Please don't ruin your friendship over a couple of kisses. It's totally not fucking worth it."

"You're worth it," Banks tells her, then to me, "No offense."

"None taken. You just beat me to the phrase." I lock eyes with Sulli. "I was going to say that first."

"But he didn't," Banks adds.

I grind my back teeth, my jaw twitching. *Fuck you, Banks.* I want to flip him off. I want to fucking *hate* him, but there is no real hatred in my heart for Banks Moretti. Even taking shots at each other, they're like water balloons, not bullets.

Sulli is having trouble containing a smile.

I give her a look.

She touches her heart. "My ego is sufficiently inflated, big thanks to you both."

"But mainly big thanks to me," I tease.

Sulli elbows my arm, but in seconds, her smile is gone. "I just want to be upfront. No secrets. No lies or untold shitty things. And you should know, Kits, that my kiss with Banks was longer and sort of an almost-naked kiss."

What? I slip Banks a sharp look.

Sulli quickly adds, "We didn't have sex."

I frown. "You think that's what I thought?" I shake my head. "Banks wouldn't sleep with you in a motel."

A wave of silence rolls through the Jeep.

Sulli takes in my words. Maybe she's realizing that I've thought about her and Banks sleeping together before. Or the fact that I know Banks cares enough not to take her virginity in a one-star motel.

I look back to Banks. "A naked kiss?"

"Semi-naked." The corner of his mouth hikes up. "It was innocent."

"How is a semi-naked kiss innocent?"

"You want the details?"

I give up on the A/C. "We have over a thousand miles for you to explain it to me. It'll be harder for you to share than for me to hear."

Banks smiles. "You're fooling yourself, man."

Maybe I am, but I'm not conceding. I brush a hand through my hair. "You're not taking back that kind of kiss either, are you?"

"Fuck no. Would you?"

"No." I would've loved to have a semi-naked kiss with Sulli. Maybe I'll have more than that one day.

We go silent for the umpteenth time.

I wipe a trickle of sweat off my temple and roll down the window. Gusts of air blow in, but I'm still burning up.

Sulli leans forward more. Her breasts rise with a deeper breath, "So what the fuck are we doing? What happens from here?"

Banks and I exchange a tense look.

I know what happens.

He knows too.

I rotate more to her. "It's your choice, Sulli. We can't tell you who you want to be with. But we both want to be with you."

"I have to pick?" Her voice pitches higher.

I nod.

Banks nods.

Sulli grips the backs of our seats and stares down at the driver's cup holder. "How can I make a choice like that right now? I literally *just* kissed you both, and it's not like I've been dating either of you."

Banks assures her, "You don't have to decide now."

I add, "You're not exclusive with either of us. We can just be casually pursuing you until you're ready." She still looks confused, so I scrounge for a metaphor. "Like you're the Bachelorette, and we're just two handsome dudes vying for your heart—but one of us is clearly better looking." I touch my chest.

"You want Windex for those mirrors?" Banks asks, fitting a toothpick between his lips.

I end up smiling. "Only so you can see me better."

Banks laughs, then tells Sulli, "One of us is clearly more humble."

I nod once.

Sulli is lost in thought. Until she looks up. "So I just casually date you both like I'm the Bachelorette until I make a choice?"

"Right," I say.

"What about the fantasy suites, Kits?"

I stiffen.

Banks frowns. "The what?" He's never seen the dating show we're discussing.

I explain, "It's where the bachelor or bachelorette spends the night with the guys or girls they're dating. I think it's at like final three, and it's implied they have sex."

His brows spike. "The bachelor has sex with the last three women he's dating? And they're all okay with it?"

"Yeah, pretty much."

Sulli is wide-eyed, her cheeks bright red. "Um…is that fucking happening or what are we…doing exactly?"

My chest tightens, and I rub my knuckles. "I think we should probably make a clear rule so no one gets hurt." I take a beat. "No fantasy suites. No sex until you choose one of us."

Banks nods. "I'm good with that."

"Yeah, me too," Sulli eases. "It's less fucking complicated."

Wisconsin farmland backdrops our drive. More fresh air whooshes into the car, rustling our hair and some loose gas receipts in the cup holder. Our set-decision should alleviate tension that's been riding with us like a fourth passenger.

But my flippant *bachelorette* metaphor doesn't mask the seriousness of what's happening. What we're embarking upon. A road where I'm in competition with my friend.

And one of us is going to be left heartbroken.

17

Banks Moretti

SWEET, SWEET *MONTANA*. Alas, we've finally made it to Yellowstone Country.

Not that we see much in the dead of night. After parking Booger in a safe spot, we click on headlamps and hike to our backcountry campsite. A place much closer to the rock face Sulli plans to free-solo.

We set-up camp.

Working quietly, seamlessly—like the three of us have done this our whole lives together—we help each other pop up the teal tent, roll out the sleeping bags, and recheck our supplies. Through our exhaustion, we zip up the tent and start to pass out.

Three different sleeping bags. Enough room not to test any kind of waters. Too tired to even overthink how I'm not on an easy path to be with Sulli.

A miracle slams down to Earth to make that happen—because that's all I've really been thinking about. How Akara and Sulli kissed. How I'm now competing for her affection against my best friend. Who also has history with Sulli that I don't have.

He's known her for what feels like *forever.*

How do I even compete with that?

And I knew a scenario where Akara and Sulli getting together could eventually come to pass, but fuck me that it had to happen less than 24-hours after I kissed her. Bad luck.

Bad at love. Throw out *Roscoe*, that should just be my middle name instead.

If I were smarter, maybe I'd just back off and let Akara jog easily into her heart, so I wouldn't be here pulling her in another direction. But if chasing after Sullivan Meadows is the foolish thing to do, I'm gonna be the biggest fool this world has ever seen.

I've gotten this far. I'm not letting her go now. And whatever happens will happen.

Come what may.

It's the thought I wake to.

Exiting the tent, I stretch my arms and yawn up at the morning sky. With the break of day, my surroundings aren't just muddled in darkness.

So I look around while I rotate my sore shoulders. Spruce trees landscape lush, yellow-green grass, rolling into hills and valleys. Wildflowers grow near the bank of a lazy river. Which I heard trickling last night, but I thought it'd look more like a tiny stream.

I go still.

Three deer wander along the bank. Massive antlers crown the largest one. Head hoisting, beady eyes lie serene on me. Like I'm just part of the scenery.

Another animal among animals.

Wildlife is abundant here. Every which way, another woodland creature pops out. Hawks cut through the air. Chipmunks scurry beneath logs. Nothing that'd bother us if we don't bother them. Though, I know the hierarchy in the animal kingdom, and I'd rather meet the peasants of Yellowstone.

No grizzly bears. No packs of wolves. No buffalo.

I'm not someone who really communes with nature. I grew up riding a bike through South Philly, not sniffing dandelions on a mountainside.

The city has been my home.

But I don't mind the crisp air or lack of traffic noise. I just wish there wasn't a fuckin' symphony in my temple right now. The banging, the thumping, pounds dully but I know it's gonna grow.

While I ignore the incoming migraine, I detach a radio off my drawstring pants and glance deeper out.

Mountains border the horizon. One cliff towers more closely and looms over our camp. That peak must be about ninety-meters high. 300-feet up.

What a long way to fall.

I unspool my radio cord, my muscles constricting the more I eye the sheer size. Looks more dangerous than the rocks in Pennsylvania.

And Sulli plans to climb that beast with no safety gear. It seems fucking impossible, but I remember why this cliff is on her list of climbs in the Yellowstone region. Ryke Meadows once free-soloed this same rock, this same route called The Bitterroot Buttress.

Her dad did it, so it is possible.

She can do it too.

I'd bet on Sulli, but that doesn't mean I won't be biting my nails to the fucking bed watching her up there.

I fit in my earpiece. Switch on comms to a frequency Akara set among Security Force Omega out west. Thatcher, Oscar, and Farrow are now in comms range, but they didn't hike to the primitive campsite last night with us. They're staying miles back at an RV campground with bathroom facilities—hell, even *showers*—and more importantly, they have easy access to the road.

My brother and the others choosing to go *glamping* is a saving grace, really.

I need them to be far away from me right now—or I could risk opening my big mouth to Thatcher and blurting out how Akara and Sulli already kissed.

I'm not gonna be the first to spill the beans. The three of us agreed to keep everything to ourselves for now. If we tell the others, it'd cause too much attention and pull focus from Sulli's purpose for being out here.

To free-solo.

Comms on, I figure since I'm awake I can at least whip up something to eat. Pretty easily, I start a fire using a fire-starter, then I boil a pot of water and dig through our breakfast supplies.

Oatmeal, *no thanks.*

Instant eggs, *not bad.*

Pancakes, *Sulli will love those.* I leave out the add-water-only mix, and the longer I dig, the less I find any kind of meat. Looks like I'm gonna be a fucking herbivore.

Wait—here's a pack of beef jerky.

I'll take it.

I rip into that dried meat, biting off a piece while I sit on a rock and mix up some pancakes for the mermaid and eggs for Akara and me.

And I rub my thumping temple and glance too many times at the tent. I'm out here whipping up food for the girl I like, and she's alone with Akara.

Good for them.

I try to think it, but my stomach roils.

Midway through cooking, Akara climbs out of the tent. "Need help?" He fits in his earpiece as he approaches.

Any heat in my soul just sputters out. Can't resent Akara. Not when I've been a supporter of him getting with Sulli for so long.

"I'm good." I fit a toothpick between my lips and flip the third pancake. I have to go one at a fucking time on this teeny-tiny fold-out pan.

Akara reaches for a pancake off a plate.

"Those are for Sulli," I say fast.

He makes a face and points at me with the floppy, half-burnt pancake. "Who are you and what have you done with Banks?"

I chew on the toothpick. "I'm the same as I've always been."

"*You* don't cook. You especially don't cook special breakfasts for anyone."

My lip nearly rises. "You sure I haven't cooked one for you before?"

"Thatcher has. You? *Never*," Akara says. "If you cooked me breakfast, I would've marked the date on a calendar and stuck OMG stickers around the words *Banks Loves Me*."

I hold his gaze. "What's today's date?"

"September 29th."

I nod to him. "Go get your OMG stickers. I made you scrambled eggs."

"Not pancakes?"

"Those are for—" *Sulli.* I cut myself off as Akara bites into the pancake.

Cringing, he spits it out in the sizzling fire. "Shit, these are *bad,* man. Like charcoal putty."

Fuck.

I try one and barely chew before spitting the hunk in the flames too.

"Here." Akara comes closer. "Let me help." He's about to take the pan from my hand, but I rock back.

"I've got it. You've already had time with her *alone* in the tent. Just let me try to make a fucking pancake." I have some batter left. And this would be a power-move on my part if I could actually cook a goddamn fucking pancake.

Akara is like a king, bishop, and rook on a chessboard. I'm just one knight trying to move in an L-pattern that makes no sense half the time.

After I toss the third pancake on the plate, I pour more batter in the frying pan.

Akara sinks down on a rock across from me. He just keeps looking at me.

"What?" I ask.

"I'm not used to seeing you this frustrated. Not much gets under your skin. Except me right now." He sends me an apologetic look.

I exhale roughly, hating being in a state of agitation. Feeling like I'm going to come up short when I pride myself on being there, without question or hesitation, for people who need me.

Quietly, I tell him, "It's the situation. I'll get over it." I pass Akara a bowl of scrambled eggs.

"Thanks." He finds a fork. "Sulli is still sleeping, you know. We weren't kissing or having some kind of marathon conversation—and I can't believe I'm even giving you these details." *I can't either.* He didn't have to tell me any of that. Akara stabs the eggs a few times, then says, "It'd be easier if you were some asshole blueblood like the Rooster." His eyes meet mine. "Then I'd just kick your ass."

I laugh. "You can still kick my ass if you want. But I'll probably put you on yours."

He shakes his head, smiling. "In your dreams, Moretti."

I smile back. "I'd take that dream. It'd be better than the shit I'm sleeping through these days."

Akara's features grow more serious. "You're having bad dreams?"

I lift a shoulder and flip the newest pancake. "Just restless ones."

While he takes a strong bite of eggs, he stares at the ground. He must be thinking hard about something. If it were related to work, he'd confide in my brother in an instant. But I'm not sure if this is about security.

"Something wrong?" I ask.

He looks up and lets out a dry laugh. "Other than the fact that we both like the same girl?"

I flip the pancake again, looks golden. "Other than that unfortunate thing, yeah."

"Unfortunate is an understatement," Akara replies into a sigh. "I hate that we're competing for her attention…her affection. Because I want it, but I'm also going to feel badly when you don't get it. And I'm going to feel like even worse shit when you do and I don't."

"Same here." I bounce my head, a migraine shooting pain in my left eye. I try not to close it. "Guess that's what happens when someone you care about falls for the girl you like."

"Yeah." He runs a hand through his hair and then answers my earlier question. "I've been having dreams."

I tense and scan him quickly. "That's what's bothering you?"

He nods once, then swigs from a water bottle. He's about to reply, but Sulli zips herself out of the tent. She's already dressed in workout gear and carries a perfectly coiled rope. "Hey, guys. That smells good."

Before it burns, I toss the golden pancake onto a plate. "Lower your expectations. Akara's food review came in and it wasn't good." I sprinkle the top of the pancake with yellow gummy bears. Standing up, I walk over to Sulli.

"Akara's not a good food critic, so it's probably amazing."

"Hey, I'm a great food critic for mainstream tastes," Akara defends. "Not your sweet-tooth concoctions."

She smiles at him, then really looks at the plate I hand her. "Did you only put the yellow gummy bears on here?"

"Yeah," I say. "Aren't they your favorite?"

Her smile is on me now. "Yeah. I just...thanks." She nods a lot. "That was really fucking sweet."

My chest rises. It's not often a girl calls me *sweet.*

Akara cuts in, "Wait until you taste it before you give him the five-star, Sul."

"He can get five-stars for the fucking delivery and presentation." She nudges Akara's knee with her foot.

Akara smiles at me. "She's giving you a participation trophy."

I close one eye. *Fuck this migraine.* "That's one more trophy than she's given you."

Akara flips me off.

I flip him off.

"Alright—none of that in my fucking presence," Sulli says in panic. She wasn't here earlier to catch our heart-to-heart. "All friendships must remain *intact* and survive the duration of Yellowstone. I have annihilated too many friendships already—I don't want to be known as the fucking Friendship Assassin."

We laugh, and Akara says, "That's too cute not to call you that."

"Stop," she groans.

He feigns hurt. "But my Friendship Assassin."

"Kits." Sulli tries not to laugh. "I want to be the *lover*, not the fighter, definitely not the killer."

The air heats as the word *lover* hangs for a much longer beat.

Sulli shifts her weight, her face brighter red. "Not that I know how to make love, but one day, I probably will."

I tip my head, wondering why she added *probably*—like she's still not sure if she'll ever lose her virginity. So I tell her, "You will."

Sulli gives me a once-over, flushing more.

"You *definitely* will," Akara chimes in.

Who's going to guide her? None of us have the answer. Only Sulli can make that decision.

Her gaze pings from me to Akara, back to me. "Cool." She nods, then shakes her head in a cringe. "Cool? Fuck me." Her eyes bug out. "I didn't mean to say that out loud or in front of you two... *fuck*."

Akara is laughing.

Hell, I'm smiling.

Instead of running away, Sulli stuffs her mouth with the golden, gummy bear pancake. While she chews with her mouth closed, she smiles at the taste, then makes a *perfect* sign with her fingers.

Take it back—I fucking rock. Move over, Thatcher, a new Moretti chef is coming to town.

Tension recedes as we joke some more about my cooking and Sulli's sweet tooth. Soon, we all end up huddled around the fire. Sitting on three rocks, we eat the last bit of breakfast I cooked.

I switch back to a lost topic. "What kind of dreams have you been having?" I ask Akara.

Sulli frowns into a swig of water. "Did you have another one?"

Akara nods, then explains to me, "Lately it's always the same dream—or at least a version of the same one." He describes the snow and the steel room. "Last night, I saw it again." He pauses, and Sulli and I exchange a concerned look.

Maybe he's not getting enough sleep.

Akara massages his hands. "Only this time, I opened the door and found you two trapped inside."

The fire crackles. Embers dying out in the soot. An eeriness falls over our camp. Akara looks rattled, and I'm too superstitious to think anything he just described is good.

18

Akara Kitsuwon

THE ANNOUNCEMENT OF my dreams sucks the last oxygen from the fire. Flames burn completely out.

I try to sit straighter.

Sulli looks to be in deep, *haunted* thought. She's superstitious. Not more so than Banks, but she's pretty spiritual. No one here is rooted solely in the kind of logic that you can see. I'm the closest one to that rationale, and even then, I believe in leading with intuition.

So if I was looking for someone to tell me, *it's just a dream, Akara; it's not real*—I chose the wrong campsite to have a fireside chat.

But I know her.

I know him.

And I *knew* my audience. I'm not looking for them to placate me. Just to share in the *what the fuck* feeling I've been feeling.

Banks bites hard on a toothpick. "What do you think it means?"

"It feels like a warning." I lick my lips, then I notice how Banks rubs his temple a lot. I eye him more. Is he okay?

He drops his hand.

I lean back, looking him over. His face screams *ouch*, but his body says, *I'm fine.*

Sulli shifts uneasily. "Could the dreams just be a sign that the three of us are fucking badass? We all saved each other in them."

I want to smile at her cute optimism. "Maybe." I stare at the burnt logs. "You know, my parents were always really superstitious. My dad more than my mom. He used to tell me how back in Thailand, my great-grandparents would consult monks and fortunetellers for everything: before a career change, before buying a house. He even believed in the whole nickname thing."

"What nickname thing?" Sulli asks.

"There's an old belief in Thai culture that malevolent spirits might harm a baby if they know the infant's real name. So parents nickname their kids."

"Nine," Sulli says in realization.

They both know my nickname, but they haven't known the significance of why I have one until now. With friends, I rarely bring up the nickname unless I'm writing a fast note and don't want to spell out *Akara.* It's easier jotting down the number.

I nod. "I was born at nine-oh-nine p.m.—they thought the number was good luck."

Banks nods back. "So you named your gym Studio *9.*"

"For good luck," Sulli chimes in.

"And narcissism," Banks adds.

"Yep to both." I smile, then watch a centipede crawl over a twig near my foot. "I always felt most connected with my culture through Muay Thai. It was my mom's profession, something she taught me—but it's funny to look back and realize there was a lot more about my life that was more Thailand than Philly, more than I even realized." I sit up more again. "I'm fourth-generation. My parents don't speak Thai. Their parents didn't speak Thai. I don't even have family still *in* Thailand to visit. Everyone is in New York. I think as a kid I didn't realize that culture isn't necessarily just a place."

Banks nods strongly.

"Anyway," I exhale a breath. "I don't know if my dad's belief in dreams is a Thai thing or just my dad." I smile more softly, remembering when I was just a kid. "Before he left for work in the mornings, he'd always ask me about my dreams and analyze them for me. He'd get so animated about it that I knew he really believed in them. In what they meant."

Quietly, like so as not to disturb any ghosts, Sulli asks, "You really believe in them too?"

"Yeah, I do." I knead my palm with my thumb. "And if I told my dad about these recurring dreams, I think he'd say, *be careful, Nine.*"

Banks sucks in a coarse breath.

Sulli stares up at the mountain looming over us. Her determination never wanes. Not even as she looks to me. "I'm still going to climb."

"I know," I say softly. "I wasn't trying to convince you not to, Sul."

She eases. "Okay, good. Maybe we should all just believe I have wings so nothing bad will happen."

Banks cracks a smile. "The flying mermaid."

"Doesn't exist," I add with a teasing smile.

Sulli stands up. "And here's my shot to prove you wrong, Kits."

"Yeah?" I look at her head to toe. "I'm glad you're going to take it, string bean!" I have to call after her because she's already walking away. On a mission to succeed. I smile more. When I turn back to the extinguished fire, Banks is watching Sulli with the same infatuated expression that I feel.

Shit.

I rise and start cleaning up our camping dishes.

How do we prepare for bad fortune when the worst outcome could be heartbreak or death?

Turn back now, Nine.

I hear my dad's deep voice. I always hear his voice in my head like a moral compass throughout my life. Guiding me.

And I just want to tell him, *I can't turn around, Dad.*

19

Sullivan Meadows

DAY 1 ON THE BITTERROOT Buttress, I mentally prepare for the ascent. Kicking dirt off my climbing shoes, I chalk my hands, a bag tied around my waist.

Akara's dreams drift to the back of my brain. I've stuck them in deep drawers and turned a lock. If I'm not focused, I'll fall, and I need to map out my route.

Moss covers the bumpy, jagged rock face. Three-hundred feet high, the foliage is concerning. If it's too wet, I might need to either find a better route or scrape it off.

Since this is a practice run with safety gear, I texted Jane, Moffy, and Charlie before I lost cell service. I told them to just meet-up tomorrow. For one, I need to climb without the added pressure of my cousins watching.

For another, there would be *zero* pressure if I weren't keeping a humongous fucking secret. *Akara and Banks are casually dating me, Bachelorette-style.*

When I see my family, I'm afraid it'll be written all over my face. I sincerely wish I were a better liar. And right now, I'd rather be thinking about this beautiful, challenging behemoth than worrying about unearthing that news.

I recheck my harness and rope.

"Knock 'em dead," Banks encourages, coming up to my side. "Or whatever climbers say."

I smile up at him. Something flutters inside my body the longer he stares back down at me. And I know, for fucking sure, that he's not looking at me like a buddy.

My face hurts from grinning. "I usually tell my sister to *scale that bitch*."

His mouth curves. "You better scale that bitch, mermaid."

"I'll try my fucking hardest."

His gaze descends my body in the hottest wave. I'm just in knee-length cargo shorts my sister bought me last year and a Camp Calloway tee, but Banks makes me feel like I'm in full glam on the red carpet. For a while there, I was scared I'd need to wear lipstick and a dress for a guy to look at me like how he's looking at me. My fear: real life actually imitates teen movies where the girl has to have a blow-out, makeup, and high heels to finally be noticed and desired.

To be me and still be longed after is one of the best experiences, one I never really knew I needed this badly.

He glances at my chalk bag. "That hooked on right?"

"Yeah." Does my voice sound raspy? "I'm all secure." I recheck again, just to be safe.

He curls his hair behind his right ear, then left, and he leans in. My heart races as he places a tender kiss on my lips. I smile against his mouth, and while I lean in more, his hand dips to the small of my back. When we break, I feel *nervous*.

Because Akara is also here.

How the fuck does the Bachelorette date like fifteen guys at once?

As Banks reluctantly steps back, he tells me, "Stay frosty."

I've heard him say that phrase to other bodyguards before. "What does that mean? *Stay frosty*?"

"Stay cool." His shadow of a smile reappears. "Stay on your toes."

I like that. "You stay really fucking frosty."

"Not frostier than you."

Akara approaches me like he's chugging a gallon of antifreeze. He gives me a look like *put me out of my misery, Sul.*

I return that with a glare. "I'm allowed to flirt, Kits."

"I'm just trying to switch the TV channel off the Hallmark Movie."

I check my harness again. "What are you putting on instead? *Stranger Things*?" It's his favorite TV show. If it's trending and popular, Kits has seen it. If it's obscure, he's never given it any time. My mom has a theory that Akara tunes into popular things because there's less risk of disappointment. He's too busy to be let down by the few things he has time for.

"*Stranger Things* would be up there." He smiles, stopping an inch away. "So would *Breaking Bad, The Walking Dead*—"

"You'd rather watch flesh-eating zombies attack me than me and Banks—"

"We wouldn't let a zombie attack you," Akara cuts in fast, then he emphasizes, "*I* wouldn't."

I smile. "Oh no, it's already too fucking late, you included him."

Akara shakes his head into a smile. His eyes descend my build, much like Banks' did. "What about if I tune into *Fifty Shades*."

I snort. "Right, like you've watched that."

"I haven't," he admits, "but I could probably show you how to knot this." His fingers brush mine as he takes an end of the rope out of my hand.

My heart skips and a strong pulse throbs between my legs. After Moffy's bachelor party this summer, I walked in on Banks and Akara's conversation about *rope* and *sex*. Mainly, Akara was showing Banks knots using a shoelace.

He's more experienced than me.

Fucking *duh*.

They both are.

I reclaim my rope, our fingers brushing again. "Maybe later."

He nods, and our eyes do a back-and-forth dance that speeds my pulse. Anticipation intensifies before he places a light kiss on my cheek. Then he touches my chin, lifting my mouth up, his lips meet mine in a softer, more sensual kiss that dizzies me.

Fuck. Breathe.

I grip his neck while his tongue slides against mine. I feel like I'm falling and I haven't even started the climb.

As we pull apart, I can barely lock eyes with Akara without blushing. I touch my burning face.

He inhales strongly. "See you, string bean."

"Yeah. Bye." I wave behind me and shake my head at myself, facing the rock and cringing. "What the fuck, Sulli?" I blow out a controlled breath.

Focus.

Concentrate.

I kick more dirt off my shoes. Shake out my limbs.

Concentrate.

I glance back one more time.

Akara and Banks stay next to each other. Spectating several feet behind me, they're two men, older than me, and I'd be more intimidated if they didn't make me feel powerful.

I liked dating Will Rochester—that first experience was a pretty good one—but I realize how small I felt around him. Like there were parts of me that I should hide a bit better.

Try not to say *cum* so often. Shave a little bit more. Strapless shirts need to go because if I show my muscular shoulders, he won't be into me as much.

Stupid.

So fucking stupid, and most of those were just my insecurities rising up like a swelling tide.

I face forward with a stronger, deeper breath.

With Akara and Banks, I feel as mighty as the mountain I'm about to climb.

Concentrate.

While they watch me prepare, I realize I'm used to their protective gazes on me while I climb. Having them here begins to calm me. My pulse eases, and the rush of the river, the chirp of birds, and rustle of leaves all fall silent.

It's just me and the rock…and my dad.

I smile up at the crag. Imagining him in his teens, using his raw strength to free-solo to the fucking top, and here I am, years later.

"I'll see you up there, Dad," I whisper, my heart filling. "I just have to practice first."

With another measured breath, I see the path I need to take like a map in the natural stone. Smiling, I grip the rough edge.

And I ascend.

20

Banks Moretti

COVERTLY, I POP THREE Advil in my mouth while Akara and I watch Sulli's first day of climbing. The pain meds aren't for my internal *oohs* and *ahhs* and *Mary, Mother of Gods* seeing Sulli do death-defying shit. It's just for the thunder-fucking headache.

Though, watching her climb is incredible and agonizing. Her strength and agility are on full display as she scales the rock over and over. Nothing I could accomplish.

Right now, the harder pill to swallow is knowing I can't do anything for her. It's all Sulli up there, and I can only protect her once she's back on solid ground.

The upside: she's still climbing with rope.

She'll be practicing for a while, until she's positive she can climb without safety gear.

Akara is beside me. Quiet. He hasn't said anything since this morning when we kissed her. With Sulli in the air and us on the ground, we only have each other's company. Cell service went to hell once we left our campsite, and our comms connection was lost too.

Akara has been sitting. Leaning against a flat rock that juts up like an arrowhead.

I can't sit down.

My arms are crossed. My nerves at an all-time high watching her attempt the same portion of cliff over and over again.

She leaps between one protruding rock to another, a cavernous hole separating them. Each time she tries, she misses the second handhold, and her rope catches her before she falls.

"She's gotta do that without a harness," I whisper more to myself.

Akara must hear because he says, "It's not a big gap. She's done larger. I think she's just unfocused."

I uncross my tensed arms. "So we're distracting her?"

"Probably," he says, but he doesn't seem worried. "She's careful. She won't free-solo until she's ready." His confidence in her—and lack of blatant outright fear—reminds me how much he's seen her climb over the years. How much he's probably watched Sulli's dad and sister also scale mountains.

I've only just recently tagged along in the past year—when Akara created his security firm and he kept putting me on her detail.

"Sit down," Akara suggests. "It's always worse if you don't relax."

Taking his recommendation, I sit back against the same rock beside him. We're almost shoulder-to-shoulder, and I flinch when she falls again. Rope catches her and she gingerly swings back to the same handhold.

"The Rooster has a girlfriend," Akara suddenly says.

"You're still keeping tabs on him?"

Ever since Sulli broke up with Will Rochester, Akara has put the shitbag on his *watch list*. Disgruntled exes coming back into the famous ones' lives isn't a far reach.

Jane's ex-friends-with-benefits did even worse than tiptoe into her sphere again. Nate, the sick fuck, stalked Maximoff and then created a scene out of *The Shining* in his bedroom with animal's blood.

Wasn't around to see it.

My brother was.

Thatcher wouldn't talk much about what he saw—much like I don't care to rehash *Sneakers*, the stalker that I encountered with his dick out in Jane's bedroom.

Sulli's ex is probably less likely to do something sadistic, but I wouldn't put it past him to say mean shit online. How he went around

Sulli's back to tell Akara not to flirt with her was pure coward shit. He could've just talked to her about it.

Respected her enough to have a conversation than play games.

Even thinking about that rich turd is like listening to two pieces of sandpaper rubbing together. Annoying as hell.

"I'm just keeping him on my radar for right now," Akara says to me, our eyes on Sulli. "He posted on Instagram."

"When?" I pull out my phone. *No service.*

"Yesterday. I would've told you, but I couldn't really figure out how to segue into that after the whole *we kissed the same girl* conversation."

I almost laugh, but the sound is knotted. "What'd she look like?" I ask. "The Rooster's girlfriend."

Akara rolls his eyes just thinking about it. "She looks like Daisy Calloway. Well, a young Daisy."

I make a face. "That fucking cock."

Akara nods slowly, gaze stuck on the mountain. "I don't think Sulli has seen the post yet. Maybe she won't. I don't know if she checks his Instagram."

It might hurt her, knowing her ex pursued someone that resembles her supermodel mom. Not that Sullivan isn't worthy of supermodel status, but she has more of her dad's features: strong jaw, athletic build, and dark hair.

I shut one eye, the sunlight bothering me more. "As much as I can't stand the Rooster, I'm glad her experience was good. Can't replace your firsts."

Akara unzips a backpack and looks to me. "You still agonizing over your shitty firsts?"

"Maybe." I force both eyes open. Because he's studying me like he has a fucking magnifying glass up to my face.

"Your first hand job was *not* that bad."

I bite the toothpick clean in half and spit out the pieces. "She got a cramp in her wrist after thirty seconds, Akara."

He laughs. "You were both sixteen, and you have a big dick. She probably didn't know what to do with it." He pulls a water bottle and slowly spins the cap off. "It's just math."

"Yeah, but you weren't there." I shake my head when he tries to hand me the water.

Akara scrutinizes me one more time before taking a swig.

"She was embarrassed as hell," I continue, "and I felt like shit after. I just wouldn't want Sulli to have to feel that her first time." I add more strongly, "And she wouldn't with me. Confidence and experience guarantee that." I'm not sixteen fumbling around anymore.

Akara rests his arm on his knee. "You don't need to convince me of anything like that. I know you'd be good for her." He glances at me. "But probably not better than me."

I watch Sulli swing to the rock again. "Only she can decide that."

He leans back. "Yeah, but it's not like she's going to take a test run."

"Which is good," I tell him. "This isn't about who's the best lay."

Akara nods, going quiet as Sulli misses the handhold again. "You weren't there, but during the FanCon tour, you remember Thatcher and I talking about how the bus broke down?"

I fit another toothpick between my lips. "Yeah?"

"There was a fortuneteller in this small town, and sometimes I think about what she told Sulli."

"What'd she tell her?"

"Something like *you're determined, a go-getter, and there's a guy who protects you strongly, and you will fall*—and then Maximoff cut her off. At the time, I thought it was *fall in love*, but that was back when she wasn't climbing. Now I think she was referring to a literal *fall*."

We're more unblinking, more laser-focused, and I want to shake my head and tell Akara he's wrong. But the energy in the air has been *off* most of the day.

If I'm honest with myself, it almost feels like we're being watched.

Hairs stand up on my neck, and I remember, "I lost my rosary."

"When?"

"This morning. I was looking for it before we hiked over here."

Akara lets out a laugh. "Fuck, Banks, you lose *everything*."

He's not wrong. "At least I haven't lost my fucking mind yet." I shut another eye.

"You're in pain?" he finally asks.

"Small headache," I mumble, breathing through my nose. "It's nothing." *Don't puke.*

He grimaces. "Doesn't look small, Banks."

"I'm fine." To switch the subject, I land on something I've thought about. "Do we know if Sulli has done more with the Rooster than just kiss?"

Akara turns back to watch her. "I don't know. She hasn't said anything to me. But that doesn't mean much since she shut me out after their break-up. I don't think she'd tell me, if she did."

I cinch my eyes closed, more from the migraine, and rake a hand roughly through my hair. "So he could have put his fingers in her." I open one eye.

Akara's jaw sets, and he passes me the water bottle. "I'm trying not to think of murder today, Banks, could you please shut up."

I pop the cap. "I'm just throwing out possibilities."

"And I'm holding onto the one we know: he didn't sleep with her."

"Right on." I put the water bottle to my lips. Taking a hearty swig, then wiping my mouth with my arm. "I don't think she gave him a blowie either. He seems like the kind of guy that'd never shut up about it."

Akara smiles. "Small thanks to that."

On the rock face, Sulli takes another leap and this time, she grabs the second handhold.

"Get some," I say under my breath, my chest swelling for her.

Akara is grinning.

Time ticks by, and as the sun starts to lower in the early evening, Sulli finishes climbing. Back on the ground, sweat drips off her forehead and she guzzles water from a CamelBak nozzle, the bladder filled with a couple liters of water.

"I think I can do it in a couple days," she tells us. "One more practice and I'll nail it."

Akara high-fives her, then tickles beneath her armpits.

She squeals, "Kits!" and squirts him with water.

A tinge of jealousy rises. *Hate that.* But I won't ever have *that* kind of relationship with her. It's not how we started. It's not really what I want with her either. Not that I've dated that much. That's Akara's wheelhouse. But I'm not Akara Kitsuwon.

I'm Banks fuckin' Moretti.

I pick up my backpack and swing the strap over my shoulder. When I go to carry Sulli's, she says, "Oh hey, I got that."

"You sure?"

"Yeah." She slings her Patagonia backpack on. "Not too heavy." She slugs my waist. "I could probably beat you in a footrace with a hundred pounds."

"Probably." I slide an arm across her shoulders while she's next to me.

She intakes an audible breath, then smiles at my arm on her. Sulli even takes my hand that hangs near her bicep and places a kiss on my knuckles.

I can't take my eyes off her, and as a bodyguard, that is *bad.* Really fucking bad. And I'm about to lean down and kiss her.

But Akara glances up at the sky. "Hey, we're going to have to jog back to make it to camp before sundown." His severity kicks my ass into gear. "I don't want us to be on the trail in the dark."

I drop my arm off Sulli and eagle-eye the path.

She nods.

"Banks, you go out front," Akara orders.

Usually I don't question a superior. At least not to their face. I've learned to shut my mouth, even when I think they're wrong. But I point out, "I'm slower than you and her. Shouldn't you two be out front and I'll take the rear?"

"That's why you should set the pace."

I nod, realizing he wants us to stick together. So I just go on ahead. The trail is riddled with fallen logs and tall grass.

Sulli is on my ass in an instant. I glance over my shoulder as I jog.

"This is nice," she says, barely breaking a sweat. "Leisurely and scenic. I fucking like it."

I laugh. "Good because I'm not busting my ass by going any faster."

"Yeah, don't do that. I like your ass how it is, Banks."

Blood pumps harder.

I wish I could spin around and just take her face in my hands. Kissing the hell out of Sulli is on my brain when I know I should be more alert.

"Watch for snakes," Akara calls to us.

Facing forward, I run as fast as I can. Having the longest legs of the three of us means nothing when I'm two-hundred-plus pounds of muscle. I'm not slow, but I lack the speed that Sulli could clock.

Wind whips around us, and my shoes crunch fallen leaves and rocks. Akara and Sulli crack a few jokes for a couple minutes before they go quiet. Just letting nature sink in.

Even with the wind, the air feels still. Strangely calm.

The thump of our feet on the dirt is a familiar noise that brings a sense of comfort. I've run miles upon miles in the military, a rucksack strapped to my back. I've run after Sulli in Italy.

Now I'm running in front of her in Yellowstone.

I stay in the moment.

I'm right here. My vigilant gaze sweeps every meter ahead. The trail widens, woods on the left, and the endless view of sky on the right. It shouldn't—and I don't know why—but Skylar pops into my head.

His face.

The one I remember.

He was fifteen. He'll always be fifteen to me, even though he was my older brother, and that fact settles heavy on my chest for a split-second.

Suddenly, a bloodcurdling sound rips through the air. Violent, like a cross between a screech and a growl. The second sound comes quicker, faster than I can even turn around.

It's a loud *thump*.

I turn to look at Sulli's six.

At Akara's six.

No.

I race back to him.

Akara has hit the ground.

And a cougar is braced on his back.

21

Akara Kitsuwon

I'M GOING TO DIE HERE.

Two-hundred pounds of animal assailed me from behind. The impact is worse than a kick in the ring. My face eats dirt. I struggle to breathe with a mouthful of earth. Claws *dig* painfully into my flesh. I grit down and elbow the animal.

Barely able to distinguish *what* it is.

Cougar, I think.

I elbow again. My pulse in my ears, I can barely even *hear*. Nails rip at me, and I know it's going to aim for my neck.

My jugular.

I'm going to die here. The sheer dread pushes my fight-or-flight instinct—I ram my elbow harder, not letting the cougar at my windpipe.

I've been camping enough times with the Meadows family to hear Ryke and Daisy in my head.

Stand tall and big and loud.

I'm already on the ground.

Don't let it have access to your neck.

I'm trying.

Never run away or turn your back.

It's *on* my damn back!

Adrenaline pumps in my ears and I can't get to my gun that's on a belly-band at my waist. My knife is closer. Clipped chest-high on my backpack strap, I reach for the hilt. Exposing my neck for a single second.

"KITS!" Sulli's deafening screams fill my ears.

"GET OFF HIM!" Banks yells even louder, and the cougar falters, *distracted*, for a millisecond. Enough time for me to unclip my knife, and I stab the cat's torso.

He lets out a wailing hiss and eases up on me. I roll out to the side, just as Sulli swings her backpack at the cougar's head. Once, twice, and then her backpack slips out of her fingers.

I struggle to stand, then freeze in a crouch as the cougar locks eyes with me.

"Don't move," Banks tells me, holding out a hand.

We're all perilously still. None of our eyes shift off the animal.

"He's going to pounce on him," Sulli warns Banks. While the cougar stalks me, Sulli tosses rocks and stones at him. "GO THE FUCK AWAY!"

The cougar doesn't turn on her.

He's after me.

I stand fully up. He lunges, and his paws crash against my chest. My back hits the dirt again, and I just start *stabbing.*

Every piece of flesh I can find, I sink my knife in and pull out. The sound the cougar makes is guttural, brutal, and I use my forearm to block him from biting my face.

His teeth are like blades puncturing through my skin. Pain radiates in my elbow, and I feel Banks trying to physically wrestle the animal off me.

He's been trying since the moment it jumped. My stomach sinks when I realize he doesn't have a gun.

Since he didn't have a band for his, I'm carrying his gun in my pack. I had more room.

My call.

My mistake.

A fatal fucking mistake.

And then the cougar lashes at Banks as he drops down to his knees.

"NO!" I yell, sitting up to see the cougar raking its claws at my friend. Banks tries to throw him off, but the cougar is close to his throat. I sink my knife into the cougar's breast. The animal writhes. Blood is everywhere.

Banks quickly reaches for my waist.

He's going for my gun.

His hand slips up my shirt, grabs the firearm from the band, and without hesitation, he rotates and fires three quick rounds.

The *pop pop pop* is layered with a growl. It takes me a second to register that the limp, *dead* cougar on top of us isn't the one growling.

The animal has already gone slack on our bodies. The weight crushing, oxygen-stealing, and I turn my head to find Sulli.

I see what made that noise, and blood rushes out of my face.

A second cougar.

And it's charging after Sulli.

22

Sullivan Meadows

STAND TALL AND BIG *and loud.*

Don't let it have access to your neck.

Never run away or turn your back.

A second cougar isn't casually stalking me. He or she is springing towards me, and I know not to turn my back to the animal. But I have nothing to defend myself. No rock is going to stop the attack.

My eyes dart to the Patagonia backpack that flung out of my hand.

My gun.

I need the gun my dad gave me.

Heartbeat in my ears, I can't hear anything or anyone as the cougar lunges.

Instinct takes hold.

I.

Just.

Run.

Feet to ground. Breath stuck in my lungs. I run.

I skid.

My fingers find my backpack and I'm fast as I reach in, but I'm not fast enough. Paws and claws crash into me, knocking oxygen from my lungs.

Fuckfuckfuck. My hand is on the hilt. Pain flares somewhere on my skin, my body, as I remove the gun from my pack and fire. The bullet rings my ears. And then I release five more *pops* in quick succession.

Growling and hissing immediately cease. All I hear now is my heavy breath. Fur blocks my gaze. His muzzle lies at my head. His body is on me.

His body is on me.

Warm blood soaks into my shirt. I try to push the animal off me, but my arm's wedged wrong.

There's just silence.

Pure silence.

It's louder and more horrible than anything I've ever confronted. "KITS! BANKS!" I yell in raw fear. They're hurt. I know they're fucking hurt. The last thing I saw was both of them fighting off that other cougar.

How much death am I lying in right now?

They can't be dead.

They're okay. They have to be okay.

"BANKS! KITS!" I scream, hot tears in my eyes. "BANKS!"

Please don't be dead.

Please don't be dead.

In a panic, I struggle to push the cougar off me. "KITS!" Hardly breathing. Am I breathing? I choke for air.

"We're right here," Akara breathes out, and just like that, the cougar is lifted off me. I try to fight off the dread as soon as I see them.

They're okay.

They're okay.

I'm silently bawling—the fear I felt crushes me more than the cougar.

My bodyguards heave the animal aside, and I struggle to regain breath. "Fuck," I choke and wipe my wet eyes with my forearm.

Crimson stains their clothes. Their skin. It's hard to tell if it's their blood or the cougars'. Akara's shirt is falling off his body, hanging by one piece of fabric at his shoulder. Blood mats Banks' hair, and they're both sweeping me, assessing quickly.

I sit up slowly, inhaling jagged breath. Their eyes plant to the gun in my hand.

I haven't let it go. It feels attached. Like a third limb.

"Sulli," Banks says, bending down, and Akara drops to his knees in a wince beside me.

"Are you in pain anywhere?" Akara asks.

I swallow hard. Adrenaline hardly recedes to make way for the throbbing in my side. "Just here." I wipe my watery gaze again and touch my hipbone. Red blood coats my fingertips. Don't know for sure if it's mine. "How badly are you two hurt?"

I want to magically take their pain away. I get they're sworn to protect me. Being in the crossfire of threats is what they signed up for, but an animal attack was never a part of that contract.

"It's not too bad," Akara says, but he's favoring his right arm. Blood trickles near his elbow. I crane my neck to get a better view of his back. Long claw marks rake along his shoulder blade. With the dirt and blood, I can't tell how deep they are.

My stomach curdles. "That doesn't look good, Kits."

"I'm okay." He's still scanning my body for noticeable injuries.

I keep trembling, more from shock than anything else. My fingers tighten on the gun. It's the only thing that feels controlled. Steady.

Banks unzips a backpack and pulls out a water bottle. A scratch runs across his bicep about as deep as the one on Akara's back. He offers me water, but I shake my head.

"You two have worse injuries," I say. "I'm certain mine are superficial cuts."

Banks and Akara share a look. "Just take a sip," Banks says. "We'll all have one."

With my free hand, I accept the water bottle and make sure to take the tiniest sip, conserving the water for them. Akara rolls his eyes when I pass him the bottle.

"We need to get back to camp," he says after he swallows water. He gives Banks the rest. "We have a First-Aid kit there."

"You might need stitches, Kits," I breathe.

He shakes his head. "I'll be fine with some gauze and bandage. It's too far a hike back to the RV camp tonight. Farrow can look at it tomorrow."

Banks nods like this is a good idea.

I realize they're both incredibly fucking stubborn, but they're also weighing pros and cons. It's their job to assess risks in situations.

Akara goes to stand, but Banks puts a hand on his leg. "Wait a sec," Banks says. "We should keep sitting and breathing until both of you stop shaking."

"I'm not shaking," Akara refutes.

"Left hand."

Akara holds it up. Sure enough, his palm quakes. "*Shit.*"

"Why aren't you shaking?" I ask Banks.

"I was. It just stopped earlier." He passes me the water again, even against my refusal. "Just focus on your breathing. We're all alright. We're all safe. It's over."

It's over.

I take a bigger swig. The water goes down like a knot.

It could have been so much worse. Maybe I should be thankful that I'm alive to tell this story, but I just see the animal I killed. I *hear* the sickening noise he or she made as they died. Lying breathless feet away. No heartbeat. I took that soul.

I shake harder.

Fuck.

"Sul—" Akara starts.

"My dad," I say in a whisper, blinking back tears. "He's been to thousands of cities. Camped hundreds of places. He's come face to face with bears, moose, *cougars*, almost every animal you can think of. And never in his fifty-years has he had to kill a single one."

It breaks me.

My spirit cracks. Fractures. Splinters off.

Tears keep welling and cloud my vision. "My little sister will hate me." I want to bury my face in my shirt, my hands, my lap—their chests.

I end up staring at the sky.

"She won't," Akara says strongly. "Winona will understand it was self-defense. If it were you or the cougar, she'd choose you."

I know that's true, but there's a part of me that also knows she'll look at me differently once she finds out.

Our dad never had to kill anything, but I took an animal's life at twenty-one. *I'm* the one who went into the cougar's home. The mountains—I don't live in these mountains. I was just wandering by.

And sure, maybe other families hunt wild game for sport and killing a cougar would be no big fucking deal, but all my life, I've been taught to preserve the wilderness and the creatures that inhabit it. My spirit has been tied to the outdoors for so long, and right now it feels as if I'm not worthy to belong here.

"It's not supposed to be easy," Banks tells me. "What you're feeling now. It's normal, Sulli."

I meet his brown eyes that pull at me with compassion and understanding. He's a Marine. I don't know how much he's seen or what he's done, but in this moment, he's holding me without wrapping his arms around me.

I breathe.

My limbs have stopped shaking, and Akara's left hand is steady. The three of us are huddled together, and once we stand up, once we make our way back to camp, all of this will feel more real.

We're slow to our feet.

"Can you walk?" Banks asks me.

Taking a few steps forward, my legs ache but they support my body enough. "I'm good." I glance to my left. "Akara?"

"I'm good, too." He's already walking towards the cougars. No limp. No shuffling. All great signs. Maybe we will just come out of this bruised and scraped up.

But the wounds are deeper than my fleeting optimism. I feel the harsh stinging across my body as Akara stops beside the cougar he stabbed. A haunted expression shifts over his face. "They're going to rot here. Or be eaten by other prey."

"Not if we bury them," Banks breathes.

I nod. "We'll come back here tonight, Kits. I have those shovels at camp." *Pooper scoopers,* Winona calls them. I packed shovels to dig latrines.

Now we're going to be digging graves.

"Okay," Akara says and looks to Banks. "After yo—"

"No way in hell," Banks refutes. "You're not following behind again. We walk side-by-side together this time so I can have your six."

Akara winces, more so at his wounds while he shifts. "I thought you hated making the calls, Banks."

"But this one is too easy."

"My vote is with Banks," I tell Akara. "And I know I'm not a bodyguard and I probably don't get a vote, but I'm creating one right now. So it's two-to-one. You're outvoted."

His smile looks like it aches to rise. "No I'm not. Because I'm voting with you."

And that's how it goes. Step-by-step, we trek to our secluded camp. All the while, I never drop my gun. The closer we get, the tighter my grip becomes. Banks and Akara keep looking at me, at the weapon, and I feel their building concern.

Shoes crunching leaves, our empty camp comes into view. Darkness has nearly set in, and I'm just on autopilot. Grabbing a couple battery-operated lanterns from our gear, I switch on the light.

One tent.

The emptiness of the tent doesn't feel as safe as the spot between Akara and Banks. I venture back out to the fire pit. Where they both are popping lids to two First-Aid kits.

Once more, Banks eyes my hand that clutches the gun. He says nothing to me and instead turns to Akara. "You're going first. Don't fight it, man."

"Hey, I'm supposed to order *you* around. Stop trying to take my job." He sits down on a tree stump.

I come up behind him. "How do you feel about going topless, Kits?" His shirt hangs by one inch of fabric at his shoulder.

"Rip it," he tells me.

To do that, I'll have to put the gun down. Instead, I decide to lean in and take the fabric in my teeth. I tear it off easily, and the bloodied shirt falls to the ground.

Akara watches me for a long second, and when my eyes meet his, I'm throttled with his worry. "Sul, you're going to have to set it down eventually."

"Not yet." It scares me how much my voice shakes.

"Okay." There's pain behind his eyes. A different kind of pain. He knows it's not okay. *I'm* not okay.

Banks comes over, his hand just covers mine for a second. Encased over my fingers and the hilt of the gun. He stays there.

My pulse is in my throat. "I can't..." I shake my head.

"You can. It's alright. I'm right here. Akara is here."

I choke out, "I need to protect myself." Is that it? I think I'm more terrified of not being able to help them again. Of losing them, of being alone.

The emptiness.

The painful, guttural *cavern* they'd leave behind. How could that ever be filled again?

Akara reaches out to me and places a hand on my back. "You don't need the gun to do that, Sulli. You can let go."

Banks never forces the gun from my grip. He waits.

His hand feels more like a comfort. So does Akara's on my back.

And slowly, I loosen my fingers and release my clutch.

Banks checks the safety on my gun, then stores it safely in a backpack. None of us can hug, not when we need to clean up and deal with our wounds. So that's what we do first.

Quietly and methodically, we use the lanterns to help assess Akara's wounds.

The worst gashes are along his shoulder blade and a bite mark near his elbow. Akara washes off the blood with water. Antiseptic, gauze, and a tight bandage—that should hold up until we see Farrow.

"If you feel dizzy at all, you better tell us," I say to him.

"I will," Akara promises.

Banks pulls off his shirt and lowers his shorts. Dried blood stains his skin. I shrug off my Camp Calloway tee and cargo shorts. Blood drips from my hair and down to my chest, soaking into my sports bra.

There is no hesitation. I can't keep it on. Gripping the bottom elastic band, I pull off the bra and let it fall to the ground.

We're all standing, and I stay between Akara and Banks. For some reason, this feels the safest. I stop shaking between their warmth and height. I pile my hair up into a high bun.

"Where does it hurt?" Akara asks me.

"My waist mostly," I whisper. "Right here." I reach down to the spot near my belly button. The blood is mine, not the cougars'.

Carefully, Akara pours water over the claw mark. I bite down in a wince, and Banks uses a cloth to wipe the blood away. Revealing fresh scratches. We rip open more bandages. Add more antiseptic to each other. I can tell they're trying hard not to cause me more pain.

The fact that they're so gentle with me just adds more emotion on top of the emotional cocktail I've been fucking drinking.

I blow out a measured breath. Among everything, I'm just glad they're here.

23

Banks Moretti

WITH A HARD THRUST, I push the flimsy, collapsible shovel into the soft earth. Hours into grave digging, sweat builds on my temple despite the frigid air tonight. A lit cigarette hangs between my lips. Embers eat the paper, and I take a quick drag, blowing smoke off to the side before continuing.

Across from me, Sulli digs the second grave, and near her, Akara rests on the ground. Forearms to his knees, he catches his breath from his shift digging. He's on "break" since we've only got two shovels.

Night air is thick with death. Among spruce trees, we found a grassy clearing for the graves, and two cougars lie lifeless, bleeding into the dirt and grass beside us. I'm more used to death than I'd like to admit.

But it still knocks me back. Almost losing Akara, then Sulli, that sucker-punched me. Thinking about how close I was to the brutal loss now is like an invisible hand around my windpipe. Every so often I feel the ghost of a hand clench tighter.

Christ, I'll take a hundred more migraines. Just don't take them.

You hear me? I look up at the sky, then back at the dirt. Shoveling once more.

Only thing that keeps my mind right and snapped to is feeling the smoke run down the back of my throat. *Alive.*

Alive.

Alive.

Each word pumps into my head as I suck in the nicotine.

"I thought you quit." Sulli's voice sounds loud in the night. Ever since we began digging hours ago, we've been quiet.

"I did." Plucking the cigarette from my lips, I keep it pinched between my fingers and skillfully dig the shovel into the dirt again.

Akara and Sulli share some sort of look.

I don't stare too long to decode it.

While Akara fits on a baseball cap backwards, he tells me, "I don't even know why you brought cigarettes on this trip."

"For nights like this." I heave the shovel back into the ground. Loose dirt comes up. "When bad shit goes down, the only thing that sounds like heaven-on-Earth is a good smoke."

"You passed that point like five cigarettes ago," Akara says with the wave of his hand to me. "Now you're just chain-smoking."

I flip him off, but I can't really disagree. Once I start, it's hard to find the will to stop. It's buried too far beneath the dirt I shovel.

"I'm digging a fuckin' grave, Akara. Let me have my moment."

He makes a cross sound, verging on a laugh. "Sure. Tomorrow they're going in the lake."

Sulli flings dirt to the side. "I'll fucking help."

"Yeah, you would," I say, wiping sweat off my brow. "Drawn to the water, aren't you?"

Her smile flickers in and out. Like she craves to feel weightless, but the situation is just heavy weight, dragging us all down. She stops digging suddenly.

My jaw hardens in a deeper frown. "Sulli?"

"What's wrong?" Akara asks.

"What if this whole trip was a bad idea," she whispers, more to the empty hole at her feet than to us. "My dad might've been right. I'm named after his best friend who passed away at twenty-seven. He was your age, Akara—to think that this wouldn't have been cursed from the start…"

"This trip is not cursed, Sul," Akara says. "You and I might be surrounded by death, but Banks isn't. Hey, he's like our very tall good luck charm."

Fuck.

I must wear my devastation on my face because Akara immediately says, "*Banks.*" Like my name is made of glass and he's cradling the damn thing in his hands.

In the tense silence, I find the empty water bottle where I've been tossing cigarette butts. Careful not to start a forest fire while I'm at it. With their concerned eyes pressed on me, I take one more long drag and ditch the cigarette.

Ghost hands wrap tight around my throat. Harder to breathe, harder to think.

I've never had to tell this story out loud. It'd been a gift to go this long without unearthing that kind of pain. But it's also agony keeping it buried in this moment.

Either way, I'm going to hurt.

"I had an older brother," I mutter those words. I wonder if Thatcher explained this better to Jane. How perfectly did he unleash the past we share? I lift a shoulder. "He died when he was fifteen. Quarry accident. Drowned. I was twelve."

Sulli takes in a breath. "Banks, I'm so fucking sorry."

I shake my head. "It was a long time ago. I have mixed feelings about everything, so I like to leave it in the past."

"That's why you didn't tell me?" Akara asks, hurt cinching his face. "Thatcher never said anything either…"

I bob my head. "We silently agreed to never speak about it." I pause to meet his eyes. "I'm gonna be honest, Akara, I never planned on telling you or anyone, really." I don't add that I'd always hoped it'd come up between him and Thatcher, and I'd just let my twin brother explain it all.

"Why?" Akara frowns.

"Because that's what we, Moretti boys, do." I force the shovel back into the ground. "We *bury* the back-breaking, head-splitting shit and don't ever speak about it." I ache for another cigarette. "Maybe because we love each other so damn much that it's hard enough feeling *my* pain—do I really want to feel Thatcher's on top of it?"

It'd cut me open tenfold.

It already does.

I add, "And then after a while, it takes too much energy to speak about the painful thing. So we don't share with anyone until it's more painful than the thing we buried."

Akara stands up. "Hey, you know I'm here, man? Whatever you want to share with me, I appreciate." He steps closer. "And I can't imagine keeping my dad's death a secret from my friends. That couldn't have been easy."

I let out a hoarse laugh. The ghost hand clenches tighter around my throat. "Easier than it probably should be."

"What was his name?" Sulli asks, then cringes. "You don't have to answer that. Fuck, you said you wanted to keep it in the past. I'm bad with words—"

"His name was Skylar," I say quickly. "And I like your words."

She lets out a soft breath. "One day, if you want to talk about him, I'll be here to listen."

"Me too," Akara says.

Pressure eases off my windpipe.

I breathe in. "Thanks," I say into a strong nod. *One day,* I hope I can tell them more. How my parents' divorce is wrapped like a vice around Skylar's death. How everything goes back to that one moment. How one night changed my whole world.

Tonight could've done the same thing.

Maybe it already has.

Like the turn of a car, heading in a new, unexpected and unknown direction. One we didn't plan or map out, but one that was meant for us.

For whatever reason, we're here together.

I lean the shovel against a tree to pluck another cigarette from the pack. "So we've got Adam Sully..." I put the cigarette between my lips. "My older brother." I light it with a Zippo and suck on the end. My eyes hit Akara and blow out smoke. "And your dad." With the cigarette pinched between fingers, I motion between the three of us. "What does that make us? Some sort of Death Brigade."

"The Death Brigade," Akara repeats with a short laugh and peeking smile.

"We all just made it out alive," Sulli tells us. "Maybe that actually makes us the Life Brigade."

"I guess we'll see." I grab my shovel and keep digging.

Not even five minutes later, Sulli curses loudly, "*Fuck.*" The handle of her shovel just broke off. I'm more surprised it hasn't happened sooner.

I look to Akara. "Too strong for her own good."

"A travesty," Akara quips. "Do we need to bury her in a third hole?"

"Fuck off," she curses, frustrated, and she collapses on her ass.

Akara and I stop joking around with Sulli, and we all take a break. Grouped together in the dark, we pass out the only snacks left in the hiking backpack.

Teddy Grahams and applesauce.

With sweaty, bloody clothes and dirtied hands, we eat together, and as I finish off a cup of applesauce, I look around at where we are, what we're doing, and I start laughing.

Sulli puts a hand to my head. "Are you concussed?"

My chest rises in a bigger laugh. "I was just thinking about how we're eating food that first belonged to a baby, digging graves with shovels meant for shitholes, and we're in a meadow with a Meadows."

Akara and Sulli flash their headlamps around the grassy clearing we chose. Sure enough, they realize we're in an actual meadow. And they both start laughing with me.

"Shit," Akara breathes into the light sound. "I needed that." He touches the back of my head.

"It's what I'm here for." I swig my water that I wish were beer. "The Meadows-in-a-meadow jokes."

Sulli sways into me like she means to slug my arm, but instead, she just leans her weight against my side. I wrap an arm over her shoulder.

Akara keeps a hand on her knee.

Laughter has faded, but resting among each other carries a solace and comfort that I'd rather not leave behind.

24

Akara Kitsuwon

AFTER HEAVING THE COUGARS in the graves, we shovel dirt on top. Covering their bodies, I crouch down while Banks hangs his head and Sulli presses her fingers to her lips.

I touch the packed-in dirt.

It was you or us.

I'm sorry it had to be you.

After a quiet moment, I rise. Banks makes a sign of the cross, and Sulli exhales a deeper breath.

"Let's go," I tell them.

They nod and follow. We make our way back to camp. It's late. We're all filthy and cut-up. Most of my pain centralizes on the bite mark around my elbow. Stinging escalates whenever I shift my arm, but I wash the ache down with some over-the-counter pain meds.

Sulli is rigging a makeshift shower. A plastic sack, resembling an IV bag, is full of boiled water that's been warming in the sun all day. She hooks the bag to a tree limb, but there's only enough water for one warm shower.

Before the cougar attack, we talked about just washing off in the river. *Now* that's not happening. I don't trust how well we've bandaged our wounds, and wading in a river with open cuts is parasite-central.

So I grab a water bottle. "You take the shower, Sul." Unscrewing the cap, I'm prepared to do a quick clean-off.

"No way." She steals the bottle, then blocks Banks from grabbing one out of his backpack, a hand to his chest. "The temperature outside has dropped too much—you'll both have popsicle dicks if you try to bathe with bottled water."

My lips quirk into a smile.

Banks makes a noise that sounds like a deep laugh.

After this crazy night, I can't believe we're still able to find humor. I should probably go check my phone now that we're back at camp with cell service. Running a security firm and a gym is a full-time gig, and the amount of missed calls, texts, and emails keep piling the longer I neglect them.

But nothing sounds better than being here. With her. With him. Painful parts of tonight will creep back when I leave.

So I stay.

Sulli looks between us. "Do you really want popsicle dicks?"

Banks cracks a smile, his eyes saying words he once told me: *Hell have mercy on my soul.*

Yeah, the dirty response is *right* there, and I just say it, "Depends on how much you like sucking popsicles, string bean."

She slugs my arm.

Pain shoots through my elbow, and I wince for real.

"Oh fuck—I'm so, so sorry, Kits." Her hands fly to her mouth, then hover over my elbow I'm favoring. "It was just instinct—like I was on automatic. I didn't think. *Fuck.*" She groans at herself.

"It's okay." I fling a strand of her hair at her face.

Amid her dirt-splotched cheeks, she turns an embarrassed shade of red.

Banks checks my elbow bandages. "It's not bleeding."

I slip him a *thanks* through my eyes.

He nods.

"Maybe you should recheck?" Sulli asks Banks. "Give it a closer fucking look?"

He does, more for her peace of mind. "He's good to go."

"But where will I go?" I tease and throw off my baseball hat.

"To hell, probably," Banks quips. "See ya there."

We smile, and our eyes plant on Sulli as I say, "Are we going to drag her down with us?"

"Only if she wants to go."

Sulli is still hyper-focused on my elbow. "How can you guys crack jokes right now?" She doesn't give us time to respond. "Does your arm hurt more, Kits? Be honest with me."

"Not much more than it did, and hey, you're the one who threw out the first joke."

Her face twists in confusion.

"Popsicle dicks," I tell her.

"I was being serious." She wipes a smudge of dirt off her cheek. "You can't deny that your dicks won't freeze if you take bottled water showers out here."

Banks runs a hand across his jaw. "I didn't deny a thing."

She holds onto her arms and shivers. *She's cold.* I'm about to go really serious and stop the chatter, but she continues fast, "There's enough warm water if we all just take a shower together."

Shower together?

I didn't think we'd go in that direction. My lips flat-line, and I look over her shoulder to Banks again. His eyes are on me.

A thousand questions spinning between us. Can we all three take a shower together? Yesterday, I would've probably said no.

But I'm spent. Exhausted. Emotionally, mentally, physically. I want the warm shower. I want Sulli to feel solid. I want Banks to not think about his brother he lost.

I want to shed the night. I want it gone and soaked in the water that falls to the earth.

"As friends," I say.

"As friends," Sulli nods and looks to Banks.

"As friends," he agrees.

I watch as Sulli pulls the Camp Calloway tee over her head. Banks steps out of his pants, and I make quick work shedding my clothes. Until I'm in boxer-briefs like Banks, and Sulli stands in panties and a sports bra. All of us bandaged up. She stares down at her chest for a second, thinking something, and then suddenly, she tugs up and shimmies off her sports bra.

Her nipples are hard in the cold. Shit, I love her tits. She turns quickly to the makeshift shower. The sack of water still hangs from the tree branch. All three of us are shivering and gather close underneath the plastic spigot. She stands between us, facing Banks.

My pulse races. Does she feel more comfortable with him seeing her tits than me? Maybe because he's already seen her naked *while* they were kissing. Yeah, maybe?

I shrug the thought off as I reach up. Pulling the string that opens the sack, a stream of water pours down on us.

Water is warm for point-five seconds, quickly chilling as soon as it hits my skin.

"Fuckfuckfuck," Sulli curses and bounces on her feet. "It's cold." Her breath smokes the air.

"Let's get this over with quick," Banks says into a cringe.

After passing around a bar of soap and rinsing, we last less than a minute under the water before we're darting out from the shower and into the tent.

No time to build a fire.

Sulli dives underneath a sleeping bag. Not crawling under, she uses the fabric more like a blanket. Her body trembles harder from the cold. Teeth chattering. Banks zips up the tent while I switch on a lantern dangling in the center of the tent, and I crawl to the right of her. I'm shivering, but not full-body shakes like Sulli here.

She groans out. "Why is it so fucking frigid?"

Banks lies down to the left of her. "Because mermaids don't swim in ice."

"That…we know…of," she chatters, then blows out a breath. "I just want…to get…fucking…warm."

"How are your popsicle nipples?" I ask her as I slide underneath my sleeping bag. Our legs skate near each other, and I can feel her goosebumps and prickle of hair.

"Probably harder than your popsicle dick." Her green, green eyes descend to my crotch.

Shit.

Blood pumps through my body, muscles flexing, and I start to warm.

Banks fixes the snagged chain of his dog tags and tells me, "Sounds like a bet." He has to know I'm seconds from sliding my hand over her tits, so I'm surprised he's playing into this.

I don't want any of it to end. "Definitely does," I agree.

Sulli turns her head to Banks. "My nipples are way harder than your dick too."

He eyes her chest, covered by a sleeping bag, and she eyes his crotch like she did mine.

For some reason, I don't mind that she's including him. I prefer it, even. *Why? How?* Maybe because in the quiet seconds between our easy banter, we're just three people laid vulnerable and bare. Dirt washed off, cut open, and even as exhaustion pulls us, we choose to stay awake and bathe in the comfort of our companionship.

"And if they're not harder?" Banks asks. "What do we get?"

Sulli shifts, her heat beginning to radiate towards me, and most likely him too. While she's lying on her back, we're lying on our sides. Facing her.

She keeps having to turn her head from side-to-side to look between us. "What do you want?" she asks.

Banks meets my gaze. "What do you want, Akara?"

Her.

But I don't want to have sex with her from a bet. It's not going to mean anything. "Bragging rights," I say. "What do you want, Banks?"

"Bragging rights sound good to me." He looks down at her. "And you, mermaid? What do you want if you win?"

"Bragging rights. Always."

Banks takes one edge of her sleeping bag, and I take the other. We pull it down, exposing her bare breasts. She intakes a shuddered breath at the cold, and her pink nipples are perked.

This isn't like the shower.

We're not just friends here.

A tangible pulse beats in the air. Hums between the three of us. We're less thoughts than we are feelings. All instinct and gut—and right now it's telling me to keep going. To not let this night end, despite the lines we cross. The boundaries that blur.

It doesn't much matter.

We neared death. We're alive.

Isn't that enough? What else really matters but us? Right here. Right now.

25

Sullivan Meadows

I'M STILL SHIVERING, but I can't decipher whether it's the cold anymore or their eyes on my naked chest. They take a long time just staring, and my breathing deepens as I look between their heady gazes.

My body squirms with overwhelming desires and needs.

And then they both touch me at the same time. Akara's thumb glides over my right nipple, while Banks' presses down on my left. *Oh fuck*, the pressure and sensitivity feels amazing. A breath catches in my throat, my limbs vibrating with pleasure and something deeper that I can't pinpoint. The something deeper that I feel—I sink into, like soft feathers nestled and cuddled around me.

Don't forget the bet.

Don't forget the bet!

I hear the loud chant in the competitive part of my brain. *Right.* I have a fucking job to do.

Reaching out a hand to Banks and Akara, I fumble against their bare thighs without looking. Trying to find their dicks.

Banks is first to help me. He takes my hand and places my palm on top of his boxer-briefs. My fingers curl around his rock-hard shaft. Fuck, he's much harder than my nipples.

Akara clasps my right hand and slides my palm up to his thigh, then his crotch. His bulge is beyond firm. I stroke him twice, and his muscles contract.

What would they feel like inside of me? Is it so different from a toy? Just imagining them so close, my pussy throbs. I shouldn't picture *both*, should I?

One day soon, I'm going to give out a *final rose* to only *one* man, and it's not fair to the guy I pick or the one I let go to be attached to both. But with what happened tonight—feeling like I lost Banks and Akara—I just want to hold onto each of them.

So maybe I'm fucking selfish. Maybe I'm doing the wrong thing and this'll come back to bite me later on, but tonight, this feels like the best, most *right* thing I could ever do.

None of us stop.

I run my fingers along their lengths, feeling the fabric molding them.

Their breath comes heavier.

Akara's thumb still circles my nipple like Banks'. Softly, Akara whispers, "You're still shaking, Sulli."

"I'm still cold." I take a breath. "And now other things too."

Banks strokes my hair out of my face. "What kind of things?" he asks, taking his hand off my boob the same time as Akara. Like they're planning this. Coordinating and in sync. Too many times, I've caught them speaking to each other through their eyes.

Bodyguard talk. Most in security have the speak-through-eyes talent, but I think the closer they are as friends, the easier it is and the more I see them do it.

Without their touch and with the air hitting my exposed skin, I shiver more. *What kind of things?* "You do know virgins can get horny, right? I'm not immune to nipple flicking. That kind of thing."

My hands rest casually on their packages, and I feel their dicks twitch at my words. I can't help but smile. Wind pounds at the tent, and a chill snakes through me along with the gathering heat between us.

"So you're horny," Banks says huskily.

My pulse drops to my pussy as if complying with his words. His eyes set on me in a way that steals my breath. He's older. More experienced. I'm sure he's aroused plenty of women. I'm not his first, even if he might be mine.

"And you're cold," Akara adds. *Cold* sounds more like *ready* on his lips. His gaze makes me feel utterly naked like there's no sleeping bag on top of my waist. His playful side has switched off in favor of something more serious and sensual.

"Really horny. Really cold…both those things, yeah," I manage to say. Probably ineloquently. How does one wax poetic soliloquies at a dreamy moment?

I have no idea. I'm not perfect with words. I'm just untamed feelings.

Not in my head enough to even be embarrassed, I just say what I'm thinking. "I feel like my skin has been shed over and over tonight, and I need warmth and something or someone to hold it together before it reaches the bone. I just…I want to be touched. Like *really* touched." My voice comes out choked at the last part.

They both slide closer until their bodies are flush against mine. I almost turn on my side, but Akara puts his hand on my abdomen to stop me. "Stay right here," he whispers into my ear. His forehead pressed against my temple. "We're going to touch you, Sulli."

Very softly, Banks asks, "How far have you gone with someone before?" His deep voice is one of the most soothing sounds in the night. Lulling me into comfort, into those feathers. A loving, protective embrace—what I've always wanted in carnal moments like this.

And it's not just here once.

I feel it twice.

"Just kissing," I say in a single breath. "That's all I've really done with someone."

They nod, and they share another look. Maybe telling each other to be careful with me. Maybe just recognizing that being touched is big and new for me, and I want it. *God*, do I fucking want it and them and their hands and overpowering, tremendous, can-barely-breathe *affection*.

Banks blows his breath into his hand, warming it before he lets his palm travel down my inner-thigh. He pulls my thigh back against him. Akara does the same with my right thigh. They spread me open.

My heart beats loud in my ears, and Banks plants a soft kiss at my neck. Akara's lips trail up my ribcage to my breast. His tongue teases my perked nipple. *Fuck yes, yes, yes.* They both knead the flesh at my thighs, near my heat but not satiating that spot. My need grows, and I writhe.

I squirm, feeling wetness gather. My back arches for them. Wanting more touch, more warmth, more emotion and *feeling*. No emptiness. No loneliness. No nothingness.

My hands have slipped off their dicks, and I go to reach for Banks' head. Anything to hold onto. Swiftly, Akara snatches my wrist midair. Clutching it tight, he pulls my hand above my head.

Banks watches my lips as they part in an aroused breath. And then his warmed fingers slide underneath my panties. *Yes.*

And between my folds. Slowly, he slips a finger inside of me, pumping in a *come hither* motion. Feeling him there, the fullness, the pressure, the sensation—I dizzy and buck up again. He watches my movements like he's studying my reaction, my arousal, and he discovers a sensitive spot, creating mind-altering friction—my legs twitch.

"Oh fuck," I curse, about to cover my eyes but my wrist jerks in Akara's hold. He keeps my arm pinned, and I drink in the way he has me. The way *they* have me so completely in their care. Being able to open myself and give myself to people I trust is more freeing than I ever realized.

I feel like I'm flying.

Like I'm powerful. In-fucking-vincible. Able to transcend time and place and reason.

Akara shifts his own hand off my thigh.

I have trouble trying to see Banks' reaction *and* Akara's. I try to watch both guys at once. My breath hitches as Akara moves his hand up to my pussy. They're not both going inside me, are they? And then I feel his thumb circle my throbbing clit.

I moan.

Akara curses under his breath.

Banks picks up speed. My legs begin to tremble and sweat builds on my skin. Their kisses return—Akara focuses on my nipples, teasing and sucking. Banks closes his lips on the soft flesh of my neck, then up to my lips. Every sensitive bud, sensitive spot feels lit by these two men.

I've never drowned before today.

I'm drowning in them. By them. With them.

A whimper leaves me, and their groans rumble the air. Instinctively, I rock against Banks' hand while he fills me. Thrusting into him and Akara. I want more pressure. I want my world to be set on fire. I want to forget everything that happened before this tent. I want there to be nothing but after this moment.

Reaching down with my only free hand, I touch the top of Akara's hand. I touch Banks' wrist, his fingers lost inside me. They both quicken speed suddenly like they're racing each other.

"Fuckfuck," I cry, so wet, almost there, almost *there.*

Pleasure mounts until my limbs quake, and my whole body tenses in a thundering climax. Toes curl and back arches even higher. I grip onto Banks' wrist while Akara's grip tightens on mine. An orgasm ripples through me, and they both slow their movements until I'm too sensitive to touch.

I try and catch my breath.

Banks kisses my lips in one beat.

Akara kisses my shoulder, then cheek in the next. "I'll be back." He releases my wrist, and I grab onto the first thing I can to stop him—which happens to be his hand between my thighs. His fingers brush against my palm, and they're slick with my wetness.

Our eyes latch. "Don't go," I breathe.

Banks has a hand on my thigh still and he pats it. "We've got to take care of some things, mermaid."

"I can take care of you both," I say in a frown. "Don't you want me to?"

"This was for you," Akara refutes.

Banks nods more than once.

Maybe it's a pride thing. They want to be sure this wasn't all about their needs but solely about pleasing me. And I get that, but the sun has been down for a while. It's *freezing* outside now. "You both can get off here, can't you? Don't run off into the cold. *Please.*"

Akara lets out a breath and sinks back down beside me. I don't let go of his wrist. "You sure?" he asks.

"Fucking positive, Kits." I glance to Banks. "You too."

"Turn on your side," Banks instructs and helps me roll onto my side. Back turned to Banks. Chest towards Akara. All of us lie underneath the sleeping bags, so I can't see their movements. But I can feel them shift as they tug themselves.

Not seeing Banks stirs me even more. It feels forbidden, only kept safe in my imagination. I know he's there jerking off, but I can't even look at his face while he's doing it. His building heat warms me beneath the sleeping bag.

I glance to Akara and then he does something unexpected.

He covers my eyes with his palm.

Can't see him either.

Only hear their heavy breaths. Their grunts.

Feel the shifting of the sleeping bag.

I reach down and start touching myself. We're all pleasure in this tent.

We're all alive.

Breath. And body. And life.

26

Sullivan Meadows

"YOU NEED STITCHES," Farrow doesn't even hesitate with the diagnosis once he removes Akara's bandages with gloved hands and sees the damage to his shoulder blade and elbow. "You should've called me last night."

Tattooed and pierced, Farrow Redford Keene Hale is usually casual and cool, unruffled by little, except when Moffy is hurt. His severity now is a knife to my heart.

Maximoff turns his head from Akara to me. His concern pummels me for the second time. The first was when Banks, Akara, and I showed up at the RV campgrounds carrying all our gear while covered in bandages and scratches. Clearly banged up, we couldn't hide the cougar attack.

I'm just thankful Kits was here to explain everything.

He's good at giving facts from an event and nothing more. No emotion to the story. I'd probably have fucked that up and rattled my cousins even more. Instead, the retelling might as well have been a security debriefing.

The RV campgrounds are quiet in the early morning. Fog hangs low at our feet, and the darkness of night is fading.

Jane told me no campers have recognized them yet. Not even at the RV rentals, where they picked out two long, taupe RVs, and Charlie actually *purchased* a mammoth-sized, sleek-black RV that could swallow the other two. Pretty much as big as the FanCon tour bus.

Their set-up is pretty awesome and more private than I expected. At RV Campsite #12, a picnic table, fire pit, and scattered chairs are strewn between the two long RVs. The vehicles do a good job of shielding their outdoor hangout area from other campsites.

And the mammoth RV sits further back up against the woods.

Right now, everyone—and I mean, *everyone*—who journeyed to Montana is congregated around the picnic table where the three of us threw our backpacks. Our appearance whipped open their RV doors and caused Jane and Moffy to rush out to me, and then SFO to sprint out to Akara and Banks.

"The bleeding stopped," Akara tells Farrow in a more authoritative tone. "It's been less than twenty-four hours. They're fine. I'm fine. We're all fine."

Moffy is still rigid.

His concern is like hardened cement. Being protective of me has been hardwired into his DNA since we were little kids. But at least he's not dialing my parents.

Farrow chews slower on a piece of gum. "I just can't see a scenario where Sulli is *this* hurt, and you don't life-flight her to a hospital."

Akara tries to push his hair back. "Come on, I wouldn't life-flight her to a hospital for a cut."

"Is it just a cut?" Moffy asks as he sits on the picnic table with Ripley on his lap. His son holds a sippy-cup and happily watches their puppy rolling on leaves.

I pull my gaze off the baby. "Yeah. Just a cut." *A big fucking one.* But I don't add that. Farrow hasn't taken off my bandage yet, but I showed him the gauze on my hip.

Oscar, Farrow, and even Thatcher are still eagle-eyeing Akara like he's acting weird. Like he *would* do everything in his power to carry me to a doctor.

But he didn't.

And I'm standing here thinking that I should've demanded that Akara and Banks see Farrow last night. Did they downplay their pain? Did I just not look closely enough?

Did we all not *look*?

But the events course through my head in raw flashes—the gunshots, the agonized growling, the dirt and heavy breath, the water and cold and then warmth, so much warmth—and nothing about that night made me want to confront all the people we care about.

I just wanted to seek comfort in Banks and Akara.

They must've felt the same.

Akara turns more to his men. "I *wouldn't* life-flight her. I wouldn't even drive her here. I wouldn't even call you Farrow. And that needs to be the end of this." He's such a boss leader.

I start to smile.

"So what you're saying," Oscar continues, "is that you don't like, *like* Sulli."

My face falls. I shift my weight. Feeling too many eyes on me. Feeling a masculine overload of protective men—too many fucking men are here. I look to Jane.

She sidles closer, her hand clasping instinctively to mine.

Thanks, Jane.

Akara glares at Oscar. "She's *right* there, Oscar."

He tosses a chip in his mouth. "I thought we were all friends by now."

Farrow's pierced brows rise. "Says the guy who hates buddy-guards."

Charlie smiles while he flips a page in a book, sitting on the steps of the left RV.

I have my fingers to my lips, my head fucking spinning. Jane's blue eyes are rapidly shifting between everyone. Like she's not missing a beat.

"Look, it was an honest question," Oscar says to his boss.

"You need to shut it down," Akara says in a tone both friendly and firm. "Sulli is just my client and friend—she knows that's all she is to me."

What?

I freeze.

I don't breathe.

He's just lying to them. He has to be lying. We agreed not to tell them the fucking truth—but after the night we shared in the tent, those words *hurt.*

Everyone—and again, I mean *everyone*—is looking at me. I must wear my utter fucking horror.

Akara's face drops. "Sulli—"

"Oh no, I get it." Does my voice sound choked? I nod a ton, my neck feels tight and collarbones jutted out like I swallowed a hundred donuts at once. *Banks?* I search for him.

He's next to his brother. And his gaze is softened on me, almost pained. Like he wishes he could come closer and wrap his arms around me. I wish he could hug me too.

Jane squeezes my hand consolingly.

I breathe in and focus on Farrow's gloves, on Akara's wounds. "Is it infected?" I ask.

"It's not," Akara says more gently to me, an apology in his eyes.

I try to take it, but his other words are still a pit in my stomach.

That's all she is to me.

I tell him, "I was actually talking to the guy with the MD."

Oscar munches on a chip. "Redford, you better check Kitsuwon for the fourth-degree burn."

Farrow rolls his eyes but continues inspecting Akara's shoulder. "You all out of original material, Oliveira?"

That's all she is to me. I frown more.

I look everywhere but at him.

"I'm saving all the good jokes for my husband," Oscar says, tossing a potato chip in his mouth. Jack Highland-Oliveira should be here soon to film me free-soloing.

I'm supposed to be climbing. *Right.* Breathing in another deep breath, I focus on my goal.

I can still accomplish what I set out to do. The weather is good. Winter conditions haven't arrived yet, and I didn't break a bone.

Fucking silver linings—I love them a waffle-lot. *I miss my sister.* The sudden thought pangs my heart.

"It's not infected," Farrow tells me.

That's good.

I take another breath.

Moffy says to me, "You could've called me last night too. I would've hiked up to you."

"I know," I say quietly. "But it was late and too dark."

Farrow is studying the bite marks around Akara's elbow. "I'm more concerned about torn muscle."

"I have full range of movement," Akara says, but his gaze hasn't left me. I feel it.

"Okay, but as your doctor, I'm recommending a physical exam instead of just taking your word on it. Also, you really need stitches. So take a seat on the table, Kitsuwon."

Akara climbs onto the picnic table next to Moffy. While Farrow rests a foot on the bench seat, he digs through his trauma bag.

"Papa!" Ripley calls out and drops his sippy-cup as he extends his arms towards Farrow.

Thatcher frowns. "Isn't Moffy *Papa* and Farrow *Dada*?"

Farrow grimaces. "Please don't ever say *dada* again."

Thatcher almost rolls his eyes. "You know what I mean."

I bend down and pick up the sippy-cup before Arkham slobbers all over it. Moffy and Farrow are kind of tense, and I know Thatcher isn't wrong about their parent nicknames.

"Maybe he's confusing you two?" Jane offers a rationale. "He's only eight-months."

"Papa!" Ripley is pulling out of Moffy's arms to reach Farrow.

"That's your dad, little guy," Maximoff says as he stands up with his son. He brings Ripley over to Farrow.

Farrow kisses his son's head, then points to Moffy. "That's your papa."

Ripley smiles up at Moffy. "Dada!" He hugs his tiny arms around his papa—well actually I guess Moffy is his dada.

We all laugh.

"Look who's a little maverick," Oscar grins. "Confirmed, that's *for sure* Farrow's son."

I miss the look Farrow gives Oscar because I hand baby Ripley his green sippy-cup. Not just any normal sippy-cup. Gray mountains decorate the sides, and a carabineer is on the handle.

The sippy-cup used to be mine when I was a kid. And I gifted this one to Ripley as an adoption present.

Moffy smiles at me.

I smile back. Seeing Maximoff and Farrow bring Ripley everywhere, on all the trips, all their daily activities and adventures, reminds me so much of how my parents raised me. I was always there with them. Constantly. Limitlessly. Until I guess I grew old enough to go on my own.

Ripley babbles to me, as though to say *thank you.*

"You're very welcome, little dude."

That's all she is to me.

I wish I would stop replaying *that* fucked up thing. Akara reminds Farrow to look at my cut and Banks' wounds, and so Farrow checks us before returning to Akara.

No stitches for us.

"You two should be good with new bandages," Farrow says, putting on a new pair of black gloves. "If any of the wounds start itching or swelling, come get me *immediately.* Not the next day."

"Sounds good," I say, dropping the hem of my shirt.

Banks nods.

"Nice ink," Oscar says to Akara, motioning to the snake tattoo along his upper chest, shoulder, and bicep. None of his wounds cut through the ink. All survived the cougar attack. Oscar quips, "What else have I missed?" He isn't in Philly as often as the other bodyguards. Maybe his compliment is just to get on Akara's good side after pissing him off.

"A lot," Akara says easily and catches my eyes that ask, *are we okay?*

I just nod. I fucking want to be.

Feelings are fucked up. Like I *know* he couldn't have meant what he said. Right? But just hearing them is messing with me.

Everyone is staring at me again, and I suddenly realize they think I'm infatuated with Akara and he's decreed *I'm not into her in that way.*

Great.

Awesome.

I take out my phone. "I'm going to call my sister." I walk away. Akara can't follow because he's about to be sutured.

Smell of campfire and burnt logs in the air, I hike down a sloped path towards the bathrooms. I hear Moffy about to follow, but Jane tells him, "Let me, old chap. I think this one is for the girls."

My lip aches to rise as Jane catches up to me.

I see her at my side, then we both glance behind us. The Moretti brothers are following. *Our bodyguards.* They keep their distance to give us the illusion of privacy.

As a gust of cold morning wind blows through, Jane rolls down the sleeves of her chunky, pastel pink sweater. "Do you want to talk about it?"

I twist my hair up in a messy bun. Part of me wants to just explode and tell Jane every fucking thing, but I can't. *I can't.* And even mentioning the bits and pieces I can say feels like sharing a lie more than a half-truth. "Maybe later?" I tell her.

She nods, understanding.

Her understanding hurts more than it should. Jane gives me a consoling side-hug. "If it makes you feel any better, even if Akara doesn't feel that way, I have a very strong suspicion that Banks does."

I dead-stop in place a few feet from the outdoor bathroom stalls. "Wait, are you saying you think Banks likes me?"

"Oui," she smiles brightly.

I'm not caught off guard that she knows. Just… "You'd be okay with that? Him liking me? And me liking him?"

Jane begins to frown. "Why wouldn't I be?"

"I don't know…is it fucking strange for you?" I slip on my jean jacket that I tied around my waist. "Banks is Thatcher's brother, and you're marrying Thatcher."

"That wouldn't bother me. You realize that your mom and Moffy's mom are sisters and your dads are brothers too?" A pair of sisters married a pair of brothers.

I smile more and elbow her hip. "You're always reminding me of that."

"It's easy to forget," she says. "No one holds it against you, and if they do, I doubt they're our friends in the first place." She hooks her arm with mine, and we continue our stroll.

For a bit, we chat about her upcoming bachelorette party and our siblings. But I still can't get over how Jane is Team Banks.

Like I'm Elena fucking Gilbert and there are *teams* in this love triangle.

Oh God.

It's not like Jane has all the information. She literally thinks Akara has permanently friend-zoned me. In her mind, Team Akara doesn't exist.

When I find a good spot for cell reception near the "information center"—which really is just a corkboard with laminated fire-safety graphics and trail maps—Jane hugs me goodbye, letting me call my sister. But as she leaves and Banks comes closer, I wait to dial Winona's number.

He stuffs his hands into his blue cargo jacket. "You okay?"

I want to nod, but I shake my head over and over. *That's all she is to me.* "Maybe I'm too sensitive. I know he wasn't trying to be cruel."

"You're not too sensitive," Banks reassures. "Akara knows he was an ass. He shouldn't have said that. Even if it was a lie."

We draw closer. "But why am I taking it to heart if I know it's a lie? I shouldn't *care*."

"You care because you love him, Sulli." Banks looks more torn up as he says those words. "Love hurts. It's just a fuckin' fact. "

My throat swells closed. "You've been in love before?"

"Once." He stares past me, just sweeping the morning campers who awake from their RVs.

Why does that hurt—knowing he's loved someone else before? I should be happy about his good experience, considering he's had a bunch of terrible firsts. At least he fell in love once. I nod a few times, and as his gaze returns to me, we move in closer.

He nods his head towards the corkboard. I follow him around the board, which conceals us from campers.

And his arms instantly wrap around my shoulders. I cocoon myself in his cargo jacket and bury my face in his collar. When I felt hurt, why was my first instinct to run straight to him?

I keep these questions to myself. Because I know their answers.

I'm falling hard for Banks.

He sways with me like we're slow dancing.

I smile at him. "I bet you were a total Casanova in high school. Three, four girlfriends that just fucking adored you."

"You'd be surprised."

"Ten girlfriends?"

He laughs. "Wrong direction, mermaid."

"A high school sweetheart, then?"

Banks shakes his head. "Just a whole lot of casual sex and no relationships." He wears a crooked smile at a thought. "I'm about as good at dating as I am in a three-legged sack race." He stares down at me. "Which is to say I fall flat on my fucking face. Akara is the one with relationship experience, if that's what you're looking for."

"No...I really hadn't considered that as a factor in..." *Choosing.* I can't even say the fucking word. "I guess what I'm trying to say is that it wouldn't bother me either way. It's not like I have any experience either."

Banks lets out a soft laugh. "Thanks, mermaid, but I'm *twenty-nine.* You have eight more years to run past where I am, and you'd think I'd learn to have a *stable* relationship before now. Something better than my parents had."

My brows bunch. "Are you worried of getting in a relationship like theirs?" I move closer to his chest as the wind picks up.

He wraps his arms and jacket more around me. "I'd be a liar if I said I wasn't. But I know I'm not like my dad, so I'm safe there."

I still don't know too much about his dad. "How do you know you're not like him?"

"Because I'm a lot of things, but I'm not selfish. And I'd *never* say to a twelve-year-old, what he said to me."

I'm about to ask him more, but my phone buzzes. "Sorry."

"Take it," he encourages. "It's probably your sister."

At mention of Winona, I touch the otter pendant at my neck. Once upon a time, I found four pendants in a zoo gift shop, and each one is supposed to represent my family. Over the years, we've passed them around, and I swapped with my sister recently.

The otter is hers.

I take out my phone and check the new text.

Banks is right. Winona sent me a message.

Sulli-Bear! Guess what I got Dad to do? He's now officially going vegan :) Want to join with us? – Nona-Frog

"What's wrong?" Banks must see my fallen face.

I pull back from him to show off the text. "My dad—the fucking *meat* lover—is going vegan for Winona. And I just killed a cougar barely a day ago." I pause, nearly groaning. "I feel like shit."

Banks almost smiles. "You shouldn't. Hasn't your dad tried to go vegan plenty of times for Winona and failed?"

That's true.

It's not public fact, but Banks is a bodyguard. Bodyguards talk, even the ones who protect the Hales and Cobalts. So I'm not too surprised he knows about my dad's short-stints in veganism.

I could just call Winona to answer her question, but now that I'm faced with the chance, I waver. I've never had so many big things happen in my life that I can't share with my little sister.

From Banks and Akara to the cougar attack.

Everyone in Yellowstone agreed that the cougar attack needs to be kept private among those on the trip, SFO, and trustworthy Luna. At least until we return home. Moffy and Jane said if we tell our parents, they'll book the first flight to Montana, which will bring a fuck ton of paparazzi with them.

Our parents are the true famous ones.

And I can't climb with the media hovering around. As much as I'd love for my parents to be out here with me, I'm not sure I should fly back into the nest this soon. It hasn't been that long since we left Philly. I've barely been out here without them.

"Don't know what to say to her?" Banks wonders since I'm stalling.

"I'm just nervous she'll bring up things I can't answer." I don't mention how I'm a shitty liar. That is already known.

His eyes are on the woods behind me, scanning the area as he talks. "Want some advice?"

"Yeah, I'd love anything."

His gaze lands on me. Older. Protective. I want to walk into his embrace again. Feel the warmth of his arms around me, but the phone in my hand feels like a barrier.

"When you talk to your sister," he tells me, "don't think of the cougar attack as a secret you're keeping from her. The things you aren't ready to tell people, they're not really secrets. They're just vulnerable parts of you that need time to be shared."

That hits me because I know he's talking from experience.

Skylar.

His older brother that he doesn't talk to anyone about. He must be one of the most vulnerable parts of Banks.

I inhale a stronger breath, smiling. "That's some good advice."

Banks smiles into a soft laugh. "I'm full of advice. Not sure if it's all good, but I don't mind giving it."

My lips haven't dropped, a giddiness suddenly surging through me. I hesitate to call my sister again, only this time it's because I don't want this moment with Banks to end yet.

I check our surroundings. No campers are hiking to the corkboard, so I look back at him and say, "I liked last night in the tent." We all haven't talked too much about what we did together. And I know it existed inside this dream world. In the shelter of the woods. Something that'll be left behind in the wilderness. Because once we're home, I'll have to choose.

"I'm glad." He smiles. "I enjoyed it too, mermaid."

My eyes glass in a bigger smile. That feels good, knowing he doesn't regret anything.

And then a faraway gunshot splinters the air.

I flinch.

"Probably hunters," Banks says, eyes on me.

"Yeah," I nod, trying to shake off the sudden jolt. "I'll call my sis." I dial Nona's number and squat down, fully hidden behind the information board and a couple shrubs.

When I look up, I catch Banks' shadow of a *grin.*

"What's so funny?" I ask him.

"The squat and talk." He gestures to my position. "Not funny but cute."

He said I'm cute. If my heart were a cheerleader, it'd be performing a winning routine right now. "Want to squat with me?" I ask.

Banks has trouble looking away. "You know I would, but I'm supposed to be protecting you. I won't see who's coming."

I can't reply, my sister cuts over the line. "Sulli?"

"Squirt," I greet, phone to my ear.

Banks turns his back to me. To give me privacy and protect me, I think.

I'm *dying* to gush to my sister about him. *Focus. Concentrate.* "You're not at school yet, are you?" I didn't calculate the time difference, but it's super early here.

"Not yet. I'm about to carpool with the babes soon." The babes are our cousins and her best friends: Vada Abbey (Aunt Willow's daughter), plus Kinney Hale and Audrey Cobalt. "Just eating a bagel with almond butter." She clicks onto FaceTime.

Fuck.

I hold the camera close up to my face. Only a small scratch on my cheek and forehead. Stuff that she'll chalk up to thorns or rocks from hiking and climbing.

I accept the FaceTime call.

Her camera is zoomed in on the bagel and almond butter. Then she flips the view to her face. Dirty-blonde hair wet from a morning shower, Winona smiles at me with almond butter spread over her teeth. "Am I beautiful, Sulli?"

I laugh. "The most beautiful land crab I've ever seen." It's an inside joke, and I hoist the camera closer to my face. *Just to be safe*. "So Dad's really cutting out eggs and diary?"

"Yeah, for real," Winona says into a gulp of water, her smile still present. "He said he'd try harder than last time. He even shook on it. And you don't have to join if you don't want to. No pressure."

I killed a cougar, Nona. Swallowing back those words, I say without thought, "Yeah totally, but I think I'm gonna try, too."

"Really?" Her voice goes high-pitched in excitement. She sets her glass down so abruptly, water sloshes.

"Yeah. Why not?" My guilty conscience is making me vegan for the wrong fucking reasons, but I've already hopped on this fast-moving train.

"Because you eat whipped cream almost every day, and last time you tried an egg-less, dairy-less waffle, you said it tasted like ass."

"Maybe I like eating ass now," I banter.

Banks turns his head slightly. He definitely heard that.

I heat up.

Winona notices. "Who are you looking at?"

"Banks. He's on-duty."

Winona raises her voice. "Banks, stop eavesdropping!"

"Nona—"

"What? Tell him to stop, Sulli. I hate when bodyguards listen into *private* conversations. It's not like we get to listen into *their* private discussions."

My sister is one of the few in my family to maintain real privacy. Her Instagram account is mostly just pretty landscape photos. Rarely, she'll post her face. She's not on *We Are Calloway*, and paparazzi seem to always be more interested in the people she's with rather than her.

"You wouldn't care if Akara was overhearing us." I glance over at Banks. He's already moving several feet away from me. Giving me more privacy.

My stomach sinks.

"Akara is more like family," Winona says. "But if he screws with you, he'll have to go through me."

"Banks' brother is about to literally *be* family," I remind her.

She stares off, thinking. "I don't know, I just feel different about Akara. It feels like he's always been around us. He's like Moffy, and I wouldn't care if Moffy overheard us."

I recoil. "Akara is *not* related to us. He's not our brother."

She bites into the bagel. "But he kinda is." She freezes. "Why do you look so freaked out? Sulli?"

"It's just fucking disturbing that you think Akara is a *brother* to me."

Winona chews her bite of bagel slowly. "Do you have a crush on him? *Sul.*" Her eyes widen. "Why didn't you tell me—?"

"I've just never thought of Kits like a brother," I interject, feeling more like the younger sister when I'm six fucking years *older.* Maybe she can tell I'm not ready to talk about Kits, because she doesn't press or pry.

She smiles. "Got it." She bites another hunk of bagel. She'd totally be Team Akara if she knew my dilemma.

It's not their choice.

It's mine.

I know.

I know.

Winona asks, "What kind of asses have you been eating that made you a convert?"

"Jerky asses, nice asses. Turns out, I'm not that picky."

Winona raises her glass. "Cheers to the nice asses."

I mime a glass and knock mine with the camera. "What's up with you, squirt? How's school going?" She talks for a while about douchebags in their classes. How with all the babes (aka the girl squad) in high school together now, along with Ben Cobalt, more eyes are on them in the hallways and classrooms.

"Mom and Dad miss you a bunch too," Winona says. "They keep buying donuts even though you aren't here, so hey, I figure they're doing better than when you first moved out. We had like five stale boxes in the kitchen then. Now we just have three. None of us eat them as fast as you."

The pang of homesickness returns tenfold.

I tell my sister I miss all of them. And I love them.

Not long after we hang up, Luna calls me.

Another FaceTime.

Only when I click into the video, I'm greeted by a potato. More specifically, Luna is a potato. She turned on a phone-filter, and I instantly laugh.

I change my filter to a tree. And we chat as a potato and tree for a few minutes. Catching up. She tells me about online college courses.

I tell her about the cougar attack, since no one has told her yet.

"No way," she inhales. "Are you okay?"

"Yeah, just a bad cut. Kits has the worst damage." We chat for a couple more minutes, before I glance through a shrub and see a pair of Vans moving *fast* towards the corkboard. *Akara.* "Hey, I gotta go, Luna."

We say fast goodbyes, and I jolt up to a stance.

Akara rolls to a stop next to the corkboard. Banks is further away now. So I focus on Kits. Who breathes hard like he sprinted here.

"Sulli." He holds a hand out like he means to explain more.

That's all she is to me. I tense. And I can admit that I fucking care that he hurt me. That it hurt. Hot anger rises and I snap, "That was fucked up."

"I know." His eyes redden. "I know. I shoved a bowl of Instant Regret in the microwave, Sul. I've been eating the thing the *entire* time Farrow stitched me."

I glance at his bandaged elbow. "I'm glad you got stitches."

His face twists, seeing that I'm still upset. "Sulli—"

"That's all you are to me," I say angrily. "A bodyguard and a friend."

Akara looks like he could fall to his knees in despair.

"And if you were *anyone* else," I continue, "you'd be out of my life right now, you know that? I've let you make me feel so fucking hurt and angry."

"I'm sorry." He's near tears. "I'm sorry. Please, I don't want to lose you." His Adam's apple bobs, his fingers thread through his hair.

My eyes burn with emotion. Maybe I've been too hard on too many people. Maybe I'm too hard on Akara right now. I want to stick up for myself, but I also don't want to be incapable of forgiveness.

"I know it was a slip," I say softly, and he eases a little. "But why was it so easy for you to say that to them?"

He comes closer. "Because I've said it too many times before, and I believed it then."

"Are you sure you don't believe it now?"

He chokes on a pained noise. "*Yes.*" He gives me a horrified look. "We…" He lowers his voice, close enough that his hand brushes my fingers. "We *hooked* up. I wouldn't do that if I didn't have feelings for you, Sul."

"You warned me you're a dick," I remind him.

"I'm not *that* kind of dick." Akara clasps his hand around mine. I let him, as he says, "I'm the dick who isn't thinking about emotions, just logical tactics—and I regret it. I never want to hurt you like that, Sulli."

I breathe in, and I curve my arms around his waist. He hugs me. I listen to his heartbeat and his soft apologies in my ear.

Since we're not hidden behind the corkboard, the embrace doesn't last long. Akara motions Banks over, and I can tell Akara is frustrated by something else too.

"Why was Oscar pressing me so hard about her?" Akara asks Banks. Hearing them talk about other bodyguards in front of me is always super fucking interesting.

Banks fixes his earpiece. "You know why. It's always been too easy to bust your balls by bringing up Sulli."

Akara pinches his eyes. "The fucking Yale boys, man." He drops his hand. "They're too talkative and observant."

Banks bounces his head.

I frown. "You guys don't think they'll figure out what's going on between us?"

Akara is still fuming. "If they keep bugging me about you, maybe."

As the sun rises and tension builds, the cold recedes. Body heating up, I tie my jean jacket around my waist.

"And the *baby*," Akara vents. "Every time I look at that *baby*, all I can think is, *Baby Needs A Bodyguard*—like a printed poster across my eye sockets. But *no*, Farrow and Maximoff don't want a bodyguard for the baby. They can protect their kid themselves." He looks to me. "Which I don't completely understand, considering Maximoff had a bodyguard when he was a baby."

"I didn't really have a 24/7 bodyguard until I was older," I tell him. "So I get it."

Akara looks to Banks for back-up.

"Baby needs a bodyguard," Banks nods in agreement.

"Exactly," Akara says, their eyes on me as they team up against me.

"I'm not sure I love the whole you two versus me thing, but weirdly, I don't hate it. Probably because I know I can kick your asses."

Banks laughs like that's wholly untrue, and now I *really* want to test out kicking his ass. I'm about to ask how much he can bench-press.

But Akara tells me, "It's not us versus you, string bean."

Banks goes to wrap an arm across my shoulders the same time that Akara goes in—and their forearms knock together.

They glare at each other. Hands drop to their sides.

Quickly, I add, "I also don't like Akara versus Banks—that is the fucking *worst* matchup." While they're on either side of me, I curve one arm around Akara's waist and the other around Banks'. Squeezing them closer to me.

They ease.

"We're cool, Sul," Akara assures me.

Banks nods.

I touch their lower backs, and their gazes roam over me in a sweltering beat. It's really fucking hot out here. I retract my hands and retighten the knot of my jacket on my waist. And I reroute to the other topic. "Just let Farrow and Moffy do their thing."

"Well, I have to," Akara sighs. "They're not budging no matter what pitch I give." To Banks, he says, "Thatcher gave me some updates on the guys back in Philly." He must be referring to Quinn and Donnelly.

"What's the word?" Banks asks.

While they talk, I study the hiking trail guide on the corkboard. My finger travels the line to The Bitterroot Buttress.

No part of me wishes to return to the rock face. The path there is cursed. And I don't want to replay the cougar attack every time we trek to the base of the crag. I'm leaving the goal unfinished.

Incomplete.

Safety is more important, and I need to be completely focused. Not halfway back in the past. And anyway, I've become more used to scrapping goals and beginning new ones. It's not that devastating.

Moffy not being able to run the Chile ultra-marathon helped me take small bumps and hiccups in better strides. Shit happens.

Fuck it all and start again.

I tap a finger to the next rock face my dad once free-soloed. The climbing route is dubbed *Rattlesnake Knuckle.*

"I don't remember him bringing home any girls since we've been living together either," Banks says to Akara. My ears pick up mid-conversation.

"Who?" I ask.

Yeah, I'm fucking nosy. Maybe because I over-share my life, and it feels like everyone else *under*-shares.

"Donnelly," Banks tells me.

Akara explains more, "Quinn said he hasn't seen Donnelly bring home any girls to hook up with."

While we trek up the path to RV Campsite #12, they flank either side of me, and I ask them, "Is that out of the ordinary for Donnelly or something?"

"Yeah," Akara says. "When I was living with him in Epsilon's house years ago, his one-night stand stole his wallet, mine, and Greer's in the morning and then bolted."

Greer Bell. He was my bodyguard before Akara. From age 8 to 16, Greer protected me, and he's currently the 24/7 bodyguard to my sister Winona. Since Greer joined security at twenty-two, he's now in his mid-thirties.

I snort. "She was able to steal from legit *security* guards."

Banks laughs with me.

Akara tries not to smile. "That's so *not* the point, you two."

"Yeah, what's the point then?" While we walk, I go to lightly slug his shoulder, then retrack. Remembering he's hurt. *Good call, Sulli.*

"Donnelly usually brings chicks home," Akara tells me, "but he hasn't been. Any change in my men, just puts me on edge. I'm just worried about him." He pushes his hair back and fits on a backwards baseball cap.

Banks reminds Akara, "And he's been sleepwalking."

Akara let that slip one time to me. So it's not news to me that Donnelly sleepwalks.

"On one hand, is he okay?" Akara muses out loud, our feet in sync as we pass the camp bathrooms. "On the other, is he fit for duty?" He touches his chest. "I'm not around enough right now to make that call."

"Then don't," Banks says, pulling out a pack of cigarettes. "Just let Thatcher keep an eye on Quinn who has eyes on Donnelly."

Akara nods, exhaling.

I understand competitive pressure from sports. But not the kind of pressure that Banks and Akara face daily. They're both in charge of human lives, but Akara is also in charge of Banks' life and the rest of SFO. If anything goes wrong, if anyone is hurt, that falls on his shoulders.

While we continue up a hill, we go quiet and I feel their eyes flash to me every now and then. Being between them is the greatest comfort but the biggest challenge I'm going to meet. For some reason, it feels tougher than any rock I'm going to climb.

27

Banks Moretti

FIREWOOD AND BRANCHES pile high in Sulli's arms. I grip an axe and a bunch of wood, while Akara *glares* at me and then Sulli. I'd say Yellowstone Country is beautiful this evening with the yellows and oranges cresting the horizon as the October season descends on Montana, but the more beautiful thing is Akara's annoyance.

Love to push his buttons and see him switch from friend to *shut up, Banks*, and it's been too easy lately. Strangely enough, it has *nothing* to do with Sulli.

"This is ridiculous. I can carry a log," he combats.

"I know you can," Sulli says. "But that doesn't mean you should."

I crack a lopsided smile. "What she said."

Akara gives me a look. "It's been *seven* days since Farrow stitched me."

"And I'm no doctor, but as far as I know, if you've got stitches, you can still break them open." I nod to him. "I'll let you hold my logs once they're out."

Akara shoots me a blunt, *fuck you* look, then whips out his phone as we make our way back to camp.

I try not to laugh *too* much. "Who are you texting?"

Sulli steps over a fallen tree trunk.

"Farrow," Akara says. "I'm asking to get them removed tonight."

He was supposed to get his stitches out tomorrow. I laugh. "Asking or commanding?"

Akara's not the kind of person to ask permission for something he wants, even if it's from a doctor.

He doesn't reply to that, just keeps texting.

Sulli and I share a smile. These past seven days have been comical seeing Akara out of his element. Taking a small step back in terms of physical labor has put him in a fucking tizzy. No lifting. No carrying a backpack. Per his doctor's orders.

Sometimes I wonder if he'd be okay with using this time to catch up on work—send emails, make business calls, all that paper-pushing shit—if he weren't competing for Sulli's time. But it's not like he's ordered me to go the fuck away.

Akara has the power to say, *Banks, your detail is changing. I'm transferring you to Maximoff for the rest of the trip.*

It'd be understandable. Farrow is on the med team. As SFO's glorified floater, I've floated over to Maximoff's detail pretty often so Farrow could take med calls.

No way in hell am I complaining about Akara's insistence to keep me on Sulli's detail with him. I don't want to be anywhere else. It crashes against me. Because I've never cared too much about where I'm told to go, I just go.

For once, I want to be rooted to something.

To someone.

Akara makes a frustrated noise at his phone.

"What?" Sulli asks.

"He's not replying." Akara touches his mic, and I can hear him through my earpiece. "Akara to Farrow, what's your location? I need these stitches out tonight."

Christ help me, I struggle not to laugh.

Farrow's reply is quick. "You're getting them removed tomorrow morning, Kitsuwon. See you at seven a.m."

Akara huffs.

Sulli looks to me since she can't hear through the mic.

"Farrow didn't budge," I tell her. "Oh-seven-hundred, we're getting our old Akara back."

Sulli nudges Akara's good elbow with hers. "Oh hey, don't fucking stress. What's one more night taking it easy?"

We all talk on our way back to the new campsite.

Moments between our friendly banter, the tension returns. And there's not just one source anymore.

Akara and I are dating the same girl; Sulli still has to choose one of us, and the three of us hooked up in a tent seven days ago—the tension is a badly mixed cocktail of awkward, painful, and hot as hell things.

At the end of the line, Akara and I have a job to do.

And ever since we packed up our tent and moved campsites, security has been harder. Right now, we step into the new camp, nestled less in the woods. Parking lot is in view, and a road curves around different camping spots.

All security risks.

Our teal tent is erected in the "tents only" section, and we've parked Sulli's Jeep a few feet away. The "RVs only" area is a good five-minute trek.

It's a better distance if something else goes down, and it also gives us privacy away from SFO and her cousins. If my big mouth spends too much time with my brother, I'm still worried I might say shit I shouldn't—and the longer I'm with Sulli, the more I wish I could confide in Thatcher.

I'm usually the one giving him advice.

But lately, I feel like I need him to remind me that I'm gonna lose her. Because I keep dreaming of a life with her beyond Yellowstone, and it's gonna kill me when she leaves me behind.

Second.

I'm always second choice, second place.

I try to leave *that* behind as Sulli and I drop our firewood outside our tent. Akara's phone buzzes with a text.

Sulli jabs a thumb to the Jeep. "I'm grabbing my toiletries, then heading for the showers." She points at me while walking backwards. "Stay frosty."

My mouth curves up. "Stop stealing my lines."

"Copyright them then!" she shouts, waving goodbye as she sprints to the Jeep like she's in a race with herself.

I watch her for an extended minute. Ensuring she's safe, then my focus pinpoints on other campers: a bright orange tent, a green tent—only two campsites down. In distance to chuck a football at us.

And they're the only other campers at this *tents only* area. We'd move further away, but this is the closest spot to the new rock Sulli is gonna free-solo.

Plus, they popped up their tents *after* us.

Back in South Philly, I wouldn't move my ass off a pub stool during an airing of Friday Night Fight (pro-wrestling), and I'm not about to move my ass now.

Name's Banks *Roscoe* Moretti. I'm a prideful motherfucker. I almost laugh out loud at my own joke like a dumbass.

Get your mind right.

Snap to.

I narrow my gaze on the campers.

They look like granola-eating, B.O.-smelling, earth-kissing twenty-somethings. Basically older versions of Ben Cobalt and Sulli's little sister Winona.

Right now, they ogle Sulli like they recognize her. Maybe not *know* her. But they at least know *of* her. And in the past week, this isn't the first time their eyes have super-glued to Sulli.

Akara slips his phone in his pocket. Sidling to me, he follows my gaze. "I found those four on Instagram."

"Right on," I say, impressed.

"It wasn't hard. They hashtagged *Rattlesnake Knuckle*, and it's not a popular tag to filter through."

Sulli has been climbing the Rattlesnake Knuckle route this week. Only with safety gear so far. She said it's a harder climb.

It's taller at over a hundred meters. 400-feet up. The rock is a slick slab with a wide fissure running through the center.

Just as I'm about to ask more about the campers, Sulli closes the trunk. Akara and I focus on her like she's the only living, breathing soul in these woods.

She sees us watching and checks us out like our staring is an invitation. "Hey." Her voice sounds raspier as she nears.

Mary, Mother of God, I'm in way too fucking deep.

Akara adjusts his earpiece, his muscles flexed. "You ready for that shower?"

Her face reddens. Don't blame her when Akara's question could imply we'll be taking a shower *with* her. Like we did after the cougar attack.

He runs a hand through his hair and his eyes drift over her for a second. "We'll be outside the door."

"Fuck, yeah. No, I knew that." She's quicker than normal hightailing it to the bathroom. And it takes me a second to catch up and jog out in front of her.

The campground only has one communal bathroom, equipped with three shower stalls. Before she reaches the knob, I open the door and check each stall. Confirming they're empty.

I nod to Akara in the doorway.

He nods back.

Sulli bypasses me to the furthest shower from the door.

"We'll be right outside," I tell her. Christ, my voice sounds fucking deeper. "Yell if you need anything."

She gives me a thumbs-up, her chest rising in a heady breath, then disappears. Tension strings between her and us, and I can't cut it. The campground isn't as private as the other one.

It's not like before.

But holy hell am I pent-up. Moments like this from an Olympian are giving me Olympic-quality blue-balls.

Going outside, I shut the bathroom door and stand beside Akara.

He leans against the brick siding. "I screwed that up," he exhales, his eyes drifting to the other campers. "I hate this campsite."

"Copy that." I pop a toothpick in my mouth. "Can't even pee in the woods without looking over my fucking shoulder."

We go quiet.

I want to ask him something. I glance at him, then scan the campsite.

He glances at me like he wants to ask something too, then looks away. "Are you going to say it or am I?"

"You are my leader." I bite on the toothpick.

Akara goes ahead and asks, "Did we have a threesome?"

I lean back too. "Is it a threesome if you and I didn't do anything?"

"Fuck if I know, man." Akara snaps a finger to his palm. "I've never hooked up with a girl *with* another guy before."

"Me either."

Akara asks, "What about two other girls?"

I shake my head. "No, have you?"

"Once." Akara frowns, thinking. "This felt so different than that. It wasn't casual or…" He has trouble finding the exact words.

"Yeah, I know," I nod, already understanding.

It was the most emotional, intimate moment I've ever had with a girl. And we didn't even have sex. *And* another guy was there.

The worst part is *liking* what we did. Because one of us isn't going to be with her. The silent fact lingers, and we share a more distraught look before our gazes return to the campsites.

"Incoming," I say.

Two campers have left the orange tent.

A dirty-blonde, curly-haired woman and a wiry, white guy with a North Face headband venture our way.

Tilting my head, I whisper to Akara. "What do you know about them?"

"They're a climbing team named *Team Apex*. They live in Bozeman, but they hop from campsite to campsite around the Yellowstone region for climbs."

Do they have ulterior motives?

Some fans are masquerading as hecklers. They go in for a simple autograph or selfie but actually wish a famous one would do something awkward or say something stupid—just so they can post a human slipup for clout with their friends.

I mean, one snapshot of a glare, and they'll just deem them *asshole celebrities.*

Truth: I prefer the clients who want me to shove strangers away from them. Like Xander and Sulli. I *love* when I can be short and threatening and not give a damn if a heckler throws a tantrum at my feet. I've had to haul asses away from Xander so that he could just simply cross the fucking street.

And while Sulli's not nearly as famous or draws as many crowds, I'll do the same for her.

Even now.

I gear up to lightly brush them off.

But I don't expect what comes out of the guy's mouth.

28

Akara Kitsuwon

"RYKE MEADOWS ISN'T welcome on this mountain, and neither is his daughter," the scrawny Team Apex guy states like this is a casual opener to a conversation. I recognize him from Instagram. His name is Lincoln and the girl beside him is Jordyn.

While he stuffs his hands in his pockets, he leans back on his heels like he nonchalantly said, *hey, how's it going?*

Jordyn nods in agreement with him.

Lovely.

We've encountered two pricks who think a *mountain* belongs to them. Growing up in an affluent neighborhood, these are some of my least favorite people to run into. For Banks, who grew up in a poor neighborhood, these are also some of his least favorite people to run into.

He glares at them like they're human stink bugs.

There's less heat in my eyes. One of us needs to *deescalate.*

Calmly, I say, "I take it you're not a Ryke Meadows fan."

Banks effortlessly sidesteps to block the bathroom door fully, but they're not paying him enough attention to notice.

Lincoln snorts. "The guy is a sellout, dude. Have you seen his Ziff commercial? He's out there chugging a knock-off Gatorade for cash, and he wants to be known as *the best* climber? Fuck that."

"It's ridiculous," Jordyn chimes in. "Climbing should be *pure*. Not something to be profited on."

"Knockoff Gatorade," Banks grumbles under his breath. They don't hear, and I try not to smile. Ziff is a Fizzle product, and he might as well have insulted the Calloway sisters. Sulli's *mom.*

Also, Ziff is quality.

I bite back an inciting retort. "Sullivan isn't Ryke," I tell them, hating that I even say these words because I'd like to defend Ryke too. But this will calm them faster, and we don't need enemies at our camp. "She's here to climb just like you two."

"Not like us," Lincoln points to the bathroom. "She's in there *alone.* Taking up the whole bathroom. There are three stalls."

Jordyn nods strongly. "Spoiled princesses shouldn't be climbing Rattlesnake Knuckle. Tell her to stick to indoor rock walls."

They both leave like that's the endnote.

Shit.

"What asswipes," Banks says gruffly. "Ben and Winona would never."

"What?" I make a face.

"Those climbers don't own this mountain," he tells me more angrily.

I almost smile. "Don't tell them that," I say like an order. "We can't have them pissed at us. It'll just distract her."

Sulli is going to eventually free-solo once she feels comfortable climbing the route.

Banks just nods, then grimaces.

"What's that look?"

"I hate how easy it is for me to take orders that I don't like."

"It's why you're good at what you do," I remind him. "Someone has to be the *yes-man.*"

"More like yes *sir* man."

I give him a pointed look. "Start calling me *sir* and see what happens."

"You'd probably get a nice boner."

With a smile, I quip, "I do love being in power."

He smacks my chest lightly with the back of his hand, and then suddenly, the bathroom door opens that he's leaning on. Banks steadies himself before falling through the opened doorway.

We both look at Sulli.

Dressed in a clean pair of workout leggings and sweatshirt, she squeezes out her wet hair. "Are you two talking about boners without me?" Her lips downturn like she's been left out.

I tilt my head. "FOMEFT is really hitting you hard." *Fear of Missing Every Fucking Thing* is Sulli's version of FOMO (Fear of Missing Out).

"I'm usually the one cracking the boner jokes."

"Beat you to it, mermaid," Banks says.

Before we can crack more jokes, I let Sulli in on what the campers said. I'm not going to hide anything from her, and she needs to know who to trust.

Definitely not them.

When I finish, she doesn't look too shocked. "Lots of climbing forums have whole threads about my dad. Most climbers dislike him for the same reasons. He's a 'sell out' or fucking whatever. It's not worth my energy. Can we just ignore them?"

"Already ignored," I tell her. But that's not completely true. It's my job to keep threats on my radar. They're in my line of sight from now on.

Over the years I've spent on Sulli's detail, I've mentally added up the number of people that were blatant assholes. Not close to the number of shits that'd spew hate towards Jane Cobalt.

But insults were hard on Sullivan. *Sulli the Sasquatch* signs and haters who were jealous of her success. Saying she wasn't deserving of gold. They couldn't see how many hours and months and years she sacrificed. All they saw was her wealth and fame.

A bright spot: Sulli has kept mostly under the radar and didn't grow up on *We Are Calloway* like the Cobalts and most of the Hales, which has given her some escape from the harsher judgment.

Her teammates on the Olympic swim team were kind to her. To her face *and* behind her back. I'd have called them her friends, but Sulli always shuts that word down. She couldn't confide in her teammates about her family. Didn't trust them fully, so to her, they couldn't be more than acquaintances.

I don't know what that's completely like. I grew up with friends in high school. Bandmates on the drum-line. Other teenagers who did martial arts. People that I actually cared about and people who cared about me.

But after my dad died, all my energy was put into my gym, and I pushed a lot of people away in favor of working to build my empire.

Returning to our camp, we start a fire, and Banks and I take turns hiking to the bathroom to shower off.

When I come back to the tent, I spend a good deal of time replying to emails, filling in Thatcher about Team Apex, and then checking in with Michael Moretti.

He arrived in Philly.

He's settled in, hopefully.

And as far as his *short* texts and calls go, he said he has everything handled. Normally I like brevity. It saves me time to do other shit, but from Banks' dad…it's unnerving.

Maybe because I haven't shaken his hand yet. Or given him a personal walk-through and rundown.

It'll be fine.

It's going to be fine.

So I shove my phone in my pocket. By the time I walk over to the fire, my stomach is growling.

Dinner for today: an add-water pouch of Beef Stroganoff for me and Banks. And for Sulli—the new vegan—a cup of oatmeal.

Sulli is already grimacing as she chews. "It's the consistency."

Banks says, "We have dried cranberries and salted nuts if you're into squirrel food."

Sulli mixes the oatmeal. "I'm more of whatever fucking animal likes chocolate syrup and whipped cream."

I lift a spoonful of Stroganoff. "Sounds like a Sulli animal to me."

We laugh.

I ask her, "Remember when you made me plug your nose while you drank your protein shakes? You took that worse than your hundred pushups a day."

"Because those protein shakes smelled like a whale's butthole. You'd be plugging your nose, too."

Banks wolfs down his food. The Stroganoff is subpar to me but not inedible. Another month here, and I'll probably be craving spicy buffalo wings or a Thai omelet.

The Thai omelet heavies my chest. Reminding me of my mom in New York. When I was a kid, it was pretty much the only thing she knew how to cook well.

I glance at a text from this morning.

> I'm doing better, Nine. No need to worry about me. Have fun in Yellowstone. Love, Mom – **Mom**

I reread I'm doing better, Nine a few more times before I put my phone up again.

Shit.

Shit.

"Team Apex is Oscar Mike," Banks says after I already see the campers on the move. They snuff out their fire and all pile into their pristine, brand-new looking Jeep Wrangler that makes Booger look like a bigger junker than she is.

I click my mic. "Akara to Thatcher, Team Apex is heading down the road towards you. Keep me posted if they stop at the RV camp."

A second later, Thatcher says, "Roger copy."

As soon as his voice is gone, the only noise comes from the crackling fire. It's oddly quiet. Team Apex has been around every night this week. This is the first time it's felt private since we left our other campsite.

Finished eating, we let the fire die out. Banks unzips the tent and crawls in first, Sulli is close behind.

"Oh fuck," Sulli curses.

"Akara. Out," Banks says quickly. Instinctively, I grab Sulli around the waist and pull her *out* of the tent.

"I'm fine, Kits," Sulli says, but she's breathing heavily. "Banks, get out of there!"

Banks still hasn't left the tent and now I'm worried about him. He's one of my men. His wellbeing matters to me. But I also know it's more than that.

"Banks! Leave the fucking tent!" I yell, and to Sulli, I ask, "What's going on?"

29

Sullivan Meadows

"SNAKES," I BREATHE hard, adrenaline spiked. "There are fucking *snakes* in there, Kits."

I know what I saw. At least three-dozen snakes are slithering underneath and around our sleeping bags inside the tent.

It has to be a practical joke.

I wish I got a better look to distinguish the exact type of snakes. Venomous or not, some fucking *creep* crept into our tent and placed them there. They couldn't have just fallen from the sky. We've been here for a whole week, and I haven't seen a single snake.

"Banks!" Akara yells again. "Get your ass out here. *Now*!"

Fuck, Kits sounds *mad*. Maybe even worried. I doubt he wants to mess around with fate after it literally bit him. His elbow is still bandaged, and his stitches are coming out tomorrow morning. Banks and I even conspired to buy him a surprise celebratory lunch. Which involved asking Jane and Thatcher to pick up a BLT at the diner in town.

My pulse races the longer Banks disobeys Akara's direct order. *I'm* definitely worried for Banks. Snake bites are nothing to fucking fool around with.

Akara drops his hands off my waist. He's about to rush to the tent when Banks ducks his head and steps outside the flaps.

In a tight fist, Banks grips five snakes by their necks. Their bodies writhe in the air. "They're just garter snakes."

I have my fingers to my temples, stunned. "What in the ever-loving *fuck*—you look like Baby Hercules." Okay, I'm a lot impressed.

Banks' brows cinch like he has no clue what I'm talking about. I don't have time to explain the Disney movie *Hercules* to him.

Akara is fuming as he approaches Banks. "I don't fucking care if there are koala bears in there. I told you to get out here."

"And now I'm out here," Banks says, eyes softened on his friend. "Akara—"

"I'm making the calls when we take risks," Akara snaps, his nose flaring. "You could have assessed the situation from outside the tent. No one was in there to save. If you came in contact with a single poisonous snake, Banks, you'd be *dead.* Think of Thatcher."

"He has Jane," Banks retorts. "He'll be okay without me."

Akara shakes his head like that's so far from the truth. "No one can ever fill that void you'll leave behind, and I know you know it. And if you won't think of him, then think of Sulli before you pull that reckless shit." He points to me.

My lungs collapse as my eyes meet the pain in Banks'. I see the words before he says them, "She has you, Akara." He turns to his friend. "When I'm gone, you'll hardly notice a difference."

"That's such bullshit," I cut in, my voice almost quaking with emotion. My heart is slamming against my body. Like it's trying to take flight and fling itself in his face. "I *care* about you, Banks." I don't forget that Akara is here.

I don't forget that these words might hurt him.

But Akara was the one to pull me into the picture, so maybe he knew Banks needed this moment, my words, my truth, my feelings out loud—even if it'd hurt him in the process.

I come closer. "I don't want to see you in pain. I don't want to see you fucking die! You mean something more to me—if you didn't, then why is the idea of never having you so fucking agonizing?"

His eyes redden. We both breathe harder, staring at one another, and then I brave a glance at Akara. He has a hand over his face. Distressed.

"Kits, I…" I pant like I'm running the longest marathon of my *life.* "…you know that choosing wouldn't be this hard if I didn't have feelings for you, too."

He drops his hand, nodding. His eyes are bloodshot like Banks'. His gaze is gentle on me. "I know, Sul."

Glancing back to Banks, I exhale, "Can you please drop those fucking snakes, Hercules? I can't take you seriously holding them."

He walks off to the woods to toss the snakes on the ground. The air lightens a fraction by my words, but an emotional string is still tethered between the three of us.

"Upside," Banks says as he returns. "I'm not actually six-feet under yet."

"Congratulations," Akara says. "You've beaten death *twice* since we've been out here. Don't test it a third time."

He cracks a shadow of a smile. "Yes, *sir*."

Akara glares. "I change my mind—Sulli, throw him in the snake pit."

Banks and I laugh, and Akara ends up smiling. He shakes his head, then fixates on the flaps of the tent.

I ask Banks, "How do you know they're all garter snakes?"

"You can thank Akara for that." Banks nods to him.

"What do you mean?" I turn to Akara. But he doesn't reply. He's even more laser-focused on the tent, walking around the perimeter in search of something.

Banks watches Akara for a second, then answers, "Akara's rulebook for Kitsuwon Securities. I think *Chapter Twenty-Nine* covered snakes and spiders."

I've heard about the monstrously huge rulebook. A doorstopper. But I didn't know he included sections on animal safety. Sounds like something Akara would do.

When it comes to his businesses, Akara goes above and beyond. I saw his drive and determination back when I was only sixteen—when he was first on my detail. He never let his phone die. Always had a charger, even found ways to access Wi-Fi in remote areas of Costa Rica—he wouldn't let a good time thieve his passions and responsibilities.

And I know I was young, but *he* was still young too. Young to own a business all by himself. Young to be a lead on the Tri-Force. Young to create a security firm. He's never let age or time or shitty cell service stop him from chasing triumph and success.

I understand what it's like running so hard after something that everything else falls to the wayside. So much of my early life, I sacrificed for swimming. And it's only since I retired that I have time to give to all the experiences I neglected.

I admire Kits because he's never been so focused that he loses sight of his other loves. His other desires. He juggles so much so well, he could join Aerial Ethereal's circus shows in Vegas.

And the rulebook—I wonder what else is inside. So I fucking go for it and ask, "When can I see this rulebook?"

Akara rounds the tent to the front, overhearing me. "When you become a bodyguard."

I huff. "So never."

He smiles at me, then tells Banks, "Let's clear the snakes and pull everything from the tent. I have to figure out how they put them in here."

My stomach curdles. I figured someone intentionally placed them in the tent, but hearing Akara confirm the presence of *creeps* creeping over our things is disturbing.

While I near the tent's entryway, I tell them, "I can help." A gray snake with long yellow stripes lies motionless at the zippered flaps. Oh fuck…

My stomach sinks.

I recognize this snake. I stepped on it before Akara pulled me out of the tent.

"Sulli?" Akara frowns.

"I squished it to death," I breathe softly. "What are the fucking odds?"

"Damn high," Banks says gruffly as he wrangles a couple more snakes in his hands. "I think there are close to four-dozen in here."

My estimation was a whole dozen off—and how the fuck did they even find four dozen snakes?! This was *premeditated.* I burn up. Pissed off that some jackasses infiltrated the place where I sleep for a prank.

So funny.

So cute.

So fucking hilarious. Let's frighten little ole Sullivan Minnie Meadows and hear her *scream.*

Not happening. If this was supposed to scare me away from the camp, it's doing the opposite. I'm going to build a fortress here and never leave.

Take *that*, assholes.

I carry the dead snake to the woods and lay its carcass down next to a rock. *Carcass.* Fuck, can I have any worse tact? What else am I supposed to call its dead body though?

A dead body, Sulli.

Right.

I'm gentle with the dead body—the *snake's* dead body. At our campsite, it takes some time for all of us to empty the tent of snakes *and* our gear.

By the time we find the slit in the back of the tent, I realize the reason Team Apex left the camp. They didn't want to be around when my bodyguards realized they pulled this prank.

"We should sleep in the Jeep tonight," Akara tells me as I duct tape the hole.

"They're not here." I squat, ripping tape with my teeth. "I don't want to run away from a stupid joke." How much I want to stand my ground—I'm kind of surprising myself. Normally, I'd remove myself from situations that involve pranksters, but I'd rather stay and risk a confrontation.

Patting tape to the hole, I add, "And if they wanted to hurt me, Kits, they would have put rattlesnakes in the tent."

Banks pipes in, "I don't think they're comin' back for the night." His South Philly lilt sounds thicker. "They seemed like fuckbags, but not idiots. Best guess: they'll return when they know we'll be hiking to the rock face."

"And," I say to Akara as I stand up, "your elbow shouldn't be cramped up in Booger all night. You'll break your sti—"

He covers my mouth with his hand. "And that was the last time you're allowed to baby me over *stitches*."

I smile underneath his palm, and then he drops his hand to flick my hair at my face. "Okay, string bean. We'll sleep in the tent." He looks to Banks. "But we take shifts."

"I'm good with that," Banks says.

But I don't love that they'll get half the amount of sleep as me. I don't argue with them. Their job is to protect me. Hindering their ability to do their job, telling them what to do—yeah, I'm not going to do that. At least, I'm going to try not to.

Thankfully for them, I'm not that bossy.

Piling into the tent together, the three of us take our respective spots.

Me in the middle.

Banks on the left. Akara on the right.

All week, we've kept our hands and lips to ourselves. Stayed put in our own sleeping bags. But with Team Apex gone and the "tents only" campgrounds empty except us, privacy has returned.

My heartbeat thumps harder as I sit cross-legged on top of my sleeping bag and dig through my backpack. Akara scrolls through his phone, and Banks texts on his. We're all quiet, but none of us make a move to sleep.

I actually don't know what the fuck I'm looking for in my backpack. I'm just stalling. Wanting this night to last longer. Sleep sounds like an enemy.

Finding a pack of colorful string, I pull out the turquoise, blue-jean blue, and apple-red thread. Might as well make a friendship bracelet. While I knot the three strings together, I'm attuned to how close Akara and Banks are.

Silence eats at me, and I just break it. "So it was a one-time thing, huh?" I ask. Akara and Banks blink up from their cells, and I just keep going. "The night we hooked up—or whatever the fuck you want to call it. It's not happening again. Not that I don't want it to or want to force you both to do something you wouldn't want." *Oh God, Sulli! Spit it out.* "Yeah, I just wanted clarification. That's fucking all."

Akara sets his phone aside, the screen flashing to black. "Do you want it to happen again?"

"It's not just about what I want," I refute and glance between them. Banks keeps looking to Akara, but I can't read their expressions. "And I'm really fucking concerned about hurting one of you in the end."

Banks lifts a shoulder. "Hell, for one of us this time in Yellowstone is all we're going to get with you. So I know I'm going to enjoy it while I can."

He doesn't appease my concerns about hurting one of them. Because we all know I will.

Letting go of the unfinished bracelet, I pull my legs to my chest and rest my chin on my kneecaps. "Theoretically, you two could just choose each other. Toss me off to the side, and then this ends a different fucking way. You know?"

They both start shaking their heads.

Akara rubs his knuckles. "I don't even want to think about this trip ending. Going back to Philly sounds like a nightmare right now. I have responsibilities there that don't burn my energy while I'm here." He takes a sharp breath. "And once were back home, I'm not one-hundred on how often I can be on your detail, Sul. Not like I am here. So this time has been priceless to me."

I knew for Akara to have it all, he couldn't be with me 24/7. That's the thing about juggling, you catch a lot of clubs, but at some point, every club is tossed in the air before you can hold it again. Creating Kitsuwon Securities added another club to his life.

It's always hard hearing him confirm, out loud, that he has to take time away from being my bodyguard. I want him to have it all, but the selfish parts of me wish I could have him all too.

Banks bobs his head up and down. "This is probably the most time I've got with you, too. I'm not taking it for granted."

Time with me.

I didn't realize how precious they really thought it was. My heart swells. Lifting me up for an enduring second. While I pick at my knotted ankle bracelet, I try hard to contain a smile. "I feel the same,"

I say softly. "Having time with both of you has been pretty fucking sweet."

It's special to be able to experience some firsts without the pressure of the media. Without worrying about stepping outside onto a street with paparazzi. Out here, I feel free and untamed. Able to be the most *me* I can be. And maybe I wouldn't be so comfortable if it weren't for Akara and Banks.

It's what I always wanted.

Yearned for.

That kind of comfort from a guy that could ease me into experiencing new things. I just never thought I'd be this comfortable with *two* guys. And after the cougar attack, there's nothing more I want than to return to that feeling that night.

The warmth.

The *warmth.*

It was nothing like I'd ever felt before. Feeling protected from the inside out.

"That clarify things for you?" Banks asks me.

"Sort of," I breathe. "You both are enjoying spending time with me, like I am with you. But does that mean we should do more than kiss again?"

"I want to," Banks says.

Akara quickly adds, "I do, too."

"Even if we're all in the same tent? Like last time?"

They exchange one look, like they're asking each other silently if they're cool with it, then they focus on me and nod. I couldn't tell whether they have experience being intimate with multiple people at once before, but with *that* look, I'm guessing being together isn't the norm.

So out loud, I ask, "Have you two been in the same room during a finger-fuck or some cock-in-pussy action before?"

Banks laughs, "No."

"Except for last time with you," Akara clarifies.

Interesting.

It eases me a little. My exploration doesn't feel like a solo journey. We're on this great, vast voyage together, and we all begin to smile because we're seeing where it'll take us.

Out here in the woods, there are no restrictions or boundaries or boxes we need to jump in.

We're free to just be.

So I forget about back home and the final rose. It's just right now in the present moment with them.

Akara sweeps me for a second. "We're just waiting for you, Sul. We're not going to push you or quicken your pace."

I laugh at that. "Kits, you know my pace is *far* faster than yours."

He scoots closer to me. So does Banks. My pulse thumps harder.

Akara slides his fingers over my ankle bracelet. His feather-light touch sends a shiver across my skin. "You can outpace both of us on foot, sure. But that's not the kind of pace I'm talking about."

That was…*hot.*

Heat envelops around me. *Warmth*—I want to reach out for it. It's swimming in the air, but it's not in me yet.

Banks skates a finger over my other ankle. His touch is just as frustratingly light as Akara's. "It's important that you set this pace, Sulli. We're more experienced than you." He pauses, then adds, "And if you wanna talk about it before we do anything—we can. It's not something that has to be jumped into without a conversation."

Akara nods. "Communication is important."

I raise my brows even more.

He gives me a look. "Even if I can be shit at it sometimes, it's important."

Taking a breath, I set my hands on my knees. "You know it's funny, I'm probably the most competitive person I know. And never once have I looked at sex as this thing to achieve. It's never been a goal."

"Do you still feel that way?" Akara asks, concern behind his brown eyes.

"Yeah, I fucking do." I smile at that thought. "I want it because I know it'll make me feel good, and I've always wanted that experience.

But not until I found someone I was comfortable with. Not until now." I run my thumb over my kneecap. "So it's hard to figure out what pace I want because I enjoy sprinting more than marathon running. But for swimming, I chose the 200m and 400m freestyle over the 50m because I always felt like the 50m was too fast. It was over too quick, you know. Does that make fucking sense?"

Akara and Banks are grinning so wide that I feel like I said something utterly ridiculous.

My face roasts.

"String bean," Akara says.

I humph at my awfully *inaccurate* nickname.

Smiling more, Akara continues on, "It won't be over too quickly. If you lose your virginity to me or Banks, it's going to last longer than a 50m."

"How long is a 50m?" Banks asks, brows pulling together.

"Olympic pace," Akara replies, "25 seconds."

Banks' face scrunches up. "What the hell? No one's fucking you for just 25 seconds."

I'm smiling like a fool. It's nice being able to talk about sex without it being weird or uncomfortable. "Sex isn't sprinting," I say. "Got it."

"Good sex," Banks corrects.

What if I suck at it? I've thought about this before and it always causes a wave of panic. I'm so used to practicing and training, and sex isn't something you can practice or train for. You just...do it. The first time could be a fucked-up disaster. But then again, that's why I waited. So there was less risk of regretting my first time.

I bite the inside of my lip. "Alright," I say. "So I choose a medium pace. Not too slow. Not too fast. 400m."

Banks looks to Akara for clarification again.

"Sulli holds the world record," he says. "Three minutes and thirty-three seconds."

Banks' smile reaches his eyes. "You're losing me with the swimming metaphors, Sulli." He cocks his head. "Just spell it out for me. Do you want me to go down on you?"

My pulse descends, responding before my words can.

"Yeah. I want that."

Fuck yes.

His grip suddenly tightens on my ankle. And then Akara's clutches my other ankle tighter. Together, they pull my legs down. My back hits the sleeping bag like a bed of feathers. I suck in a gasp, my hips already arching.

30

Banks Moretti

BEFORE YELLOWSTONE, I've never done anything sexual with a girl while another guy watched or was involved. Didn't even contemplate it. But after the cougar attack, I didn't hesitate. Didn't think about firsts or *befores*. It just felt right.

Like now.

It *feels* right.

And I go with my instincts and slide Sulli's leggings down her thighs while Akara leans into her lips and kisses her deeply. My cock stirs, blood pumping vigorously south.

Watching them should piss me off. I should be red-hot in rage that he has his teeth between her bottom lip and his hand riding up her shirt.

But I see the way she drinks in the sensation, and her pleasure is my pleasure. Doesn't matter if Akara's the one giving it to her, I realize. Sulli isn't the only one experiencing new things in this tent—all three of us are having *very* new experiences.

Firsts for everyone.

Cheers all around.

As I tug her leggings to her ankles, she lets out a ragged noise. Akara breaks from her lips, and her eyes dart down to *me*.

"Banks," she breathes, voice raspy.

Veins pulse in my erection, just hearing her say my name like that. *God fucking damn.* "Yeah?"

"I can blow you." She offers a blow job to me, the first she'll ever give. Her neck turns a shade of aroused red from Akara's hand. His palm is moving underneath her shirt, probably massaging her breasts.

"You don't need to blow me, mermaid," I tell her as I yank her leggings off completely. I toss them to the side. Her white panties have tiny donut designs all over them.

Her eyes flit from me to Akara. "Do you two not want to see each other's dicks while we're doing stuff or something?"

I hadn't even thought about that.

Akara tells her, "He can whip it out of he wants. I don't care."

"Same," I say.

His dick or any dick doesn't bother me. I fucking have one.

Akara explains before I can, "Banks just doesn't like blow jobs." I forgot he knows this about me.

"You want one?" Sulli offers to Akara. I imagine watching Sulli's lips wrapped around his dick, and I harden more. *Yeah, looks like I wouldn't mind watching that.*

"You first," Akara says.

She nods, okay with this.

Total, raw attraction draws me to her. I kiss her thigh, up to the hem of her panties. She shudders. Akara sheds her shirt and her bra. His lips return to her perked nipple. His eyes hit mine as I press a palm to her thighs and guide them open.

"Fuck," she moans, bucking up each time Akara flicks his tongue over her nipple.

I cup her pussy. Fabric separating my hand from her skin—but she's soaked through. My muscles contract, dying to rock into Sulli. Christ, I want to taste her so badly. More than that, I crave to get her off and see what makes her squirm the most.

I bite the inside of her thigh and watch her lips break apart in throaty arousal. Her hand dives down to my head. Gripping a handful of my hair.

It's a scorcher. A thousand blazing degrees in this tent.

She said *yes* to *me* going down on her since I asked, but this is her first time being eaten out. And I'm not fucking sure she wouldn't want Akara first.

I have to be sure.

Before I peel down her panties, I ask Sulli, "You want me here first?"

Sulli presses a hand to her forehead. "Can't you two just pick? I just don't want either of you to fucking read into that choice, and I don't mind either way."

Volleying that decision to us isn't that fucking simple.

Akara's gaze hits me again. Mine hits him.

We both want to go down on her. I'm waiting for him to tell me to move my ass. Maybe he's waiting for me to just concede all together.

She wants us to pick.

One of us has to give in, and she tenses the longer we take.

I'm about to throw in the towel, just so she doesn't have to make the painful choice. But Akara suddenly says, "She said *yes* to you to begin with, Banks. You're already there."

I nod, "Right on."

He nods back.

Sulli instantly relaxes. And I slip my fingers under the band of her panties. Drawing the fabric down her thigh and leg slowly. I savor the way she watches me like she's pinning each movement to memory. Maybe to get off to later on.

Everything about Sulli is a fist around me, stroking me with heavy friction, and I soak her in too.

Her eyes are on mine, then Akara. She's watching the way we consume her. Akara kisses her cheek, her nipple, and as I remove her panties, he grips her thigh and spreads her open wider for me.

Careful of her bandage, I clasp her hips, and I lower my head, trailing rougher kisses down the inside of her thigh. I ascend to her pussy.

She watches.

Hell, Akara watches not only Sulli but the way my lips move to the promise land. All the while, his hands roam over her, and he kisses her breasts, ear, lips. Leaving no skin untouched.

The second I kiss her pussy, she squirms.

"Fuck," she cries.

She tastes fucking amazing. My tongue strokes her clit before I suck the bud and really go to town, and she loses it. Sulli moans so loudly that Akara covers her mouth with his hand before trying to kiss the sounds away.

Her legs jerk, back arches, completely overwhelmed. She was already so aroused and swollen to begin with, I'm not surprised she's jet-packing to a climax.

I'm hungrier. Akara is a little rougher, making out with Sulli. Our fingers dig deeper in her flesh. Starved for her, and she gets wetter, warmer. Her eyes nearly roll.

A groan rumbles in my chest.

Akara makes a deep noise.

I toy with her clit again. She writhes, crying out in pleasure. Shifting her legs, until Akara braces one leg open, his arm hooked under her knee.

Her hand flies to my head and to Akara's bicep—but Akara seizes her wrists, pulling her hands above her head.

"Fuckfuckfuck," she cries.

The intensity is driving me insane. My cock is ready to burst through my boxer-briefs.

As soon as I suck deeper between her thighs and she eyes him and me and the way we have her, she explodes into a peak. Her high-pitched moan could wake RV campers five-minutes away, and Akara is quick to shield her mouth with his hand again.

She's loud.

I smile. *Love that about her.*

And I loved going down on her as much as she loved me down there. Best fucking feelings: mutual attraction and satisfaction.

We watch her come down, and Akara kisses her wrists before lowering her arms.

"Holy fuck," she breathes, then laughs in awe. "So that's what that feels like?"

We're all smiling, until car lights suddenly roll towards our campsite. The air sobers. My gaze narrows.

"Shit," Akara curses. "They're back."

Team Apex.

Sulli quickly reaches for her leggings.

I help her shimmy them back on. Akara grabs his radio and asks for updates from SFO.

When Sulli is fully dressed, I grab my gun and leave the tent. Adrenaline doesn't help my erection right now, it presses painfully against the fabric of my boxer-briefs. Lengthy strides take me to the road beside Booger, and I watch as Team Apex's Jeep Wrangler rolls towards me.

I feel exposed in the light, but fuck it, I hope I'm doing a damn good job at glaring them down. Six-seven and pissed off, they don't want to mess with me right now.

The Jeep comes to a halt and then they do a quick three-point turn and drive back in the direction they came.

Good.

Stay gone.

I turn around, and Akara is standing beside the tent.

As I duck and crawl back inside, I tell him, "They must've thought we'd be asleep."

"They'll be back again," Akara says, following me.

Sulli looks between us while we zip up the tent. "I know we probably shouldn't risk doing anything, if they come back, but I'd feel better knowing I got you guys off too."

"I'm fine," I tell her.

Akara nods, "We shouldn't risk it."

"You're both as hard as fucking rock."

I raise a shoulder. "It'll pass." Yeah, I'm pent-up as fuck, but I enjoyed seeing her come and getting her off more than I'll enjoy coming right now.

"Kits?" Sulli asks.

"Another time." He fixes a loose wire in his radio. "It's not important."

"Your needs are important to me."

He smiles. "I'm not saying *never*. Just not now."

"Alright," she says understandingly. "But maybe we don't have to sleep *in* the sleeping bags? Could we risk that?"

I look to Akara. He's the boss.

He nods. "We can do that."

We all crawl under the sleeping bags like a blanket, and Sulli rolls onto her side, facing me. She buries her head into my chest and then reaches behind her and pulls Akara's shirt. He scoots closer until his chest is flush to her back. His eyes meet mine.

We're not kissing.

We're not really even holding her.

And yet it feels fucking intimate. I realize in this moment that I've never had this. I've fucked a lot of women, and most of the time it's been un-sensational. Forgettable, even. I always thought I was bad at love. But maybe I just never had it to begin with. Never had intimacy like this.

That hits me.

"I'll take first shift," Akara whispers to me. "Get some sleep, Banks."

It's hard to close my eyes.

But I take his orders and try to drift asleep.

31

Akara Kitsuwon

THE SMALL NEARBY TOWN consists of a general store, a diner, and bait & tackle shop that has a pet store in the back. Sulli pulls Booger into the parking lot of Fish Hooks, and I adjust my radio.

"Sulli, you sure you want to do this?" I question. "It might just piss them off even more."

She narrows her eyes at the store challengingly. "If it's a prank war they want, it's a prank war they're going to fucking get."

Banks and I confronted Team Apex this morning, and they pretended not to know anything about the snakes. But as soon as we turned our backs, they snickered like high schoolers that got away with shit. In that moment, I was all for retaliation. But that's also a different side of me. The side that doesn't own a security company and doesn't need to deescalate threats.

"We've got your six," Banks tells her.

I nod at that as we all climb out and head into the store. *Shit,* the smell hits me first, almost bowling me over: a strong, clashing odor of fish bait and pine chips used for hamster cages.

"Jesus," Banks scrunches his nose.

Sulli's on a mission, aiming for the back of the store that says "PET SHOP" on a poster board. I sprint to slip out in front of my faster-than-lightning client.

"Slow down, Sul." I skim a hand against her hip, near her ass, as I move in front. I've never touched her like that before this trip.

So I don't think it's my words that make her feet suddenly stop. Her gaze flits quickly around the shop like she's seeing if anyone saw me touch her.

Fish Hooks is empty.

Part of me wouldn't really care if someone saw.

You should care, Nine. I hear my dad—at least imagining what he'd tell me, that moral, paternal voice guiding me through life.

I know I should care. Because it'd complicate things, and I don't want to force her hand and have her choose me just because we were spotted together.

Shit, though, I want to touch her in public.

It's killing me not to.

We make it to the counter. A sticky note taped to a bell says, *tap me for service.*

I tap twice.

Ping. Ping.

Sulli bounces on the balls of her feet, and her eyes flit to Banks. "You alright?"

He's slipping on a pair of dark-tinted sunglasses and just gives her a single nod. *Migraine,* probably. Not just a passing headache. I stiffen the longer I watch him.

How many has he had recently? I hope that I'm not wrong and these are just infrequent. I could just be more attuned to his health than usual since we've been spending more time together.

I motion to the parking spot. "I left a bottle of Tylenol in the glove compartment. I can grab it for you."

He puts a hand to my shoulder. "I'll get it."

Before he leaves, a gray-bearded man pops out from an *employees only* door. "If you're here for snakes, we're all out."

"Shitbags," Banks mutters on his way out.

Sulli frowns. "Someone bought *all* your snakes?"

I zone in on the empty snake habitats. "How many did you have?"

"About fifty of 'em," Gray Beard says, nametag reading *Chuck.* "Some organization for birds of prey is using 'em to feed their eagles."

Sulli and I share a look. Yeah, that's bullshit.

"We're not here for snakes." I push my black hair back, fitting on a red baseball cap backwards. "Do you have crickets?"

He nods. "Sure. Sure. How many?"

"As many as you have," Sulli says. "I have a colony of toads." She says it with as much seriousness as she can muster—which isn't a lot.

I lick my lips to try to stop from laughing.

Chuck just shrugs. "Whatever. Don't care what they're for as long as you're paying. Wait here." He disappears into the back.

Big Sky adventure brochures—rafting, fishing, kayaking—are displayed in dozens on the counter. Resting my bad elbow on the surface, the ache is small. Stitches came out yesterday, and Farrow said all of our wounds are healing well.

Angling more towards Sulli, I tell her, "You're still a shit liar."

"Hey, I'm keeping *us* secret, right? So I'm at least worthy of a bronze medal in Lying." She glances at the storefront's glass windows. Barrels of fishing rods and mannequins in fly-fishing gear obstruct most of the view from outside. "You think Banks is okay? How long does it take to grab some Tylenol?"

She's thinking about Banks right now.

It dumbfounds me how much that doesn't bother me. Jealousy is smothered beneath my own concern for him. And I'm happy Sulli cares about his wellbeing too.

I click my mic. "Akara to Banks, you alright?"

Banks responds quickly. "Liquor guy called back for the bachelor party. I'll be in soon."

Thatcher, Banks, and I have been texting each other in a group chat called *The Losers Club* since way back when the Moretti brothers joined security. And we'll text whenever we don't want shit heard over comms. Well, recently, Thatcher used the group chat, and I was around Banks when the messages were rolling in.

How's the bachelor party planning coming along? –Thatcher

Don't worry about it. I have it handled. – Banks

Maximoff has already finished organizing Jane's bachelorette party. – Thatcher

Banks almost choked on his toothpick. He turned to me like a wounded animal, and I knew he hadn't done a single thing to prepare for his brother's party yet.

October 20th is less than 2 weeks away. Just let me know if you need extra hands. I can help – Thatcher

Stop stressing. I have it covered. – Banks

I made some calls for Banks using his phone. Including one for the liquor store. Banks is great at a lot of shit, but he procrastinates on tasks he's unfamiliar with. Like planning an expensive party that's more than just a six-pack and a few dozen wings.

So I helped my friend.

Lifting my mic to my mouth, I tell Banks, "Take your time."

Banks and Sulli—they seem to always find time alone together. A rare moment where Banks is on the phone and I'm not? Yeah, I'm *coveting* these extra few minutes alone with her.

After I drop the mic wire, I fill Sulli in on Banks. *Looks like I can't stop talking about him with her.* It's impossible.

And the only real reason I want to divert the subject off Banks is *fear.*

I'm afraid the more we discuss him, the more she'll choose him in the end. Like I'm really just the friend to Sulli. It's what I've always been.

He's the romance.

I push past my insecurities because I really don't want to be a dick. And I feel like an asshole *shunning* Banks from our conversations when I actually want to confide in Sulli about him.

Once I finish mentioning the liquor guy, her brows bunch. "You think the bachelor party stress is making his headaches worse?"

"I don't know." I frown. "Have you seen him have a lot?"

"Before we left Philly, he definitely had one. He told me it was just a headache."

"Me too," I nod. "But more recently." I easily scan the store.

"So it can't be *us*, right—if he had headaches before the road trip? This whole…situation isn't causing him physical pain?"

I smile softly. "This situation?"

She tries to lower her voice. "Us in the tent."

I smile more. "There was *zero* stress in that situation, Sul. Trust me." Banks was *into* her, and I know because I was watching her being eaten out and her getting off from him.

Which almost annihilated me.

And shockingly, it was a euphoric annihilation. Not a resentful, angry, pissed off one. I almost heat up remembering it all. And yeah, I wished I could've been the one between her legs, but I liked being against her lips. Kissing her.

Touching her.

It didn't feel like I was losing anything. Just a part of something more. Something she enjoyed, he enjoyed—I enjoyed.

Plus, I hate that Banks is so hung-up on his shitty firsts. He deserves to be happy—and shit, it makes me happy seeing him have a good time and even having a good time with him. Last night was fun.

I'm feeling the moment out.

New experiences don't send me hitch-hiking backwards. I'm not as free as the wind as Banks, but I try to kick myself out of my comfort zone. If I stayed in there, I'd never do half the things I've done.

Give and take punches and kicks for Muay Thai. Bungee jumping with my dad at fourteen. Open a gym at eighteen. Snowboard black diamonds. Swim with sharks with the Meadows family.

Chase after Sulli.

Some piece of me wishes I could be a cocky asshole and say, *she loves me more than him. I have this in the bag.*

But I don't think I do. In order for me not to go out of my mind, I try to stop looking at this like a competition.

I just want to have this time with her.

At the small-town mountain store, Sulli breathes easier with my reassurance. She rifles through a bowl of Montana stickers. She's one hundred percent looking for a gift for Winona.

I spin a rack of postcards next to Sulli, then take one out and flick it on her nose.

She tries hard not to match my smile. "You don't want to start a nose-flicking competition with me. I'll beat your ass, and then you'll pout."

"But I thought you loved winning against me?" I flick her nose again.

She steals the postcard. "Yeah, because you're the biggest sore loser I know. Victory is that much sweeter when you whine—"

"I don't *whine*," I scoff with a smile.

"You whine." She grins.

I glance at her lips more than once.

She bites the bottom one. "Fuck." She turns her head away from me.

My pulse skips. "What's wrong, Sul?" I tilt my head.

Sulli peeks up at me through her long brown hair. "Sometimes I think I was dreaming it—you and me together—and then you look at me like that, and I remember it's real." She inhales a bigger breath. "It's pretty fucking overwhelming, but you probably know what this feels like already."

I'm confused. "What do you mean?"

"A friend-turned-lover." She cringes at her sudden use of *lover*.

I smile, "You don't want to be my lover?"

"Kits," she groans. "You know what I mean."

"Okay, lover."

"Fuck off." She snaps the postcard to my nose.

We both laugh.

I spin the postcard rack but look at her. "I've had friends who I ended up dating, but no friend has been like you. I've had vested interest in your wellbeing for so long, Sul. It's just a different feeling. More…intense."

Can't live without her.

She spins the rack now. "Do you think it'd be easy for you to just go back to being friends with me?"

I tense.

Is she already breaking up with me?

And before I can respond, she says, "Because sometimes I feel like I'm waiting for you to change your mind at any time. Like you could just pull that switch and go back to how things were with us."

My stomach plummets. I don't want Sulli to feel like I could rip a rug out from under her. To press rewind. It devastates me even imagining myself doing that to her.

Am I capable of it?

Yeah.

To her?

No.

But I can't blame her for feeling this way when I kept asserting how our friendship was just that. Friendship. Written in cement. Carved in marble. Etched in the center of the Earth.

"I'm *not* going to pull that switch," I say from my core. "I promise you, Sulli. I don't just want to be your friend."

Her green eyes smile before her lips. "Yeah?"

"Yeah," I nod. "And it's not snowing, so this can't be a dream."

"Have you had one of those in a while?" she wonders, looking more concerned.

"Actually, no," I admit. Now that I think about it, the last one was the night before the cougar attack.

Her brows rise, just as surprised as I am. She opens her mouth to reply, but Chuck returns with three shopping bags filled with containers of live crickets. They're loud as shit. He shows us the self-checkout pad, then trots to the back.

Sulli refuses to let me pay. "It's my idea."

I still have my wallet out. "I can put this on my business card."

"How does this relate to your security firm?"

"It relates to you," I remind her.

"No," she snaps. "I have money." From her trust fund. And she contends, "You'd never put up a fight before."

"That's because you weren't my girlfriend before." The word *girlfriend* comes out, and I eat another bowl of Instant Regret. Because I feel bad for *Banks.*

What is this guilt?

I wish I didn't care that much about his feelings in all of this, but I can't shut it off.

Sulli looks thunderstruck.

"I meant date," I correct. "I'm dating you, and I wouldn't let a date pay."

"Is this a date?" she starts to smile.

"A casual one," I nod. Definitely not what I'd do on a normal date. Buy crickets for revenge. But Sullivan Meadows is an American princess, so I never thought this would be normal.

She smiles. "Alright." But she swipes her debit card in the pad. "I'm paying for my date this time around."

"Fine," I sigh with a smile, then slip the card into my wallet. Before we leave, the two of us linger near a rack of canoes on the far wall. She must want extra time with me too. My chest rises, and we both set down our shopping bags.

Sulli pretends to inspect the three-person canoe. Mostly, she keeps glancing back at me.

I ask, "What's on your mind?"

Her fingers skim down the canoe's vibrant green exterior. "I just hope you know that I'm supportive of you and your businesses. I don't want to hold you back, and I don't blame you for bailing."

It's hard to inhale. "Is that what you think? That I'm bailing on you?"

She brushes her hair out of her face. "No…I don't know. I guess in a sense you technically are, but it's understandable. And I understand you want more than just to be my full-time bodyguard."

I don't want more than that.

But I do.

I hate that I do.

I've wanted it for my dad. For myself. Since I was eighteen and I started my own gym, I've wanted it all. And it's been *hard.* I've met setbacks and roadblocks and now creating a new company has its own challenges. But no challenge is harder than saying goodbye to Sulli.

Connor Cobalt's voice rings in my head: *Be a full-time bodyguard or be a businessman. There's a great chance you won't be able to do both.*

That time hasn't come yet. I refuse to believe it has.

"I'm still your bodyguard," I remind her. "Nothing's changed." *Yet.*

She nods, but she doesn't look fully convinced. "To be fucking crystal, I want whatever brings you the most happiness. If that means leaving my detail for something else, I'll understand." She pauses. "I wouldn't say it won't hurt. Someone once told me that *love hurts,* so that's probably why it wouldn't be that easy."

Love.

I breathe in. "Who said that?" I smile teasingly.

She hesitates, wavers, shifts her weight. "Me?"

Banks said it.

Fucking Banks.

I can't even be upset. "You wouldn't even win bronze in Lying. You'd get a cheap tin-bottle cap with the words *Loser* in marker."

She shoves my arm with a smile.

I smile back, then get more serious. "I appreciate your support—I always will, but it's not easy for me to just walk away either. I love being your bodyguard, Sulli. I want to be on your detail as much as I can, as long as I can." As I edge nearer, I glance at her lips; she glances at mine, and I say, "And I want to kiss you."

My fingers tighten on her wrists at her side, and her breath hitches.

"A friendly kiss, or…?" She smiles playfully but it falters as she stares at my mouth.

My lips drop to her ear, giving her more. "I've heard you come, Sul. I've *made* you come. And every night, I go to bed picturing myself inside of you. So *no,* not a friendly kiss."

Her chest rises in a deeper inhale. "Should we buy some rope?" Her eyes lock onto mine in greater challenge.

"But, string bean, you have enough rope to climb with."

Her face flushes. "You know what I mean."

"Do I?" I'm being a dick and giving her a hard time, but I can't help it.

"Kits—"

"What would you need the rope for?" I want to hear her say it. The air thickens between us, arousal brewing.

"I want to know what it feels like." She glances down to her wrists where my hands still clutch them tight. "I like when you do this."

I step closer. Our bodies flush up against each other, and I bend down just slightly so that our lips are a breath away. "Do you like when I kiss you?" I wonder.

"Yeah. I like that, too." She pulls back to see my eyes. "Do you like when I kiss you?'

"*Sulli*," I groan and lean into her lips, kissing her deeply in a better reply. She sinks into me. Her back knocks into one of the canoes, and while we kiss, I step her to the side so they don't tumble. Crickets chirp loudly around us.

I could stay in this moment forever. Never leave.

Never really want to.

But then I hear a voice that punctures my reality. Rips me from it.

"I'd say I hate to interrupt, but I don't. And I need to talk to my cousin for a second."

Sulli and I break apart.

Shit.

In her shock—at the sight of Charlie fucking Cobalt—she stumbles *into* the rack of canoes.

They all go down like Jenga pieces. Too quickly to even try to right them, but I stop one from falling on Sulli. Canoe upside-down, Sulli and I hold it above us, our pure shock on each other.

How did I miss him coming in the store?

I ease my gaze on Sulli. Trying to reassure her. But her cousin just saw us making out—this is *bad.* Another canoe drops on top of the one we're holding.

Sulli and I support the impact, but I hear a louder *crack.*

We look up and see the large fissure.

"You can put the canoe on your business card," Sulli tells me.

I'd laugh if behind the canoe wasn't a complete shit show.

"What the hell?!" Chuck yells from deep in the store as we pull the canoe off our heads. But he doesn't emerge to check on us.

Setting down the canoe on top of the others, footsteps pound through the store's entrance. "What's goin' on?" Banks asks, looking between all of us.

Oscar Highland-Oliveira stops short by Charlie and eyes the canoes. "Everyone alright?"

Anger surges. Oscar doesn't always provide his location change, and usually I let it slide because he's dealing with a difficult client. But after the cougar attack, I specifically told him and Farrow, *you go anywhere, use comms and give your location, no excuses.*

Besides this event being avoided, I should have that intel in case of real emergencies in Yellowstone.

I zero in on him. "Why didn't you tell me you were on your way here?"

Oscar frowns, skepticism in his eyes. "I lost connection on the road. By the time I came back, we were already here, and Banks just saw us parallel-park outside."

Charlie stares through me.

I don't avoid his gaze. I've never been intimidated by him, and I've always found ways out of impossible situations. But my mistake isn't a typical one that I ever make.

I've given a twenty-two-year-old the perfect ammunition to cause ultimate chaos.

Right now, I want to press Oscar harder and tell him that's not good enough. That he should have still radioed in once he was here, but I'm worried that if I sound as angry as I feel, it'll be too suspicious.

Not that it matters. Our secret is already half-blown now that Charlie saw us. He could implode everything right here, right now.

Oscar has no allegiance to me when it comes to gossip, and if he knows I kissed Sulli, he'll blurt it to the other Yale boys in less than a heartbeat. Shit, he'll probably radio them about it right now.

And Banks…

He eyes me for a large second, confusion and questions pinging in his brown irises. *I fucked up*. Everyone's going to know I kissed Sulli, and it'll push him to the side. And then if she chooses him in the end—it just complicates things for her.

It's messy.

So messy.

And only Charlie Cobalt has the ability to make it less complicated. Seeing as how I was once his bodyguard for a total of *two* months, I'm not holding my breath.

32

Sullivan Meadows

HOLY FUCK.

Holy FUCK?!

Charlie saw Akara kissing me—*Charlie*, the one cousin out of all my cousins who is a complete fucking wild card. It's almost worse than Moffy finding out. He'd just do the whole big brother overprotective routine and then settle on being happy for me, like he did with Jane.

I don't know what Charlie will do.

I don't even know what he's *thinking*.

Fuck.

Fuck.

Fucking *fuck*.

Charlie casually turns to his bodyguard, acting like nothing transpired. "I just have to talk to Sulli." He glances between Akara, Banks, and Oscar. "And I'd like to talk to my cousin in private."

"I'll be outside," Oscar says. "I can see you through the window."

Banks and Akara don't agree to that distance, but they take the crickets and head towards the other side of the store near the tackles. Out of earshot, but within better eyesight. They whisper to themselves, and I know Akara has to be updating Banks on this royal fuck-up.

"Charlie," I whisper-hiss. "What are you doing here?"

"What am I doing here?" His brows arch. "Shouldn't I be the one with the first accusatory statement?"

I let out a frustrated noise. Communicating with him feels so fucking out of my wheelhouse sometimes. Like I need *Jane.* "I just wanted to know why you stopped by the fishing store."

"I came to find you." He shoves his hands in his wrinkled slacks. His white button-down is half-untucked and unbuttoned. "I'm not here to watch you climb, remember?"

He's here to try and rebuild my friendship with Beckett. "Seriously?" I say. "You couldn't have waited until I got back to camp to stage this fucking coup."

Charlie tilts his head. "It's not a coup, Sullivan. I was coming to guilt you into talking to him. Make some story up about how he's having a bad day. Blah blah blah." He waves a hand. "But I have a better idea now."

No.

He smiles wickedly. "You call my brother, and I won't tell anyone you and Akara are fucking."

"We're not *fucking,*" I whisper angrily. "We just *kissed,* and fuck you—don't talk about me like that." The way he said *fucking,* he made it sound…meaningless. And it's never been to me.

Charlie rolls his eyes, but he eases up. "I believe you aren't *sleeping together.*"

I exhale a tense breath. "Thank you."

"Only because you're a terrible liar."

I glare. "So you're blackmailing me? Your own cousin?" I am a *little* shocked. I thought there were some lines Charlie drew in the sand. Or maybe I was just untouchable to his tactics because I used to be Beckett's best friend. Now I'm not.

He lets out a tired breath. "He's my twin brother. I'd blackmail my own father if it meant making him happy."

I snort. "As if you could blackmail your dad." I can hear Uncle Connor replying to his son, *that's very ambitious to think you can blackmail me, and it's also completely out of your capabilities.*

Charlie says, "Which is probably for the best, since I wouldn't want to have to try."

It is kind of sweet what Charlie would do for Beckett. In this fucked up way. And I do care about Beckett, but for some reason, I can't easily erase the hurt he caused. I remember a word.

Forgiveness.

Why is it so hard for me? I'm so quick to cut people out. With no look back.

That scares me.

It scares me even more to let Beckett back fully into my life. To know he could hurt me again. And his words have been scarred inside my heart.

The second you retire from swimming you're all of a sudden drinking alcohol and passing out—at least I'm not pointlessly destroying my body.

He's never criticized me as a way to deflect off himself before. He was purposefully cruel, and I'd never *ever* fucking attribute that word to Beckett Joyce Cobalt.

Cruel is so far from what and who he is.

Addiction.

It runs in my family, and I want to be empathetic towards Beckett and what he was going through back then, but I'm *afraid.*

Beckett and I have always built up each other's confidence, and in that moment, I realized he was the one person that could tear me down to the ground. So even if I forgive him now, I'm giving him the ability to hurt me again.

"Sulli, this offer is going to expire and self-destruct in ten seconds," Charlie says and looks to his watch, timing me. "Ten…nine…"

"Okay, okay," I say quickly. "I'll call him."

"Right now," Charlie states firmly.

I make a face. "Now?"

He lets out an irritated noise. "That's what I said."

"Can't I have a couple days?"

"No."

"One day?"

"We're not bartering. You have no leverage in this transaction." He takes a seat on an overturned canoe. "You now have five seconds."

"Ugh," I groan and pull out my cell phone. "If you weren't family, my bodyguard would have you pinned on the ground right now."

Charlie barely blinks. "The bodyguard who was too busy sucking your face to notice me? That one?"

Oh my fucking God!

I've lost the verbal tennis match that I didn't even want to play.

Quickly, I squat to talk on my cell, but I also want to sink into the ground. Let me just become a puddle on this floor.

I pinch the bridge of my nose as my phone rings.

"Sulli?" Beckett sounds concerned. Because why else would I call after all this time? Maybe he thinks I'd only reach out if I were on my deathbed.

Then again, I didn't even call to tell him about the cougar attack. The room is stifling all of a sudden. I feel like a jerk. It's been too long, and I don't know how to do this anymore. I'm the Friendship Assassin. Not the Friendship Necromancer. I don't know how to bring a friendship back to life.

I want to hang up.

"Sulli?" Beckett asks again. "Are you okay?" On the background of the call, I hear classical music. Songs to *Romeo & Juliet*, the ballet he's cast in. Unsure of his schedule, I can't determine whether he's at a rehearsal before the performance or whether he's backstage during it, but I also can't see him dipping out of an actual show just to talk to me.

Just like I wouldn't dip out of a swim meet to talk to him. Our dedication has been a link that ties us, an understanding that no one else really gets. And it feels good to be understood so deeply by someone.

Charlie clears his throat. I glance over at the canoes, and he gestures at my phone to speak.

"Um..." I swallow hard. "Yeah, I'm alright. I fucking guess. Charlie just blackmailed me into calling you." I don't even know why I told him the truth. It's just not natural to lie to Beckett.

He sighs heavily. "I apologize on Charlie's behalf." He must move somewhere quieter because the music falls more hushed. "Shit, I'm sorry," Beckett says, "this isn't how I wanted you to talk to me again."

"Well, it's fucking happening." I stare at the dirty floor tiles.

"Is he watching?"

"Yep."

Beckett laughs a little. "Then I'm sorry again. I'd tell you to hang up, but he probably won't find this call sufficient enough. Do you want me to hang up? You can pretend to keep talking for a bit."

Beckett is kind.

My dad used to always say that all the Cobalt boys are mischievous in some way. All but one.

Beckett.

Honest and kind. Though, he can be extremely blunt. I know that. And after he snuck around doing drugs, I'm not so sure my dad would say *today* what he used to say *back then.*

But right now, Beckett's kindness rushes back into me, almost as a reminder of the Beckett I grew older with, my best friend.

"No, it's okay," I whisper. "We can talk for a second."

My pulse ratchets up. On a steep incline.

The second you retire from swimming you're all of a sudden drinking alcohol and passing out—at least I'm not pointlessly destroying my body.

I push that memory back to ask, "How's ballet?" I want to ask whether he still "loathes" Leo Valavanis, his rival in the company, but those extra words lodge in my throat.

"It's challenging lately, but I like that about this performance we're on." He pauses. "How's swimming?"

"I'm climbing. Not swimming."

"I know, but your first love is swimming. First loves just don't go away." He uses *love* in context of a thing, a sport, an ambition—not a person. Beckett doesn't want to fall in love with anyone.

First loves.

The plural has me struggling not to picture both Akara and Banks. And I struggle even more not to share all that's happened with Beckett.

He's the one person I'd always confide in. Where everyone else has their number ones. Their friendship groups. Beckett is my person. And now he's just…not.

I settle with, "You're not going to ask what Charlie has on me?"

"I thought about it," Beckett says, "but I don't really deserve your secrets, and I think I need to earn this one."

I pinch the bridge of my nose harder, emotion trying to swell up. "I'm so fucking bad at friendships," I mutter to myself, but I know he can hear. And I ask, "Have I shut you out too long? Am I being unreasonable?"

"Yes," Charlie says.

"No," Beckett tells me on the phone. "I love you, Sulli, because you don't take any bullshit, and I flung a lot of shit at you." He sounds choked up. "I'm not any better at friendships, you know. I compete with every guy at my company. I have protective blinders up every time I talk to someone. Like they can't see below the bottoms of my eyelashes. I'm tired…so fucking tired of feeling on guard all the time. You're my best friend. I don't have to have any blinders with you." Except when it comes to cocaine.

He's never talked to me about it. I don't know if he will ever confide in me. It hurts to think we could become friends again, but not like before. Not the kind of friends who'd share everything in our lives.

The pain in my chest blossoms like an ugly glower. "I have to go," I say suddenly.

"Okay. I understand." I hear him take an audible breath, but his voice sounds tight. "Tell Charlie he's an asshole for me."

"Will fucking do."

"Bye, Sul."

"Bye, Beckett." I hang up and rise to a full stance.

Charlie stares from me to the cell in my hand like he can manifest his brother in this bait & tackle shop.

"We're even," I say.

Charlie's lips press together, and then he says, "For every day I have to keep your secret, you have to call my brother."

Anger flares. "That wasn't the deal, Charlie."

"It's a new deal." He pulls a sweater over his head, the color of winterberries. While he fits his arms through the holes, he adds, "Take it or leave it. It's up to you."

I have a feeling he'll just find a new creative way to get me to talk to Beckett if I don't.

And anyway, this deal is in my favor. I have more reassurance that he won't tell anyone about the kiss. Not if there's something consistently in it for him.

He has to know he gave me some power. Maybe he even wanted that.

I don't try to descend inside Charlie's head. All I do is hold out my pinky finger. "Deal."

He stares at my finger.

Rolling his eyes, Charlie locks his pinky with mine.

33

Banks Moretti

CHARLIE COBALT SAW Akara and Sulli kiss.

Fuck my motherfucking life.

I'll admit a seed of jealousy was planted somewhere on this trip, but it *barely* grew. It was a sprout.

My little sprout-ling of jealousy just ate fertilizer and grew into a giant beanstalk with the world's longest thorns. And somehow, it's growing inside me. Twisting around my organs.

Green doesn't even look good on me. I prefer blue. But I can't help it. I'm stupidly envious.

Truth: I wish Charlie caught me kissing Sulli. It wouldn't solve a goddamn thing, but it'd help the knot in my throat.

"This doesn't change anything," Akara whispers as the three of us hike through the dense woods. He carries Sulli's rope on his arm while Sulli grips her harness and a water bottle, sweat dripping down her temples. She just finished practicing Rattlesnake Knuckle for the day.

And everyone from the RV camp was there watching. Her cousins. And Oscar, Thatcher, Farrow. I was quietly pissy and in my feelings, but only Thatcher and Akara could tell. Sulli probably could more once she was on the ground.

Now that the RV *glampers* are off to their cushy pads, Akara is ready for my "silent brooding" to end and he's pushing me to talk about it. So now I have to *talk* about the green monster inside me. He already knows it's there.

While we pass towering tree after tree, Akara tells me, "Charlie's not going to tell anyone as long as Sulli keeps calling Beckett."

"And I will keep calling," Sulli assures me. "I'm following through."

Tendons in my shoulders and neck pull taut. Still tensed, I whack a branch out of my face. "Even if you call Beckett every minute of the day, I don't trust Charlie to keep his word." And then what—everyone knows Akara and Sulli kissed. My chances with her have plummeted to the darkest depths of the deep sea.

I knew my chances already existed there.

I've been chasing rejection from the start. But it doesn't change the despair inside me, which feels like a fatal wound, the final blow.

"Hey, I barely trust Charlie too," Akara admits in a friendly tone, "but it doesn't change things between the three of us." He's still trying to deescalate my jealousy.

A rough laugh sticks to my throat. "If this is a race, Akara, you're at the fucking finish line."

"That's not true." Sulli stops in her tracks on the slope of a wooded hill.

Akara and I halt further down the incline and turn to face her.

She gives me a hard look, then Akara. "I'm not going to base this decision on what other people know. If I did, I would have picked Banks days ago when Akara friend-zoned me in front of everyone." Her gaze hits mine. "And Jane thinks you like me."

Akara whips his head to me. "Did you tell Jane something?"

I honestly can't remember what I said to Jane at the motel.

"No," I say, then scowl in a grimace. "I told my brother Sulli and I kissed—"

"You idiot," Akara snaps.

"Hey, *hey*." Sulli races down the hill. Coming between us fast, she puts a hand to my chest and then Akara's. We're actually not moving in towards each other. We're just glaring. But I'm not gonna move the mermaid. I like her where she is.

To Akara, I say, "That was *ages* ago. Back at the motel before I even knew you two kissed."

Akara's shoulders slacken, relaxing.

I add, "My brother promised he wouldn't tell anyone. Not even Jane. She probably just thinks I like Sulli because I do. I'm not as good at hiding my feelings as you."

Akara runs his fingers through his hair, then mumbles, "I guess that's true."

"If it makes you feel any better," Sulli says to Akara, "if my little sister knew about this situation, she'd be cheering with Akara Kitsuwon pom-poms." Before my stomach plummets at *that* news, she swings her head to me. "And Jane's firmly Team Banks."

Yeah, I'm smiling.

Akara makes a face. "There are teams?"

"Unofficial fucking ones," Sulli pats our chests. "Just so we're clear, I'm Team Akara and Team Banks right now. Equally."

I believe her. She truly cares about me and Akara, and she's not going to needlessly string one of us along. When she knows who she wants to be with in the end—she'll tell us.

Akara snaps a finger to his palm, eyes on me. "So Thatcher knows you kissed Sulli. Charlie knows I kissed her. That sounds almost even."

"Almost," I agree. Because we both know Thatcher's more likely to take this secret to his grave than Charlie's likely to keep this secret to tomorrow.

Continuing our hike, we reach an area in the woods that has the best vantage of the Team Apex campsite, while we're out of earshot. All three of us crouch behind two large boulders.

I pass Sulli a pair of binoculars.

She puts down her harness and peers through the binoculars, looking out for movement. Before Sulli began her climb today, we released crickets in Team Apex's tents.

Now we wait.

Hopefully they'll spend as much time clearing out the insects as we did the snakes. I light a cigarette, and both Akara and Sulli shoot me disapproving looks.

I blow smoke away from them. "What? You two have never had a smoke during a stakeout before?"

They're trying not to smile.

Times like these, Akara would smoke a cigarette. He's a social smoker. But he must really want me to quit because he doesn't ask for one.

"I think I see their Jeep," Sulli whispers in eagerness. She lowers the binoculars to double-check.

Sure enough, the Jeep Wrangler is headed to their campsite. After everything, I need a win. Let this be one.

Akara's phone buzzes loudly in his pocket at the same time Sulli's chimes. She fumbles to remove it from her backpack on the ground, while Akara slides his out.

I take the binoculars and peer through.

They're piling out from the Jeep. Looks like they're aimed for the campfire, carrying bundles of logs. Thankfully they're not searching for the cellphones ringing out in the distance.

I'm about to ask Akara and Sulli who's calling, when my phone pings.

Xander Hale is sending a text to a group chat with Thatcher and me.

Rare.

He's only sixteen.

When we were his full-time bodyguards, he was supposed to only use the thread for emergencies since he's a minor and we report to his parents. Sometimes, though, he'd recommend us fantasy TV shows and books to watch. More so lately, our text communication is about boxing since Thatcher, Farrow, and I started to teach him on our days off-duty.

But the message I'm staring at now has nothing to do with Jon Snow or Frodo Baggins, the dweeby-looking elf, goblin thing, or sparring when we come home.

Banks. Thatcher. PLEASE don't let Donnelly get fired. It's not his fault!! – Xander

What in the fuck happened?

34

Akara Kitsuwon

SOMETIMES I HAVE TO remind myself that I don't work for Price Kepler anymore. Now that I own my own security firm, he can't fire me from Triple Shield. But Price isn't a bad guy. He's been there for Daisy Calloway since his early twenties.

Young.

So young.

And now I'm young, just twenty-seven to his forty-some-years, and I'm protecting Daisy's daughter. I've respected Price. Admired what he built. Having the Tri-Force—three leads to rule them all—awarded his men power alongside him.

He gave me power as a lead in his firm.

He respected my calls, my decisions. And when I told him I was creating a security firm, we were cordial.

But the minute Triple Shield had egg on their face from losing the girl squad in Anacapri—he began resenting me for building Kitsuwon Securities. Which looked shinier, better, newer, *younger*.

Recently, my firm has had missteps with temp guards screwing up and Charlie getting robbed at the Carnival Fundraiser. So Price should feel better.

Instead, he's just *patronizing* me ten-times more. Like my company is a liability to his company and a liability to these families.

That enrages me.

And as he lays into me over the phone right now, you'd think I was back in Philly and a brand-new bodyguard on *his* fleet.

My grip tightens harder on the cell. Pretty fast, I get the gist of what happened.

What I know: most of the parents were gathered at the Hale house, and they invited Price and the Epsilon lead over to talk about security at Dalton Academy, the prep school that the girl squad and Ben attend.

They heard a *splash*. When they ran outside, they saw Ben in the pool. Apparently, Xander and Ben were having an argument. Donnelly got between both teenagers to deescalate the situation, and Ben fell in the water.

Price thinks it's Donnelly's fault, and if the Alpha lead hadn't been there, I doubt this would even be a fucking issue.

Over the phone, Price is still fuming. "Paul Donnelly isn't being paid to interfere with their personal lives. That's not how we do things, Akara. That wasn't his job, and it's an abuse of a bodyguard's power—"

"An abuse of power?" I cringe and speak hushed. "Come on, Price, that's an over-dramatization of the situation and you know it." I lean back against the boulder but turn my head around the rock. I have a partial view of Team Apex in the growing dark. And while Banks has binoculars loose in his clutch, a cigarette burning between his lips, Sulli is between us on the phone too.

"Nona, slow down," Sulli tries to whisper, a finger to her ear. Even though it's not that loud in the woods. "You what? He *what?*"

Banks' eyes dart from her to Team Apex.

Currently, the rock climbers are chatting and throwing wood on a fire. The cricket prank in Montana is happening alongside major *high school* drama back in Philly. Xander Hale is the only minor who agreed to be a client in my firm, and I didn't think it'd be a point of contention until now.

"Ben's bodyguard wasn't there," Price emphasizes to me again. "They're teenagers. It shouldn't have been Xander's bodyguard versus *Ben*."

My nose flares. He's acting like Donnelly *purposefully* pushed Ben Cobalt into the pool. From the way he rehashed the details, it sounded like an accident, and I need Donnelly to recount the story himself.

Price hasn't told me *why* Ben and Xander were arguing or whether Ben is upset with Donnelly. He hasn't even brought up the parents' reactions. He's just fixated on the fact that Donnelly butted into *family* drama.

I lower my heated voice. "Have you talked to any of the parents?"

"No, not in length, but if Ben were my son, I'd want Donnelly fired *today*. I don't want him near my bodyguards or the minors. Put him somewhere he's not around Epsilon. Because the longer he's on Xander's detail, the more contact he has with SFE and the kids."

My jaw tics. Laughter from Team Apex cuts my gaze back to their campfire. They still haven't crept into their cricket-infested tents.

"You can't tell me?" Sulli says into her phone, looking horrified. "Is it fucking bad? Alright, I know…I know."

Banks reaches over Sulli and flashes me a text on his phone.

> Banks. Thatcher. PLEASE don't let Donnelly get fired. It's not his fault!! – Xander

That's a better indication that Xander still wants Donnelly to be his bodyguard. I nod to Banks while I tell Price, "It's not your decision on what happens to my men. It's going to come down to the clients. It always does, and if Xander wants—"

"What about his father?" Price interjects. "You really think Loren Hale will want Donnelly on his detail after tonight?"

"I'm not going to assume *shit*, Price. You haven't talked to Loren. I haven't talked to Loren. And if your men can't be professional with Donnelly and my bodyguards, then that's on you." I'm boiling, but I keep my voice leveled, and before he tries to interject, I add, "I have calls to make. You need something, contact Thatcher."

I hang up and dial a new number.

Sorry, Thatcher.

But I have to delegate, and Price's venting is a waste of my time. It's also a waste of Thatcher's, but his single-word responses will have Price clicking *end call* faster than if he were talking to me.

Sulli slumps down against the boulder. No longer watching Team Apex as she listens to her sister rehash the drama. How is Winona even involved?

Confusion grows on my end. As I put my phone back to my ear, I peer over the rock again. No new movement.

Banks blows smoke behind his shoulder, then keeps hawk-eyed on our rivalry with the other climbers.

The line clicks. "What's up, boss?" I hear *whassup*. Not only is his South Philly accent thicker than Banks', but he sounds in a rush right now.

"Hey, Donnelly. We need to talk about what happened quickly. Are you still at the Hale house?" I look more at Sulli than Team Apex since Banks has eyes on them.

She whispers, "But you're alright, squirt?"

Donnelly says hurried, "No, I'm off-duty. Already told Thatcher. I left the gated neighborhood about fifteen minutes ago. Is this about Price? I dunno what his beef is, boss, but he looked at me like I committed murder."

"What happened?"

"I was on-duty, you know. Just protecting Xander at the Hale house." No other client really requests bodyguards to go on-duty in the gated neighborhood, except Xander. I listen as Donnelly continues, "And he'd been outside near the pool talking to Ben." *Talking* sounds like *tawking*. "They were arguing because Xander wants to enroll in Dalton Academy after Christmas break, and Ben thinks it's a bad idea."

Shock stiffens my joints.

Xander has always been homeschooled.

"He told Ben he feels confident about it. Ben is just worried about him. He thinks he'd get peer-pressured. But they got heated since Xander wants to at least try and Ben isn't letting him do that," Donnelly pants like he's jogging.

Now I'm worried about *him*. "What are you doing, Donnelly?"

"Trying to beat the PPA." He grunts in a sprint. "I only had enough quarters for seven minutes, and I parked four blocks away to go grab a hoagie."

The PPA is Pennsylvania Parking Authority.

He rushes to say more. "And then Ben brought up what happened with Kinney at school. When he said that something like that could happen to Xander—Xander got upset."

I'm surprised he knows about the Kinney Hale incident at school. It happened months ago. But as the head of security, her parents gave me all the details. I even learned that Kinney told the Rainbow Brigade first.

Don't know how Ben or Xander found out, but I'm guessing Kinney told more people. It's mostly likely that Donnelly was in the room when she confided in Xander. Because clearly Donnelly's not asking me *what* happened to Kinney.

He continues, "Once Ben and Xander got closer to each other, Xander gave me a *look*."

"What kind of look?" I ask.

Banks glances at me, interested in my call because of Xander. And if we weren't trying to keep hidden from Team Apex, I would let him listen.

"Like *back me up*," Donnelly pants. "And I know we're supposed to stay out of family stuff, but you shoulda seen him, man. And all I did was step between them. Ben wobbled backwards. I didn't touch him, I promise. He's six-five and looked unbalanced, and I felt bad the moment he fell in. I startled Bambi, but I *didn't* touch him. I tried to help him out of the pool, but Price came in and acted like I was some…" He trails off. "I didn't touch him."

I'm irate. That Price would make Donnelly feel like a fucking axe murderer. "Hey, I believe you. You're not in trouble. Just log in your account of the event, send it to Thatcher. We'll have a security meeting when SFO is all back together."

"Sure thing." He inhales a sudden sharp breath. "You've gotta be kidding me."

"You get a ticket?"

"Yeah. Parking restrictions ended only three minutes ago." The car beeps over the line. "Got a hundred-dollar hoagie in my hand." He's referring to the cost of the fine.

"Kitsuwon Securities will pay for the ticket," I tell him, even though my company will be in a deficit the more I throw cash around. Hiring Michael Moretti wasn't cheap.

"Nah, I'm off-duty. I got it."

"You're driving a security vehicle." I watch as Sulli starts saying goodbye to her sister.

"Farrow let me borrow his Audi while he's gone. That's what I'm in now."

He should pay the fine then. But I'm uneasy about it.

I've noticed that Donnelly has been tattooing more while he's off-duty. He's even brought some of his tattoo clients to the apartment. And I'm not positive what he's blowing his money on.

Right now, he sounds like he has enough to cover the fine, so I don't argue with him.

Once we hang up, I tell Banks, "Xander's okay."

His shoulders ease.

Sulli ends her call with Winona and rotates towards the boulder. "Have they moved?"

"Still warmin' their cold hearts," Banks mumbles, cigarette between his lips. Yeah, sure enough, they're all just gathered around the fire. Still chatting.

Still laughing.

Their vocal happiness is almost as infuriating and grating as my talk with Price. Like five sets of nails scraping a chalkboard.

I pocket my phone. "Is Nona okay?"

"No." Sulli winces, looking between us, her voice grows hot as she tries to whisper, "She *punched* some fucking bastard in the hallway at school, and she won't tell me why. Just that he did something disgusting. She said that she can't explain more because Kinney told her in confidence or something."

Shit.

I go cold.

The incident at school—Kinney must've also told the girl squad.

"You know what happened?" Sulli realizes off my expression.

I nod, and I'm going to tell them. From my angle, the guy involved is a security threat, and if Xander really does go back to school, I'll need to tell the rest of SFO: Quinn, Banks, Thatcher. And I can see everyone finding out and Sulli being the only one in the dark.

She's the last to know a lot of things with her family, and I have the power to change that.

Quietly, I explain, "At Dalton, a guy followed Kinney into an art supply closet and showed his dick to her. He pressured her to touch his penis to *prove* that she's a lesbian."

Sulli's jaw is on the ground.

Banks mumbles Italian curse words.

"Fuck him," Sulli growls after shock wears off. "Good fucking job, Nona." To us, she reminds us like we forgot, "She punched him."

Her dad must be flipping out. He's been concerned Winona is being too much of a hothead like him. She can shift from a fun-loving sparkler to an explosive rocket. Sulli is more sparkler than firecracker, though she has that in her too.

I sit off of the boulder and tell Sul, "What goes around comes around."

Banks nods, "Good riddance." He passes Sulli the binoculars.

Eyeing us, she doesn't focus back on the other climbers yet. "That's not all." Sulli looks scared, alarmed, worried.

Banks asks, "What's wrong?"

"She got in trouble, didn't she?" I realize.

Sulli nods. "A two-week suspension for punching that fucking creep." We have no time to react. Team Apex suddenly unzips their tents.

As they crawl inside and start shrieking, the three of us rise to a stance. More visible to them as they race outside of their tents, shaking out their hair and clothes.

The one thing we're not going to do is run away.

Banks takes a drag of his cigarette.

And the climbers shout loudly, "Fuck her!" and "That Meadows *bitch*!"

I bite down hard. Glaring.

"You want to say that to my face!" Sulli shouts.

They look over at us, as we stand up on the hill.

And after a death-match staring contest, they ignore us and start cleaning out their tents.

Banks says, "Looks like both Meadows sisters got revenge today."

We should be clapping and celebrating, but the news about Winona looms heavy. And Sulli still seems tensed.

"There's something else," she says ominously. "Now that Winona doesn't have school, she said my parents agreed it'd be okay if she flew out here." Sulli looks from me to Banks. "I said *yes.* I couldn't say no. I wouldn't…" She pauses. "My sister is coming to Yellowstone."

Shit.

As if things couldn't be more complicated.

I reach out and steal the cigarette from Banks' mouth. Putting it to my lips, I take the longest drag, filling my lungs. I pass it back as I blow out smoke.

And we watch Team Apex huff and puff around their camp, the only source of victory at the moment. And it's fleeting.

Sullivan Meadows

MY BODY IS ON FIRE.

Not the sexy kind of fucking fire, but more like the itchy can't-stop-scratching-my-armpits kind of fire. It's so un-sexy, but I don't much care because there is no relief from these ant bites.

After our cricket retaliation, I thought we finally won. Four days of no response. Until last night. Team Apex went up a notch in the prank war and let loose fire ants into our tent.

Knowing Moffy is deathly allergic to fire ants made me even angrier. He wasn't there (thank fucking God), but if Akara, Banks, or I had been allergic, the prank would've killed us.

I was so angry, I tried to not even give them the satisfaction of any reaction. Instead, the three of us just casually ditched the tent and slept in Booger last night.

Now, I feel myself reacting.

"I can't believe we're letting Team Apex win," I say in frustration. We walk down the rows of RVs for rent. Banks and Akara flank me on either side, while the sales associate charges out front. He has the *perfect* RV to show us. Unless it comes with water balloons that I can sling at those climbers' faces, it won't be perfect.

Maybe it's easier to concentrate on this pseudo-competition between Team Apex and us, than the romantic one where I'm playing referee and judge. It's definitely helping calm my nerves, and considering

Winona is coming to Yellowstone *today*, I'll take anything to help scrub the words *love triangle* off my forehead.

"They're going to keep escalating," Akara tells me. "We have to walk away." He's in protect-Sullivan-Minnie-Meadows mode, which does not fit into a prank war.

Banks is rubbing lotion onto his arms. "Agreed. Next they're going to do something that'll be harder to clean. Like squirting silly-string in our tent—"

"That's a great idea!" I clutch Banks' bicep. "They'll never see it com—"

"No," Akara says. "It's over."

I slouch, limbs deflating with my fucking hopes. "I hate losing."

"We know," Akara and Banks say at the same time. They give each other an aggravated look, and then Banks passes me the bottle of lotion.

I take it just as the sales associate, Neil, stops in front of a white travel trailer. We already told him our basic needs. Sleeps 3 and weighs less than three-thousand pounds.

Booger has pulled four-thousand pounds of trailer behind her before, but for this trip, I'm not testing fate by setting new records.

"You can have a look inside," Neil says, waving to the trailer. Akara goes in first and I follow. As I scope the area, Neil gives a play-by-play of what I see. "Bathroom in the back. Kitchenette in the middle and at the front is a Queen bed. The dinette area converts to a single bed."

Banks brushes up against me as he squeezes into the small hallway. Our eyes hold for a long beat, a knowingness that we're sort of together in a way. *Dating.* My lips lift, and I heat up a bit. I wince when he hits his head on the top of the trailer.

"Oh fuck." I cup the back of his head. "Are you alright?"

"Yeah." His shadow of a smile appears while he ducks, his eyes on me.

I'm still touching his head. Gripping his soft, brown hair, I'm really fucking loving the way he's looking at me right now. His smile keeps growing.

My heart flip-flops.

I'm giddy, until I question how much of an insensitive asshole I'm being. Because Akara is right here. Watching.

His Adam's apple noticeably bobs like he's swallowing a rock.

I don't want to hurt him.

I don't want to hurt anyone.

Someone is going to get hurt, Sulli. I know. I fucking know, but I just hate that I keep sinking a knife in their hearts before I've even chosen.

Thankfully, Neil helps segue the moment. "Take a look around."

There's not much to see, and I'm about to scratch this one off based on Banks hitting his head, but he beats me to it.

"Don't worry about me," he says. "It's not like I'm doing jumping jacks in here. I'll just be racking out, and I'd rather not let Booger carry a bigger trailer." He rests his ass against the kitchenette counter and bends his legs a little, giving his neck a rest from ducking. "See? I'm good."

Akara is already shaking his head, then drops his voice to a whisper. "We need to get a bigger one."

"Why?" I frown. "This is close to perfect."

He already knows my sister wants to sleep in a tent, and she understands why I'm switching to an RV.

Akara explains, "The Yale boys are going to ask where we're all sleeping in this thing."

"Fuck," Banks says, realizing the same thing as Akara. But I still don't see the problem.

My frown deepens. "I don't get it. I'm taking the single and you two are cramming in the Queen. Right?"

Banks points to the dinette area, a table and two cushioned seats. "That doesn't have a mattress."

"So?" It still *converts* into a bed. There's another cushion stored somewhere. The table lowers and the extra cushion goes on top. Winona won't bat an eye, so why would Farrow and Oscar?

"The Yale boys won't believe I let you sleep there over the bed," Akara says. "It's going to draw attention."

"Cumbuckets," I mutter and ignore a weird look from Neil. "Fine. We can find something that has a bunk."

We all exit, and Neil claps his hands together. "We find a winner?"

Akara takes over, knowing that I don't love small talk. "Unfortunately, it's just a little small for us. We'd like to see another."

Neil nods and looks between the three of us. "Maybe if I knew your situation better, I could help." He eyes Banks' height like that's the sole problem. I've always been the one given a double-take for my height, so I know how it feels. But definitely not to the extent that Banks gets.

Neil asks him, "Are you sleeping in the bed or the single?"

"Wherever," Banks says.

"The bed," Akara and I refute together.

Neil narrows his eyes at me. "So the couple is in the bed." He looks to Akara. "And you're on the single."

Couple.

Couple!

Cum-nugget, he thinks Banks and I are together. It was me holding Banks' head that gave Neil that conclusion, wasn't it? I roast a shade of red. "Um," I say, feeling Akara's hurt in the air. "We're not a couple."

Banks' jaw tenses.

Fuck.

I'm fucking this up.

"They're actually both taking the bed," I say quickly, motioning from Banks to Akara. "We're all just friends here."

"Good friends," Banks says.

"*Really* good friends," Akara adds like he's trying to top Banks.

Okay, lots of testosterone is pumping into the air right now. I am both turned on and worried that they're going to start testing the boundaries of their friendship.

I am not a Friendship Assassin. If I repeat it enough in my head, maybe it'll be true.

Neil looks a little freaked out but he covers quickly by pointing to another trailer. "This one might be better suited for three friends."

As we follow him, my phone buzzes.

Sulli-Bear! I'm pulling in to the RV place now. Can't wait to see your gorgeous face <3 – Nona-Frog

She adds a ton of nature emojis, and my chest swells like I'm about to rush downstairs on Christmas morning. My sister is here. Then I suddenly remember all I'm keeping from her.

Cougar attacks.

Bachelorette-style dating with my bodyguards.

Hey, at least I'm still vegan.

My stomach sinks regardless. I've realized that I won't be able to hide the cougar attack. Clothes conceal most of our healing wounds, but we still have visible scratches. Plus, the bite mark on Akara's elbow is in plain sight. She'll ask.

I won't lie.

And so I'll finally have to come clean.

I quickly text her back a big smiley face and hearts.

Akara whispers into his mic, and I think he's probably giving our location to Winona's bodyguard. Greer Bell is on Security Force Epsilon, which means that for the first time this whole trip, someone from Price's Triple Shield is here.

It's going to put a strain on Akara, seeing as how his company is in an unofficial competition with Price's.

Even though Price Kepler has been my mom's bodyguard for *so long*—before I was even born—my parents still weren't upset that Akara jumped ship and started his own firm. My mom was really fucking excited for him. She said it suited him more being his own boss.

As Neil stops at a sleek black trailer, I hear off in the distance, "Ca-Caw! Ca-Caw!"

I cup my hands to my mouth. "Ca-Caw! Ca-Caw!"

My little sister rounds the corner with the biggest smile. Her backpack thwacks against her as she races towards me. Her copper-haired bodyguard jogs next to her, not having a hard time keeping up with my fifteen-year-old sister.

I close the distance and we hug tight. She's only an inch shorter, and with thick-soled Timberland boots, we're the same height. Wearing cargo pants and a men's baggy, khaki-colored button-down knotted at her belly button, she looks pretty fucking cool.

"How was the flight?" I ask as we break away. "Are you hungry? I've got snacks in Booger."

"I had food on the plane." Nona bounces on her feet, dropping her backpack to the ground. And she holds out her hand.

I smile big as I shake her hand into a fist-bump, then it devolves in a much longer sequence. A secret greeting formed one muggy summer at Camp Calloway. Two hip-bumps, we throw our arms in the air, rattling them to the sky, then spin in two circles. Crouching low, we're face to face again and flutter fingertips to fingertips. Then I hook her elbow with mine and we skip 'round, howling at the sky.

And we don't pull apart.

Instead, we draw nearer, our foreheads pressed together in a huddle. My arms around her shoulders, her arms around mine. This close, she's all I see.

I'm all she sees.

Private. At least for us. We're fucking aware other people are watching. They're always watching, but in this moment, in our huddles, it's just me and my sister.

Winona whispers with a smile, "I wish you would've been on the plane ride here—Greer was *rolling* at my farts."

I laugh, smiling so much my face hurts, realizing just how much I missed her.

"They smelled *horrible.* I tried to hold them in."

"You did?" I whisper skeptically.

"I did," she grins. "My stomach hurt when we landed I tried so hard. I didn't want to asphyxiate every passenger, they were *that* bad, Sulli." We laugh together. "This one prick behind us thought Greer was the farter. It got so bad that the guy told Greer to stop passing gas, and I told him, *sir, I've been farting, not him.* The guy looked like he saw a ghost. He said nothing, just shrunk backwards in his seat."

We laugh again, and as the sound fades, her brown, hazel-flecked eyes rest softly on my green. It's my turn to share in our safe, private huddle.

I could bring up something funny. Like how my boob itches from at least three ant bites. But that's not really what I need to share. What I *want* to share.

Because I want to tell her the truth about what I did. I'm just scared of my sister's reaction.

Foreheads still pressed together, I drop my gaze. "After a practice climb on this route called The Bitterroot Buttress, Akara, Banks, and I were hiking back to our camp...and two cougars stalked us."

Winona holds her breath. I'm not looking, but I feel air vacuum between us.

"I killed a cougar, Nona." Pressure mounts on my chest like the animal is back on my body. "I used the gun Dad gave me, and I killed her." I finally raise my eyes to hers.

Tears are streaming down her soft cheeks.

"Why are you crying?" My voice breaks.

"I'm crying because you're crying." Her chin quakes. My face is wet.

I try to laugh but it cracks. "I'm sorry, Nona." I'm so afraid she's going to look at me differently, but her wet lashes and glassy eyes stay on me with condolences and love.

"I don't think I could've done it, Sulli." She cries with me. "I would've let the cougar kill me."

"Stop."

"No, I would've. And it's good. It's good that you were the one there..." We're both nodding to each other, foreheads together, sucking in snotty tears. "It's good," Winona breathes, "because Mom and Dad can't lose either of us. And I can't lose you, not to an animal, not to a mountain—I just can't." We shift our heads and come together in the tightest hug, tears soaking each other's shoulders.

We stay like that for a few more minutes. And she asks if I got hurt. I tell her about everyone's wounds, but that we're all okay.

She's not disappointed in me for taking an animal's life. She's just happy that I'm alive. Weight eases off my chest.

When we separate, we dry our faces with our shirts, and she rests her head on my shoulder for a beat. For once, I feel like the older sister. And I realize it's her fear of losing me that causes this change.

WHILE AKARA DOTS ALL THE I'S AND CROSSES THE T's, all the paperwork involved in renting an RV, Winona and I loiter around the office's vending machines. We unscrew bottles of Ziff and chat about her suspension.

I've done a decent job hiding the love triangle because she hasn't said a thing or even done a double-take.

Score for Sulli! I could pump my fist in the air.

I smile into my Ziff.

Off to the side of us, I hear Banks say, "Greer, nice beard."

It pulls my attention to my sister's bodyguard. Sure enough, Greer has grown a somewhat thick beard. It's the same copper-red as his hair. He has a muscular build, and his left earlobe is bitten off.

When I was little, he used to tell me a shark bit him. Eight-year-old me was very fucking fascinated by that fact. As I got older, I called him on his bullshit, and he admitted it was a bar fight at eighteen and some drunk guy took a chunk out of him.

He won the fight apparently, but it's still horrific in my mind. And that's also when I realized why my parents didn't try to force him to tell me and Nona the truth when we were kids.

It's kind of hard to believe Greer had been my bodyguard for eight years. Since he was twenty-two and I was only eight, we weren't friends. But he wasn't a jerk, and he's still really nice to my sister.

More so, I think Akara and Greer were friends at a certain point. Honestly, I can't say for sure. It's hard to grasp the bodyguard relationships from my vantage. But I can't imagine they weren't at least friendly before Kitsuwon Securities. They spent a whole ton of time together on my family trips.

"But they *did* ground you?" I ask Winona since that part has been vague.

"Sort of. Dad said when I get back, I can't be on the internet for the weekend." She shrugs with a smile. Our dad has to know that's not much of a punishment for Nona. She's rarely on the internet. "Mom said he smiled when he heard who I punched. But he's all like, *I'm not trying to fucking promote violence in this household.*" Her imitation is spot on.

I laugh. "So they didn't want to fly out with you?" On this trip, I've talked to my parents only a handful of times, mostly to check-in, say hi and *I'm alive.* Our phone calls have been nowhere near the almost daily that I'm used to, so I don't know where their heads are at.

Winona sips the sports drink, then wipes a dribble down her lip where a scar lies. "I wondered the same thing. I thought they would've wanted to see you climb." She begins to smile. "But Mom told me this is your great, wild adventure, and you need this time without them."

My eyes burn and well with emotion.

She knew—my mom knew this trip would be more than just the spirit of climbing. That it'd *become* so much more.

I smile into a soft laugh. *Thanks, Mom.* I feel like I'm on the right path, even if it's an uncertain one.

36

Akara Kitsuwon

SULLI IS AT LEAST a hundred feet off the ground. As she ascends Rattlesnake Knuckle, the crack in the slab of rock widens so much that her legs stretch further and further apart. Firmly rooted between the fissure, she releases a hand off the rock to shake out her right arm.

She still has on a harness.

And rope.

She's solo climbing, placing safety gear up the rock face, and once she reaches the top, she'll rappel down and clear it all.

I remind myself that she's safe if she falls—because the nervous audience watching her climb right now is making *me* more edgy and apprehensive.

There might not be a football stadium of people gawking at Sulli, but there are a *lot* of eyes and even a few cameras.

From Jane, Maximoff, Charlie—to Farrow, Thatcher, Oscar—to Jack Highland-Oliveira, his sixteen-year-old brother Jesse—to Greer and Winona—and we can't forget about the baby and the puppy.

And I saved the *shittiest* for last: Team Apex decided to observe Sulli for the day like they're suddenly fans. They've parked their asses on a hill. Adding to a broiler of intensity that burns up inside of me. My gaze cuts between so many people.

When really, I wish I could just focus on Sulli. It wouldn't be that bad if everyone knew we were dating. Because at least I could've kissed her before she ascended. Shit, I've watched her climb *countless* times throughout my life, but it's hitting me how different it's been in Yellowstone.

I want to smother her with affection. To hold her cheeks and whisper dirty things in her ear. To put my lips to hers before she climbs four-hundred feet in the air.

But with everyone here, it's like I'm only her bodyguard.

Her friend.

Like we've shot backwards, and I can't paddle to the place I want to be. That feeling settles inside me like a chainsaw. *Just friends.*

Only friends.

I've never hid my affection in a relationship. I hate this. And the worst part: *this* is all either me or Banks will ever get with Sulli. One of us will never know more.

On the grass beneath the cliff-face, Banks is standing beside me, toothpick between his lips. He gives me a look like I'm pacing around the rock and biting my nails.

All I'm doing is running my palms back and forth. Under my breath, I tell him, "I liked it better before." I catch his gaze for a second. "When it was just the three of us."

"Yeah." Banks nods about five times. "Me too."

We both go rigid. Watching *Winona* climb a traditional route parallel to her older sister. Placing gear, she's the lead climber while Maximoff is her belay, climbing about six-feet below.

While Winona stops at an anchor she just placed, she grips a Canon camera strapped around her neck. And she films Sulli.

Jack should be up there.

He's climbed and filmed Sulli before. But apparently at the RV camp yesterday, he tore a muscle in his shoulder playing basketball with most of SFO and Jesse.

I wasn't there. But as the story goes, Oscar raided every RV for ice, even knocked on other campers' RV doors to gather *more* ice. Ensuring his husband had proper first-aid.

Jack's seventeen-year-old shaggy-haired, surfer brother is here to help shoot, but Jesse isn't that skilled at rock climbing. Winona ended up offering to get some footage for the production team. She loves photography, but mostly, she was just excited to climb next to her sister.

I run my palms together a few more times, glance at Banks. Glance at Team Apex. Glance at her cousins. Glance at Ripley. *Baby needs a bodyguard.* Glance at SFO and Jack's cameras. A tripod is set-up near me and Banks. The lens is aimed at Sulli.

Jack adjusts the camera on the tripod. His teenage brother is squatting closer to the rock face, filming from a different angle.

My eyes flash back to the rock at sudden movement. *Winona.* She drops her Canon. Hooked to her neck, the camera thumps against her chest, then she slips.

Maximoff pushes off the rock with his feet, giving her slack as the rope catches her fall.

Sulli never flinches. Still focused, she rises.

"Watch out for those fire ants! I hear they can be bad around here!" Lincoln on Team Apex *yells* up at Sulli.

Now she flinches, and instinct propels me towards these *idiots.* I'm boiling and running, and Banks is hot on my heels. Just as livid, and we're not even twenty-feet on them when they bolt.

Racing away like—

"Fucking cowards," Banks growls the words I feel.

Breathing hard, we glance back at Sulli.

She's rappelling.

I head quickly to the tripod. "Did she slip?" I ask Jack.

He shakes his head. "I think she was freaked out."

I frown, and Banks' eyes tighten on Sulli, more concerned. Like a boyfriend would be. Jealousy bites at me.

Banks is on my side. Better to have him overly concerned about Sulli than only partially. That's what I'm telling myself.

I rest my hands on my neck, hot with frustration from so many directions. And I whisper to Banks, "We should've cut them out on Day 1, not had a prank war."

"It's too late now."

What was I thinking?

Probably, *have fun with Sulli.* Yeah. I can't help it—I enjoy having fun with her, spending time with her, kissing her. I remember shopping for crickets, trying to pay for her, taking her on an afternoon date.

Regretting the prank war means taking back those moments, and I won't return those. Not for any price, not for anything. So I shelve the bowl of Instant Regret this time.

But Team Apex *can't* distract Sulli while she climbs. If she'd been free-soloing today, she could've fallen and been severely injured or died.

My muscles tighten. "Next time they come back to watch her, we threaten them," I tell Banks like an order.

He nods, "Don't have to tell me twice." He's all-in.

Intimidation is literally our best bet.

SULLI SAFELY ON THE GROUND, WE ALL START packing up to leave.

I help Sulli coil her rope, and Banks hands her a water bottle. Close by, Jack is on his knees packing up the tripod in a case.

He catches my eyes. "Same old, same old, right?" he asks in a staple-Jack-Highland-smile. Bright and charismatic—the kind that made me not trust him. Now, I know that smile as purely genuine.

But being real, constant positivity is off-putting to me after a while. I wouldn't hang out with the sunshine Care Bear every day of the week, so I take Jack in small doses. It's one of many ways we've maintained a good friendship after a rocky start.

Same old, same old.

He's trying to be casual and friendly while production is intermingling with security. I like Jack, but I *hate* production.

Cameras impede security. Their presence is a bullseye on all clients. Passersby will see the camera crew before the famous person and immediately run over to play *spot that celebrity.*

Luckily, we're not in the city right now. And there aren't many threats around.

I smile back. "The same old shit never really gets old for me." I could watch Sulli climb and swim every day for the next hundred years.

He nods, snapping buckles on a black case. "I've been meaning to tell you, there's a new crew member on *We Are Calloway* who's single. She's super cute. I talked you up for a solid ten and gave her your number."

My stomach pole-vaults in the ground. "You what?"

Sulli definitely overhears. She turns her back to Jack and me.

Shit.

Banks looks between us like pain is rushing in, a hole in a boat that I can't plug fast enough.

He wants to comfort her. I know he does.

Jealousy gnaws harder at me, but a part of me wishes one of us could hug her right now without drawing suspicion.

"I gave her your number." Jack frowns at my distraught reaction. "Is that okay?"

I'm barely breathing.

Jack thinks I'm single.

But I'm actually taken.

Mentally, physically, emotionally closed off to anyone but Sulli right now, and the thought of uttering the words, *I'm single* to Jack is going to kill me.

It'll be like casting that into the universe. Breathing reality into it. And then I'll wake up in Philly without her.

Single.

And I can't lie again. Not like last time. It eviscerated me, and it'll eviscerate her.

I try to deflect. "You're still wingman-ing for me as a married man?"

He stands up. "It's actually easier now to send women in your direction. Her name is Jennifer by the way."

Sulli takes the largest swig of water. Her back still to me.

Awesome.

Another *Jennifer*. Sulli already saw the first Jenny before Yellowstone, and now there's another waiting for me back there.

"She might call you," Jack adds.

Perfect.

Just perfect.

I force a smile and run a hand through my hair. "Thanks," I say into a nod, about to add a *but.*

Sulli just thuds to her ass on the ground. My whole body clenches in pain. Like I emotionally kicked her.

Shit.

Just shit.

Banks crouches down to Sulli, and quickly, I say the rest to Jack, "But I'm not interested. Can you tell her that for me?"

"Yeah, no problem." His attention swerves as Jesse approaches.

"Kuya, don't lift that," Jesse says, jogging faster. "Let me help."

I slip away and walk around Sulli. Facing her, just as Banks stands up.

She inhales a strong breath. "Two Jennifers?"

I hold out a hand. "One Sullivan."

Her lips rise, and she clasps my hand. I help Sulli to her feet.

Unfortunately for me—Jane, Maximoff, and Winona crowd around Sulli. Pushing me and Banks further back from her.

Once we start heading to the RV campsite, I lead out front, and Banks jogs up to my side. I can feel the stress emit off him like toxic smoke.

"What's wrong?" I ask, readjusting my radio. The trail back to camp hasn't been cleared in a while, and I'm careful not to trip on rotted logs. "Is it Sul?" I glance back, but she's still chatting with her family.

He shakes his head, but mention of Sulli causes his eyes to find her too. "Caterer just called and said he's fresh out of oysters, and I'm now fresh out of fucks." He unzips his outer jacket like he's heating up. "I'm thinking about buying a tombstone to bring to the bachelor party. Seeing as how I've died about a billion times trying to plan it."

Jack overhears. "Why are we even having oysters at this thing?"

Banks says, "Because I'm a dumbass and asked Charlie fucking Cobalt what he and his brothers would like to eat."

"It sounds like he's messing with you," Jack says. "He'll eat anything you give him."

I'd ask how he knows, but he's married to Charlie's bodyguard. And he's doing a personal travel videography for Charlie, which has given Oscar and Jack more time to be together. Plus, the newlyweds have been filming *Suddenly Famous*, a miniseries that I'm surprised Oscar agreed to do. More media attention makes the job harder and being Charlie's bodyguard is already near-impossible.

Banks makes a wounded noise. "I'm getting punked by a twenty-one-year-old."

Sulli slides between Banks and me. "Charlie is twenty-two."

"Same difference," Banks says.

His words fall into quiet, and our eyes drift to each other. None of us touch or flirt. A longing exists. A desire to just…*be*. I didn't realize how free I felt with Sulli and Banks until it was taken away.

Now I feel caged.

I brush a tense hand through my hair. I'm just waiting until we head into our own RV and break apart from everyone else. So we can be ourselves again.

37

Sullivan Meadows

AFTER A CAMPFIRE AND s'mores with my family and our bodyguards, everyone splits up and heads to their respective outdoorsy lodgings.

"Sweet dreams, squirt," I tell Winona while she slips into her sleeping bag.

"I love you *s'more* every day, sis," she says in a yawn.

"I love you *s'more* every minute." I smile and reach into her tent. "Avo-cuddle." I wrap my arms around my sister. Winona squeezes back even tighter.

When I exit, I zip up the flaps. Outside the entrance, Greer unfurls a foam mat and thermal sleeping bag on the dirt. So far, Greer seems to have played nice with Security Force Omega. He even joined us at the campfire and made a marshmallow-less s'more.

Banks thinks Greer isn't starting shit because he's the only Epsilon bodyguard here. Outnumbered. But Akara said it's because they all have a common enemy right now.

Team Apex.

After those fucking creeps heckled me while I was climbing today, every bodyguard is on high alert. I hope Team Asshole just sticks to fucking with me. If they go after Winona…

I bristle.

And grimace.

I don't want to even think about it. Greer is planning to crash under the stars in the October cold. I'm guessing it's the best vantage to protect my sister, and I feel better knowing he has her back.

Greer nods to me. "Night, Sulli."

"Night," I say as I pass, and Banks follows at my side. Anticipation grows on our trek to our trailer, nestled in the woods next to my forest-green Jeep. It's felt like fucking *eons* since we've had any sort of privacy from my family and his friends.

"After you, mermaid." Banks holds open the door for me.

My lungs are light as air as I breathe in. "Thanks." I can't stop fucking smiling, but as I start to draw curtains closed over the half-windows, I spot Akara alone at the dying campfire. A phone is pressed to his ear.

I know it's a business call.

"He's been on the phone for a lot longer than usual." I glance in concern to Banks.

Coming up beside me, Banks peers out the window and mutters, "Don't envy his job one bit." He looks to me. "He's been coordinating temp guards for the bachelor-bachelorette parties. All of us are going off-duty that night, so we need extra hands, and Akara is waist-deep in *logistics*."

"You're not a logistics kind of guy?" I ask, drawing the curtains shut, but I fucking swear Akara glances to the trailer just as I do.

"No, intricacies like that are mind-numbing to me." Banks brushes past my frame to reach a panel above the dinette. My heart palpitates as his chest skims along my boobs. While he pushes a few buttons, he continues, "I don't know how Thatcher and Akara do it half the time." Warmer air blows through the A/C above the queen-bed in the back. He cocks his head to me. "I'm a follow-through with Akara's logistics kind of guy."

I nod a lot, smiling so fucking much. "Yeah, I can tell."

His mouth curves up in a crooked, sexy smile the longer we stare at each other with a quiet understanding. That we really like each other's company.

That we both want to be together rather than all alone.

Banks glances at the locked door, then at me as he edges closer. Not much space in the tiny trailer to move, we're already close enough that I feel heat radiate off his six-seven build. He curls a strand of hair behind his ear that tries to get in his eyes. Eyes that haven't abandoned me. Eyes that speak Encyclopedias-worth of words and attraction.

He's such a beefcake.

My beefcake.

Those overwhelming feelings swell up in me—how much I really, *really* want Banks to be mine. It's easier to come to these conclusions when I'm alone with each of them. Harder, when we're all together.

With Banks this close, more warmth bathes me. Maybe he shouldn't have turned up the trailer's heat. It reminds me of *water.*

Being so focused on climbing has just put swimming on the backburner, but it's something that I'll always enjoy, always love.

Out loud, I realize, "It's been a while since I've been swimming."

He holds my gaze. "You're the kind of mermaid who'll die if you don't get wet?"

That sexual innuendo was so good that I smile bigger. "I'm totally a need-to-get-soaking-wet kind of mermaid. Preferably by large bodies of water."

He bounces his head in a nod. "I've seen a large body around here somewhere."

We're both grinning, our eyes on each other's lips, but I'm surprised when Banks nods to the door. "You want to go before it gets too cold? That hot spring we all found along the river hasn't moved."

He's asking me out.

I inhale, and air feels so paper-thin like I'm breathing in helium. High on this moment. "Yeah, I'd fucking love that." And then I look to the curtains I shut. *Akara.* Guilt creeps in, and I'm wincing.

Banks notices my switch in mood. "We can invite him along."

I feel torn. Conflicted. And I shake my head. "That's not fair to you."

He shrugs, hands spread open. "I'd like more time alone with you, but I know doing it will hurt my best friend, and while we're out there, you'd be thinkin' about how you're hurting him too, probably even more than me. I've lived with a lot of pain in my life, and I'd honestly just rather do the least painful thing."

"Me too," I say in a quiet breath.

So we agree to wait for Akara. After packing towels in a backpack, we find ourselves on the ground. Not even on the mattress. Side by side, we lean against the queen-bed, our asses on the floor, like it's more comfortable than blankets.

Banks seems like someone who adapts well in any odd situation, any odd place. From a dingy motel to primitive camping to a tiny RV, he hasn't complained really or asked to turn back.

It's attractive, how much he's up for anything.

"When I was a kid," I tell him, "I used to watch this movie over and over on rainy days." Our eyes meet. "*Little Giants*."

His lip lifts. "I've seen that one."

"Really?"

"Yeah, surprisingly." He slides his arm across my shoulders, and everything about the maneuver lights up my body. His touch is chock-fucking-full of *I'm so into you* and *let's never let this end*. He asks, "That's the kid's movie about football?" Off my nod, he explains, "I played football growing up, so I watched it a bunch."

I draw more into him. "So you know Becky the Icebox? She's the daughter of the coach and the only girl on the football team." Off *his* nod, I tell him, "I related to her in a lot of ways when I was young—she wanted to compete with the boys, but she also had this stupid crush on Junior, who just saw her as the Icebox: a friend, plus a great football player."

Banks listens.

"And I'd yell at the fucking TV, *Look at her, Junior!* And as much as I loved the movie, I hated that ending."

"Why?" His brows pull together. "I thought Junior finally comes around and gets with Becky."

"But that's after she decides to be a cheerleader." I tuck my legs closer to my chest. "I get the whole message. She wanted to be a princess and a football player. Becky *and* the Icebox, and girls can be both things, but I guess I only identified as the Icebox. And it made me feel like one day I'd need to become the cheerleader in order to get the guy in the end." I add, "Maybe that's partly why romance was never on my radar growing up. I didn't want to be hurt knowing that me, as I am, isn't fucking attractive enough to the guys I liked."

Banks looks deeper into me. "For what it's worth, I never liked Junior."

I break into a shocked smile. "No way, didn't every guy want to be Junior?"

"I thought he was an idiot." Banks smiles more, seeing mine. "Boys are stupid at that age. And then most turn into bigger stunads." *Stunad* basically means an idiot. I remember that Italian-American word since he uses it a lot. "But I'll fuckin' admit, I did some Junior-like things as a kid too."

"Like what?"

"I practiced how to kiss using my hand."

I touch my chest with a laugh. "Fuck, so did I." We're both grinning again. "Although, it probably didn't help me much. I feel like it's nothing like the real thing." I clutch his bicep, more seriously. "Be honest, am I a shitty kisser? Because I've only kissed…" I trail off at the unspoken, awkward thing.

I've only kissed *three* guys, and one of them happens to be dating me too.

Banks tenses, under-fucking-standably. With an exhale, he pushes through that awkward bit, and I love him for it.

My heart palpitates again.

"You're not a shit kisser. I think if two people are feeling each other, it's harder for the kiss to be bad." His confidence edges along that crooked, sexy smile. "I've had enough *bad* kisses to know that kissing you is like a touchdown during a Super Bowl."

I breathe in. "That's a good line." I eye his lips, my pulse drumming.

"First time I've used it." He nods to me. "And it's true."

My whole body is vibrating in desire, in want. Turned *on* like a million-watts, and I ache for his rough grip, wanting him to explode forward.

Just as he moves in, the door unlocks.

Akara is frozen, keys in his hand. Like he walked in on Banks taking my virginity. That did *not* happen, but it'd be a royal fucking lie to say I haven't thought about him inside me.

But I've also thought about Akara inside me too.

My heard is whirling, and I'm still turned on. Quickly, Banks and I scramble up to our feet together. "We're going to the hot springs, Kits." I toss the backpack at him.

It thuds at his chest and falls.

Fuck.

38

Akara Kitsuwon

OKAY.

Okay.

Breathe.

I've seen them flirt before. Shit, I've seen Banks eat her out already. Jealousy claws at my heels, but I kick it away fast.

I'm hanging onto my relationship with Sulli. Confident in my feelings for her and her feelings for me and what we share. Regardless of what she has with Banks.

I clear a pit in my throat. "I just ran into Jane." I pocket my keys. "She asked me if I wanted to crash in Charlie's RV tonight. So you two could have privacy."

Sulli rests a hand over her face, hiding from the train wreck I just experienced. "Oh my fucking God," she mumbles. "*Jane*." She drops her hand with a sigh. "Now I feel badly about complaining about the bride-to-be—who is so fucking rad that she'd try to orchestrate a way to get me alone time with the guy she knows I like."

Banks can't hold in a smile.

"Now how is *this* fair?" I ask him. "You don't see Charlie trying to whisk you to his RV so *I* can have alone time with her."

"No," Banks says, "he's just the one who'll probably tweet to the world, *Akara and Sulli are in a relationship*."

He has a point.

Still, I'm envious that Jane is playing wing-woman to Banks *and* Sulli. While I'm scrounging in the depths of every hell trying to find time with Sul. At this point, if a demon said they could give me an extra hour with her, I'd be willing to pay any price.

But I also hate knowing I might've taken something from Sulli and Banks. Why am I not jumping for fucking joy that I cut their little floor-flirting thing short? What's *wrong* with me? I should be so happy that I interrupted them when *I* have deep feelings for her.

You care about them, Nine.

Yeah.

And I also just want to be here. I've wanted to be here with *her* all day, and I'll even take Banks here with us. "So hot springs?"

Sulli comes closer. "Wait, what'd you tell Jane?"

"That I *love* eating string beans."

Sulli slugs my side. "*Kits*."

More deeply, I say, "I told her that I need to protect Sulli, and I'm not going anywhere."

Sulli inhales a lungful. I know I might need to reassure her more than Banks will have to, since I constantly have to step out, but I could live forever just coming back and reminding her, telling her, *showing* her how much I care.

How much I desire her.

Need her.

Sulli moves a step closer to collect the backpack at my feet. The trailer is so small that her body wedges between ours. *Shit.*

Her skin feels hot.

I'm hot.

Her eyes roam me and him.

My gaze journeys over her six-foot athletic build. Blood pumping down to my cock. My muscles flex, and I glance over at Banks.

He's giving her the longest once-over, then his gaze lifts to mine. We're wondering the same thing: *are we going to do this again?*

Why wouldn't we?

The moment decrees *go for it.* Out here, the three of us are leading with zero inhibition. No constraints.

I can only find one reason to stop: someone will be left with these memories to mourn. Me or him, but right now, I push that back.

It's just the three of us. There is no tomorrow. Just today.

Sulli grabs the backpack but while she rises, her tits press up against *my* chest. Ass against Banks, and I rake a hand through my hair and lick my lips.

She drops the backpack.

My chest rising and falling heavily against her, I tell her strongly, "Go lie back on the bed, string bean."

She mutters, "Holy fuck, that was hot."

I smile, trying not to laugh. "Sulli, *go.*"

Dazedly, she drifts back until her legs hit the queen bed. She sinks down, and I look to Banks while we both pull our shirts off our heads. "We're not taking her virginity," I tell him more commandingly.

Banks slips me a smile. "So now you're ordering me in the bedroom too?"

I flip him off, my lips rising. We focus entirely on Sulli. She has on loose-fitting pants, and an old Aquatic Club shirt. While we near her, I imagine Sulli stripped bare, her back arched and lips parted—like she'd been in the tent.

"Hold up." She breathes shallowly, and we both stop a literal foot away. So close that I could reach down and tear her pants off.

Banks rubs a hand across his jaw.

I try to read her expression. All I see is arousal, but to be positive, I tell her, "We don't have to do anything, Sulli—"

"It's not that, fuck." She presses a hand to her temple. "I'd just rather see you two come since I haven't *seen* that yet, but don't feel pressured or…" She trails off because Banks and I are already shedding our slacks.

Down to boxer-briefs, she nearly falls backward on the bed in a pant. "Oh fuck."

I absolutely *love* getting girls off. If they're not falling asleep in exhaustion from coming multiple times, then I haven't touched them or fucked them right.

Banks asks me under his breath, "Stay back?" He's not asking if he should stay back. He's asking if *we* should. I've communicated enough with him through security to understand.

I nod. *Stay back.* Sulli is about to have more than just a strip tease.

We shed our underwear. Rolling the elastic down my thighs, I step out of the clothing. Banks does the same. We stand buck-naked, and her green eyes pin right on my cock. Then his. I glance to his crotch and realize we're both hard.

Her raspy breath fills the quiet. She looks back and forth between mine and his. I palm my long shaft. I love my dick. The *morning-afters*, I've been told it's the perfect size, but that's partly because I know how to use it well.

Banks has the length and width that'd fit his height, which is to say, he's much larger than average. He's said it's caused him more problems if he hits the cervix.

While my hand creates friction and Banks strokes himself, Sulli unbuttons her pants. An aroused knot balls up in my throat. I crave to push her back against the bed and strip her myself. Honestly, I crave more than that, but even if she asked, I wouldn't go get rope.

I've never tied up a virgin.

And Sulli is…she's *really* inexperienced to me. Which isn't bad, but I just want to be cognizant of that fact. A man's hand on her body is a brand-new touch, and she had two pairs of hands on her in the tent, so she got overwhelmed fast.

I watch Sulli zip down her pants in the camping trailer. Her fingers dive between her legs and underneath the cotton of her panties. I blaze alive, muscles contracting, and I rub harder and rest my other hand on the dinette table.

Banks' breath is heavier when she bucks up her hips. He curses, "Fuck."

I slide my ankle against her ankle and break her legs open. Even if she's clothed, her knees spread apart, and she bites on her bottom lip, rubbing her clit faster. Eyeing our cut muscles and abs back down to our hands as we jerk off. "I feel like," she says throatily, "I feel like I need you…in me."

I breathe through my nose, almost coming. I slide my hand up and down. Friction pricking every nerve in my body, and I can't tell if she's speaking to me or Banks or both of us. But I tell Sulli, "I feel like I need to be in you."

"Fuck…me," she cries out softly. "Please."

Banks grunts, gritting down on his teeth as arousal slams into him.

I'm close enough to Sulli that if she sits up more, she can touch me. And I glance at Banks, just to tell him I'm moving forward. Once we exchange a single look, I cup the back of her head, bringing her up.

With her hand still between her legs, Sulli eyes my cock that's at perfect height to her lips.

"Only if you want to," I remind her.

"I do, *fuck*," she cries out while I replace her hand with mine. *She's so wet.* Her gaze stays on mine while I slip a finger inside of her.

She squirms, eyes nearly rolling. "*Kits.*" Hearing her say my name like *that* is going to stay with me for weeks…months…*years.*

Sulli has a good visual of Banks as he continues to jack off, and once her eyes open, she watches him, then she asks, "How should I…?"

I guide my hard length to her lips. "Use your tongue first."

She runs her tongue around the tip. "Like this?" Her innocence in bed reminds me to *go easy.*

I nod and hold her chin. "Now open."

Sulli opens her mouth, then stops. "What if I bite you—?"

"You won't." *You might scrape me.* But I'm not going to be a dick about it if she accidentally uses her teeth. She was less in her head when she was watching Banks, so I tell her, "Watch Banks."

The suggestion almost *eases* Sulli. Maybe she was afraid she wasn't paying enough attention to one of us. While she watches Banks, I slowly slip between her lips. Her mouth open, she stops thinking and just goes with the feeling.

Standing tall above Sulli, I pump my finger inside her, and I cup her cheek while I rock against her mouth, only a few times. Her breath catches, and I pull out.

"*Fuck*," she moans, writhing. She watches Banks root a hand to the side of the trailer and come hard in his palm. Sulli clenches around my finger.

I didn't even want to try putting two in her. And seeing her hit a climax sends me to mine. I stroke once and release in my hand.

We're all heavy breath.

"You okay?" I ask Sulli.

She's smiling and collapses back. "Wow."

"I feel that," Banks says in a laugh, grabbing his boxer-briefs. None of us forget the hot springs. Putting on clothes, we head out to the river.

The thirty-minute hike leads to us stripping down again. Dipping into the warm water of this primitive, natural hot spring, like a small alcove in the river. Not found on any website or any map.

Steam rising, I kiss Sulli.

And then, Banks kisses Sulli.

We make out with her. We talk. We crack jokes. We laugh. Waiting until the last second to leave. And when we're running back to the trailer to beat the freezing cold, biting at our flesh, the air hangs thicker. Heavier.

I open the trailer.

Back to reality.

Almost.

Sulli takes the bunk bed. Refusing to let us take it since we're taller and it's cramped. So Banks and I share the queen bed. Lying side by side, I stare up at the ceiling of the trailer.

An hour later, Sulli peeks her head out. She sees me awake. Banks stirs, rubbing his eyes in the semi-darkness. The moon shines through the trailer.

Sulli is quiet. Saying nothing, she crawls between us on the bed. My pulse slows, and I turn on my side and spoon Sul, then she burrows into Banks' chest.

Having her safe in my arms, I finally fall asleep.

39

Sullivan Meadows

FUCK THE RAIN.

Five days of thunderstorms have constructed a huge roadblock on my goal. Rain means slippage, especially on the slick, flat slab of rock I'm trying to scale. With these miserable weather conditions, I haven't been able to climb Rattlesnake Knuckle since the day Jack filmed. And that day was supposed to be my *last* practice climb with gear.

Now, I'm not even confident about free-soloing without another dry run.

Jane and Maximoff flew out to Yellowstone to watch me free-solo, and now they're not going to get the chance. They fly back with everyone tomorrow. I feel a little bit like I wasted their time, and it's hard not to beat myself up over it, even if them watching me climb wasn't my goal.

I haven't failed.

Not yet, anyway.

I still have time to free-solo at least *one* of my dad's old climbing routes. So as long as I free-solo Rattlesnake Knuckle and get to experience something my dad once did, I'll have succeeded what I set out to do.

I keep telling myself that even as the rain pours harder outside.

Rain isn't such a deal-breaker for Thatcher and Jane's bachelor and bachelorette parties today. Their best man and man of honor booked the event at a fucking *humongous* Montana lodge, set on a ranch with acres and acres of land. Also complete with a brewery and a spa.

The people at the front desk even handed me a map.

I told Jane that I hoped she didn't choose Montana just out of convenience for me. If she wanted her bachelorette party in Vegas, I would've flown there. But she said they'd been looking for a resort-style place like the lodge, and it fit everything she wanted.

It's five-star worthy luxury.

Considering I've been roughing it in a tent and then RV trailer for almost a month, I'll gladly take some pampering.

Jane's bachelorette party has been morning mimosas and pedicures, and now afternoon mud facials, and soon, a dip in a mud bath. Staring at my unshaven legs reminds me that I haven't used a razor in a solid week. One day of no shaving and I'm a fucking cactus. So my hair has *grown.*

I remember the hot springs.

Five days ago, where my legs brushed up against Banks, then Akara under the water. And neither one took their hand off my leg. Banks actually pulled my legs *on* his lap.

I smile.

Those memories are scorched in my brain. I want to be with Banks.

But I want to be with Akara.

You can't have them both, Sulli.

The thought always sinks my stomach and spirits. I know I can't be in two relationships at once. It's different while we're here. It'll always be different in the privacy and beauty of the wilderness.

Home has never felt so uninviting.

I want to stay out here forever. But I'll need to pick soon. I can only procrastinate for so long before I'm being totally unfair to Akara and Banks.

Shaking away the stress of *choosing*, I try to just enjoy this time with the bride-to-be.

Moffy asked me to plan a game for the party. My one task as a bridesmaid: I had the lodge staff print out pictures of dicks. They side-eyed me, but in my fucking defense, some were vegetables.

During pedicures, the *Dick or Not?* game landed Moffy first place.

No one was surprised, since he's the only guy at the bachelorette party. He's stared at his junk his whole life.

We all fawn over Jane. As it fucking should be—she's *always* doting over us, but it's really hard to get Jane to concentrate on herself.

Even on a day we planned for her. She fuels all the stories about us as if we're the center of the universe.

Like now.

"My brother said he's been talking to you more," Jane says in an effervescent smile that sparkles her blue eyes. The brother she's referring to is *Beckett.* Mud masks on our faces, we walk together to the poolroom inside the spa. Our next stop is the mud bath. She asks, "Have you two patched everything up?"

"Not exactly." I pick at the dried mud on my cheek. It feels weird when I scrunch my nose. "I just call him more often."

"You should call him today," Jane suggests. "He might be feeling left out since he couldn't make it here."

I haven't called him yet today. But I planned to do it *after* the bachelorette party. "Today is your day—"

"I don't mind," she cuts in. "Seeing you two be friends again would make me happy."

It'd probably make a lot of people happy. Including *me.* But I'm not sure I can click my heels and go back to the way things were.

At her persistence, I say, "Alright, I'll be just a sec. Don't play *Never Have I Ever* without me." I slip out of the poolroom while she heads to the mud bath. And I find some privacy in an empty massage room.

What is glaringly different: the temp bodyguard hovering around me. No Akara. No Banks. The temp is older, mid-forties, and buff like a pro-wrestler.

"I'll probably be a few minutes," I tell him.

He nods, scoping out the hallway.

Very professional, very vigilant. I'm pretty proud of Kits for finding a way to hire Michael Moretti. So far, from my perspective, the temp guard that Michael trained is really confident in his abilities. Which makes me feel safe.

I shut the door, and the temp waits outside in the hall.

Wearing a bathing suit and a towel tied around my chest, I hop up on the massage table. Full-length windows have eerie views of a mountain range. All rain and fog.

After dialing my cousin's number, we start to talk.

"I wish I were there," Beckett says. "A brewery sounds more fun than having to remind Leo he's not Romeo for the fifth time. He still thinks he's God's gift to ballet."

Beckett, along with all of Jane's brothers, were invited to Thatcher's bachelor party. But he had to pass because of his ballet schedule. He's not the only one who couldn't make it, though. Joana Oliveira had a boxing match in New York, so she's also MIA. I'm a bit bummed that I can't hang out with her again. When we were all stuck in Scotland, it was nice having someone else be on the "I'm not a Beckett Cobalt fan" train with me.

Lifting my feet to the table, I tuck my legs to my chest. "Maybe Leo is overcompensating for a small dick. You know what they say, *big ego, little dick*."

He laughs. "That's never true."

I'm smiling. It's weird I'm smiling talking to him. I've lost count the number of phone calls we've had since Charlie blackmailed me. Around ten? Maybe more. There have been days I've called him twice.

Though, he still hasn't brought up cocaine or the cruel words he said to me. That topic is a shadowed figure sitting in the corner of our conversations.

"How's climbing going?" Beckett asks.

I pick at the frayed strings of my anklet. "It sucks I haven't free-soloed yet."

"Perfection doesn't happen overnight."

My heart pangs, hand tightening on the phone. Those are words we used to say to each other growing up. When we were twelve and doing push-ups in the living room. When we were fourteen and watching our siblings go off to school, while we stayed back for homeschool. When we were sixteen and we declined invitations to parties. To trips. To fun things.

Perfection doesn't happen overnight.

Being perfect is a fucking drain. I let out a sigh, "One day, we're going to be old and gray and look at each other and ask, *was it all worth it?* And I hope we'll say yes."

Beckett takes a breath. "In that scenario, are we friends?"

"I guess so." Lightning cracks outside, and I check the time on my cell. "Fuck, I have to get back."

"I'll tell Charlie you've successfully filled your obligation today," Beckett says, trying to be casual but I catch a hint of sadness in his voice.

Pain swells inside my chest. Even if Jane suggested I call her younger brother, I didn't feel like this call was an obligation. I don't know when that changed, but I wanted to call him.

Before I can utter those words, Beckett says a quick bye and hangs up.

I stare at my phone for a solid two minutes before I pry my ass off the massage table. *Leave it all behind.*

Leave Beckett behind.

He hasn't even apologized. We haven't even really *talked* about what needs to be said. I try to mortar all the bricks back up between my heart and my friend who could hurt me again. A wall that no wolf—not even me—can blow down. But with each phone call, I wonder if I've built the wall out of twigs and straw this whole time.

I'm in a daze coming out of the massage room and wandering down the hall. Right before, I reach the glass doors to the poolroom, Moffy rounds a corner in a mud mask and dark-green swim jammer, which is basically competitive swimwear. Tightly-fitted, resembles boxer-briefs but covers the thigh.

"Hey," Moffy says, empty-handed.

Literally, he just had his son in his arms the last I saw him. "Where's Ripley?" The little dude has spent all morning with us. He even kept sipping out of his sippy-cup every time Moffy took a drink of lemon water. It's fucking adorable how much he loves his dads.

"I just handed him to Farrow," Moffy explains.

And I almost smile picturing how that went down. Considering Moffy is wearing a mud mask, his husband probably busted his balls. I've never seen anyone get under Moffy's skin like Farrow. Growing up, if anyone fucked with Moffy, they usually ended up with a black eye.

But after seeing Maximoff fall for Farrow, it made total sense why they click. He's needed someone who isn't afraid to be honest with him. Just like Jane has needed someone who's as logical and considerate as she is, to be balanced as two people could be.

And me…

What do I need?

Those words linger in the back of my head as I tell Moffy, "I thought maybe his teeth were still hurting." Earlier, Ripley was chewing on cold celery that Farrow packed him, just in case of teething issues.

"Not that I could tell," Moffy says but glances back at the exit like maybe he should go double-check.

"Oh hey, I'm sure he's fine."

"Yeah." He nods a ton, eyes on me. "Babies aren't allowed in the poolroom, so I thought he should spend quality time with his dad."

"You mean his *papa*?"

Maximoff groans into a smile, "Jesus, I still can't believe he's mixing us up."

"Or he's getting you both right."

"Maybe." Maximoff cracks a knuckle and blocks the *push* bar to go to the poolroom. "I have to leave Montana and be back in Philly for Janie—"

"I know," I interject, thinking he must be feeling guilty. "I don't see it as you choosing her over me."

He's still rigid. "But the day before you free-solo, call me, text me, send me a goddamn rocket flare or something. Because I'm gonna take the first flight out here—"

"Moffy," I cut in.

He adds fast, "Free-soloing is a big deal, Sulli. I want to be there."

My lungs flood. The fear in his eyes is palpable. "I'm not going to fucking die."

"Yeah, I know that." He nods more, but Moffy is someone who'd try to protect me from the mountain if he could. Being miles and miles away while I'm free-soloing is like riding backseat, not even in the passenger seat, and Moffy loves being behind the wheel.

I want him there.

As much as I'd actually love my dad and mom to watch too.

Because Moffy is another safety net. The illusion of one anyway, and it is easier to breathe and climb knowing he's present.

"I'll call," I tell him.

Maximoff brings me into a hug. "I love you, Sul."

I hug back. "I love you too, Mof."

I hate how much this feels like a goodbye.

And the bachelorette party isn't even over yet. By tomorrow, everyone will be on a flight home. Even my little sister will be gone.

When we push the door, I scan the poolroom. A normal Jacuzzi sits off to the far end where Winona, Vada, Kinney, and Audrey are having an intense discussion.

I eye them in confusion as I wander to the mud bath: an in-ground pit of gray mud as big as the Jacuzzi. Luna is already chin-deep while Jane keeps her arms clean and sips on a goblet of light-colored beer.

While Thatcher is at the brewery three-floors below us, he's been sending up tasting-sizes of beer he thinks Jane would like.

It makes me wonder what Akara and Banks are up to at the bachelor party. If they're getting super wasted now that they're off-duty or if they're just relaxing. I wish I could be a million places at once. With them and also right here. So I never miss a thing.

"What's up with the girls?" I ask Luna and Jane as I shed my towel.

Jane peeks over her shoulder. "High school drama, I believe."

"Glad to be rid of that," Luna adds.

A familiar *pang* hits me again. Moments when I realize I didn't have a normal teenage experience. No walking down high school hallways and trying to beat the bell in the morning. I chose a different path, and I have no regrets, but a part of me will always dislike missing out on something. An adventure untaken. But to succeed in swimming, homeschool was the better option for me. I couldn't walk both roads.

I plop my feet into the mud.

Moffy sits on the ledge, his ankles submerged, but I lower onto the Jacuzzi seat inside the mud bath near Jane. Gray sludge rises up to my chest as I wiggle my way into the thick, warm goop. Mud cocoons around my body like a comforting hug. Almost like I'm being held together.

I breathe in strongly.

And I cringe at the rotten-egg sulfur scent. Fuck that stinks. Even the spa's lavender candles and incense can't drown out the stench.

"Okay, I'm gonna do it," Luna suddenly declares, hoisting herself onto the ledge.

Jane perks up. "Right now?" She looks excited for Luna.

Moffy looks on edge. "You need help constructing the text?"

Am I the only one really fucking confused here? I look between the three of them. How out of the loop am I?

Luna wipes mud off her hands with a towel. "Uh-huh, I'm sure. I have a text ready with the pic."

What picture?

As she grabs her phone, I ask, "What's going on?"

Luna looks over at me. "You know my galaxy tattoo, the one I keep hiding from my dad?"

"Yeah," I say, remembering Luna showing me the intricate thin-line tattoo that snakes up the side of her ass and down part of her leg. Right now, mud hides her inked skin.

"I can't keep it a secret anymore," Luna says. "*Celebrity Crush* posted something on their Twitter account about how I didn't show my legs all summer, and I don't want my dad to jump to conclusions like I'm…" She exhales sadly.

Jane tells me, "Like she's hurting herself."

I nod, more understanding. It sucks that the media is forcing her hand in this. But I think it's good that Luna is coming clean, even if

Uncle Lo is going to *flip*. Honestly, I'm impressed at how long Luna has been able to shelter a *visible* secret. It's literally written on her body.

The cougar attack is written on mine, but it's not something I want to keep quiet when I go home.

"So you're telling your dad now?" I ask Luna.

"Yep." She unlocks her phone screen. "I'm mostly just worried about the fallout with Donnelly. I don't want him to get in trouble for a tattoo that *I* asked for."

Moffy chimes in, "Donnelly said he was cool with you telling Dad."

My jaw drops a fraction. "When?" How did I miss *that* too?

"Earlier this morning," Luna explains, "I talked with Moffy, Farrow, and Donnelly about telling my dad today, while we're all here. I think it'll give my dad some time and space to process."

Jane lifts her beer goblet. "Cheers to courage."

I want to smile, but little ole me is sitting here with a huge ass secret. And it'd be nice to have advice from Moffy and Jane like Luna has been getting lately.

Luna taps her finger to the goblet in cheers, then taps her phone. "*Sent*." She looks more nervous as reality sinks in. "I did the right thing? Dad had to know?"

Jane holds her gaze. "Better from you than from the media."

Moffy nods. "It was time."

I try to give Luna an encouraging smile. "You got this, Luna."

Jane's phone buzzes the same time as Luna's. While Jane smiles at her screen, Luna is frowning at hers.

"Shit," Luna curses. "He's asking me *who* did it?"

"You should tell Dad the truth," Moffy says.

Luna inhales, then types out a message. I scoot closer to Jane as I catch the bride-to-be swooning at her phone.

She smiles over at me, then flashes me her screen. "Thatcher's mom stopped by to check on Lady Macbeth and the others. Thatcher texted me the pics she sent him."

Her cats.

Thatcher messaged Jane a photo of their fur babies rolling on the carpet like cat burritos, and they're making silly faces. I laugh. "Are they strung out on catnip?"

"On love, apparently," Jane says, unable to stop smiling. "They adore Gloria. Thatcher said his mom grew up feeding strays and bringing them inside."

Gloria. That's also Banks' mom. Obviously, but I find myself hanging onto Jane's words for different reasons now. I want to know more about Banks and the woman who raised him.

Is she cool? Does he have a good relationship with her or is it more strained like the one with his dad? Things…I don't exactly know that deeply, but I really, *really* fucking want to.

There is a path where I never do.

Where I never get closer to Banks, and that sits inside me like a ball of misery and desolation. Like some post-apocalyptic scenario that I didn't choose.

I'd never choose that.

But I may.

I try not to wince even thinking it, and I concentrate on Jane.

She shows me another cat photo. "Ophelia is licking her lips after a tuna treat."

Adorable, but my eyes immediately jump to the text message sitting above the photo.

I'm going to push inside your wet pussy, honey. – Thatcher

Suddenly it's a million degrees and my eyes have popped out of my fucking head. Do I alert Jane and make the situation awkward? Or do I ignore the fact that I just read a dirty text from her future husband, one that is super direct and assertive?

"Uh…" I stammer.

Jane frowns, then follows my gaze. "Merde." She's beet-red and clicks out of the text thread.

Maybe I should go to college and take up Acting 101 to save other people from myself. "I didn't see anything," I lie.

She smiles, but her face is as red as mine. I mean, we're all pretty open and talk about sex, but it's not like I've ever heard Thatcher tell Jane that he wants to stick it in.

"That is a big fat lie, Sullivan Meadows," Jane notes sweetly. "But I appreciate you lying on my behalf."

"What'd you see?" Moffy asks me.

I look to Jane, wondering if she wants this unleashed.

"A sext," Jane answers.

"You sext?" Luna smiles but glances nervously at her own phone. Waiting for her dad's reply. Uncle Lo might just be drawing out his reaction to put his daughter on edge.

"Sometimes." Jane studies the way Luna stares at her phone. "Did your dad respond?"

"Just now, he did. He said, *we'll talk more when you're home. Glad you're okay, and remind me—what's Akara's number again?* He's going to call Akara." Her head whips to Moffy. "This is bad, right? If he's calling Akara, then he's going to get Donnelly fired."

"Kits won't fire him," I cut in. "He wouldn't."

Moffy nods. "And Farrow will vouch for Donnelly."

"Plus," Jane adds, "Uncle Loren already has Akara's number. So he's most likely trying to make you sweat it out."

Luna's shoulders loosen. Relaxing more, she dips back into the thick mud.

All this talk of Donnelly reminds me of something. "I heard that Donnelly hasn't brought anyone back to his apartment in a while," I tell my cousins. "No hookups or dates. Akara and Banks said it was strange for him."

The air thickens more than the mud.

What the fuck? You'd think I dropped a heavy-duty explosive, when I thought I was just giving a tiny morsel of bodyguard gossip that I could share with family. No one says anything. Jane is looking to Moffy, who looks to Luna.

"What's going on?"

Now Jane is looking to Luna.

Luna draws a muddy star on the stone ledge, but her amber eyes ping between all three of us before landing on me. "I wanted to tell you for a long time—I really did, but I couldn't. The more people keep finding out, the harder it is to keep."

My frown deepens, heart starting to race. "About what?" *Drugs.* I can't help but jump to secret drug usage because of Beckett.

"A year ago," Luna begins, letting her light-brown hair get matted with mud, "Donnelly and I hooked up—just oral. On *me*."

My brain explodes. *Holy fuck.*

She continues fast, "If my dad ever finds out, it could be ten times worse than whatever his reaction is to Donnelly tattooing me, so I've been *trying* to keep this under wraps. Different people just keep finding out on accident, but I've hated that you don't know."

That actually makes me feel better. But when she lists out *who* knows—Jane, Maximoff, Thatcher, Farrow, Oscar, and Jack—my stomach somersaults knowing just how on the outs I've been. I guess Charlie and Beckett aren't aware either, but I always thought Luna and I were closer after rooming together.

With how poorly I lie, maybe Luna felt like she couldn't trust me. I guess I can't fault that reasoning. I wouldn't want to accidentally cause her or Donnelly pain if he were to get fired.

"You can't tell anyone, *please*," Luna pleads. "Not even Akara." She barely pauses. "Donnelly is way older than me, so *murder* might actually be on my dad's agenda if he finds out."

Yeah, I can't see that going well considering Uncle Lo was really hard on my parents for their age-gap when they were dating. But maybe time heals all, and he's changed.

Luna has these soft, pleading doe eyes.

I want to do right by her. By my friends. To have good friends means that I need to be a good friend too.

Secret-keeping isn't usually my strong suit, but I'm going to try to gain more experience on that front. "I won't fucking tell, I promise." I shift closer to Luna in the mud. Like moving in liquid cement, it takes effort, but I slip between Luna and Jane, and Luna and I curl pinkies in a bigger promise.

My mind is gathering more logic. *So if Donnelly and Luna hooked up once, and Donnelly is strangely not seeing anyone, does that mean…*

Oh.

Fuck.

Luna and Donnelly.

They're…dating?

Moffy already looks concerned. Big brother mode is on.

I come out and ask Luna, "Are you and Donnelly in a secret relationship or something?"

Jane rests her chin on her fist. "Exactly what I was going to ask." So Jane and Moffy have no clue about this. They only knew about the hookup from a year ago, and with that info, plus the rumor I just told them, they theorized a secret relationship like me.

Luna shakes her head profusely. "Nonono."

"We'd understand if you are, and you can trust us," Jane says, setting down her phone and goblet on the ledge. "We've all been there. Except Sulli, of course."

Fuck my life.

I *have* been there. I am currently right fucking there. Although we haven't exactly settled on labels. Probably because I haven't been able to choose who'll go from short-term dating to long-term boyfriend. Not to mention, they might just choose each other in the end.

I pick up a handful of mud. Avoiding direct eye contact with *everyone*. Thankfully they're all so focused on Luna, they don't notice my bad acting.

"There's no secret relationship happening," Luna tells us. Her gaze stays on her older brother for a longer beat. "I've been honest with you. I wouldn't lie when I told you it was a one-time thing."

I'm the real liar.

The bad liar.

Right here.

Me.

The wolf in sheep's clothing.

"I believe you, Luna," Moffy says strongly. "It's just a weird coincidence, and those happen all the damn time, trust me. I've been through misunderstandings and doubts."

The HaleCocest rumor. I cringe remembering how the media thought Moffy and Jane were hooking up. So fucking gross. It was even worse when some of our family didn't know what was real either. A lot of security facts were stacked against Moffy.

Luna eases, then frowns, thinking harder. "Donnelly and I don't really talk much outside of group events and some of the tattooing sessions we've had. I don't know anything about his dating life." Her frown deepens. "I'm just as confused as all of you."

I say unhelpfully, "Maybe he got an STD and he's waiting for things to fucking clear up."

Jane's eyes go wide. "Is that what Akara said?"

"What? No!" Oh fuck, I am so bad at this. I don't want to start a rumor about someone having an STD. "It was just a guess. A *bad* guess. Wipe it away from your memories."

"It's gone," Jane says with a breezy flick of her hand.

Luna's lips have downturned. "You really think no one would sleep with him if he had an STD?"

"Luna," Jane says. "The memory is wiped."

"Oh right." Luna scoops up handfuls of mud and plops them on her head. "Memory erased." She looks like *Carrie* from the movie, only instead of blood, she's drenched in mud.

"Bachelorette game time," Moffy decrees.

Fuck yes! Time to win. I pick myself out of the hot mud bath. Sitting on the ledge, ready for total domination.

Jane cups her beer goblet again. "Wait, while we're on the topic of bodyguard relationships, have you given any more thought to Banks?" She's volleying the conversation back to me.

"Banks?" Luna frowns.

"He likes Sulli," Jane says.

Luna draws a newly wet mud mustache on her face over her dried mud mask. "I thought Akara likes Sulli."

The wind shifts in my sails like I'm being spun sideways. Am I still breathing?

"Akara said he just sees her as a friend," Jane notes.

"Huh," Luna tilts her head. "But Banks likes her?'

"Oui."

This can't be happening.

If I utter a single word, I'll be caught in my lie. My lips have cemented together, and I try to be all cool. All casual. I remember how easy it was for Akara to skate through his lie like it was nothing, and hurt blossoms in my chest.

It shouldn't be easy to lie about this. To lie about them.

Because I lo…I *care* about them both. Fucking immensely.

Luckily Moffy pries the conversation off Banks and Akara and refocuses it onto the bride-to-be. Moffy doesn't know it, but he's definitely helping me be better at secret-keeping. Thank God for the man of honor.

40

Banks Moretti

AS THE BEST MAN, it's my job to make sure my brother is having a good time at his own bachelor party. But Thatcher Alessio Moretti is making that task harder than I thought he would. I'd have better luck flying my ass to the moon.

He hasn't touched his beer and we're at a fuckin' *brewery*.

At least he keeps sending ice-cold lagers to his fiancée.

"Thatcher," I lean into his ear, clamping a hand on his strict shoulder. "You can drink more than the baby sips you've been taking. We've got temps and SFE here." I hate to give that much credit to Epsilon, but if it'll ease my brother's stress then I'll be spitting those words all day.

Montana Moose Foot Brewery is on the ground floor of this enormous lodge. Complete with barrel-drum tabletops, leather barstools, and mounted bison heads. Bougie, but also something my brother and I would've walked into if we had the cash and the people didn't side-eye us to hell.

I'd love to give myself kudos for the venue, but Jane and Thatcher basically chose it themselves with an assist from Maximoff.

We bought out the brewery for a "private party" for the whole day, and right now, various cliques pack the bar area, leather sofas, and tabletops. From my cousins at the bar—Morettis, Piscitellis, and Ramellas—to the Cobalt brothers at an entire sofa section, and to Omega at the high-top tables.

It's like high school all over again.

My brother and I currently occupy a tabletop dead-center of the brewery. Right now, it's the worst damn place for Thatcher to be. He has a perfect view of all the guests, which is causing him to act more like a bodyguard than a man about to be married.

Thatcher stares at the beer, a dark porter on draft, that I shove at his chest. "Her *teenage* brothers are here, Banks. If anything happens to them—"

"It won't," I cut him off.

His eyes peel to the sofa area. Eliot and Tom Cobalt are in some deep whisper-conversation. Nothing good is going to come from that, but I'm not advertising my pessimistic thoughts right now. I'm a fucking rainbow of joy for my brother today. He deserves the hype man, not a Debbie Downer.

But Christ, it's hard when I'm playing babysitter to Cobalt brothers *and* I'm a goalie playing defense as I try to keep Tony Ramella from approaching my brother. Lord knows Tony will throw out some dumb comment that'll tank my brother's mood.

Which is already too uptight to begin with.

"You should *drink*," I try to encourage. "You're not on-duty, and you won't see Jane later. We're not meeting up with the bachelorette party." The thought sours my stomach because I'd love nothing more than to hang out with Sulli in a brewery, spa, barn, fucking horse-manure stalls—I'll take anything, being honest. As long as I can spend more time with her.

"Agreed," Akara says, approaching with a couple beer flights. "You need to enjoy this, Thatcher. You're only getting *one* bachelor party."

Thatcher doesn't ease at those words. Not really sure what'll take the ice out of his bones tonight. "What's the word on the security meeting?" he asks Akara. "SFO is finally together now, we could have one in five before the gents are drunk."

Akara checks the time on his watch. "Maybe in twenty."

I wag a finger, then pound the table with *said* finger. "*No work*. No meetings. This is a fucking party. Can you two please shove the pencils and calculators in a drawer for *one* night?"

Akara fits on a black beanie, smiling. "Hey, I'll do whatever the groom wants."

Thatcher shoots me a look. "If we're not talking about work, what do you want me to bring up?"

"Phillies, Eagles. Hell, I'll take an hour of Jesus and Mary and rehashing the birth of Christ."

Thatcher almost smiles.

There we go.

He grips the porter but doesn't drink yet. "What about Sulli?"

I stiffen and shift, then scratch the back of my head. My brother is making casual conversation like my dumbass suggested, but I didn't think he'd surface Sulli.

Akara is the one to say. "What about her?" He does a much better job not looking like he has spiders in his pants.

Thatcher's gaze slices between us. "One of you likes her, one of you said you're just friends. I thought you two would've talked it out by now."

Lying to my twin is the biggest sin of my life. It's more painful than any migraine. Like drinking gasoline by the gallon and lighting a match in my lungs. So I struggle to clarify the truth. That Akara hasn't actually friend-zoned Sulli.

That we're both dating her.

That I'm still likely to be heartbroken in the end.

"No conclusion yet," Akara says to Thatcher, skating by a lie into a fucking gray area that I'm not sure I could find as easily.

Thatcher retorts, "Go talk about it then." His South Philly lilt comes out in his simmering ire. He wants both of us to get our heads out of our asses. "If you need time alone, I can find Farrow."

It's surreal how buddy-buddy he is with Farrow. So much so that Farrow is one of five groomsmen. Along with me, Akara, Charlie, and Beckett. Never really saw a friendship with Farrow and Thatcher coming, not for how long Farrow really *despised* my brother. Probably for good reason since Thatcher had to single Farrow out, but I think pretty highly of Farrow that he was able to see the good in my brother in the end.

It means a lot to me, even if I'm not as close to Farrow.

Akara reaches up and clasps Thatcher's shoulder. "It's *your* bachelor party. We're not going anywhere, man."

Thatcher nods once, but he sets down his porter again.

Akara mimics one of my cousins, "So how about them Eagles?"

We all laugh.

Though, my brother is *still* scoping out the venue, mostly hawk-eyed on the Cobalt brothers.

We're not alone here for long. Oscar, Quinn, and Donnelly leave their tabletop once they see our beer flights. "Don't mind me," Donnelly reaches for a small tasting glass and downs the beer in one gulp.

"That's not a shot, bro," Oscar says into a laugh.

"Where's the stout?" Quinn asks, inspecting the flight.

"I'll get it," Oscar says, eying the bar. Pretty sure, he's more likely heading that way for his husband. Jack is flagging down the bartender with zero to little luck. His brother Jesse seems to be chatting his ear off too.

Before Donnelly can down all the beer, Akara steals two from the flight and hands them both to me.

"Thanks," I say.

If my brother's not going to drink, I'm doin' it for him. I take them both like shots, too. Warm liquid slides down the back of my throat, and then I tell Thatcher, "The temps are actually trained well, so you really shouldn't worry about anyone."

That statement shocks him out of his vigilant stance. "What?"

"I said—"

"I heard what you said." He stares at me like I've grown three horns. "Just didn't think you'd be praising Dad."

"If it gets you to enjoy yourself tonight, I'll kiss his fucking feet, if I have too."

That gets me a major eye roll. "I'm having a good time."

"Says no one."

"Says me."

I pick up his beer glass again, and he grabs the thing out of my hand and puts the rim to his lips. He takes a baby sip that causes *me* to roll my eyes.

"Fucking hell," he curses.

My muscles tense and I follow his gaze to the Cobalt brothers. Eliot has pulled a flask out of his jacket. No one on Epsilon will stop them from underage drinking. They'll just report it to the parents tomorrow.

But Thatcher made it very clear that Jane's under-twenty-one family members were only invited to the bachelor party on the stipulation they wouldn't drink.

Sober Cobalt brothers are difficult enough. We don't need shit-faced ones too.

Thatcher takes a step forward.

I put a hand to his chest. "I've got it."

He gives me a look.

"This falls under best man duties." I point at myself. "Me, best man." I point at him. "You, *not*."

He glowers at me, but I'm so not affected by my brother's broody nature.

I add, "Jane would be really upset if she found out you spent tonight corralling her brothers."

He lets out a resigned breath. "Fine. But if you need me, use your radio." SFO all have their comms on an Omega-only channel. Even though we're all off-duty, it makes it easier to stay relaxed in case there really is an emergency.

"Copy that." I smack his chest, then hightail my ass to the sofa area. Charlie, Eliot, Tom, and Ben all stop talking as I approach, and I don't waste a minute to plop myself down in the tiny space between Tom and Eliot. They have to scoot out of the way so we're not thigh-to-thigh.

Eliot's pint of soda almost sloshes on his lap. He curses under his breath.

"Hey, gents." I pull out a pack of cigarettes from my pocket. "We having fun here?"

Charlie has his feet kicked up on an expensive-looking coffee table. My mom would've dragged me by my chicken-wing if I did that growing up. He tilts his head to me. "Depends on your definition of fun." His yellow-green eyes pierce through me.

As though saying, *I know Akara and Sulli kissed, and I know you're protecting that secret too.*

He could let loose that fact at any moment. With his family around, he might be more inclined to ignite drama *for fun.*

I'm on edge for a second and shove my cigarettes back in my pocket. Thatcher might only be six-minutes older, but I've definitely shirked a lot of responsibility onto him. So he always feels older, and I didn't grow up with a lot of little brothers. Just younger cousins. Rarely gave orders to anyone, just took them.

Still, I can handle the Cobalt brothers who've strewn themselves over the leather furniture like they're cigar-smoking, heaven-dropped and hell-raised American gods.

I have to believe that for my brother's sake.

While I turn to Eliot, I say, "I saw your flask. How about you give it to me, and I won't cause a scene?"

Eliot grins mischievously. "What if I want a scene?"

Ben leans forward on the opposing couch. "Come on, Eliot. Just give it to him."

Tom's the one who reaches into Eliot's blazer and pulls out the flask. "What are we to deny a thirsty patron?" He hands it over to me.

I untwist the top and take a small sip. It's only wine. "Thanks for the vino. Tom's right; I was thirsty." I stand up and take the flask with me. In and out quick.

I just became a certified firefighter tonight. Extinguishing flames every which way. I laugh at my thought as I tip the flask to my lips and continue through the packed brewery.

Fuck no.

I eagle-eye Tony Ramella. He saunters away from the loud pack of cousins at the bar. He's laughing at a conversation he pulls away from, but he's aimed for Thatcher.

Swift as a motherfucker, I cut off his path.

His laughter slowly fades on me, but his shit-eating grin lingers, which makes me want to shove his face in literal shit. He's shorter but tries to pull himself higher. "What's up, nephew?"

A brittle laugh sticks to my chest. "The day I call you *uncle* will be the day I'm dead and buried and you resurrect me as a fucking ghost. And then, I'm only gonna say it right before I murder your ass." I swig from the flask.

Tony grimaces. "Jesus, Banks." He shifts his weight, his eyes tightening in emotions that I don't recognize. "You're still pissed at me?"

I'm unblinking. "My brother almost *died* in a fire trying to save you when you should've *never* gone back in there at all, so *pissed* is putting it mildly."

Tony's nose flares, staring at the ground. "I'm sorry for what happened, and if I could take back that night, I wouldn't run into the fire." His eyes meet mine. "Can't we put this in the past?" He's about to touch my shoulder, but I smack his hand away. He lets out a short, frustrated laugh. "I expected this from Thatcher, but aren't you supposed to be the shy one?"

I glower.

Fuck him, man.

Fuck him.

I was a shy kid, but that attribute should *not* be attached to me at twenty-nine when I've never been a shy adult. "Aren't you the dickish one?"

Tony snorts. "That's right, you're the *funny* one." He swigs his beer. "Before you came stomping over here, I was just going to ask Thatcher if he wants a whiskey flight. On me and the Ramellas." He gestures to our family at the bar.

I make eye contact and the guys nod to me.

"Hey, paesan'!"

"Youse heard about them Eagles, Thatcher?" a cousin calls out.

"That's Banks, you scustumad'." Another cousin called him *stupid.*

"Fuck me, sorry, Banks!"

Tony laughs and tells our cousins at the bar, "It's the same thing. They're basically the same person—one is just getting married first."

They all holler and cheer for Thatcher.

Every word out of Tony's mouth rakes across me. Grating my brain like shredded meat. It shouldn't eat at me that much considering I've heard all that horseshit growing up, and I thought I moved past it. The off-handed "they're like the same person" comments.

How I'm one half of one person instead of a whole fucking individual. While I silently fume, I know not to cold-cock Tony and tear apart our families. I manage to corral Tony back with the others at the bar. Leading him away from Thatcher.

"Gloria's really officiating the wedding?" a cousin asks me.

"Yeah," I answer, "with Rose." Both my mom and Jane's mom will be marrying off the happy couple. I make a quick exit after I diss the Eagles, knowing they'll *boo* me away.

"Get outta here!"

"Ah fuck youse, Banks!"

I leave, just as Akara approaches.

He eyes my cousins and the curses that trail after me. "You need backup?"

I shake my head. "They're harmless." Though, I think of *Tony.* I dig in my pocket for a cigarette. "Christ, I can't believe Tony is Connor Cobalt's bodyguard." I stick a cigarette between my lips. "Why doesn't he just *can* his ass already?"

"Because Tony's related to his future son-in-law," Akara says like the answer is clear as day. "If he tells Price that Tony isn't working out, what is your family going to think of the Cobalts?"

They'll think that the Cobalts only care about the Cobalts, and not the *whole* family. Which includes the Ramellas.

They'll never forgive the Cobalts.

"Fuck," I mutter, cigarette in my mouth while I fumble for a lighter.

Akara shakes his head. "I wish you would quit."

"I already did," I remind him.

He tries not to smile and digs in his pocket for his buzzing phone. "I wish that stuck." His face sobers as soon as he sees the name on his phone screen.

"Who?" I ask.

"Loren Hale wants to talk." He checks his watch. "I have to call an SFO meeting."

"Now? Really?"

Akara says, "Your brother wants to hold one too. Think of it as a bachelor gift to him." The fact that they're both so ready to jump into a *meeting* during a party reminds me that they're best friends.

"Fuck it." I light my cigarette. "Let's get some."

41

Akara Kitsuwon

OUTSIDE THE LODGE, the Montana land rolls towards foggy mountain peaks, and a fall breeze passes through the ranch. Quinn Oliveira zips up the hoodie underneath his blazer.

I like Quinn a lot, but man, do I wish he didn't take after Farrow. The maverick, the rule-breaker. It's hard enough having one on the team. It's even harder when Quinn tries to go rogue—because I really don't like being tough on him. He's the *only* guy on Omega who's younger than me. So disciplining him feels like disciplining a little brother.

I'd rather just guide him. Teach him.

Thankfully, he's here for the team meeting and I didn't have to go flag him down somewhere.

I snap my finger to my palm while all of SFO gather on stone stairs that lead to the brewery we just exited. I stand before them. At the bottom, but I don't need to be towering over them to wield authority.

They know I'm at the top.

Thatcher and Banks sit side by side on the middle stair. Banks smokes on a cigarette, ignoring Thatcher's side-glares, but they're both quiet, waiting for me to start.

As I look between them, it's easy for me to say that Thatcher is my best friend. I've always been closer to him. We've been leads at the same time. Dealt with shit that Banks never had to, but when I think of Banks, I inhale a stronger breath and I can't help but picture what we've been through recently.

Not just the intimate parts. The cougar attack. The way he's been there. He's always there. How much I've *relied* on him. And needed him.

I've known that I can't live without Sulli.

But it's starting to feel clearer and clearer how much I can't live without Banks, and I hate the scenario where our friendship gets decimated.

It's the most plausible outcome.

The most likely thing.

Because if she chooses Banks, I can't stick around and watch him be with her. No more than I know he could stomach watching me with her.

Too painful.

Even thinking it draws down my face, and so I try to regroup.

Farrow has Ripley on his lap. *Baby needs a bodyguard.* I swallow those words. If I had more time, I'd definitely fling that issue into today's meeting, but it's not important right now. And I want this to be quick because we've all been drinking and it's still Thatcher's bachelor party.

"So here's the deal," I tell them, "as of now, you've probably heard about the incident at the Hales with Donnelly accidentally causing Ben to fall into the pool." I'm guessing this is why Loren Hale wants to talk.

Donnelly hangs his head, his hands cupped together. Oscar squeezes his friend's shoulder.

"We *all* need to be more careful around the minors," I tell them. "Epsilon protects them, and the *only* client on our list that's under-eighteen is Xander. So they feel a sense of entitlement to their well-being, and they're going to feel threatened if we overstep or make any kind of mistake, even one with no potential harm."

They listen closely, and I know they don't like hearing me talk about *playing nice* with Epsilon. Trust me, I'd love to play dirty, but for the sake of the money I'm putting into Michael Moretti and training my temps, I have no wiggle room to go into legal battles with Price's Triple Shield.

My men don't need to be punching Epsilon. Let them take the first swing.

I add, "We win this by doing our jobs better than Epsilon. That's how it's going to be." I focus on Donnelly. "You can't get between family members. Do it in private, I don't care. But don't do it where anyone on Triple Shield can snitch on you."

He sits up straighter. "Got it, boss."

I nod and address everyone, "They're going to try to make your lives harder with the parents. Don't give them reason to."

Oscar nods strongly.

Farrow nods.

Quinn, Banks, and Thatcher all nod.

"Papa!" Ripley says up to Farrow, which causes the men to reroute focus onto the baby.

Oscar grins. "Look at him, using his words."

Ripley is wiggling out of Farrow's hands, and then the group of men all let out groans.

Oscar plugs his nose. "The kid had an explosion."

"No shit," Farrow says, then playfully gasps at Ripley. "You need a changing, little man?" Ripley wears a silly smile and touches Farrow's cheeks.

Farrow combs a hand through his bleach-white hair, before standing up and hoisting Ripley on his waist. He catches my gaze and motions to the door.

I nod to him, letting him dip out early.

I'm seconds from letting the others go back to the party when my phone rings. *Loren Hale.* I was just about to call him, but I tell everyone, "Meeting's not over. Hold on." I put the phone to my ear. "Akara Kitsuwon speaking."

"Akara," Loren says, his voice sounds like razor-knives. "I *just* found out something about one of your bodyguards that's disturbed me."

I freeze, looking up as my men watch Farrow leave through the doors. "Which bodyguard?"

"The one who's already written on my shit list—and if my son didn't like him so goddamn much, there wouldn't be a problem."

Donnelly. I glare at him on the steps.

He sinks down on the stair like I've just put him in time out.

"What'd he do?"

"He tattooed my daughter's ass. When did this happen and where were they?"

Shit.

I know about the galaxy tattoo, but I don't have all the details Lo's asking for. I narrow my gaze even more and bring my phone down, muting the speaker so Lo can't hear. "Donnelly, when and where did you tattoo Luna's ass?"

Every head jerks in his direction.

"This summer." Donnelly slips a cigarette behind his ear. "I did most of it in her bedroom."

"What?" Thatcher glares.

"*Bro*," Oscar groans more, "her bedroom?"

"It wasn't like that," Donnelly defends.

Banks slides me a furtive look. Yeah, I know that look—the one that says, *who are we to judge?* We've been dating Sulli. And her dad finding out she's been with *two* bodyguards, not just one, could be catastrophic.

But I'd rather take on Ryke Meadows than Loren Hale as the father of the girl I'm dating. Any day of the week.

I unmute Loren and put my phone to my ear. "It happened this summer, and he tattooed Luna at your house. She requested the tattoo."

Loren is quiet on the line.

SFO are holding their breaths.

I wait.

"My kids are *young*," Loren says sharply. "Luna looks *younger* than her age, and she's a *young*, impressionable *nineteen*." He's emphasizing these words very strongly here. "My son is a *young*, impressionable *sixteen*. My daughter didn't have a single tattoo until Donnelly. And now my son's favorite hoagie place has changed."

I don't think Xander ever had a favorite hoagie place.

Loren keeps going, "Tell him to back off. He's not their best friend. He's their *twenty-eight-year-old* bodyguard. And he's going to be roadkill if he *ever* sees my daughter unclothed again. I don't give a shit if it's just for a tattoo. I'm not an idiot—I know how that spirals into other things."

"It hasn't, it won't," I assure Lo. "Donnelly is professional." With a few more reassurances, I hang up, and I tell Donnelly, "You're on Loren Hale's permanent shit list. You're not getting off."

He nods a few times. "You transferring me?"

"No. Xander wants you on his detail, and Loren doesn't want you to leave. But you need to tone down the buddy-guard routine. Just do your job. Don't take him to Wawa anymore."

"He wants to go, though."

I sigh. "Just try not to influence him." It might be hard because Donnelly doesn't seem to be doing anything. He's just *cool* in the eyes of Xander Hale.

I pick up my beer mug. "Before the meeting ends," I tell them, "I want to say *cheers* to your Omega lead." I gesture to Thatcher who starts to smile.

Banks, Quinn, Donnelly, and Oscar pick up their drinks.

"Congrats to Thatcher, for being the second bodyguard to do the impossible and be with American royalty. Can't wait to be there and see you cry as Jane walks down the aisle."

Everyone laughs.

"Thanks," Thatcher smiles more, swigging his drink with the rest of us. But as the liquid slides down the back of my throat, I realize a third bodyguard is going to do the impossible and be with another American princess.

I'm just not sure who it'll be anymore. Me or Banks. Any way I turn it, it feels like a total tossup.

Sullivan Meadows

OCTOBER 30TH. HALLOW FRIENDS Eve. The day I fucking *finally* free-solo.

Yesterday, the weather cleared for my final practice run, and I breezed through the route. Every handhold, every path to the top is engrained in my mind. So much so that I could climb Rattlesnake Knuckle blindfolded.

There is only one thing left standing in my way today.

The asshole climbers.

I thought we shook off Team Apex, but they're back. And they're placing foldout lawn chairs about a tennis court away from the base of the crag. Close enough that I'll be able to hear their jeers and heckling while I climb.

I dip my hands in my chalk bag. Standing at the base of the crag, I try to *ignore* Team Apex and mentally focus.

This is *it.*

The last day that I can possibly free-solo in the Yellowstone region this year. The last day that we'll even be here. Grand Teton will have to wait for another time. A cold front is rolling into Montana and Wyoming, and more than the winter conditions, we have to drive back to Philly for the wedding on November 1st. We leave tonight with plenty of time.

I seriously *cannot* let Team Apex distract me. If I bail today, there's literally no other opportunity to complete my goal before next year. I don't want to stall. I feel like all I've been doing is stalling out of *safety*, and I just want to climb.

Besides the unwanted campers, only Akara and Banks are my spectators. I called Moffy this morning because I honestly wasn't sure if the weather would hold up enough. And I didn't want him to fly back here just for me to pull the plug. He understood, but I could tell that he wishes he were with me.

It made me feel good that he's still thinking of me. That being physically away again hasn't wiped me from the minds of the people I love.

I chalk my hands another time.

Akara and Banks whisper behind me, and my stomach does twists and turns whenever I remember the end of the trip will mark the end of whatever we've been doing. And I'll ultimately have to decide between them.

Concentrate, Sulli.

I smack my hands together, chalk pluming. I shake out my arms, then realize they're both fixated on Team Apex.

Akara catches my wrist. "Wait before you climb, Sul."

I frown. "What's the plan?"

"We kick their asses," Banks tells me strongly. "Then you climb that big rock."

"What are you gonna do, just walk up to them and say *fuck you* and deck them in the face."

"Yeah." He bobs his head. "*Exactly* that."

Akara detaches his radio on his waistband. "You're not going to be a part of the ass-kicking, string bean. Just stay *right here*."

I scoff. "I'm a lover, not a fighter *anyway*."

And I want to maintain absolute focus on my climb. Revenge might derail me. It's definitely set me back more than once this trip.

Akara smiles, flinging my hair at my face. "There's my Sulli."

My Sulli.

I instantly smile. "Go be my Kits, *Kits*," I tell him, "and kick their asses."

He bows, then picks up my hand, kisses my knuckles. "Will do, m' lady."

I shove his shoulder, and he smiles more while Banks is vigilantly observing Team Apex. But I notice how his eyes flit to me in a strong pulse of sadness.

I haven't chosen yet.

I didn't just pick Akara, but I can understand him thinking I might be on the road there.

"Did they make hot cocoa?" I question as Lincoln pulls out a thermos like they're ready to watch a new theatrical release.

"Fuck them," Banks says coarsely.

Akara marches forward, signaling Banks to follow, and I stay at the base of the crag, watching my bodyguards charge Team Apex.

Gaining distance on them, Banks approaches hotly and smacks a cup out of a hand. Hot cocoa goes flying.

"Hey, we have every right to be here!" Jordyn yells.

"Come back *later*," Akara sneers. "You know what you're doing. That's *life* or *death* for her."

"She's choosing to free-solo," Jordyn snaps. "That's not on us."

"Bullshit," Akara curses. "You're here to heckle her."

Lincoln shoots up from his chair and angles towards Akara. "Fuck—"

Banks swings, and Lincoln goes down like a sack of flour. His friends hurriedly lift him up, his bottom lip already swelling. "Jesus," one of them screams. "We're going. Alright. You psycho."

"Get the fuck outta here." Banks feigns another hook and they all stumble to a quick exit. Some even leave behind their chairs as they trip over their feet. Running away from Banks and Akara. But mostly Banks. No one else wants to be punched.

I smile as they return to my side. "Nice job, Hercules," I tell Banks.

He curves an arm over my shoulder. And my whole body sings as his head dips and lips meet mine in the most breathtaking kiss. It's his hand that steals all my fucking senses—his hand that slips up the nape of my neck to my jaw. Holding my face protectively.

The kiss feels long but I know lasts only seconds. We break apart and I touch my tingling lips. He whispers, "I'll be waiting for you down here."

I inhale. "Alright." Why do I not even want to leave anymore?

Banks looks like he wants to say more. Loving words scream inside his eyes and wail to be let out, but he cages them, his breath rising and falling heavily.

His staggered breath begins to stagger mine. I never really knew how this kind of *love* could be written in someone's gaze before they say the words, but I see them *so clearly* in Banks.

"I'll come back to you," I whisper.

It's a promise that I shouldn't make, but I'm feeling more than thinking.

He nods a lot, his lip rising. "Happy Hallow Friends Eve, mermaid."

I smile. "Maybe this'll turn out to be the best one."

"Third time's the charm," Banks says, and then he glances at Akara, who hangs a few feet back from us.

They switch spots, and I tell him, "You weren't so bad back there, too, Kits."

Akara takes off his beanie, pushing his hair back. "Well, I would've punched that asshole, but now I'm waiting for the lawsuit."

I forgot the bodyguards get sued often. Assault charges are common, even if it's all in an effort to protect my family.

Banks calls out, "I'll help you with the paperwork."

Akara smiles back. "You better."

I try to keep upbeat, but I just see their friendship. It's good and solid and has history before me. I hope that it still survives after me too.

They might choose each other.

Maybe they should. Maybe that's how this all needs to end. But my insides feel *crushed* with weight even imagining going back to the start. Losing the romance and love I've longed for.

Akara focuses on me. "Concentrate. Don't let me or Banks or any nagging thought distract you up there." He cups my cheeks. "Okay?"

I cup his face with my chalky hands. "Okay." I tap his face, creating handprints.

He smiles, then drops his hands, kissing my cheek. "See you, lover."

See you, Kits.

I can't even say the words. My mind is on the ascent. My path. My route. I've rotated back with a clear head, and I breathe in and grip the first handhold of rock. Pulling my body up with my muscles, I ascend.

I move fast.

Precisely.

My limbs know what to do and where to go, and I just go. Wedging two fingers in the tiny fissure, I find a better foothold and shimmy up the crack that widens with every twenty feet. Until I'm over two-hundred feet off the ground, and I can fit my whole body in the fissure. I do a split and shake out my arms. Balancing all the weight on my legs.

And I glance down.

Akara and Banks are specs in the distance. Wind whirls, but it's not too gusty. I smile up at the last two-hundred feet of ascent.

What my dad once did.

I blow out a breath and keep climbing.

Fear is nowhere to be found when my confidence has propelled ahead. Dousing all reservations. I push harder to make better, faster ground, and when I've reached the top, I pull myself onto the ledge of the peak and stand up.

Feeling how small I am in this big wide world, I take a seat on the highest ledge. Not afraid of heights, I look every which way.

And I try to picture my dad up here in his young age. "I did it, Dad." I'm more excited to call him, to tell him everything, when I know I should also be soaking in the moment. My smile flickers in and out.

I can barely make out Akara and Banks waving up at me.

I wave down to them, but their voices are inaudible.

And I look up at the clear blue sky. I stare out at the gorgeous mountain ranges, and I glance at the emptiness beside me. Then back down at the people waiting for me at the bottom while I'm alone at the top.

Climbing four-hundred feet has never felt so far away before.

It shouldn't fucking feel like that.

This was a goal I completed. An achievement. A pump-my-fist-in-the-air *success.*

I hate this loneliness. This was the exact *opposite* of what I thought I'd feel once I free-soloed. So I stand up, grab my rope that I left here for the rappel down, and I step into my harness.

All I want to do is run into their arms.

43

Akara Kitsuwon

WE'VE BEEN ON THE ROAD for hours, and Sulli's mood hasn't lifted much since she descended the rock. Not even as we packed up all our gear and left Yellowstone. I thought she'd be happy after free-soloing Rattlesnake Knuckle. She killed it in under thirty minutes, and that half-hour felt like a full century.

Banks and I were barely breathing. Like maybe for every breath we held, we could give her more. When her feet touched the earth again, I surrounded her first, and she looked like she was about to cry.

"Sulli," I whispered, my heart hurting seeing her that upset.

All she said was, "I thought it'd feel differently."

I hugged her.

Banks hugged her, and I tried not to get in my head at how long she *really* hugged him. It's good that he's a source of refuge and comfort for Sul.

So good.

Very good.

Not a problem at all.

I tap the steering wheel, taking glimpses of the rearview mirror. Just to see Sulli in the backseat. She's been staring solemnly out the Jeep's window. Quiet as ever.

From the passenger seat, Banks glances back at her too with the same heavy concern as me. I didn't know what she meant by *I thought it'd feel differently*, and she was too upset for me to press her on it.

Night has now descended, and the only noise comes from the forest-green Jeep as Booger bumps over potholes on the poorly paved road.

"Sul?" I call back. "Do you want to talk about it?"

She rests her chin on her knees. "I don't know how to explain it."

"Try us," Banks replies.

"I just thought…" She exhales a heavier breath. "I just thought it'd be a powerful moment, being *up there* after free-soloing. A spot my dad once free-soloed too, and it…it wasn't. It was fucking lonely, more than any speed-climb I've done. And I guess I'm used to getting out of a pool after an achievement and being near people. Even running through a finish line, I can turn into another person's arms—up there, I was just *alone*." She says the word from her core, like it's full of a cruel nothingness.

Like it's worse than death.

I'm used to being on my own. More than Sulli or Banks. After my dad died and my mom left for New York, I just had myself to go home to.

Being alone isn't an unfamiliar concept to me, but I've built my whole life around a team of men. Around protecting a girl 24/7.

Around people.

Banks and Sulli have never known life without companionship, and I've been constructing something close to that so I don't have to go back to a life without it.

So I'm never really alone anymore.

She adds softly, "Maybe it's because I put pressure on the free-solo to *feel* something rather than look at the times and my speed. I don't know…"

I swallow hard, her hurt pushing through my sternum. "It's okay for things not to work out exactly how you planned," I remind her. "I know it's hard, but sometimes pivoting turns out better than you expect."

"Like you did with security?" Sulli knows my goal wasn't to be in security work. But my gym wasn't an instant success, and I needed money and a backup plan.

Turns out the backup plan was almost better than the goal.

"Yep," I say. "Just like me and security."

Banks nods, then tells her, "Hang on to the moments you did enjoy. Fuck the rest."

Her lips begin to lift a little. "I like that slogan. Fuck the fucking rest." She leans back, crossing her legs on the seat. "The climb isn't the only reason I'm bummed."

I adjust my grip on the steering wheel. Tension stretching in the knowingness of the silence.

Red flush ascends her neck. "It's over once we're home, right? I have to choose."

I nod slowly, my muscles stiff. "We can't really keep up this bachelorette thing in the city, Sulli. People will figure it out."

Banks adds, "I can't keep a secret from my brother for that long."

"Alright." Her voice is small. "I'll figure this out, I fucking promise. I'm not trying to string you guys along."

We both assure her that we understand.

My muscles are tensed, palms sweating. How do I relax when I could be going home and losing her?

Bank runs a hand across his jaw, then his leg, looking back to Sulli. "Are you leaning one way or the other?"

"I mean, *honestly*, I go back and fucking forth all the time." She covers her eyes. "And I just think, W.W.F.M.J."

I make a face in the rearview. "What?"

Banks pops Skittles in his mouth. "What Would Farrow Moffy and Jane Do?"

"It's missing a *D*," I tell him.

She peeks out a smile. "No, it's *Wise Words from Moffy and Jane*." She leans forward as Banks offers his pack of Skittles. She takes a handful of candy. "I think about what advice they'd give me if they knew what situation I'm in. I think Moffy would just ask me how I feel a lot, and Jane would tell me to make a Pros and Cons list." She tosses Skittles back in her mouth.

"That's a good idea." I nod to my backpack at Banks' feet. "A notebook and pen are in there."

Banks looks at me like I've lost it. "Really?'

"Yeah, she should make this decision with a clear head."

"This isn't a spelling test, Akara," Banks snaps, but he's already unzipping the backpack. "There should be some emotion behind it."

"I didn't say there wasn't. And it's a spelling *bee.*"

He flicks me off.

"Hey," Sulli puts a hand on our shoulders. "Remember, you two could just choose each other. That's another option."

Banks and I exchange a tense look. Yeah, that is an option, but in that scenario, Sulli loses the most. That hurts to think about, so I push the thought back.

Banks passes Sulli the notebook and pen. "Only if you want to."

She flips open a page and slides back in the seat. Clicking the pen over and over.

"You can take your time, Sul," I say. "Don't stress about it."

"No, I've got this." She scrawls down on the notebook for three minutes, and I try to concentrate on the road.

What is she writing?

I have no idea how the matchup between me and Banks is faring. So I pry. "How's it going?"

"Lots of pros on both columns. Zero cons."

I smile.

Banks is smiling too.

I tell her, "Come on, Banks has a ton of *cons.* He definitely farts in his sleep."

Banks tells her, "And Akara's feet smell like spoiled sour cream and chives."

She laughs, "Fine, alright. I'll put the sleep-farter and feet-smeller in your cons, but they're just going to equal each other out." She scribbles, then pauses, sniffing loudly. "Do you smell that?"

"My feet have no scent," I defend.

"No, Kits..."

I already see it. Severity crashes against me as the front hood of the Jeep engulfs with a thick layer of smoke.

Shit.

44

Banks Moretti

THE JEEP SMOKES AND backfires. A rhythmic, repetitive popping sound that I recognize. And I'm thinking, *too easy.* I packed some tools and cleaner in case of any mechanical issues on the road trip. I'll give the carburetor a clean and we'll be good to go.

So we pull over on the side of the road in the dead of night. I pop the hood, and I'm inside her for fifteen minutes, finding problem after problem after fucking problem.

"Is it bad?" Sulli asks, shining a flashlight for me while I check the camshaft and remove the valve covers. Akara is further away, trying to locate a fucking morsel of cell service in a dead-zone.

"She's running lean," I explain to Sulli as I work, "which means too much air is flowing in the engine. The air intake boot has ripped, and it's causing unmetered air in the engine. Plus, the main vacuum hose broke." I remove another valve. "It's the power brake booster feed line. *And* the spark plugs are worn out." I did a routine check before we got on the road, and none of this shit looked *this* fucked.

"Can it be fixed?" Sulli asks.

I wipe sweat off my brow with my bicep. It's cold outside, but *I'm* running hot. "Anything can be fixed. It just depends on the parts I need to fix it." I crank the engine and then motion her closer to me. "Shine the light over here." The valve spring windings are harder to see.

She presses up to my side and angles the light downward. I observe the intake and exhaust valve operation opening and closing, and I check the spring windings.

Fuck.

"It's bad," she realizes off my scowl.

"We can add broken springs to the list." I glower at the pushrods. *Fuck.* "And a bent pushrod." I expel a coarse breath. "It's restricting the movement of the valve." If I had a towel, I'd throw it right now. I reach into her and do a final carburetor assessment.

I back up, my chest collapsing in realization. "I think she needs a new carburetor."

"So you can't just clean it?"

I shake my head. "There's no point wasting time trying. She already needs a new air intake boot. It can't be fixed out here, but if we get her to a shop, they *might* have the parts we need."

Akara comes back, hearing that last bit. "No service. I can't say how far away the nearest town is."

"Where are we?" I ask him while I lean back into the car and return the valves to their original spots.

"Minnesota."

"Fuck," Sulli mutters, smacking her flashlight that flickers out.

Akara points his cellphone flashlight at Booger, helping me see. My oil-stained hands move around her innerworkings. I pry off the tracker her parents placed on her car—and it's dead. Battery must've died, who knows when.

"I can run down the road," Sulli offers. "Maybe I'll find a town or gas station, or even cell service. Then we can call a tow truck and get Booger to the nearest shop."

My muscles are flexed, seeing holes in her plan before Akara points them out.

"We'd have to run with you, Sulli," Akara reminds her that we're not just two guys she's dating—we're her bodyguards.

"Then run with me."

"That means leaving the Jeep on the side of the road, which we *can't* do."

Her Jeep isn't just any old car. It belonged to Adam Sully. Fans have even created an Instagram page for the thing. It's famous. It's sentimental.

Akara and I know what the Jeep means to Sulli—what it means to her dad—what it means to the Meadows family and the public.

Leaving it behind is like deserting another person attached to Sulli.

We can't.

I shut the hood, and Akara tells her and me, "Three options: we all three push the car to the nearest shop, or Banks pushes while Sulli and I run ahead, or I just run ahead and you two push."

I hate making the tough calls, and luckily, it's not my job to choose. "What do you say?" I ask him.

"We don't need two people to run, but you'd gain more ground having two people push the car. So Option 3: I run. You two push." He looks to Sulli. "You okay with that?"

"I wish I could be the one to run, but I fucking get it." She nods, knowing she can't run alone like us, even if she's the fastest runner. It's the fuckin' pitfalls of fame.

With the plan in order, we get to work.

Hour one, sweat drips off my brow. Muscles ache, but I fucking push next to Sulli. Barely any cars pass us in the middle of the night on a mostly empty, deserted road. The few vehicles that stop only cause Sulli anxiety. I always block her. I always talk to them, and when they acknowledge they can't help, they take off.

Hour two, we worry about Akara.

"He could've tripped," Sulli says between her teeth, pushing the back of the Jeep next to me, "and broken his ankle or something,"

"We'd pass him," I grunt. "We're going the same way."

Hour three, my legs start cramping. My fucking back throbs. I grit down, using all my force as I shove forward. The longer we keep at it, the Jeep feels heavier, like we're trying to move a Humvee, then a tank, but I never stop.

Sulli never stops.

I'd push through any hell if I needed to, but the question is, is all we've got even enough?

"How many miles…" Sulli pushes the Jeep with her back, using her quad muscles, "do you think we've gone?"

Five klicks. "Maybe 3 miles."

I check the time on my watch.

Zero four hundred hours. The sun isn't close to rising. It's *early* on October 31st. An Unhappy Halloween. Because my brother is supposed to be getting married bright and early at zero nine hundred hours tomorrow.

We have only a little more than twenty-four hours to make it back to Philly, and I'm currently hundreds of miles away.

Sulli takes out her phone. "No service."

Dammit. Sweat drips down my temples, my jaw.

She switches around, using her hands again to push. Sulli grunts and bites down, her biceps cutting sharp as she shoves harder.

She knows.

She knows how important being back in Philly is to me. She'd probably kill herself to get me there.

"Pace yourself," I say in a heavy breath.

"We can make it," she grits down with all the force she exerts.

My eyes burn, holding something back. "Don't hurt yourself doing it."

She only applies more effort, her face reddened, shirt caked with sweat. "Let's go...faster."

I breathe harder.

Hour four, she glances over at me with reddened, glassy eyes.

"We still have time," Sulli says, voice choked, "...if we just ditch Booger, we can run, meet up with Akara, call an Uber, book a flight—"

"No."

"We have to leave her, Banks!" Sulli shouts tearfully, standing up and letting go of the Jeep for the first time in four hours. "I'm not letting you miss your brother's wedding because of a stupid fucking *car*."

I've never heard Sulli insult her Jeep before. It means something more to her than I can even understand. "It's not a stupid fucking car," I snap back. "Akara said you *cried* when you were sixteen and your dad gave you the *one* thing he had left of his best friend. You cried snot-nosed tears, and you've told me multiple times that you *promised* your dad that you'd take care of this car—Adam *Sully's* car. You promised him."

She's crying now. Fighting more tears, she rubs a hand under her running nose. "And that's your *twin* brother," she retorts. "The guy you shared a womb with. The guy you went to war with. You've spent twenty-nine years of your life with your twin, and you've told me *multiple times* that you can't wait to stand next to him on his wedding day. Your brother. Your twin."

We're both breathing even harder.

And I'm falling more and more in love with her.

"One is a memory," Sulli says in tears. "The other is a person who's still here. *Please* don't miss his wedding to save a Jeep that might be fine on its own. *Please.*"

I'm used to taking the selfless roads where *duty* is concerned.

I'm bound to Sulli's needs. Not my own, and she's trying to throttle me, shake me, to place myself above her. I think about how much it'll break my brother if I'm not there, and that just about breaks me. I'm placing him above the Jeep.

I'm about to step away from Booger when we hear a *ding ding* of a bicycle bell. Dawn is nearing, but even through the darkness, I make out Akara.

He pedals harder on a pink child's bike, fit with a basket and ribbons out of the handles.

He's in one piece. It's one of the first times I almost smile.

Sulli exhales relief. "What happened? You're alright?"

"Yeah, I'm okay. You both are good?" He jumps off the bike, coming next to us and assessing our ragged states. Sulli nods enough that Akara doesn't press, and he just explains, "The nearest gas station had cell service. I called a tow truck, but the closest one available is really far away. It'll take *four* hours to get here."

"Fuck," Sulli and I say in unison.

Akara seems less concerned. "The shop is actually closer. It's only another mile away. I called them already. It opens in an hour, but no one picked up. So I bought a bike at the gas station—it was the cashier's nieces, and I went to the shop, banged on the door, and got ahold of a mechanic. I told him the Jeep's model, and he said he has the air intake boot and carburetor we need."

Now I really smile. "What are we waiting for?"

Akara smiles, and we share a bigger one with Sulli before we all return our hands to the Jeep. One more mile to go, and we push together.

All three of us.

For once, the Jeep feels light as air.

45

Sullivan Meadows

WE REACH THE SMALL Minnesota town after pushing Booger for five hours. Exactly twenty-four hours until the wedding, I feel hope surge knowing that we can still drive to Philly in time.

Pumpkins are set out beside a burnt-red garage. Ghosts hang from the trees, and fake cobwebs are stretched between toolboxes inside. The sky lightens to a morning blue, but the sun is still hidden.

It's quiet in the garage. The doors are open to the lonely road while we wait near Booger. After the mechanic brings out the parts, Banks pops the hood, and they talk and start to work their magic.

I'm exhausted. My whole body is sore, but I'm less physically spent and just emotionally wiped out. Akara pockets his phone so he can hold my hand, but before our fingers even clasp together, everything comes crashing down again.

Banks comes over to us fast. "It's the wrong carburetor for this older model. He thought they would match, but it's not gonna fit." He uses the bottom of his white tee to wipe grease off his hands. "We can order parts, but he said they won't be here for another two days."

I butt in, "Booger stays here. She *stays here.*" I convince myself that nothing bad will happen to my Jeep if we desert her. She'll survive, and I'll *never* forgive myself if we don't do everything possible to make it to Jane and Thatcher's wedding.

That's my cousin. My big sister. I can't miss her walk down the aisle. Banks can't miss his twin brother get married.

I'm a bridesmaid. Banks is the best man. Akara is a groomsman. We're *all* in the wedding party and supposed to be a part of the ceremony.

I add strongly, "And we don't have time to argue about it. Salvaging her isn't a part of the plan anymore." It hurts when I think about the day my dad gave me the keys. How he started crying with me. My dad rarely cries like that—like something was torn open in him for a second and he was brought back to a place in the sky where he released the ashes of his friend.

He gave me the Jeep because he said I'd get more use out of it. He didn't want the car to languish in a garage.

I still remember him saying, "Adam Sully took his car around the country, and he'd want someone to go on just as many adventures in it. It's yours, Sulli. Just promise me you'll take care of it."

I promised him, but no matter how painful, I'd break it for Banks.

Softly, Banks asks, "Are you sure?"

"I'm more positive than I've ever fucking been," I tell him with everything in me, my voice shaking with emotion. "I love you more than that car."

His chest rises, lips parting at my declaration. I told Banks that I love him. It just came out. It came out in front of Akara. Fuck!

Fuck.

I'm dying inside, seeing Akara's face contort in heartbreak. It hurts like a hundred knives stabbing my lungs. And I'm not that dense that I'd fling an *I love you* at Akara right now. Because he'll just see the words as a pity thing.

Even when they're true.

"Kits," I start.

"It's okay," he chokes, swallowing hard. "I'll call a tow truck for the Jeep, so it'll get back to Philly without us." His eyes stay on me, mine stay on him, and he says, "It's not a new realization, Sul. I've known how you feel about him."

"Do you know how I feel about you?" I breathe, my throat swollen.

He nods with a sad smile. "Yeah." He nods again. "You love me too, string bean. It's why you haven't picked yet."

Yeah.

I sniff back snot that tries to drip down my lips.

"We're going to get through this," Akara tells me and also Banks, and even though his words encompass our current car situation, it feels like he's speaking about so much more too.

We whip out our phones.

Akara books a tow-truck to transport Booger, so the Jeep is set to arrive back home in a few days. But we need to find a way to get ourselves to Philly much earlier than that.

"Nearest airport is a two-hour drive," Akara says.

I scroll through my phone, looking for taxis, Ubers, Lyfts. Anything that will get us from point A to point B.

Banks is looking for flights.

Akara breaks away and speaks to the mechanic. I barely pick up their conversation as Akara asks, "Is there any local we can call to take us to the airport?"

The mechanic chuckles. "If you find someone 'round here to take you there, let me know. I'd like their number."

Fan-fucking-tastic.

"No ride shares are in range," I tell Banks.

He eyes Akara, who disappears into the back of the shop with the mechanic. "Akara will think of something. He always does."

Five minutes later, Akara returns and opens the glove compartment of Booger. He pulls out an envelope stuffed with cash—*his* cash that he brought for "emergencies"—and he jogs back to the mechanic. Vanishing again.

One-minute later, he comes out and dangles a set of keys. "Let's go."

"You bought a car?" I ask, my heart swelling up.

"Yep."

I could kiss him, but I think the way I'm looking at Kits means more than any kiss. He smiles down at me, his eyes roaming over my features.

He tells me and Banks, "I paid all cash and bypassed the paperwork. We can get out of here now."

Wasting no time, we all unload our crap from Booger. Transferring our bags to an old, black Honda with wrinkled and ripped, black leather seats.

Before noon, we're on the road.

I drive first since they're both on the phone.

"Slow down, Sul," Akara says in the passenger seat.

"I'm only going fourteen-over," I refute. "I won't get stopped."

"It's not going to matter," Banks says from the backseat. I glance through the rearview. He's looking at his cell. "There's only one flight back to Philly. And it leaves tonight."

"What time does it say we get in?" I wonder.

"Give me," Akara leans over and holds out his hand for Banks' cell.

Banks says to me, "We'd arrive at oh-six-hundred." He passes his cell to Akara.

So…6 a.m. The venue is only a half-hour from Philly. Wedding is at 9 a.m.

It's perfect.

"I'm booking it," Akara says.

I slow the car to the speed limit. We have time then to make it to the airport. But if I wreck this Honda, I really will never forgive myself.

46

Akara Kitsuwon

THE DRIVE TO THE AIRPORT is painful. Like being in a slow-moving train that I know is about to crash. And it has nothing to do with being late to the wedding. I'm *confident* we'll be there with hours to spare. Even without a private jet.

We did visit that avenue. Sulli called her uncle, but Connor couldn't find a pilot available in our area. At least not in the window we're working with.

But I've pinned down four other possible commercial flights with short layovers that we could take at last minute. Just in case our current flight is delayed.

Sulli is in love with Banks.

The thought crawls over me every few minutes and digs into my flesh.

Be happy for them, Nine.

How?

How can I be happy when I love her too? I *love* Sullivan Minnie Meadows, and I don't want to let her go. I've even contemplated whispering the words in her ear. Shouting them with all I have. Making *sure* she knows how much I love her, so I've put everything on the table.

If she chooses him, I don't want it to be because she's unsure of how I feel.

But the timing isn't right. I'm not alone with Sulli. Banks is here too. And I'm more aware that going back to Philly feels more brutal than it should. The closer to the airport we are, the less relieved I am.

Sulli parks on the third floor of the parking deck. Only a few cars dot this level, which gives us plenty of privacy as we climb out and pop the trunk of the Honda. Sulli is digging in the backseat, gathering her backpack and things.

I scope out our surroundings, and as Banks pries a duffel from the trunk, I take the bag from his hands—*something's wrong.*

He cinches one eye closed, wincing at fluorescent, parking deck lights that flicker on as dark clouds roll across the sky.

I solidify. "You're in pain?"

Banks roots a hand to the side of the car.

I drop the bag. "Banks—talk to me."

He hunches over, gripping the side of his head. "*Fuck*," he grits through his teeth.

My pulse spikes. I dig into my pocket, about to call 9-1-1.

"Banks?" Sulli crawls out of the car and races to him, a hand to his shoulder. "Is it your head? Just sit down. Sit down." She helps him lower against the tire of the Honda.

He rests his head back against the car. Both eyes cinched shut.

I tell him, "I'm calling an ambulance—"

"No," he chokes, breathing hard through his nose. "Don't." He reaches a floppy hand out to steal my phone. I easily hold it out of his clutch.

Sulli squats next to him. "What do you need? Tylenol?"

He nods stiffly.

Sulli races back to our bags and starts digging in them.

Panic has already shot off in me. "Your head hurts?"

He nods. "Like a nail-gun to a…" He can't even get out the words. He turns his head and pukes on the concrete. "Fuck," he groans and spits.

"I have water," Sulli calls out, rolling the bottle to me while she keeps searching for Tylenol.

I grab the water and crouch down to him, my hand on his shoulder.

He bangs his head back, face stuck in a grimace.

"Can you drink something?" I ask, popping the plastic lid to the water bottle.

Banks feels for the bottle, but I put it in his hand. He squirts some water in his mouth, swallows hard.

I grip my phone again. "You need a doctor—"

He shakes his head.

"*Banks*, I can't just let you sit here and mask whatever's happening with pain meds." My voice is shaking. I'm angry that I haven't pushed him to see a doctor earlier—like Farrow. *Farrow.* We've been around a fucking doctor for *weeks*, and I never brought up Banks' headaches.

And I'm afraid that this is just a symptom of something bigger that's happening right *now.*

Banks opens one eye to glare. "My brother…"

He knows if I call an ambulance, he'll be stuck in a hospital, and he'll miss the wedding. We all will, because there's absolutely *no way* I'd leave him.

He's one of my men.

But it's more than that.

"I can't let you risk your own life to make a wedding—"

"*My brother*," he forces, his eyes bloodshot.

"Thatcher would understand," I retort.

He shakes his head. "I can't do that—"

"You could die," I cut him off hotly, standing up. "You could fucking *die*, Banks. Your migraines could be a symptom of something bigger, and you could end up flat on your back *unconscious* and *seizing.* And I love you too much to let you die out in the middle of fucking Minnesota!" My pained voice echoes through the parking deck.

Shit.

I look around quickly for strangers.

Sulli is safe.

No one else is here.

I told Banks that I loved him before telling Sulli I love her. Awesome.

So very awesome.

I push my hair back. My heart rate accelerates even faster, and Banks tilts his head, looking up at me from his slouched spot against the tire. His knowing, understanding gaze just punctures me more.

Very gently, he says, "It's not a brain aneurysm."

Sulli comes back, kneeling beside Banks. She helps him with the pain meds, but she eyes me like I'm the one barfing on the ground and in need of assistance.

I lick my dried lips, then go to massage my knuckles, but my phone is in my fist.

They both know my mom has been in the hospital for brain aneurysms. She's had *six* over the course of her life. Surgery for three. Same symptoms that I just saw from Banks right now.

Sensitivity to light.

Nausea.

The day she had her first seizure, I found her in the kitchen. I was eighteen. I'd just lost my dad a year before, and I thought I was about to lose my mom.

After she got a diagnosis, she chose to move back to New York. Family upon family are all there, cousins and aunties and uncles who are closer than close. Family that my parents left when they had me and ended up in Philly. Family that I didn't grow up around.

It was always just me and my mom and my dad.

Thais look after their elderly parents, and even though she wasn't old yet, I thought my mom would let me help her. Be there for her. Take care of her.

But she chose New York and her brothers and sisters a year after I opened my gym in Philadelphia. A year after I sunk my dad's life insurance into a business that I couldn't abandon.

A year after I committed myself to the city where *she* raised me.

She left, knowing that I couldn't follow.

I was nineteen.

And she keeps me briefly in the loop about her health, but I hate feeling like she left because she didn't want to burden me. Some days, I just miss my mom. I worry about her regardless if she's a mile away or a hundred.

And now I'm afraid for Banks.

"You can't be sure it's not a brain aneurysm," I tell him, "or something worse."

Banks washes down paid meds, forcing his eyes open on me. "I've had migraines since I got back from my deployment." He takes a sharp breath. "It's been like this since I was twenty-two. There's nothing more to them than this. I promise." He's not as pale. He's able to speak.

"Have you ever seen a neurologist?" I ask.

He shakes his head.

"*Banks,*" Sulli says in shock. "I'd slug you right now."

Banks tries to smile, but he's trying not to puke again. "Doctors are expensive."

"I pay for your health insurance," I remind him. "And it's fucking good and expensive *for me.*"

His lip manages to quirk. "Maybe I just don't trust them."

"That sounds more accurate," I say, my phone still in my fist. If I let him get on a plane and something were to happen to him mid-air, I couldn't live with that. It'd be the worse decision I've ever made.

But if it's only a temporary migraine and I send him to the hospital where he misses Thatcher's wedding…

Shit.

What am I going to do?

I flip my phone in my palm.

Trust yourself, Nine.

I pocket my phone. "Can you stand?"

Banks relaxes seeing the threat of an ambulance gone. "Yeah." He weakly picks himself up with Sulli's and my help. And once he's able to stand on his own, we grab the bags. He tries to pick one up, and I shove his chest.

"What is it you always say?" I ask him, then snap my finger. "*No way in hell.*"

Banks cracks a weak smile. "That saying doesn't work for you, Akara. You'd find some way in hell. That's why I follow you and not the other way around."

I almost smile back, but I won't fully breathe until we're in Philly and he's standing on two feet. "Promise me, when we get back home, you'll go see someone about your migraines."

He gives me a nod. Barely a promise.

But I accept what I can. Right now, we have a plane to catch.

47

Banks Moretti

MY PHONE IS HEAVY in my hand. I stand at the huge glass window, overlooking a half-a-dozen idled planes. The sun has gone down; lights blink around the tarmac, and rain batters the glass and the pavement and my fucking *soul.*

The airport is packed with restless and sleeping bodies. Electronic boards read *delayed, delayed, delayed.* Sulli has been making calls to her family. Her sister steamed her pale-yellow dress and has been holding onto the garment bag. Every bridesmaid is going to wear a different pastel, cotton-candy color.

Every groom has a different pastel, cotton-candy-colored tie. My mom has my black tux, my mint-green tie, and Akara's pastel pink. They're helping us so when we arrive, we'll just slip right in and carry on.

Except the storm that's tearing through Minnesota isn't letting up. Rain rolls down the glass I stare out of, and high winds thrash suitcases off carts, lying sideways on the tarmac.

This is going to be the hardest call I've ever made in my life.

And I don't want to make it.

I wish to God I didn't have to.

My finger presses his number, a thousand pounds of lead in my stomach. And I lift my phone to my ear.

He picks up on the first ring. "I'm looking at the flight tracker right now." He's been staring at it all night. I know my twin brother.

"What's it say?" I ask, choked.

The line is loud with our pain.

"It might not be delayed for long," he says, his voice just as tight. "It could pass through in enough time."

"Thatcher." My voice breaks. I pinch my eyes, my chest heaving. *It's too late.* I can't get the words out. "I'm sorry, I'm sorry, I'm sorry." I breathe out the apologies like a cathartic release, but it's not enough to take away the iron fist around my vital organs.

Thatcher sniffs loudly, a sharp sound in his throat like he's holding back tears.

I catch Jane's soft, consoling voice in the background. "I'm here."

I smear a hand down my face. "I'm sorry," I whisper, shifting my weight. "I'm so sorry."

"No, I'm sorry," Thatcher chokes out.

"What do you have to be sorry about?" I question, my nose flaring and eyes burning. "Huh? You're not the one missing..." My face twists, chin quakes. *This is happening.* This is really fucking happening.

"It's out of your control," Thatcher says in a deep, shaking breath. "And I'm sorry if you think I'm pissed at you—I'm not. You know I can't be, not for more than a second."

I wipe the wet streaks off my face. "I want to be there."

"I want you here."

Tears well up again. Heaviness bears down on my chest. "I physically can't make it."

"I know. It's okay."

I shake my head to myself.

Imagine growing up with someone from the first breath to twenty-nine. Sharing every milestone together. We're bonded by something stronger than friendship or family. Something deep and unseen. For the rest of our lives, we'll be tied together in this world. And I'm going to miss one of the biggest moments of his life.

I never imagined I wouldn't be there.

"It'll never be okay," I tell him.

"I can postpone the wedding," Thatcher says, and I hear Jane voice her agreement in the background.

I feel sick, worse than the migraine I endured earlier. "You aren't doing that Thatcher *Alessio* Moretti," I say in a whisper. "You *can't.*" I go on and on about how there are too many people involved in the wedding. Too many family members. All the work Jane did. And I end with, "I'd never want you to change everything just for me."

"I'd change my world for you," he whispers back.

I'd do the same for you.

It all crashes into me. "You shouldn't have to." I wipe my nose with my hand. "I'll be alright. You'll be alright. Sky will be with you."

Mention of our older brother breaks Thatcher. I hear him choke on a sob. I stare harder at the tarmac, fighting more tears. "I'll see you and Janie when I can." I take a breath. "I love you."

Thatcher inhales. "I love you too. Be safe."

I breathe in more and add, "Tell Ma and grandma I'm fine. And tell your future brother-in-laws to record everything. Every angle."

"I'll tell my future sister-in-law," Thatcher says softly. "Audrey will do a better job."

I wipe at my face again. "Good."

Good.

We stay on the line for a moment longer, and then we say our official goodbyes and I hang up. I'm frozen solid for a second.

Gutted.

And then I feel a hand on my shoulder. Another on my waist. Akara and Sulli come to either side of me. They don't say anything. The three of us just stand together. Looking out at the lights on the tarmac. The pain ebbs and flows inside me, and I feel them trying to carry it. To take it away.

Christ, I can't imagine being here alone. With no one. The thought is more painful, so I hold onto the soothing reality.

They're here with me.

It'll be alright.

48

Sullivan Meadows

WE REACH THE STEPS of the stone mansion, resembling some kind of royal, Tudor castle with roses etched into wooden arches. Stunning, fucking *majestic*, and perfectly fitting for Jane.

Brass knockers decorate the humongous oak double-doors, and they're already cracked open. Inside, a white-gloved server greets us with a tray of espresso martinis, and I know the reception is halfway over.

Winona has been texting me updates so I can track how much we've missed.

The ceremony has ended.

Dinner has been served. Plates of sea bass, bread and butter, beef tenderloin, chicken marsala, cavatelli: a pasta that Banks pronounced *gavadeel'*, and more are eaten and washed clean.

So at least Banks, Akara, and I are heading to the outdoor reception without blindfolds. We know what we're barreling into.

Not pausing to grab espresso martinis, we quickly pass the server and half-jog, half-walk down the long castle hallway. Oil portraits of historic, 1700s Philly are framed on dark-wood paneling. Chandeliers that probably cost more than a Rolls-Royce hang above our hurried pace.

We're wearing the same grimy clothes we had on in Yellowstone. The same ones we wore when we pushed Booger down a deserted road. Same ones we had on at the airport, then the plane, then our taxi ride here.

No time for showers. Just a quick swipe of deodorant and a swish of mouthwash. My hair is piled into a bun, and I've lost the ability to catch our scent hours ago.

I'm sure I smell just fucking *wonderful.*

But none of that matters. Every second we miss the reception is another memory gone.

"Screw this maze," Banks grunts as we end at a fork in the hall. I peek into the grand ballroom where the ceremony took place. Littered with colorful dahlias, bright-blue cornflowers, and baskets of baby pink verbenas. Flowers I couldn't name if it weren't for Jane showing me the floral list.

My heart pangs, seeing the venue's staff take away stacks of chairs. I can almost picture the romantic, sentimental ceremony. The smiles, tears and tissues, and Jane smiling so brightly up at her groom that her cheeks turn a rosy pink.

Banks opens a door that might be an exit.

It's a broom closet.

He groans, "Mother of Christ."

To reach the gardens, we have to go through the venue. Perfect for privacy and security but fucking hard for three latecomers who just want to be *there* already.

Akara switches a knob on his radio. He must hear something because he says, "Take a right."

Banks blazes ahead, and I'm right behind him.

Seconds later, we find stained-glass double-doors that lead to the outdoor gardens. Chilly tonight, guests wear coats since the sun has just disappeared. Fairy lights are strung up between trees, and the dance floor is crowded.

As soon as the three of us exit the stone building and enter the party, the song switches. It's in that sudden moment of silence that someone from Banks' family spots him and yells, "BANKS IS HERE!"

A giant metaphorical spotlight shines down on us.

If I didn't feel out of place in my jeans, T-shirt, dirt-smudged cheeks, and messy bun—I definitely fucking do now.

Banks grumbles, "Aunt Tami."

Thank you, Aunt Tami.

One good thing comes from the immediate attention, Thatcher and Jane are *running* towards us. Jane hikes up her wedding dress to gain speed.

My eyes immediately well when I see my cousin in her wedding gown. The bodice is a pastel baby blue with multi-colored, glittering rhinestones. Baby blue tulle upon tulle fills the bottom of the dress with more gems sewed throughout.

She looks like a fairy princess.

And when her arms fly around my shoulders, it's hard not to burst into tears. "I'm so sorry, Jane," I say at the same time she says, "I'm so glad you made it."

I wipe roughly at my face. "I didn't make it."

We break away and she brushes the remaining tears off my cheeks. "You're here, aren't you?" She must see the guilt in my eyes. "It's not your fault, Sulli."

It is my fault. I could have finished climbing a day earlier. A week earlier. Fuck, the trip could have been postponed until *after* the wedding. Until next year. Banks would have made it in all of those scenarios. I would have made it. Akara would have made it.

It will always be my fault.

No matter who tells me any fucking differently. No matter how many times Banks professes that it's not, the guilt will stay in my heart where it belongs. I've learned a lot over this trip. How forgiveness is hard for me. It's going to be even harder to forgive myself.

"You're going to regret coming," Thatcher tells his brother. Jane and I both catch their conversation and look over. Thatcher has an uncharacteristic smile on his face. "*Everyone* wants to hear this story. You're going to end up talking to more family than me."

Banks grimaces. "How about we do another twin-switch for a couple hours?"

"Hell no. I'm going to be the one dancing with my wife." Thatcher grins wider and then his face grows more serious. "You were right." He takes a beat. "I felt him there."

Banks nods more than once, too choked to speak. He must be referring to Skylar. I watch as Banks pats the necklace against Thatcher's chest: two gold horns.

And then Thatcher brings his brother into another tight hug.

Right as they pull apart and Thatcher hugs Akara, Jane squeezes my hand. Grabbing my attention as she says, "Your parents have been worried about you."

I suck in a tight breath. *My parents.* I had a quick phone call with them at the airport, so I know their worry is at the top of Mount Everest right now.

I give Jane a smile and squeeze her hand back. "Congratulations, Mrs. Moretti." It's been wildly speculated in the media if she'd take Thatcher's name.

She told me her decision weeks ago.

Jane Eleanor Moretti.

She dropped the Cobalt. But in her words, "Being a Cobalt isn't in name. It's in blood and heart." I believe that as much as being a Meadows is in spirit.

My cousin lights up at hearing me call her a Moretti, and I hope to feel that happiness one day. Completely swallowed up in someone else that you love sharing everything. Time, companionship, clothes, down to a name.

But a prick of anxiety nips at me. My ribs tighten thinking about that choice.

A name.

Kitsuwon

Moretti.

I'm not talking about marriage. That's not even on my fucking radar. I just want the feeling, the relationship, the romance, and I definitely wish I could just *detach* from the doom and gloom of losing one of them and enjoy Jane's wedding.

So I try my best to forget.

Jane and I give each other another hug before I leave her side to hunt down my parents. As soon as I shift away, I'm surprised when

Akara doesn't follow me. Instead, a temp bodyguard edges closer like he's been silently instructed to take my detail.

Glancing around for Kits, who's left Thatcher and Banks' side, I find him speaking to an older-looking man who's well over Akara's six-foot-two height.

Michael Moretti.

Akara is finally able to formally greet Banks' dad.

49

Banks Moretti

COUSINS SWARM ME, and thank Christ I'm great at brevity because I fling cliff-notes versions of what happened every which way.

While my brother and Janie make rounds thanking guests, I position myself near a cluster of red rose bushes. As far from the outdoor heaters as possible, which warm the *three* fully stocked bars, the packed dance floor, a three-piece orchestra playing Italian classics, a crooner singing way too much Sinatra (Sorry, Grandma)—plus a DJ, four dessert tables, and several round, wicker tables for guests.

I'm hoping to shake off some of the extreme talkers, but apparently, everyone wants to freeze their ass-cheeks to come hear my story.

Staying in one spot isn't working, so I just slip between chatting guests. Moving like a shadow throughout the gardens. And my eyes return to Akara and my dad. They speak near a pond where pink rose petals float across the water.

Really looking at my strict, hardass dad stops me in my tracks.

My nose flares.

I was twelve the night my brother died. Twelve the night that my gutted, grief-ridden dad looked me in the eye with this dark hollowness and said, "You're the dispensable one. It should've been you."

It hurt to hear when I was a kid.

But as an adult, looking back—for my dad to tell his twelve-year-old son that he wished he died over his fifteen-year-old…it's *unthinkable* to me. I'd never do that to someone, let alone a *kid.*

Sucks for him, I'm still alive.

And I'm not planning on going anywhere.

My dad laughs at something Akara says, and Akara smiles back, a hand to my dad's shoulder who laughs more. Looks like they're already hitting it off.

Good.

I only ever told Sulli and Akara half the story about what my dad said. Because I genuinely want good things for Kitsuwon Securities, for my best friend, and I'm not sure what Akara would do if he knew my dad told me I should've been the one to die.

I take in the reception around me.

Smiling faces. Dancing bodies, and I've always felt like air. Able to go anywhere, but I feel in limbo. Purgatory.

Stuck.

But my lip curves, seeing my brother twirl Jane towards the dance floor. His happiness tries to lift me. Maybe if I lose Sulli, it'll be enough just to be happy for him.

Who am I kidding?

I'll be devastated if I can't be with her.

I shove my hands in my blue cargo jacket.

Uncle Joe comes up next to me. Besides me and Thatcher, he's the only other person to reach six-seven here. A hand to my shoulder, his hoarse voice is nothing but kind as he says, "Whadda you doin' here all alone, huh?"

"Moping, I guess." I sigh, trying to look anywhere but at the happy couples. Goddammit, there are so many. *Weddings.*

Uncle Joe squeezes my shoulder. "You're here. Family's all together now. Fuhgeddabout the rest."

I nod.

"Come, let's have a drink."

Having a lot of love for my uncle, I always do what he says. And I forget about the rest. For now, at least. Following him to the bar, we cheers over glasses of whiskey on ice. I smile, and after he's caught in another conversation, I spot Farrow near a frozen ice sculpture of a lion.

I excuse myself and jog over to the neck-tattooed maverick. "Hey," I nod.

He's digging in a diaper bag, a strand of bleach-white hair in his eyes. His pierced brows lift to me, but his hands keep moving. "Nice to see you made it here. Jane thought you might get lost through the mansion."

"I did," I admit.

Farrow's smile stretches into a laugh. "No shit?"

I bounce my head, then smack his chest as he rises. "Thanks, by the way." I pause. "For being there for him."

Farrow filled in as *best man.* He stood next to my brother. He handed him the ring.

I add, "And I know Charlie and Beckett were up there too, but that's not the same as having a friend. It meant a lot to me that my brother wasn't alone."

Farrow's smile softens. "Anytime."

"Hey, Farrow!" Loren Hale calls from afar, who has Ripley in his arms. They must need something in the diaper bag, so I nod goodbye to Farrow and dip out.

I end up on the edge of the dance floor where my four-foot-eleven Grandma Carol sips on a glass of brandy and shimmies left and right to Sinatra. "Banks!" she exclaims as soon as I approach, and I bend down and kiss her rosy-red cheek.

"My boys are all together." She cups my face as I'm bent down. "Oh, don't youse look so handsome."

I've never seen eyes that smile as brightly as hers. None of us would've made it without her in our lives.

I stand up fully. "You look more beautiful than I look handsome, Grandma."

She waves her hand like I'm full of shit. "Let's dance. Youse hear that?"

Sinatra. "Andrea Bocelli?"

My mom snorts, coming up to us, "You go to Yellowstone and come back a smartass."

"Hey, Ma," I greet, and my grandma is still grinning as I spin her again. With my hand still in Grandma Carol's, I kiss my mom's cheek. "You look beautiful tonight."

She doesn't even glance down at her black sequined pantsuit. She's just smiling at me like she knows I've been through the ringer and need all the love I can get. "Banksy. We missed you." She reaches up and cups my cheek. "Don't get into any more trouble. Not without your brother."

Trouble.

I laugh. "I thought we were the good sons."

"Still are. Always will be." She kisses her fingers to reach up to place them on my cheek.

The women who raised me are my world.

I dance with my mom, with my grandma, and I look around for Sulli—but I can't see her. Not even as my mom's wife, Nicola, sneaks up behind her. They laugh and kiss, and my grandma asks me, "When's your turn to find that special someone, Banks?"

"Yeah," Nicola chimes in, "any lucky girls recently?"

Sulli.

Can't say that. Can't even say if it'll last past tomorrow.

Before I find an answer, my mom adds with a smile, "Or any lucky guys."

She's trying to be inclusive, *just in case.* I try to crack another smile, but it flickers fast. "You three are trouble when you're all together. You know that?"

They grin, and my grandma passes around her brandy as they dance.

Right when I turn my head, I finally spot Sulli.

She just now detaches from the chatty girl squad, and she's heading to her parents.

Sullivan Meadows

UNDER THE TWINKLING fairy lights, my mom and dad linger next to a chocolate fountain. Goldilocks sits cutely at my mom's feet with a bow around her collar, tail wagging. With my mom and dad's parental eyes on me, I'm pretty fucking positive they've been staring at me since I arrived.

They wanted to give me a moment with Jane, and my appreciation is second-chair to my urgency to see them. To talk to them. Especially since all the younger girls trapped me into rehashing the story in *grave* detail.

I'm not a good fucking storyteller.

Kinney even said, "Blah," at the end.

That was my review.

Blah.

My trip to Yellowstone was *not* blah. It was…it is…

I inhale deeply.

Maybe there are no words. Maybe it's just a feeling. Maybe it's always just been an inexplicable feeling.

As soon as I near, my mom wraps her arms around me. I know everyone says Aunt Lily gives the best hugs, but in my biased opinion, nothing beats hugs from my mom. Secure and warm and full of unyielding love.

"My peanut butter cupcake." She kisses the top of my head, a couple inches taller than me in her heels. "I'm so, *so* happy you're home. And you're safe—"

She cuts herself off to pull back and check my face. Dirt and scrapes exist, but the scratch from the cougar attack is hidden underneath my shirt. Her green eyes are the same bright color as mine and they carry years of wisdom, risks, and explorations.

"I'm sorry, I smell," I say.

"You smell like adventure." She wags her brows.

I laugh and rub my running nose with my sleeve. "So I smell like royal shit."

"You smell like the woods," my dad says, and he leans in for a hug. His hugs are pretty fucking close to bear-hugs. Rough, protective, and full of strength. I want to siphon off that last bit of strength from him. To get through this.

When we break apart, it's hard not to look around at the guests that keep gawking at me. There are so many more people here than just my family. So many more people here than the mountains I left.

"Hey, Sul," my dad says. "You don't have to fucking stay here. If you want to leave—"

"I can stay." *For Jane*, I should stay.

He nods slowly, his intense eyes zoning in on me for a second. His strong worry is like the waves of an ocean, crashing against me in rough swells. "You've had a long fucking day. Are you alright?"

Pressure compacts on my chest. Usually now would be the moment I'd gush to them about how it's my fault Banks missed the wedding. How I'm in a B*achelorette* scenario and the final rose is coming up. And I'm going to hurt Akara or Banks. How I free-soloed *one* measly rock face the whole trip and it feels like it wasn't *enough*.

I want to tell them I survived a cougar attack with two people I'm falling in love with.

But I can't say any of it. It feels too raw. Like if I touch it, the words will explode in my heart and shatter me apart.

In the end, I just nod to my dad and say, "I'm alright." I shrug. "I'm running off Lightning Bolt! energy drinks and adrenaline, so just waiting for the crash."

My parents share a look I can't decipher. Have I been gone so long that I can't even read their looks anymore? Or am I changing so much that this is a new look I've never seen before?

I can't think too long.

My mom flicks my nose playfully. "I have a theory." We share a smile.

Her theories are my favorite.

And very softly, she tells me, "When you crash someplace where you feel safe, you'll wake up happy in the morning."

I take a big breath. "I think I agree with that one." I wipe a smudge of dirt off my cheek. "At least tonight, it sounds good to wake up in my own fucking bed for a change."

Everyone is supposed to be staying overnight at some five-star hotel near the venue. A car service is even shuttling guests to the hotel in case they're too hammered to drive.

My dad tells me, "Nona saved you a piece of vegan coffee cake at one of the tables. It's not like the real fucking thing, so just beware."

I smile.

Jane is so thoughtful to include a separate little vegan cake for guests. It's even the same coffee flavor as her big wedding cake. I could go back to eating dairy—but I love how going vegan has excited my sister so much.

After a couple more hugs, we part ways. I find my sister again just as Jane gets ready to throw the bouquet. Chatting for a bit, we catch up about more than just Yellowstone, and I try the vegan cake.

Not sweet enough for me, but my stomach appreciates any food at the moment. I scarf down every bite during the bouquet toss.

The bundle of pastel flowers flies in the air and lands right into Audrey's hands. Not anywhere near me. *It doesn't mean anything, Sulli.*

Yeah.

It's definitely *not* a sign that Akara and Banks are going to choose each other.

Not a sign at all.

I hate being superstitious, but I fixate on Jane's thunderstruck little sister. She hugs the flowers to her chest with a swoony look.

I laugh and *my* little sister darts away, bouncing on her feet to congratulate her best friend.

Akara finds me by the round table near the dance floor as I lick cake crumbs off my fingers. His smile reaches his eyes as he lands by my side. "You can take the girl out of the wild. But you can't take the wild out of the girl."

I suck icing from my thumb and then slug him in the shoulder with my free hand.

He barely moves. "I rest my case."

"Hey, it's not good cake unless I'm licking each little crumb off." I look him up and down, about to ask how things went with Michael Moretti, but his expression shifts to utter affection as he cradles my gaze. I slowly pull my thumb from my mouth, my pulse double-beating. "Kits…?"

We're interrupted by an MC on the mic. "All those beautiful couples, come onto the dance floor. This is your slooooow jam."

Unchained Melody by The Righteous Brothers begins to play, and I back up from the edge of the dance floor where Akara is in a frozen stance.

His eyes only rest on me.

As couples join hand-in-hand and singles drift away, the dance floor becomes more open, and I notice Banks standing by himself only a few feet from Akara.

He turns his head, his eyes on my eyes, and I breathe harder, looking between Akara and Banks.

Banks and Akara.

As the most romantic fucking song plays, this is the part where the girl runs into the arms of the man she loves. Where I pick who I want to be with.

Instead, there is just an aching longing to run towards both.

We all seem to be breathing in at the same time, and I break the synchronicity and find Winona again. My fifteen-year-old sister leans against the dessert table where there's a massive chocolate turtle spread. I slip my hand in hers.

She smiles and drags *me* onto the dance floor before I can drag her. We twirl each other, passing Akara and Banks, but I feel their eyes on me the whole time.

I can't forget them.

I've tried all night. And a huge part of me never wants to forget. Forgetting them means forgetting how they make me feel. And I always, *always* want to remember.

51

Akara Kitsuwon

ONCE THE RECEPTION begins to end, Sulli tells me she wants to go home instead of crashing at the hotel. Tonight, nothing sounds better than being far away from all of these people. Away from everyone. Everything was simpler in Yellowstone.

My responsibilities bear back down on me here, and I'm tempted to just sideline them for one more night. Tomorrow will be a different day. But I can let those worries roll off my shoulders for a handful more hours.

As wedding guests leave the gardens and trickle back into the stone mansion, creating a slow-moving line through the stained-glass double-doors, I find Banks saying goodbye to an uncle at a dessert table. Nothing but crumbs and half-eaten coffee cake left.

Once his uncle leaves, I tell Banks, "I'm taking Sulli back to her place."

She's currently hugging her parents one last time, and I left a temp to watch her for a minute.

Banks glances to her, and he downs a glass of sparkling water, which I know he hates. "She choose you, then?" Pain already grips his voice.

My muscles tighten. "No." I laugh under my breath. "Almost the opposite, actually." I spread out my arms. "She asked me if I thought you'd want to come with us back to Philly."

So there's *that.*

Back in the city, Banks is more of a floater than her 24/7 bodyguard, and it's more unclear to Sulli when Banks will follow her around. I make those decisions.

Surprise reaches his eyes. "What'd you say?"

I lick my dried lips. "I told her I'd ask you."

His brows knot into a harder frown. "This was your one shot to get her alone and you fucked it?"

I nod slowly. "I guess so."

What I don't tell Banks is that I want him to come along. That maybe, after all of this, the thought of leaving Banks here, alone, in a hotel room tonight sounds like an asshole move.

I'm cutthroat, but not when it comes to him. I've accepted the fact that he's my exception, and I don't want to be an asshole to him. Ever.

WE'RE THE ONLY HUMANS AT THE PENTHOUSE where Sulli lives.

Two fluffy Newfoundland dogs and a few cats greet us at the front door. "Hey there, Orion." Sulli hugs Luna's dog and rubs behind his ears.

Banks grabs Arkham by the collar before he darts out, and I shoo a few cats away to shut the door behind us.

Once the door closes, the weight of the past 48-hours descends heavy on my muscles. We've all traveled across the world before, but this expedition was layered differently. Delayed flights, the car breaking down, the plane ride, and socializing at a wedding causes aches and weight, but so does the sheer emotional toll.

That part of our journey is unlike anything I've felt in a long time.

Like we've all jumped in a washing machine of happiness, heartache. Hurt, laughter. Joy, pain.

Loss.

After my dad passed, I've fought *so hard* not to lose the things that matter to me. My gym. My job as a bodyguard. My position as a lead, my own security firm, Sulli's friendship.

And the trip to Yellowstone has been a crash course in Hanging On.

Hanging on to the people I love.

Hanging on to what I want out of this life.

I'm afraid of an ending more than I've ever been afraid of a beginning.

Sulli rises to her feet, rubbing a knot in her shoulder.

I fix the tangled cord to my mic. "Banks and I are going to do a quick sweep of the penthouse." I want to switch-on a different, less serious setting, but safety first.

Usually I wouldn't feel the need to check every inch of the 9,000 square foot penthouse, but Jane's wedding date is public knowledge. If someone were to *attempt* a break-in, it'd be tonight. It'd take some bribery and incredible Mission Impossible shit for them to sneak past the building's security, but I'm not taking any chances.

Sulli nods. "I'll feed the animals and meet you both in the bathroom. We can wash off the travel stink." She's already gone for the pantry before either of us can point out that we have our own bathroom in our own apartment three-floors down.

I think even if I weren't dating Sulli, I'd still find a way to *stay.* To walk that blurry line between friends and her bodyguard like a pro.

The difference now is that I want to wash off *with her.*

"Take the kitchen first," I tell Banks, and then I leave them to cover the east side of the penthouse. Checking rooms mostly. Opening doors and closets. I'm quick about the sweep. Every step feels weighted, energy draining.

So by the time I enter Sulli's bedroom, the rushing water from the bath is the sweetest sound I've heard all night.

Steam billows out of the bathroom's cracked door.

Pausing for a second, I don't enter right away. I sweep Sulli's bedroom. Decorated pretty plainly like she spends little time here, except for her bed. Topped with a turquoise velvet quilt, tons of kitschy pillows—shaped like cupcakes, donuts, mermaids, crabs, and more sea creatures—are stacked so high, you can barely see the mattress.

I'm smiling as I open her closet. Pushing aside her striped T-shirts, no one is hiding behind her jackets either. I do another quick sweep of her room.

A weight bench in the corner looks worn-out, scratched, lovingly used. My eyes latch to Sulli's shelves of medals and trophies. Some of the awards I saw her win. Her Olympic gold medals dangle right next to medals she won in amateur competitions when she was twelve.

I wonder if after tonight, this'll be the last time I enter her room. If she picks him, I'll finally make the hard choice and permanently transfer Banks to her 24/7 detail. I'll throw myself into my companies like I need to do anyway.

Not see her as often.

Barely see her.

Rarely see her.

Pain shoots through me. I grind down on my teeth, and I hear a soft *splash* from the bath like someone is climbing into the water.

Footsteps sound from the hallway, and I glance at the door as Banks slips into her bedroom. "West side clear," he says, and his eyes skip to her shelves of medals.

I see the way that Banks looks at them. Like each one is a piece of Sulli he hopes to protect. It's the same way I look at them. Pride. Love.

Devotion.

It's clear.

So *very* clear.

One of us is going to be obliterated.

Banks meets my eyes with the same raw understanding.

There might be pain tomorrow, when she does choose, but tonight there's a bath. Heat and warmth. Her company. *Loss* isn't here yet.

We're still hanging on.

I run a hand through my hair, then drop it to wave to the bathroom door. "After you," I say.

Banks smiles. "Even when you let me lead, I'm following." Before I can reply to that, he's pushing through.

Hot steam hits my face. A huge, soup-bowl-style bathtub sits underneath an iron chandelier. Sulli's bathroom is more industrial than elegant. Green planters hang on brick walls, creating a more serene atmosphere.

I was wrong about Sulli already climbing *into* the bath. Still fully clothed, she's knelt beside the tub. Her hand dips into the water, testing the temperature.

She looks over her shoulder, seeing us enter. "Oh hey," she whispers. "It's still too fucking hot."

"Why are you whispering?" I ask in a soft voice as I unhook my radio from my waistband.

Banks does the same, winding the cord around the device.

"Fuck, it's just habit," she says a little louder. "When I was Luna's roommate at the townhouse, I tried to be quiet, even if I'm not any fucking good at it."

Banks eyes the tub, then the shower. "Where do you want us, mermaid?"

"I thought…we could all share the tub." Flush ascends her neck. "I'm too tired to even stand up in that thing, and you two are probably feeling spent—*unless* you want to take the shower."

"I'll take the tub." I already pull my dirty shirt over my head.

"It's good with me, too," Banks says, shedding his tee. He tosses his shirt at the wicker hamper, but it lands on the concrete-slab sink counter. "*Unless*, you think my six-seven ass can't fit."

Her eyes glitter, lips lift, like she just heard a challenge. "We can *all* fit." She rises to her feet and unbuttons her jeans.

Banks and I watch Sulli snap off her bra, slide off her panties—all the while, we're stepping out of boxer-briefs. Vapor kisses my bare flesh as the three of us stand naked in her bathroom.

I never thought this would happen.

But I'm not shocked that I'm here. Not when the air between us is unfettered and peaceful. Why would I run away from that?

I study the bath for a half-second. Figuring out how to maneuver in it will be like a human puzzle. The tub is striking, almost like the focal point of the room. It could comfortably hold three people, but we're all six-foot or over.

"You first," I tell Sulli. "Stay in the middle." Steam coasts over the gentle water, and she reaches out for Banks' hand. *Doesn't mean anything.* She didn't just choose him. He was just closer.

Banks helps stabilize Sulli as she plunges each foot into the bath. She has good balance, so I know it's partly just to touch each other.

My gaze melts over Sulli, dripping down her athletic body. Every inch of her is defined muscle. Her legs are leaner than her broad-shoulders, and the dark hair on her pussy is fueling my need.

Sulli catches me staring. "What's that look?"

I want to run my hand over every inch of you. "You're a total babe, Sul."

Her lips tic up in a cute smile.

I smile back, and I imagine cupping her tits, pinning her to a bed, driving *deep* between her thighs. And her overcome face as she unravels in the intensity.

The pleasure.

My cock twitches, and I absentmindedly palm my length, still holding her gaze.

A shallow breath expels between her lips. Hot and bothered, she twists her hair up in a tighter, messier bun. I swear she mutters a soft, "Fuck."

She's twenty-one.

And a virgin.

Sometimes I forget she's a lot younger and inexperienced until these small moments where she's overwhelmed at my confidence, assuredness, forwardness.

She lowers down into the bath. Water laps at her tits.

I look to Banks. "You next. I'll squeeze in after."

He's clumsier climbing into the tub, and Sulli grabs onto his thighs before he slips. He sinks down, legs bent and spread open so that she can fit between them. I do the same. The hot water feels *amazing*, and every ache in my muscle screams at me to just *relax*.

We shift around until we're all in a comfortable position. With my legs spread, my ankles practically hook with Banks' ankles, our knees bent out of the water. I rest my back to one side of the tub. Still close to being chest-to-tits with Sulli.

I watch her dip her head beneath the water. Very close to my cock, and then she pops up, combing her wet hair back out of her face.

Shit.

She's beautiful.

Sulli leans back against Banks' chest. His arm moves underneath the water, maybe around her waist. Whatever he does, she looks *deeply* satisfied, easing completely like putty, and that makes me smile.

Sulli squirts some soap into the water and swirls the suds around with her fingers.

My muscles slowly unwind in the hot bath. Relaxation sinking me down. I skate my hand along Sulli's leg. The hair on her calf feels softer in the water, but I love the prickly Sulli as much as the fuzzy Sulli.

"Goddamn," Banks exhales as his eyes flutter shut. His arms grip the lips of the tub on either side of him. "I could just fall asleep here and never wake up."

Sulli slides a palm over his bicep. "No falling asleep then. I want you to wake the fuck up."

"Me too." I splash water at him, but Sulli's face gets doused instead.

Her brows rise. "You do *not* want to start a splashing fight with me, Kits. I will tidal wave this bathroom."

Banks chimes in, "Good thing mermaids don't drown."

Sulli smiles.

And I lean forward a little. Her tits brush up against my chest as I tell Banks, "We don't need to test that one."

She splashes *me* this time.

I grab her wrist before she can try a second time. Her breath hitches. Shit, my body goes into a full-body alert. Screaming words.

Want.

Need.

Sulli.

I notice more clearly how Banks drops his arm into the water. How he pulls her back tighter to his chest, and he must clasp the inside of her thigh, spreading her legs wider—because her knees knock into the sides of the tub and an *aching* sound leaves her lips.

I harden. Veins in my cock throbbing. She's open right in front of me, but the water is murky with soap.

I glide my hand up her hip, over her abs, to her tit, thumbing her soft nipple. Letting it harden from my touch.

She pants softly, her head lolling back against Banks' shoulder. He drops his head down to kiss her. I watch him slip his tongue into her mouth.

The bathroom suddenly feels stifling hot. All steam.

All feeling.

All arousal.

Make Sulli feel extraordinary is on the agenda. Banks must get the memo too. Our hands move in hot, ravenous waves over her body. She bucks her hips, "Kits. *Banks*. Fuck…*yes*." I'm not even inside of her.

I lean forward and take her nipple between my lips, sucking gently and then firmly. Her body shudders, and I keep her other leg opened as she jerks in arousal. "Oh, fuck." She whimpers, and her fingers thread through my hair.

I reach up to touch her head, but my elbow knocks into Banks'. *Shit.*

"Sorry," I say, pulling back from her tit.

He cracks a smile. "It's not you, it's me." He's shifting behind Sulli, who's just trying to catch her breath. "I'm trying not to poke her in the ass."

I tilt my head. Didn't realize it, but she is kind of sitting on his lap.

Sulli rests fully against his chest, breathing hard. "I don't mind being poked in the ass. I like feeling you guys. It's really fucking hot… knowing how hard you are."

I rub my lips—am I regretting being in front of her and not behind?

Banks moves her wet hair to the left side of her shoulder, exposing her neck. My blood pumps harder when I watch him sink his lips to the nape of her neck, sucking deeply.

Her aroused eyes—they're on me.

No bowl of Instant Regret this time.

Her lips part in a heady breath, and I take her wandering hand and guide her palm to my erection. Underneath the water, her fingers curl around the hard length, and she nearly squirms in need.

Her grip around me and her flowing desire is churning mine on high-speed. Banks kisses her neck hungrily, and I clasp her jaw in a strong hand. Our movements rougher, she forgets to jerk me off, and I don't need her to.

I kiss her like I'm famished, nipping her bottom lip, and I massage her tit. She arches up her hips, her legs jolting in my hold and his hold. We keep her spread open.

"Oh...*fuck*," she moans. "Please..."

I'm on fire, burning in the water.

Banks kisses the most sensitive spot of her neck, and his eyes flit to me while he sucks. He's watching *her* hand find my cock beneath the water again. She rubs me a few times. I'm watching him drive her crazy. Her body keeps trembling in needy waves.

This give and take is like walking into high voltage. All shockwaves and electrified energy.

I suck her nipple again, and she lets out a raspy breath. Her hand is friction on my length, but I crave to sink between her legs.

Something changes in the room. The temperature kicks up ten notches, and our movements grow more passionate, more urgent. Like this could end.

Like some unforeseen figure just overturned an hourglass and time drains with the sand.

My lips find hers once more, and our kiss siphons oxygen. Banks and I knock elbows again, but this time I don't apologize. His face is inches from mine as he sucks on her neck, and as his hand cups her breasts, I can feel the tops of his fingers against my chest.

I break from her lips at the same time Banks pulls away from her neck. She breathes ragged breath as her hand slips from my length and grips onto my thigh.

My hard body is pressed against hers while I breathe beside her ear, "We can slow down."

"I don't want to slow down," she says, very raspy. "I want this to last forever." She touches our hands under the water that hold onto her thighs. "I want to have sex." She takes a breath. "Tonight."

She's a virgin. The thought blares in my head. *Be careful with her.* I know she's not even on any kind of birth control.

Banks looks her over. "Sulli—"

"If that's something you two want," she spits out quickly. "I know we had a rule—no P-in-the-V action until I chose. But tonight just feels…"

"Perfect," I finish for her.

Her eyes wash over mine. "Yeah." Her breasts rise in a bigger breath. "It's perfect. Or is it just me?"

"It's not," Banks says the same time I say, "It's not just you."

She nods strongly.

Banks and I share a look. *Feel the moment.*

It feels right.

That should be all that matters.

52

Sullivan Meadows

AKARA LEAVES THE TUB completely naked.

Oh my fucking God. My chest rises and falls heavily while I watch him, his shoulder and upper-chest beautifully inked. Water drips off his body as he steps on my teal bathmat. Behind me, Banks reaches down and unplugs the tub.

"Are we fucking leaving?" I ask, a little more than just bummed. I don't want to go. Everything has been perfect right here. Being so close. So warm.

The water.

Banks.

Kits.

Them. And us.

"No, I'm just letting some of the water drain out," Banks says in a way that makes me think he knows what he's doing. More than me.

"Have you had sex in a bathtub before?" I ask, but my eyes flit to Akara. He's squatting down and rummaging through his pants' pocket.

Banks rests an arm on the lip of the tub. "This'll be a first for me."

"Same," Akara says, standing up with something in his hand.

I'm grinning. "Look at that. You both are virgins, too."

Banks wears a crooked smile and laughs hard.

"Let's not go that far," Akara says, and as he strides to the tub, I see what's in his hand. Two condom packets. *This is happening.* My abs clench expectantly. Excitement rushes through my veins like I'm just about to take the starting block before a swim heat.

"How does this work?" I ask.

The intensity of their gazes bears down on me suddenly. I quickly add, "I'm aware of how sex fucking works—"

"We know you know that," Banks says, assuring me.

"Plus"—I lean my head back against his shoulder, staring *up* at him—"I know a ton of fucking positions, too. Porn really helped with that."

The way he looks down at me is with a headiness that steals my breath, and he grows harder against me. My pulse descends between my legs. "What kind of porn does a mermaid watch?" he asks huskily, eyes falling to my lips.

"Different things," I say, a little distracted by Akara. He steps into the bathtub again, condoms still in his fingers. The water keeps draining, my naked body more in view and the cold nipping at my skin.

"Even DP," I add. *Though that's not usually a regular go-to for me.*

Akara stiffens.

"Double penetration," I clarify.

"I know what DP stands for, string bean." He sinks down into the tub. Our bare knees knock into each other. Banks plugs the drain back up, leaving only a couple inches of water. It feels like I'm sitting on a sandbar with a layer of ocean.

I take a breath. There's a reason I brought it up, and I think Akara's connecting the dots. So I just come out and say it, "In case you both don't want to choose who goes first, I just thought I'd throw that fucking out there as an option."

Banks puts his hands atop my head. His face is caught between amusement, a laugh, and a little shock.

"That's very considerate of you, Sul," Akara says, kneeling in front of me. His cock looks harder than I've ever seen it. He cups my kneecap, carefully parting my legs. "But you're not taking two dicks at the same time when you've never had one."

"Go big or go home," I say into a grin.

Banks laughs, his chest rising and falling against my back.

My grin falters as my breath shallows, especially as Banks' hand slips to the inside of my thigh. He pulls my left leg open more, like he did earlier tonight.

I *really* fucking love when he does that. And I loved how Akara had possession of my other leg earlier too.

In the water tonight, I just feel so safe with them. Like I really could bask in this pleasure and emotion for eternity.

Can I live in this tub? *I have everything I need here.*

Banks and Akara talk through their eyes for a single second, and then Akara tells me, "Unless you have an issue with it, I'm going to take your virginity. Banks is going to watch."

Fuck, wow.

"It was that easy to make the decision?" I thought there'd be a longer debate between them.

Banks looks down at me. "I'm not small."

"Neither is Akara," I point out the fucking obvious which is staring at me and making me squirm with desire.

"It's going to fit," Akara tells me like he thinks that's my hang-up.

"Fuck, I know it will *fit.*" Talking about their dicks entering me is lighting up all my sensitive nerves. I ache more and more for their touch. I want their hands roaming my body again.

"My size might hurt you if I go first," Banks explains. "I'm bigger, Sulli. Hell, it still might hurt the first time me and you have sex, but at least you'll be more ready to take me if you still want to."

"I want to," I say, not missing a beat.

Akara's brows are furrowed. "Would you rather Banks go first?"

In Yellowstone, I've imagined having sex with each of them a million different ways. In some, Banks takes my virginity. In others, Akara does.

So I say the truth, "I've pictured either way, but if you two think it'll hurt less this way, then I want you to go first, Kits."

I can tell they were hoping I'd say that because they both ease.

Akara rips the condom packet with his teeth, and Banks runs his hand along my thigh, his arm curved around my waist, and as my leg dips, he stretches it back again.

I'm not certain how opened I need to be or if I should tilt my pelvis up for Akara. "How should I…?"

"I've got you." Banks' lips brush my ear. "Just relax." He hooks his arm underneath my thigh, lifting it a little higher to my chest. Cold air isn't biting my skin. My body warms at Banks' touch.

At the way Akara is watching me.

He slides the condom along his shaft. *That's going inside me.* My heart beats madly in my chest.

Banks' hand descends between my thighs. "She's still not wet," he tells Akara.

"What?" My face is full of confusion. "That's impossible. I'm *beyond* fucking aroused." I stare at my pussy that has betrayed me.

Akara edges closer, kneeling between my spread legs. "Water washes away natural lubricant."

Right.

I knew that, but the fact must've been slow to arrive since I'm really caught up in them. And I don't have much experience having sex, clearly.

Now I realize why Banks probably drained the tub. So they *both* knew this fact too, which sends my pulse beating even harder. Older. More experienced. Strong but definitely *not* stronger than me. I can bench press more, I know it. Still, they were ready to take care of me.

An overwhelming comfort washes over me. Like protection is all around me. A private oasis right here with them.

Banks kneads my tender breasts, while Akara kisses the inside of my thigh. When Banks' mouth touches *that* spot on my neck, my pulse drops and I clench hard.

"There it is," Akara says, slipping his finger inside me. He pumps a couple times, his thumb circling my clit, which flutters my eyes—*fuck ahh.*

"Please," I beg. "I need…"

Banks' muscles flex underneath me. A deep, gruff noise catches his throat that makes my legs twitch.

"Sul," Akara groans.

I reach a peak. My toes curling. Not just one time either, they keep touching, rubbing, creating hot friction until I meet a second combustion.

I'm theirs. Take me away. I've never felt this kind of pleasure in my life. I want to devour them whole, but they devour me first, and I'm more than okay with that.

Akara removes his finger, then grips his length in a firm clutch. "We're going to give you what you need, Sulli. Just breathe."

I remember to exhale.

Akara scoots closer. His hand slides down my knee, then he lifts my leg over his tattooed shoulder. *Oh my God.*

Heat stoked between all three of us, Akara leans close to my face and kisses me ravenously on the lips, his tongue slipping hotly against my tongue. When we part, his forehead presses to mine. "Tell me if it hurts," he whispers.

"I will."

He glances down at our bodies, and I must not be aligned perfectly because Banks lifts up my ass so I'm at a better angle. I settle back more against Banks' chest. Letting him take more of my weight. His hands stay on my hips, and I lift up my head, our mouths meeting instinctively. He kisses me strongly. I kiss back wanting more, more, so much *more,* so this never reaches an end.

With his lips on my lips, I feel a pressure against my heat. Lost in the moment until my pulses races—keenly aware that Akara is easing into me.

I wince at a sharp pain, breaking the kiss.

"Okay?" Akara asks, a tender hand to my chin.

The pain fades fast. "Yeah," I breathe out. "Are you in?"

"Not all the way." He still doesn't move. "Sul?"

"Yeah?"

"You're wincing. Are you sure it doesn't hurt?"

"It doesn't anymore. I promise." I try to relax my face.

"Is she wet enough?" Banks reaches down to my pussy.

"She's soaked," Akara assures.

Banks rubs my clit in melodic circles, heating me up to a boil. The bundle of nerves isn't too sensitive to the touch yet, thankfully, because I want him to keep his hand there.

My body is singing, and I reach out, gripping Banks' bicep for support. Even though I'm not in threat of falling, I feel like I'm floating already.

Akara runs a hand up and down my thigh. "I'm going to ease in a little bit more."

My cheeks have roasted a shade of red called Sullivan Meadows is A-Roused. I really kind of love how they're discussing me. Like my wants and needs are both of their priorities.

Akara thrusts his waist forward, pushing deeper inside of me, and I gasp at the pressure, new and different, and his warmth, the fullness, reaches pleasure-points. My gasp cuts into an overwhelmed breath as he rocks again, then I wince.

He stops.

Banks even stops rubbing me.

"Go, *go*," I rasp. "Please…I need…it doesn't hurt, really."

"Really?" Akara asks, skeptical. I get why. I like experiencing *new* things, and I'm very comfortable with them to where, *maybe*, I wouldn't brake right away. But that's a big fucking maybe, and that's not what's happening.

"It's just different, a good different."

Akara cups my cheek, studying my features for a second.

"I just might be anticipating things too much," I explain. "Just, fuck…please keep going." I look up at Banks. "I promise I'm alright."

He plants a kiss on my lips again.

Akara kisses my leg hoisted over his shoulder. And then, he drives deeper. I watch him disappear inch by inch inside me. The leg-quaking feeling ascends upon me again. He slides out quicker than he arrived, then takes the slow-trek back in.

Fuckfuckfuck. The fullness is overwhelming.

I whimper as he does it again. Out. In.

Out. In. He rocks his hips. I forget what I should be doing to help. I just drown in the moment.

In the way Banks kisses my neck and toys with my perked nipple. Sensations light up around me. Every nerve-ending reached by them.

Akara's breathing has labored, and I drink in how his whole body flexes. His abs, his biceps, and I wish there were a mirror so I could see his ass.

And he has undeniably gorgeous quads.

He's in me.

He's in me.

"Kits," I cry. "I…"

"You what?" he breathes close as he rocks, his hand on my hip. Banks hoists my ass up more, and Akara hits a deeper spot. I see stars.

"You can't handle it?" Kits breathes; his voice is literal sex. "You want more?"

All I can do is nod. Such a goner of fucking *pleasure.* Akara is a dreamboat.

Banks whispers in my ear how beautiful I am. How hot I am, how hard he is, and I think I mutter a *keep going* to him. Because fuck, his words are shots of adrenaline.

I want more.

In and out. Akara fills me fully again, this time he takes harder, shorter thrusts. Changing the tempo. His pace, his rhythm is hypnotic.

As I buck up against his chest, Banks tightens his grip on my leg. My body trembles from the friction, and I cry out, "Fuck!" The intensity, the way they're consuming me—water drips from the creases of my eyes.

Banks makes a heavy noise.

Akara groans, "*Sul.* You're so fucking wet." Arousal flexes his muscles. "You feel how hard I am?"

I feel him.

I feel him in more ways than one.

"I'm not stopping." He sits up more and thrusts in short, deep spurts again, watching himself enter me. He takes my hand that tries to grab the tub, and he rests my palm on Banks' other bicep.

I hold on.

Banks nips my earlobe. How he keeps finding places that tingle my toes, I'll never understand.

I want to tell them how good Akara feels. How good Banks feels. But I can't form words. My body is alight with new, raw sensations that overtake my other senses.

Warmth.

So much warmth.

A need burrows in me, Akara nearing it but not quite. I moan again, this one more distraught. "You want to come?" Akara asks.

I nod.

He stops thrusting to kiss my lips gently. And then he says, "Words."

"Please…" I squirm in their hold.

"Please what?"

"I…need…"

He pumps in a new mind-numbing rhythm.

I cry out again. "I…I can't…"

"Can't what?" Akara breathes.

You know what, Kits!

"*Please*," I cry, "I want to…"

I can feel Banks smiling behind me. "The mermaid is lost for words." His voice is so husky that I feel myself become more soaked.

Akara bites down as arousal pummels him. His chest rises and falls heavier. He's in me, so he must've felt the stimulated rush. His eyes reach mine as he speaks to Banks. "I want to hear her say it."

I can barely catch my breath. *I want to say it.* I love a good challenge.

Banks tells him, "Should've known you'd be bossy in bed."

"A boss in life…" I breathe out. "A boss in bed."

Akara gives me a look. "You could say that but not *I want to come*." He looks over my shoulder to Banks. "She must not want to come."

"Must not."

"Hardy-har-ha—"

My voice catches as Banks touches my sensitive clit. Akara drinks us in for a second before he eases fully into me again. "Sulli—"

"I want to come," I say hurriedly, my voice carrying loudly. "Fuckpleaseplease."

His pace quickens. So does Banks'. They work me over until I'm water. Flowing with them and the pleasure that builds between us. Banks kisses me, and Akara makes love to me.

As I gasp on breath, shuddering in overwhelmed rip tides, I wonder how I can ever lose the closeness that I feel with them after this.

Their hands are voracious but caring. Bodies soulful against mine as emotion spools around us, a current to each breath, each strong heartbeat.

Fullness. Friction. Feelings all light me up in ways I've never experienced. Until I'm riding my orgasm to the summit.

I cry into pure bliss. *Oh fuck!*

Akara's breathing heavies, he groans as he comes, pumping a couple more times before sliding out and gently resting my leg down. Banks eases my thigh to the tub too.

As I relax from that high, I watch as Akara removes the condom, ties it off, and leans over the tub, putting the thing on the tiles. Banks unplugs the drain again. And I realize the water is a slight pink.

"You popped my cherry," I joke to Akara.

His smile plays across his lips. "You okay? Anything hurt?"

I see how they both assess me. As their eyes peruse me, it's obvious they're making sure I'm emotionally and physically okay. And I almost get teary-eyed because I *love* how much they care about me.

This has been even better than I dreamed. I even love the awkward beginning where I didn't understand the tub drainage.

I'm not trying to act like it's my millionth intimate experience. It feels like my first time.

"Nothing hurts," I breathe. "I just feel full inside."

Even if he's not in me anymore, that feeling hasn't waned. Carefully, I rise to my feet, then I rotate before sitting back down in the tub.

This time, my back is to Akara.

My eyes lock with Banks.

Something sensual passes between us. A simple phrase from me to him.

Your turn.

HELL HAVE MERCY ON my soul.

I press my knees to the warm, empty tub. "Again?" I ask.

"Again," she rasps, her eyes coveting me as much I covet the hell out of her.

I hesitate, though, because I really don't know if she should be having sex with me after she just had that kind of deep sex. I don't want to hurt her.

She just had a perfect first time, and I'm fucking terrified I'm gonna ruin this experience. I glance over at Akara.

He pulls her wet hair into his hands. Twisting strands into spirals that fall loose. A strange calmness hangs in the air between me and him. A respect and a type of love that I can't explain, but everything feels easy tonight when you'd think it'd be the biggest clusterfuck alive.

Come on, Banks.

I just ask, "You sure you're not too tired, mermaid?"

"I'm wide-awake," she professes, arching her hips a bit. "Can you…?"

I edge closer, my hand sinking down her leg to the inside of her thigh. I pull her down some, and Akara shifts her hips. His brown eyes flit to me as he wraps an arm around her collar, then kneads one of her breasts.

Christ.

I'm dying to be inside Sulli. Sweat glistens across my skin, and it's not just my sweat either. I brush a hand across my unshaven jaw as our heady breaths fill the air again.

In most situations, I think she'd normally have passed out after getting pounded by him—at least if I were a chick, Akara would have knocked me out after *that* fucking—but she seems to be running off adrenaline for the moment.

Her eyes are pinned to my length. My cock throbs uncomfortably. It took mental endurance not to come when I heard her cry out. I'm painfully hard. *Fuck, I need a release.*

"I want you inside me," she says in a pant. "...if that wasn't fucking crystal."

I smile. "It came through clear." I slide my fingers against her heat. "I want inside you, too."

She bucks up. "Banks." Her eyes almost roll.

A deep noise rumbles in me. *Fuck.* She's really sensitive, but I'll find a way to make this last a long while for her. For us.

Akara hands me the condom packet, and I do a quick double-check to make sure he grabbed mine. Last thing I need is this shit ripping while I'm inside her.

I spot the size. *Good to go.*

Akara tilts her chin back and they kiss softly while I sheath myself. He catches her lip between his teeth, and I align my waist with hers, clasping and lifting up her hips. Her bikini tan line is cute.

It'll be better for her if she's lost in Akara for a second, so I'm glad they're kissing.

I edge my fingers into her entry. Her arousal pumps my blood harder. *Jesus.* She breaks from his lips in a pant. And once her eyes descend down to me, I remove my fingers and grip my shaft.

"Breathe," Akara coos against her ear.

She inhales, her eyes fastening to mine—like the very first time we kissed. And I don't desert her gaze. Not even as I slowly push inside her pussy.

She is so…fucking…*tight.*

Fuck.

The pressure is almost immediate. Wrapping around me in a vice. Her thighs tremble as I slowly slip in, our eyes still latched.

"You alright?" I whisper.

She nods, lips parted. She reaches for Akara's hand, then mine.

It's in the soft seconds of her breath. His. Mine. That I feel like this moment is transcendent. That there's no going back after this. I thrust, but I don't give her the full length, and still, an involuntary noise flies from her lips.

A cry.

A whimper.

Those noises are gonna fuck me up. Holy hell, are they like a drug. I want to hear more. I rock against her in a slow, hungered movement.

"*Please,*" she moans, about to buck her hips, but Akara grabs her waist to keep her from taking more of me. If I hit her cervix, she's *never* gonna want to have sex again.

I'm careful with every emotion-packed second, every sweltering beat, and I extend the moment to earth-shattering minutes upon minutes, soaking in the feeling of being inside her. And then Sulli explodes. Her eyes roll, body shudders, and she *clenches.* The pressure around my cock is like being knocked out with a baseball bat. I'm struck to the fuckin' moon as I come, and I flex to keep from a natural instinct to push deeper and milk the climax.

Can't go any deeper.

I breathe hard, my cock twitching as she keeps pulsing against me. "*Sulli,*" I groan, and gently, very fucking gently, I pull out.

She's exhausted, trying to smile. A smile passes through me, my mouth curving. That feels good. Akara rotates the faucet, refilling the tub with warm water after I discard the condom.

We all ease back.

"That was…" she says in soft breaths. "…so fucking…amazing." Her eyes close fully. "I can just sleep here."

Akara and I share a smile.

"I'm living here now," she yawns. "The tub is my new home."

I stretch my arm over Sulli. "Rent will be cheaper."

"Spacious," Akara quips. "I can *definitely* fit my whole office in here."

"You would be thinking about your fuckin' office," I laugh at him.

He splashes water at me as the tub fills.

Sulli curls up against him. "Mmhhh. So many donuts."

"Sad to say, we can't live here, mermaid."

"The water though…"

Akara and I exchange another look. This time, our smiles fade, knowing this is drawing to a real close too soon.

We wash off. Dry off. Sulli is half-asleep.

Akara says, "We're taking you to bed, string bean."

I stand up and easily lift Sulli into my arms. She cocoons her head into my chest. "I can sleep here, too."

I'd like that, but she needs an actual bed. I step out of the tub, careful not to slip. Akara tosses the used condoms in the trash, grabs a couple towels, and follows me into her bedroom.

He knocks off the majority of her pillows before I can lay her gently on the mattress. She curls up into the velvet quilt, and sudden-fear springs open her eyes. "You two are staying over, right?"

I bob my head. "Right." I'm not about to ditch Sulli after making love to her. I crawl in next to her on the bed and wrap an arm around her broad shoulders.

"Of course," Akara says, but he's texting on his phone.

"*Kits…*" Sulli's concern mounts.

"I have to set an alarm, Sul. Your roommates might come back early. They can't see us leave."

That sobers the room. More reminders that this isn't lasting. What feels like a *forever* type of moment is just an illusion. Forever ends tomorrow.

She pushes wet hair off her forehead, turning on her back. "Can you set it for 5 a.m.? I'll just wake up at that time too."

His eyes flit to her. "We're not running out on you."

"I know. But this way it won't feel like you are."

I kiss the top of her head.

Akara nods, then returns to the bed.

Sulli curls up against my chest, and Akara holds her against his. He presses his lips to the back of her neck. Once more, sleep comes for her, but this time she doesn't fight it.

None of us do.

54

Sullivan Meadows

WHAT HAVE I fucking done?

I'm hopelessly in love with two men. And today I have to make a choice. Last night, I thought it'd be an impossible one. But this morning, when I watch them leave my penthouse, everything starts to become clear.

I think I've made my decision.

But before I confront Akara and Banks, I need to make one stop. I dress quickly, still feeling the soreness between my legs. Like they're still inside my pussy. It's a new, strange feeling that I don't hate. Maybe even like.

I text Akara where I want to go today and hit send. *Fuck, there's something else*. It'd be crass to text him about it, so before he can respond, I decide to call.

He answers on the first ring. "Sul?"

"Hey, sorry. Did you get my text?"

"Yeah. When do you want to leave?"

"Soon." I put my phone on speaker and grab a pair of running shoes from the closet. "Do you think you could put a temp on my detail today?"

The air strains. "Is everything alright? Last night—"

"Was fucking perfect," I say quickly. "Better than anything I could have imagined. It's just I think you two should talk things over while I think things over alone." *In case they want to choose each other.* That option still exists.

He exhales a breath of relief. "Okay, yeah. That's a good idea."

My stomach does a somersault. Nothing about this is going to be easy. I might have made a decision, but it's not simple or easy or will leave everyone happy.

Not in the slightest.

He adds, "Gabe will be over there in five minutes to take you." Gabe is one of the better temp bodyguards that pre-dates Michael Moretti, though Oscar mostly uses Gabe to protect Jack.

"Thanks, Kits."

BECKETT'S BEDROOM IN HIS NEW YORK APARTMENT is a mixture of deep blues and gold tones. He's a minimalist through and through, but his style still shines bright in the abstract gold etchings framed perfectly on his wall. I get lost in them for a second.

He returns with a couple cans of Fizz Life. When he notices me observing the etchings, he stares longer at them, then goes to the wall. He adjusts the frame by a hair.

I don't mention that the frame was perfectly aligned before. Or else he might spend the next five minutes readjusting.

Beckett comes over to me, soda still in hand.

Seeing him in the flesh is so different than our phone calls over the past weeks. We didn't even FaceTime. Just heard each other's voices.

He's all lean muscle, and a shadow of stubble lines his jawline like he hasn't shaved yet this morning. Most girls swoon over his floral tattoos inked down his arm, his dark-brown hair with a good amount of wave, and his unique yellow-green eyes.

His jeans are ripped today at the knees, and I recognize the Carraways band T-shirt as one of their first merch designs.

He's twenty-two.

My best friend.

Former best friend.

He hands me the can of soda. "Charlie really didn't put you up to this visit?"

I pop the tab and hear the familiar fizzy sound. "He really didn't," I say. "I'm here of my own free will. I have something to tell you."

I want his friendship back—and I figure, if I want it to be what it was, then I need to confide in him like I used to. And I want that. *God,* I fucking want that.

His brows rise. "Before you start, I have something to tell you too." He motions to his bed. "Take a seat."

"This is a sitting kind of conversation?" I plop on his mattress, crossing my legs. Being in his room feels more comfortable than I thought it would, but his declaration seizes my pulse. Deadens it for a second. *Is he going to tell me he doesn't want to be friends?* Maybe something happened to him.

Something I missed again.

"It's an overdue kind of conversation," he says. "I just didn't want to have it until I saw you again." He winces. "And I probably should've been the one to come to you, but ballet and…" He stares down at the can of soda in his hand. "That's a shit excuse. It's all pretty shit, really." His eyes flit to mine. "When I started using cocaine before shows, I always thought about you."

My mouth falls open for a second. *He's talking about cocaine.* My hand is cold from the condensation of the can.

He continues, "I kept imagining what you'd do. Not what you'd say to me, if you knew about it. But if you had a drug that wouldn't disqualify you from competition, and it'd take away all your pain, make you a better swimmer—I wondered what you'd do."

"It'd be an easy out," I say. "I wouldn't have done it. We always said we wouldn't."

"Not even if you didn't retire?" he asks me, brows knitted. "Imagine you're still competing for the next ten years, Sul. Imagine you didn't medal. Imagine you're still fighting for that dream at thirty, and your body isn't the same as it was. What then?"

I'd take it.

For gold, I would take anything.

"You're not *thirty*, Beckett."

"I've been dancing since I was four, Sul. My body is fucked."

Tears pool in my eyes. "You're at the top of your career. You already have gold."

He takes a small sip of his drink and swallows hard. "I guess that's the difference between you and me. You can get a medal and call it a day." He shakes his head. "I can't live without ballet."

Ballet for him isn't just dancing. It's the art. The whole performance. The craft. The audience. The passion. The soul. I don't try to convince him that he can live without it. But there's an expiration date—and I don't want the day he ends ballet to be the end of him, too.

"Are you still using?" I ask.

He shakes his head and sets his Fizz Life on the desk. "No. I made a promise that I wouldn't." His eyes hit mine. "I'm not going to bullshit you, it's *hard*."

"I know. I get it now."

That almost breaks him. Tears filling his eyes. "Do you?"

"Yeah," I say. "I'd have taken it, if I was still competing, but that doesn't mean it's not fucked up. And I would want you to tell me to fucking stop."

He rubs at his eyes. "I'm glad you were mad at me." He takes a step forward. "I'm so, *so* sorry, Sulli, for what I said to you."

I inhale sharply. I stopped waiting for this apology a long time ago, and so I didn't think I'd hear those words now.

He continues, "I don't think you're pointlessly destroying your body. I think you were just experiencing shit at twenty-one, like a twenty-one-year-old should."

I rub at my eyes. "So why'd you say it then?'

"Because I thought you'd understand why I was using. Maybe I even convinced myself you'd agree with me. It's why I didn't tell you earlier. I thought…if you were on my side, you'd get heat from my brother, my sister, Maximoff. I didn't want it to be us vs them. I didn't want to put you in that position. When I realized you were already on their side, I was angry. So I lashed out."

Silent tears slip down my cheeks. All this time…Beckett thought I'd betrayed our friendship first. That I chose them over him.

"I'm sorry," I say, rising from the bed.

"No, you were on the right side, Sul." He bridges the distance and we hug. "I need to stop using. I've stopped."

"Good." I part from him as guitar chords sound from another room. Tom must be practicing. I dig in my pocket and dangle out the turquoise, red, and blue friendship bracelet. "For you. I made it in Yellowstone. I thought about giving it to you if this day ever came. And I honestly thought it might take years, but I'm happy to say, *it didn't*."

He holds out his wrist, his lips rising. "Me too. And I thought about giving you my friendship fries if this day ever came, but Eliot just ate the last bag I'd been saving."

Beckett used to always share his fries with me. It's always been his favorite mid-day snack. And so we used to call them Friendship Fries.

I smile big and tie the threads of the bracelet around his wrist. "I'll just take some imaginary friendship fries."

Once I finish the knot, Beckett asks, "What do you need to tell me?" He smiles more. "I want to hear it all. I feel like I've missed decades of your life."

It kinda fucking feels like that for me too. I don't know how to do this, so we both sit cross-legged on his bed, and I just start from the beginning. The funhouse where I told Banks and Akara that it'd be cool if they took my virginity. The motel where Banks kissed me. Then the morning run where Akara kissed me too.

I talk about how we've been dating. *Bachelorette* style. How they make me feel. Our easy banter, even when we're all together. How scared I was to lose them in the cougar attack.

How they're so different, but I like that they're different and not the same. And every day with them just makes inexplicable sense.

I leave out the other sexual moments. Just for now.

He listens.

He's always been really good at listening.

We move down to the floor and bring in snacks as I continue talking. My throat grows scratchy, but it's like everything just flows forth. I only stop when I reach the wedding.

"And we agreed," I say. "That today I'd make a decision." I circle my thumb on the soda can rim. "I think I've come to one. But first, I wanted to hear how stupid you think I am—"

He smiles. "Why would I think you're stupid?"

"Because I decided to become the fucking bachelorette to *two* bodyguards!"

"To me, and this is just my opinion"—he puts his hands on his chest—"it sounds more like you were in a polyamorous relationship."

I frown. "A what?"

He scratches the back of his head. "How to explain this…?" He takes out a green M&M. "This is you." He sets a blue M&M beside it. "This is Banks."

"That's his favorite color," I note.

He smiles a little as he chooses an orange one next.

"It should be red," I say quickly. "Akara's favorite color is red." *Well, candy apple red.* But I don't go into that much detail.

Beckett glances at the friendship bracelet I made, the same colors I listed, and we both laugh hard. He shakes his head, "You're so in love."

He says it like a disease.

"You want to cure me?" I ask him, tossing the green M&M in my mouth. Fuck, I'm cheating on my vegan streak just this once.

"No. You're too far gone." He smiles, replacing the green M&M. "Stop eating yourself."

"But it's so much fun." I swig my soda, a pit of anticipation forming in my stomach. "You can keep going."

"Okay, Akara is red." He puts the red M&M at a diagonal to my green. With the blue M&M, they resemble a little triangle of candy. "There can be all different kinds of poly relationships. You can have partners that have other partners." He moves a yellow and orange M&M next to Akara's red.

I'm immediately shaking my head.

He laughs. "This is a demonstration."

"I don't even want to imagine it."

He brushes away those extra M&M's. "Or you can have a *closed* relationship. Where however many multiple partners you have, they're only romantically connected to each other. It sounds like that's what you, Banks, and Akara had in Yellowstone."

"But we weren't in a relationship. We were just casually dating."

He tilts his head. "*I* casually date. And I would never talk about my dates how you talk about Akara and Banks—but you can use whatever labels you want, Sul."

"I am interested in these labels though." I point to the three M&M's. "What is this fucking called?"

"A triad." He crisscrosses his legs on the floor.

"Even if we didn't do anything sexually, the three of us would still be a triad?"

"Yeah. It's not about sex," Beckett says. "You can be in a relationship and be a virgin your whole life. People tend to only think about relationships with what they know, and it's bullshit, Sul. Two people, three people, *ten* people—if you can make it work, and it's consensual and loving, why would that be wrong?"

Wow.

I take a deep breath. "I just didn't think it's possible for three people to all be together in a serious relationship." And I know that was my ignorance. From what Beckett tells me, there are people in the world in happy polyamorous relationships.

"I didn't say it wouldn't be hard. There's lack of time. Jealousy. But every relationship, even monogamous ones, have complications. In the end, it just takes effort and commitment. That's the hardest thing for *all* people—commitment."

It's an overwhelming thought to have this new possibility. This new option. I stare down at the M&M's. "But what if the green one had sex with the red one and the blue one?" I blush a little, meeting Beckett's eyes.

His brows have risen. "You lost your virginity?"

"Last night," I say. "It was fucking epic."

He laughs. "I'm glad. They didn't hurt you?"

I shake my head. "They weren't…*together*. I mean they were together in the same room but not together in me. And sorry for the TMI." I don't even know why I apologize. Maybe because we haven't been talking much lately, but sex isn't an off-limits topic for us. Even if he's super private about his sex life with most people, he's shared with me.

"I asked," he says into a shrug. "I just want to make sure they're not assholes to you."

"They're not. You know I'd dick-kick them if they fucked with me."

He pops an orange M&M in his mouth. "Yeah, but I'd want to dick-kick them, too."

My smile falters for a second, and then a sweeping feeling surges through me. "A triad?"

He takes a sip of his Fizz Life. "It doesn't matter though, does it?" he asks me. "You said you already made a decision. Who did you choose anyway?"

My stomach overturns. "No one."

"What?" he frowns.

"I was going to just choose their friendship for them and walk away."

He gives me an iconic *what the fuck* face. "Now *that* is stupid."

"I didn't know we could all be together!" I collapse backward on the fuzzy rug. "And what if they don't want that option? A triad. What if it sounds too complicated and too difficult and too *different*?" I'm an American princess. If I profess to the world that I have *two* boyfriends, I'm going to be fodder. Maybe Akara and Banks won't want to put me through that—even if I'd want it.

Fuck, I want it.

I want them.

Both of them.

"They may not want to do it," Beckett says, honestly. "It's not for everyone."

We talk more about the ins and outs of polyamorous relationships. Beckett gives me a crash course—and I ask if he's been in one. *No*, only casually dating. But he's had threesomes, which weren't relationships. Just sex.

This isn't just sex.

It's why it's hard.

There are emotions and love…so much love involved. That inevitably, if we can't all be together, there's going to be pain.

OUR SECRET RENDEZVOUS point could have been warmer. I'm freezing my ballsac off. I zip up my cargo jacket and stuff my hands in the pockets. The top of a hill at Camp Calloway overlooks camp cabins, the canoe rack next to a glittering lake, and a bunch of trees. Endless seas of yellows, reds, and oranges in the November fall.

Akara rocks on the balls of his feet and blows warm breath into his hands. He glances out at the road, and I hear a voice through my radio.

"Gabe to Akara, I'm on the way with Sulli. Be there in about five."

"Copy," Akara says into his mic.

Our eyes latch. We haven't spoken the unspoken words.

One of us will be leaving this hill without her.

"Have you told her you love her?" Akara asks me.

I shake my head. "I didn't want to do that to you." It felt wrong to bring up my love for her when Akara's been fighting to be with her too. Like playing a winning hand in the middle of a game. And this isn't a game to me. My feelings for her are clearer than the skies today. They've been clear for a while now. I ask him, "Did you tell her?"

"Truthfully, I wanted to tell her without you there, but it never felt right. And it didn't feel right with you there either. Like either way I'd be hurting a friend."

I nod repeatedly. "So we're both dumbasses."

He tilts his head, smiling. "Basically."

"Do you think we should tell her?" I kick some pebbles on the ground. "At least then whoever she doesn't pick can rest easy knowing they did and said all they could."

Akara nods slowly.

My chest tightens. I can't shut up about this. He needs to hear it now, not after. "And if it's you, I'm going to have to ask for some sort of reassignment—"

"Stop." He grimaces.

"I can't watch you be with her, Akara," I say, hurt already compounding against my ribcage.

His eyes are bloodshot, fighting something back. "You watched me be with her last night."

"That was different. I was with her, too." I let out a frustrated breath. "And I don't know why you're giving me a hard time. You're going to quit her detail, if she chooses me." I hate that outcome too. I hate not having him as a friend.

"Yeah, I will," he says. "But maybe I like the scenario where I keep the girl and I keep you. Fucking sue me, I'm greedy."

I smack his chest. "I think you get sued enough, man. I don't need to add to it."

He laughs. "Shit, I can't believe you're making me laugh." His humor fades and the air sobers for a moment. "Either way, we lose each other, don't we?"

I fit a toothpick between my lips. "She's worth it."

Akara nods. "Yeah, she always has been."

Tires crunch gravel, and we both turn to watch the security vehicle drive down the road. The SUV parks near ours. Sulli hops out, waves to Gabe, and the car heads back to where it came.

She blows out a breath. Her hair billows in the wind and she hugs her arms to her chest. I want to bring her into my body, warm her, but Akara and I are rooted in place.

"Sulli—" Akara starts.

"Before you two say anything," she interjects and holds up a hand. "I want you to know that the time I spent with both of you in

Yellowstone has been undeniably some of the best times of my life. And whatever happens after today, just know I love you both." Those words rush through me.

I glance to Akara. *Is he going to say it first?*

He looks to me. Waiting.

She smiles. "Oh hey, I know you both love me, and I love that you care about each other enough to not hurt one another by saying it." She eyes me. "So I'm officially the *second* girl you've ever fallen in love with, huh, Banks?" She says it very fucking proudly.

Hate to ruin her good time. But I'm grinning like a fucking fool.

Her smile fades. "What?"

"You're not the second, Sulli."

Her fingers touch her lips, confused. "Wait, but you said you've been in love once before."

"Yeah." I nod strongly. "With you, mermaid."

"All the way back then?" The realization chokes her up for more than a second.

I nod, but I don't want to say anything else. This isn't a hand I'm playing. It's just the truth, but I can feel Akara's tense energy beside me.

She looks between us. "I care about you two too much to drag this out any longer. That's why my decision was already made this morning." She exhales before she says, "I was going to choose your friendship."

Was. Past tense.

My blood ices over. I don't know whether to be fucking destroyed or overjoyed by this news.

I bite on my toothpick. "So in that scenario, we both watch you be with some other guy?" I wonder.

She shrugs. "Or I could stay single forever. Who knows?"

"I don't like it," I say gruffly.

"Neither do I." Akara tugs on his beanie and nods at her. "What's the new verdict, string bean?"

She puts her fingers to her lips. "It's...unconventional. I didn't even think it was an option until I talked to Beckett today." She drops her hand. "Would you both want to be in a relationship with me… together? A triad. A *closed* triad."

It's like she's speaking in Spanish—which she's *fluent* in and I'm definitely not. "I don't know what any of those words mean," I say and glance to Akara.

Akara shakes his head. "No clue."

Sulli looks over her shoulder at the road. "Fuck, I should have brought the M&M's." *Don't know what that's about either.* She lets out a frustrated breath. "I'm sorry. I'm not good at this or at words."

"It's okay, Sul," Akara says. "We're listening."

"You have all my attention, mermaid."

She smiles softly. "Alright, so basically, we'd be in a relationship. Like what we did in Yellowstone. Only there's no end date that we'd have to worry about. No choice that has to be fucking made. We're all just…together."

I've got a lotta questions, but I'm not the logistics guy. Mostly, all I hear is *we're all just together.*

My mouth curves in a smile that Sulli hangs onto.

I go where the wind blows me.

It's sent me here.

To Akara. To Sulli. To home and love.

I'm ready to be rooted down, and this doesn't feel like a consolation prize, having him here too. It feels like I've won it all.

My best friend.

And her.

I glance to Akara, hoping he'll feel the same. But I see more questions in his eyes. And unlike me—he is that logistics guy.

56

Akara Kitsuwon

"I'M IN." BANKS BARELY hesitates. I didn't think he would.

They both look to me for my answer. I could back out, and if I do, I lose her. But I'm more scared of losing *this*. The ability to have what we had in Yellowstone. That's like a dream. And I'd think I'm stuck in one, but it's not snowing.

This is real.

"Slow down," I hold out a hand. "How does this even work?"

"I can explain everything," Sulli says, "But mostly, we get to choose our relationship. We define the boundaries. No one else." She grins. "Wild, right?"

Banks smiles.

I try hard not to feed off their excited energy, but I can feel my lips already rising. "This might not work," I say realistically. "I mean, what do we even call each other?"

She touches a hand to my chest. "You're my boyfriend." She puts a hand on Banks'. "You're also my boyfriend."

I narrow my eyes at Banks. "Does that make you my boyfriend?"

Sulli smiles. "Not unless you like that term with each other," she says. "If you're not romantically involved, it's like a V-triad, I think that's what Beckett said. It's not a triangle, and in a V, I'm the hinge between you two. You can call each other metamours. Closer than a friend but not quite a boyfriend."

Metamour.

Banks is my metamour.

Strange, but interesting. I've literally *never* heard that word until today, and it sounds like something from a fantasy novel, not real life. I'm tempted to open my phone and look up *metamour.* But then again, Sulli said we should define our relationship.

We could call each other Pop-Tarts for all it matters.

Shit, I'm already confirming this in my head like it's real. Like I want this.

Because you do, Nine.

I breathe in deeply.

The pain I've felt this entire trip has been from the idea of losing one of them. Banks or Sulli. This outcome has the least amount of pain, but it's also going to be the hardest for her. I don't want to burst her happy bubble, but I need to make sure this is everything she wants.

"Sul," I say. "I can't be your boyfriend in secret."

Hurt crosses her face. "You wouldn't be." She looks to Banks. "Neither would you. I would tell *everyone* that I'm proudly in a poly relationship. And even though I learned what that is this morning, it doesn't change my feelings for both of you that have existed far fucking before it."

"The media—"

"Fuck the media," Sulli says.

"Sulli," Banks interjects. "Akara is right. You have to just give it a second thought. This won't be your normal bout of attention. It's going to drive a lot of focus onto your life."

She swallows hard. "And I know it's going to be tough. The media cannibalized my dad for dating my mom, just because of their age difference, and my dad has always been unapologetic in his love for her. They stayed together, despite the headlines, the lies, the rumors—they never let the media tell them who to love or what to do with their lives." Her eyes well up with conviction in her voice. "I wouldn't be a Meadows if I didn't unapologetically go at life at a hundred-and-fifty-miles per hour. No brakes." She exhales, "I'm tired of playing it safe."

Sulli is wrong.

She is really good with words. Those ones wash over me like a euphoric cleansing. Before I can speak, she adds, "And the other option is losing each other, and that sounds infinitely worse. I'll take tough over lonely. Any day of the week."

Wind picks up harder. To block the gusts, we close the distance between each other. A huddle forming. "If the three of us are going to be in a relationship," I say—which causes both of them to smile wide. I roll my eyes. "—then we have to agree to something."

"Anything," Sulli says and clasps my hand.

Banks puts a hand on my shoulder.

Strength pools within me. Love surrounds me. For how much I lost in my life, I've gained everything today.

"We don't make this into some big announcement," I tell them. "If someone asks, we be upfront about it. We feel the moment."

"Feel the moment," Sulli nods, squeezing my hand.

"Feel the moment," Banks agrees.

Feel the moment.

57

Sullivan Meadows

THREE HOURS OUTSIDE Philly, I climb with my dad. He didn't tell me why we needed to climb this route at the quarry, but he said *meet me fucking there.*

So I'm here. But my dad is *nowhere* to be found. Now I start to wonder if this has to do with the cougar attack. I rehashed the story to my parents yesterday after Booger arrived—safe and sound—back in Philly. There were tears, very long hugs, and a general happiness that I'm alive. My bodyguards are alive.

No one was left behind.

Maybe this is actually a safety lesson. He's about to sneak up on me like a cougar. I glance over my shoulder. Nope, don't fucking see him anywhere.

I walk along the base of the flat limestone. Akara and Banks trail behind but there's some security issue back in Philly that they're whispering about. Today could have been a different outcome. Alone.

Lonely.

Instead, I have boyfriends.

My boyfriends.

I'm smiling when I press the phone to my ear. The line clicks. "Hey, where are you?" I ask my dad.

"Look up."

120-feet in the air, my dad is sitting at the top of the rock, his legs dangling over the crag.

"I thought you wanted to climb together?" I frown, confused.

"Meet me up here."

"But I've already free-soloed this one a bunch." Winona and I would practice at this quarry all the time. It's one of the easier rock faces.

"This will be different," my dad tells me. "I fucking promise."

HE'S RIGHT. EVERYTHING IS DIFFERENT ABOUT this free-solo climb. I'm stronger after weeks of training on a harder rock face. But that's not why I move in breathless, light strides. It feels automatic, like I'm here but not here. I just go.

On the hardest portion of the rock, I'm supporting myself with just two fingers. My feet find good leverage in a crack, and then I continue on. The last ten feet is a breeze.

I'm barely breaking a sweat by the time I hike a leg over the edge and find firm solid ground again. I don't move from my knees, and the intensity of those one-hundred-and-twenty feet just annihilates me. Because I look up and I see him.

My dad. Scruffy, weather-beaten face. Hardened jaw and eyes, the most loving dad I could've ever asked for.

The person I've wanted to connect to all this time. He's on his feet now and watches me with this heavy understanding.

I sit. "Why did that feel so different?" I ask him.

He squats down beside me. "This has always been my favorite rock to fucking climb." He takes a beat. "Because I would climb it with Adam Sully. I'd meet him at the top." He puts a hand on my knee. "Climbing can be lonely, Sul. The best climbs aren't."

My chest rises in a deeper inhale. I hated the climb in Yellowstone, but I loved this. I *needed* this. "Thanks," I tell him. "It feels complete now."

He touches the top of my head. "No more climbing my routes?" The joy in his voice is palpable.

I laugh. "Don't sound too upset."

"I just want you to be happy, Sulli," he says. "That's all I've ever fucking wanted since you were born."

I think about how different my life is from when I left. He hasn't exactly asked about my love life, and parts of me just wish he would, so I can tell him. Even though his reaction is the one I fear the most. His approval means everything to me, especially when I know I'm going to combat a lot of harsher judgment from the world.

I want to believe he'd like Akara and Banks with me, but I can't know for certain. I'm still his daughter, and he's still fiercely fucking protective. He might flip his shit if he knows I'm with not one but two bodyguards.

I end up saying the truth. Even if it's not all of it.

"I am happy. Really fucking happy."

We hug.

And then we descend.

Once back on the ground, we remove our rappelling gear and Akara and Banks approach from their spots. My dad carefully winds up a rope.

"Sir," Banks says easily.

"Hi, Banks," he nods, friendly enough. "Akara."

"Hey," Akara says.

A weird silence stretches, and my dad frowns for a second, eyeing us. He can sense something's off. Because it definitely is. I want to lean into Banks' chest. I want to grab Akara's hand. And each second the three of us are here alone with my dad, it feels like I'm keeping a lie.

Feel the moment.

I've got this.

"Dad," I say. "I have something to tell you."

I edge closer to Akara and Banks until I'm standing between my dad and my boyfriends like a referee in a coin toss.

My dad's confusion builds as he glances from them to me.

I take a breath. "So, Dad, I'd like you to meet my boyfriends. Akara Kitsuwon and Banks Moretti."

I almost want to shut my eyes to avoid his reaction.

But I can't.

My eyes are wide fucking open.

ACKNOWLEDGEMENTS

The Like Us series has reached beautiful, adventurous, *wild* Book 8. We're incredibly thankful for all of you, the readers who've taken a chance on our work, for picking up these books when there are so many out in the world. For sticking with us and these families up to the eighth novel.

It means so, so much to us. The Like Us series has had our hearts and souls for years now, and to see it still going strong because of you is a precious gift.

Thank you so much Lanie, Jenn, and Shea—our Fizzle Force FB Admins—for all the time & love you've put into celebrating and supporting *Wild Like Us* and every book we've ever published. Thanks to our beautiful mom who has been our biggest cheerleader since we were little girls. We couldn't do this without you. We love you all a waffle-lot.

Thank you to the Fizzle Force and to our patrons. Every reader who's been on Patreon—you've all changed our lives. And we wouldn't have reached Book 8 without you. Your love for these characters continues to inspire us and invigorate us. We are so grateful for each of you. Whenever we feel burnt-out or sad or doubtful, you all unknowingly remind us why we love to write. The spirit of writing and creating stories and characters is never lost. To see how these books, bonus scenes, extras, podcasts resonate with all of you is still surreal to us. Not a day goes by where we don't look at each other and go, *wow.* We feel so lucky.

Writing this series has been a true joy and a source of *love* for us for so long. These characters often remind us that life is short, and there is no better life than to be surrounded by people who love you unconditionally. We hope these characters can be there for you if you ever need them like they're here for us. And we can't wait to keep writing more ;)

All the love in every wild universe,
Krista & Becca

PRONUNCIATION GLOSSARY

The Italian used in this book is an Italian-American language developed by Italian immigrants. It is an incomplete language and uses Italian, English, or both. Different Italians speak different dialects in certain areas, and what is used in the Like Us series is prominent on the East Coast. Words may vary in pronunciation and spelling in different communities.

gabbadost': pronounced gaa-baa-dahst (Origin: capa dura/capa tosta)

gavadeel': pronounced gaa-vaa-DEEL (Origin: cavatelli)

paesan': pronounced pai-ZAAN (Origin: paesano)

rigott': prounounced ree-GAUWT (Origin: ricotta)

scustamad': pronounced skoo-stoo-MAAD (Origin: scostumato)

stunad: pronounced stoo-NAAD (Origin: stonato)